Hell and High Water
An Appalachian Trail Adventure

BY JOSEPH HAROLD

Dedicated to my hiking partner, LoGear who always walks beside me, even if she is several meters ahead, and to my girls, who inspire me every single day. Lastly, to Xander, my little fox. Your loss will be felt the rest of my life, being able to imagine what could have been, was my therapy.

Contents

CHAPTER 1
ARMY TRAINING, SIR - MONDAY, JUNE 4TH

The sun was peeking over the mountain outside the window of Sergeant First Class Clayton Collier's bedroom and spreading its bright yellow light on the project in front of him. It was early June, and the morning was just shaking off its nightly chill in the valley next to Blue Ridge Mountain. He was packing for a training evolution down in Georgia and he was trying to decide on whether he needed two sets of extra batteries for his headlamp. His wife Lori stirred in her warm slumber and opened one eye. "Do you think you packed enough gear, Sergeant Collier?" she chided him playfully. "It's only a five-day deployment. You don't need to pack everything you were issued."

He reached over and patted her hip lightly. She was just as beautiful as the day he had met her, long ago on a path in the wilderness. "You know what I always say, baby. I would rather have it and not need it, than need it and not have it. As long as I can handle the weight, I am going to be ready for anything." This was his usual mantra. His pack was always full and heavy, but he never complained or tried to lighten his load, and he was usually able to dig out what someone needed in any situation.

"Just don't forget the pouch," Lori said lightly, already drifting back towards sleep. The pouch was a small thing, made of brown leather and stitched with waxed string, with a cord of rawhide, long enough to wear around his neck. Inside were three locks of braided hair. One each from his children's first haircuts. The other is from Lori. There is also a Twenty-sided die, a tiny quartz stone in the shape of a heart, and a little glass ladybug.

The D20 is from his son, an avid gamer. The ladybug is from his daughter, in reference to her childhood nickname. The heart stone was found by Lori when they were on their month-long honeymoon, traveling the country and exploring every park they could. Clay took this amulet on every deployment, long or short. It was already around his neck.

Clay had been in the U.S. Army for nineteen years. His current duty assignment, watch leader of the guard unit at Mount Weather Emergency Operations Center and Chief of Security, was going to be his last. He was looking forward to retirement after a rewarding career. This upcoming deployment was a short survival training session that would run him and his watch section through an annual refresher course on how to stay alive in the bush with limited supplies. The training was taking place in the Chattahoochee National Forest north of Atlanta, Georgia. His squad would be leaving in an hour for the ten-hour drive down to the training area, where they would practice several survival skills, like shelter building, fire making, and resource gathering. His job guarding the Emergency Operations Center didn't usually need many survival skills, but having those skills was part of being in the army and he liked to keep himself up to date on all the latest techniques.

The OpCen had a very special mission. Underneath the normal base buildings was a special secret city, full of everything needed to keep the government running when terrible things happened. He didn't go down below very much as his main function was to keep curious tourists and sometimes lost hikers away from the fence line. Everybody knew that something unique went on at the OpCen, but preventing unauthorized entry was his job.

Clay fastened the buckles on the rucksack and shouldered the pack. He bent over and gave Lori a kiss. She kissed him back and mumbled something that sounded like "see you soon, baby." He headed out the door and down the long hall of the old farmhouse. He peered into the first bedroom on his left. Inside everything was neat and tidy. Asleep under a thick comforter was his firstborn, Brittney. All he could see was a fall of reddish-brown hair sticking out. Brittney was twenty years old and had just finished her third year at Virginia Tech, where she was working on a degree in botany. She loved the outdoors and everything that grew in them and spent a lot of her free time hiking the nearby Appalachian Trail. Clayton went over to her bed and laid his hand on where he guessed her shoulder was. "I'm on my way, darling. I'll be back in five days," he whispered into her ear.

All he got from her was a slight shake of her head and a soft "love you" whispered back at him.

He exited the room and passed the old bathroom on the left. The last room, this one on the right just before the steps, was his son, Shane's room. He looked inside this room and as usual, it looked like a hurricane had just passed through. The unmade bed was empty, as he had expected. Shane had just spent the weekend hiking and camping on the trail up north. He had gone out with some of his recently graduated high school friends as a little celebration for just completing their senior year. Shane planned to follow his sister to Virginia Tech next fall, but he also planned to enjoy his "Last Summer of Freedom" as he put it, by spending as much time as possible doing whatever he felt like. He was due to return later today.

Clay descended the steps and turned into the hall which led to the front door. The old farmhouse was over 150 years old. They were located across the Shenandoah River from Blue Ridge Mountain, where Mount Weather was located. The farm had once belonged to Lori's grandfather who had raised a number of crops and some dairy cattle before selling off most of the land and retiring. They had kept the place when he died and when Clayton was lucky enough to get his latest assignment; they had moved in. It was perfect. A mere twenty-minute drive to work each day and the area was beautiful. Blue Ridge Mountain rose to the east, huge and green. Before that, the Shenandoah River snaked its way at the foot of the mountain, working its way into the valley from the south. The river was a great place to play — perfect for canoeing and swimming. The Appalachian Trail came from the south to Ashby Gap where it crossed Route 50 and worked its way to the north through the mountains. Here it traveled over a series of fourteen hills called the roller coaster, due to the short but steep ups and downs of each hill. Clay had spent a lot of time hiking that trail and had done the whole thing from Georgia to Maine when he was nineteen, a couple of years before joining the army.

As Clay walked out the front door, a desert-colored Humvee pulled up in front of the house after coming up the long driveway from the road. Clayton approached the vehicle, threw his ruck into the back and walked around to the passenger side where a young guy with spindly arms and legs and dark brown hair was exiting. "Morning Sarge," said Corporal Jimmy McAfee as he jumped into the rear of the Hummer. "Great day for some survival, ain't it?"

"Every day is a great day for survival, Corporal," Clay replied. "If not, we'd all be dead."

Clay settled in and looked over at the driver, Private Mike Taylor, and gave a nod. Private Taylor gave a two-finger salute and put the rumbling beast into gear. Gravel spurted out from under the Hummer's tires as they headed down the driveway, turned right and shot off for the highway and their next five days of adventure. Clay looked over his shoulder to the old farmhouse. He didn't realize it at the time, but it would be another two months until he saw it again.

CHAPTER 2
SURVIVAL OF THE FITTEST - MONDAY, JUNE 4TH - TUESDAY,
JUNE 5TH

After meeting up with another Humvee which contained the remainder of his crew, the group headed down the highway in a two-vehicle convoy at a steady sixty-five miles per hour. Private Taylor turned on the FM radio that he had installed in the Humvee, pushed a few buttons and turned up the volume. The tinny voice of an announcer came out of the speakers affixed to the dashboard.

"... *showers will be possible for the next couple of days in the valley and up over the mountain.*

In other news, Richard Flaherty held another rally in Norfolk, Virginia today. The crowd became violent as protesters stood outside the venue, yelling and blowing whistles. Men in full military outfits entered the crowd of protestors and started beating them with their weapons. No one was arrested, but several protestors needed medical attention. Flaherty's violent rhetoric has become more and more intense and his support of using pseudo military personnel to quell anyone who disagrees with him has increased in the last several days.

The Baltimore Orioles lost their game last night against the ..."

Clayton reached up and turned the station on the radio to the local classic rock station and the guitar intro to *(Don't Fear) The Reaper*, by Blue Öyster Cult came flowing out of the speakers. "That's more like it," Clayton said, as all the occupants started nodding their heads to the beat. The next ten hours passed in a blur as they listened to music and talked about the training they were heading to. They didn't talk about politics or the trouble that seemed to be brewing in Virginia and all over the country. They wanted to forget about all of that and concentrate on practicing the skills of survival.

#

Two Humvees moved down the dirt road with a cloud of dust rising behind them and came to a stop on the shoulder next to an already parked vehicle. Standing just off the road were four soldiers in uniform. One was an army officer. Second Lieutenant Jason Pierce had a very stern face for someone only a few years out of West Point. His short black hair was always cut in the highest of highs and the tightest of tights and his uniform was always crisp and clean, even after being out in the bush for a week or two. He was the instructor for this survival course, and he didn't like anyone having any ideas of their own. It was his way or the highway. There was no room for improvisation. The soldiers exited their vehicles and Clayton threw a salute to the Lieutenant "Good afternoon, sir," he greeted his superior. "Watch team Bravo ready for training," he added with false gusto. Clayton never really liked the Lieutenant, but always acted professionally when they were together. The Lieutenant's presence was the only downside to these survival training sessions. Pierce returned the salute with a distasteful grimace that seemed to always be on his face and said, "Have your men get their gear and be ready to move out in five minutes." Pierce turned to his men to give them their final instructions as Clayton and his men got to work unloading the Humvees and donning their packs.

The men from the other Hummer were the rest of Clayton's watch team. Staff Sergeant Kell Sumpson was a large Black man with bulging muscles straining his uniform. Staff Sergeant Sumpson looked like a football player, and he had actually been a pretty good linebacker during the two years he had spent at college before deciding he wanted to serve his country and join the army. He was Clayton's second in command during their watch routine and Clayton relied on him a lot and liked him as a person. They had spent quite a few off-duty hours hanging out together at each other's house and got along well. Private First Class Jason Webber was a short squat fireplug of a guy. He was only nineteen and had been in the army only a brief time. He was always laughing and joking, and it was sometimes a challenge to get him to be serious about a situation. The last of the team was Private Anthony Masvanni. He was a tall, sinewy, Italian man from Staten Island, New York. He had a haunted look in his eye from time to time and Clayton was pretty sure he hadn't had a very good childhood. Tony had joined the army to get away from the poverty and violence he had endured growing up in one of the rougher parts of the island. The six soldiers were ready to go in four minutes. Lieutenant Pierce looked them over, nodded his head, turned and started off into the woods. The group followed the Lieutenant in single file. As they started up a rise on the forested slope, they heard the other soldiers firing up the Humvees and driving off. They were on their own now. They weren't expecting to see those vehicles again for another five days.

The wooded slope rose steadily, and the group easily climbed through the mix of oak, maple, and other large trees. They followed no trail but knew which way they were headed since they had studied their maps for a few days and a simple compass bearing got them on their way. The day was starting to end after their ten-hour drive. They would continue to hike after dark for a few hours in order to get to their first planned camp. The moon was full and due to arrive shortly after sunset. Since the sky was still clear, they may not even need their head lamps to make their way through the forest.

Lieutenant Pierce was a serious man who exuded an arrogance that belied his low rank in the officer corps. It seemed that he looked down on the group he was tasked with training, and this was evident to each of the men. Of course, he was an officer, while they were only enlisted, so everything was kept professional. *Sometimes you can learn just as much from an incompetent person as an expert*, thought Clayton as he adjusted his load and concentrated on picking his next step in the rocky hillside. Right now, Pierce was setting a relentless pace. They had about ten miles to cover before making camp and it was mostly bushwhacking through woods that were rather thick in some places.

As they crested the hill and started moving along the ridgeline, they could see a small hamlet in the valley below. Everything looked so peaceful from up here. It was hard to realize all that is going on in the town and in the houses. Who is fighting with their wife? Who is making love to their husband? What is the newsman talking about on the television? Up here, everything is simple and complete. Find a place to sleep. Eat some food. Walk more miles tomorrow.

The men continued along until they came to a trail. The sun was low in the west now and it would be gone within the next half hour. Darkness was just another obstacle that they would overcome. This trail led to another, which would eventually lead to the Appalachian Trail, fondly referred to as the A.T. Springer Mountain is where it officially starts on the southern end. From there it crosses fourteen states until it terminates at Mount Katahdin in Maine. This training mission wouldn't go near the A.T., but Clayton felt the connection of the trail that he thought about nearly every day as he crossed it going to work. He remembered hiking through this forest twenty years ago as he traveled the approach trail to Springer Mountain. The excitement of a new adventure just starting was coursing through his body and he was practically running as he made his way up the steep steps in Amicalola Falls State Park. Just getting out into the woods brought a little of that excitement back and he was feeling pretty good right now. He loved being out there.

#

Twilight was dwindling as they saw the bright moon rise in the east like a huge ship coming over the horizon. It was bright and full and provided ample light. They could see the trail easily and didn't turn on their lights just yet. They walked along in silence, enjoying the night and listening to the nocturnal sounds as the inhabitants of the forest went about their business. It was warm and a little humid and each had worked up a bit of a sweat as they carried their loads and negotiated the ups and downs of the Georgia Appalachian Mountains. After two hours of traveling, they descended from a small ridge into a flat plateau that had wide spaced oak trees. There was a stream on the south side of the flat that gurgled happily through the forest on its way to its salty destination far away. Lieutenant Pierce called a halt and ordered the men to set up camp.

The men were carrying no firearms. They had the basic needs of survival and not much more. Within or attached to their packs, each man was carrying: a lightweight sleeping bag called a patrol bag, a sleeping pad, some cooking containers, and a few bags of Meals Ready to Eat or MREs as they are always called. Their packs also contained: a compact first aid kit, which included water treatment pills, some personal hygiene items, and a poncho for rainy weather. For sleeping, they had a bivy sack to put a sleeping bag into, which is the most portable tent someone could carry. It was waterproof and durable. They each had some sort of light, mostly head lamps, and some extra batteries. On their belts, they all had a nice combat knife, a compass and two 1-quart canteens. Each man also carried a team item. Clayton carried a small hatchet. Kell carried a collapsible shovel. Taylor carried the maps they would need for the surrounding area. Webber carried a small tarp and Masvanni carried a more extensive combat first-aid kit, with tourniquets, bandages, morphine and other items that they hoped they wouldn't need. This was all the gear they would need for the next five days. One of their practical tests was to forage and harvest wild edibles to supplement their — sometimes unsatisfying — MRE meals.

Each man selected a space within the clearing to set up his sleeping area. The ground was relatively level and there were not a lot of rocks. Their sleeping setup ended up looking like the spokes of a wheel. In the center of the wheel, they cleared a space to make a fire. The fire was a valuable resource out here. It could sterilize the water from the creek by boiling it to kill all the bad bacteria and make the water safe to drink. It could heat their meals, and best of all, the fire just made them feel good. They had removed the leaves and sticks from the area, piling them out of the way for later use. They dug into the topsoil a bit, also saving that material. They planned to restore the area to how they had found it when they moved on. This set up was safe enough to not let the surrounding leaves catch fire but didn't use rocks that would be harder to restore back to the natural site of the area.

The group got the fire going, ate an MRE meal and settled in for the night. Two men would stand watch, moving out into the bush in an ambush position while the others slept. Every two hours a new team would relieve the on-watch pair until dawn arrived. Since there were seven men in the group, the Lieutenant would sleep through the night without standing a watch. No big deal to the guys, they were used to it.

Clayton took the first watch along with Private Taylor. Taylor was a quiet and rather standoffish twenty-year-old man from Atlanta. Clayton figured it would be a quiet two hours and he was right. Before he knew it, he was waking up Corporal McAfee for the second watch. McAfee and PFC Webber would take the next two hours staring into the darkness as the night creatures prowled the forest looking for food, or mates, or both. There wasn't too much else happening out there in the Georgia woods in the early part of June.

#

The morning light slowly crept into the camp and the soldiers each came awake without any prodding. They quickly and quietly ate a cold breakfast and broke camp. After they replaced all the items they had moved to make camp, there was no evidence that they had just spent the last seven hours hanging out there. They were a good team, and it didn't matter if they were doing their shift at Mount Weather or surviving in the woods; they had worked together long enough to have built that modicum of respect and familiarity to know what needed to be done and to get it done.

The Lieutenant came over to Clayton when everyone was packed up and handed him two maps. Each had a different set of objectives, with a meetup at the when the tasks were complete. Clayton would be traveling with PFC Webber and Private Masvanni. Staff Sergeant Sumpson would lead McAfee and Taylor to the day's rendezvous. Lieutenant Pierce would move from one group to the other throughout the day and observe their completion of the objectives. Before dismissing the men, Pierce held up a burned match in front of Clayton's face. "I found this over by the tree next to the fire," Pierce said with a smirk. "You were supposed to restore the site to perfection, with no sign of our use. I'm going to deduct points for this lapse."

Clayton looked at the Lieutenant for a few seconds and said, "Yes sir. Won't happen again." As he turned away from the Lieutenant, Staff Sergeant Sumpson caught a glimpse of the eye roll Clayton tried to hide. He smiled at Clayton, and they each turned to their groups.

Both teams' first objective was to find water and make it safe to drink. Each of the men still had at least one canteen full, but knowing where the water was and getting to it was an important skill. This first task was pretty easy. The nearby creek provided the source and the pills each man carried made the water safe to drink. That task completed, the two groups each went in a different direction for their next task.

The next objective on the list was to navigate through the forest to a set of coordinates and build a small debris shelter. Clayton and his crew proceeded to the east over a slight rise. There was no road or trail to follow here, and the brush was thick in places. Poison ivy was scattered across the forest floor. Even with these obstacles, each man maneuvered through the woods easily, following the bearing they had calculated until they crossed a stream, headed up a hill, and found their objective — an open area within the forest containing less underbrush and lots of material to work with. Each of the three men moved off in different directions to collect sticks and branches. They started off by selecting a level spot to erect their shelter. They crossed three logs they had gathered in a tripod with two short ends and one long one. Along this long beam, they placed numerous small sticks to create the framework of their roof with a decent space to fit all three of them inside. It would be a little cramped but spooning helps save body heat they say. On this frame, they started dumping large handfuls of leaves and other debris they had collected. After twenty minutes or so, the shelter was ready. The squad climbed inside to test the fit. It would do just fine.

About an hour later, Lieutenant Pierce came stumbling through the forest. He moved into camp, thinking he was being stealthy, but the guys were ready for him. They had started hearing him about ten minutes before he arrived, so his entrance was no surprise.

"Hello, L-T. How did the other guys do?" Clayton asked.

"You'll find out in the debriefing," the Lieutenant replied snootily. "Now drop your canteens there and crawl into your contraption," he sneered, pointing to a spot in front of the shelter. The men all climbed into the shelter, settling themselves — not quite spooning, but close none-the-less.

The Lieutenant picked up two of the canteens, opened their caps and started pouring the contents onto the shelter. This continued until the six canteens were laying in a pile empty. The three grunts relaxed in their shelter and Webber started to snore — either real or staged, Clayton wasn't quite sure — as they stayed dry as a bone. They knew how to make their shelters water resistant, and this was no exception. Disappointed he hadn't stumped the team, the Lieutenant called them out, ordering them to dismantle the shelter and restore the area. They completed that task in about ten minutes and then they refilled their canteens in the nearby steam. They prepared to head to their next objective, which was to make a fire using primitive methods. They would use this fire to purify their water later.

They started navigating to the next waypoint, as the Lieutenant headed back into the woods, following his own compass bearing back to the other group of trainees. The objective was a narrow gully with a cliff on one side and a trickle of water running through at its deepest point. As they went, they started collecting material to make a bow drill, along with tinder and kindling which they would use as fuel to create a fire in a primitive technique.

They were also on the lookout for anything edible that they could augment their bland MREs, which they would be eating again that day. They each only had three MREs apiece. Not really enough to provide the calories needed to hump these Georgia mountains, complete their tasks, and keep their heads straight, but a little starvation never hurt a grunt. They could handle it. Clayton found a few wild strawberries and Webber stumbled into a patch of ramps. He gleefully picked a good handful, all the while describing how he would sauté them up in his canteen cup and flavor his meatloaf meal with some oniony goodness.

After another hour of traveling through the underbrush, they found the small gully and set about their next task. Masvanni was good with a knife, so he got to work creating a bow drill set, while the other two used the materials they had gathered to sort the sticks by size and build a bird's nest of tinder, which would take the ember and coax it into a flame.

The Private quickly created a fireboard, spindle and handhold from a piece of cedar he had found. Webber had found a nice bow shaped stick, and he tied a piece of paracord loosely on each end. Before too long, everything was ready to go. Masvanni had the honor of going first, since he had crafted the device. He put all the pieces together and started slowly moving the bow back and forth, turning the spindle in the notch in the fireboard. Gradually, he started to move faster as smoke started to rise from the board.

All the men had done this before, and after another minute or two of spinning, Masvanni checked the board, blowing lightly at the dark notch. He was rewarded with the subtle glow of an ember. Carefully, the Private lifted the board and tapped the ember into the bird's nest that Clayton was holding. Clayton lightly blew into the tinder bundle, moving the material around to keep the air flowing, while still giving the ember something to burn. As he blew, the smoke became thicker and thicker. Suddenly a flame erupted from the bundle. Clayton quickly moved the flaming bundle under the teepee of small sticks that Webber had constructed.

Taking his time, Webber delicately added twigs and kindling to the small fire. Treating it like a baby, until the flame was stronger. As the fire grew, he would place a few more sticks, increasing the size of the sticks until he was placing thumb sized pieces onto the fire.

They had a nice fire going and were each boiling a canteen cup full of water by the time Lieutenant Pierce came walking into the clearing they were using for this stage of the course.

"I see you got the fire going," he pointed out the obvious. "I hope you used the bow drill and didn't cheat," he sneered. Clayton bit his tongue on his preferred response and instead lifted the bow drill for inspection, which had clearly been used recently, with its dark notch showing the wear of Masvanni's efforts.

The Lieutenant nodded his head and checked their progress on the water purifying. "Once you finish with the water, douse the fire, return the area to a pristine state and continue on to the bivouac for the night. I'll see you there," he commanded as he headed off to the east, back into the woods.

The men completed their task and when they too followed the same route the Lieutenant took, the gully looked just as it had when they had come in from the west.

The final walk to the second night's camp was a little more technical than the other treks. They had to navigate around a small swamp and negotiate a cliff of about fifteen feet before they entered another clearing where they would be spending the night. As they approached, they saw the other men already setting up for the night.

Each of the men took their own positions and stowed their gear for the night. Tonight would be a fireless one, so they each ate an MRE as the sun set on the squad. They then settled into the watch rotation for the night. The training was going very well so far. Tomorrow would be another challenging day.

CHAPTER 3
FUBAR - WEDNESDAY, JUNE 6TH - THURSDAY, JUNE 7TH

Clayton's eyes were closed, but it seemed like someone was shining a very bright flashlight into his eyes. He moved his head aside and slowly blinked awake. The whole campsite was as bright as day. He glanced at his watch and saw it was 0200. Not the right time for the sun to be shining. He quickly came out of his bag and looked around. The bright light was coming from the south, and it wasn't the sun.

"That's where Atlanta is," said McAfee as he approached Clayton, rubbing sleep from his eyes. "I wonder what is going on. I was on watch and facing north, when I not only saw the forest light up with the brightness, but I felt it. It was sudden and surprising."

"If I'm not mistaken, that sure looks like a nuclear detonation," said Sergeant Sumpson. "What the fuck is going on? I was looking almost directly towards the city when it lit up, I'm having trouble seeing right now. Just giant spots in front of my eyes."

The Lieutenant came over and started ordering the men to pack their gear, but they had all already moved into action as soon as they realized something was not right. Within three minutes, they were packed and ready to go. "We have to head back to the road and see if we can find the Humvees," said the Lieutenant.

"Roger that," they all replied together as they made a quick check of the map, checked their compasses and started back down the way they had come up at the end of the day. Each man wore a worried expression. Clayton didn't know what was going on, but he planned on finding out.

#

The seven men had navigated in the dark until actual dawn arrived, then continued on after a short break to eat some food and refill their canteens. They covered ground quickly as they made their way back to the drop off point. The group was walking down an old fire road that led to one of the forest roads. The afternoon sun was dappling through the trees as they moved along. As they saw a lightening in the trees ahead that signified a clearing, Clayton spoke softly to Corporal McAfee, who was on point, telling him to hold up for a minute. They all gathered around in a circle.

Clayton wanted to approach with caution. Through the trees, they could see a small parking lot, and it appeared that there were some cars in the lot. As they had started down the hillside a while back, Clayton had heard what sounded like a car door slamming.

"L-T, I think we should do a reconnaissance first, before we enter the parking lot," suggested Clayton. "I think I heard activity coming from the clearing as we came down the hillside."

"What could be there besides someone who can help?" the Lieutenant replied. "We don't need a reco."

"L-T, the situation has just become fucked up beyond all repair. Nothing is as it was just ten hours ago. I'm pretty sure we have been attacked and we are now probably at war," Clayton responded. "I highly recommend a cautious approach. We have limited weapons and no reason to blunder into the area."

At this point, Corporal McAfee moved back to the circle. He had done his own short reconnaissance and thought he had seen something. "I'm pretty sure there is a Humvee parked in the lot. It appears to be in the middle of the circle, but I couldn't tell if anyone was in it or near it," the Corporal reported.

"That's settled then, our rescue is at hand gentlemen, follow your leader back to civilization," Lieutenant Pierce announced as he started forward.

Clayton was still hesitant. Something wasn't right. He motioned to McAfee to go with the Lieutenant and then looked over at Kell to get his assessment. He nodded his head and looked to PFC Webber, signaling for him to stay put and keep near him. Clayton looked at Masvanni and Taylor and did the same.

Lieutenant Pierce moved along the trail and entered the parking lot. He immediately saw the Humvee in the lot and two men in uniform, standing next to the vehicle.

Pierce started walking faster and said, "Boy, am I glad to see you guys. I'm going to need to take your Hum —" The man on the right raised his weapon and sent a three-round burst into the Lieutenant's chest. Everyone froze for a second, not understanding what was happening.

McAfee spun around and started running back towards the woods. Another burst of rifle fire brought him down.

Clayton signaled to Kell, who grabbed Webber and moved to the left, trying to circle around the parking lot. Clayton and Masvanni headed the other way, drawing their knives, the only weapons they had. Clayton ordered Taylor to stay put and remain alert.

Clayton advanced to the clearing from the woods and heard the Humvee driving off.

Kell and Webber appeared across the way and the group converged where Pierce fell.

A quick check confirmed their suspicion that he had been dead when his head bounced off the ground.

McAfee was still alive, but he had been hit high on his back and when they turned him over, blood was frothing out of his mouth. There was little they could do to help with their limited first aid kit.

Masvanni pulled a morphine ampule from his kit and gave him a quick shot. As the Private dug out some bandages and started working on the Corporal, McAfee's breathing slowed and then ceased altogether. McAfee was dead, too.

"We really need to figure out what the fuck is going on," said Private Taylor, who had joined back up with the others. His voice was a high pitched whine, which showed his fear. "My family lives in Atlanta. I need to go see what happened."

"We'll figure it out soon enough, Private," replied Clayton. "Something really bad is happening out there. Who were those grunts? Their uniforms looked like ours, but from what I could see, something was definitely off about them. We need to assess what we can do and be careful in our movements and interactions with anyone we encounter. But first, we need to take care of these two," Clayton added, nodding to the Lieutenant and McAfee. "We can't take them with us, but we won't leave them to the animals. Let's get started on some temporary graves. We will come back for them once we have sorted out what is going on."

#

They wrapped the men in their ponchos and placed them inside their bivy before digging one large hole about three feet deep. They carefully placed the two KIA soldiers into the pit and covered it with dirt. While three men filled the pit, two others walked down to a nearby creek and started bringing back football sized stones to cover the grave. This would protect the area from digging animals and act as a marker for the soldiers temporary resting place, making them easier to find when the time came. After that detail was complete, they all moved to a small clearing within the woods and gathered in a circle. They each took stock of what they had amongst themselves, figuring out what they had and how long it would last. They had gathered the Lieutenant's and McAfee's gear and checked what they all had. Each man now only had one full MRE and a random food item from the dead men's issue. They had broken down the two fallen soldiers' rations to divvy up amongst the surviving squad. They each still carried a knife, and their team items (hatchet, shovel, maps, tarp, and first-aid kit) were all accounted for. The first-aid kid was slightly more depleted than it had been yesterday, but still contained materials that could prove useful if needed. The Lieutenant had a satellite signaling device that had the ability to send an SOS signal back to the training base and send text messages back and forth. It hadn't worked since the bomb had gone off. It turned on, but all it would do was flash the word "*searching* ..." in a continuous effort to find a satellite. Shit was getting real. Even though it wasn't working now, Clayton stowed it in his ruck, hoping it would start working later. "We need to head off the mountain and get to a town or village. Find out what is going on," Clayton said to the guys.

"I think we should head towards Atlanta," Taylor interjected. "I need to find out if my family is still alive. Whether they still exist or if they are just dust in the wind."

"I don't think that is a good idea, Taylor. If that was an atomic bomb, there will be fallout to be careful of and avoid. Once we get somewhere that has information, we will find out what has happened to your family," Clayton persuaded. "That's the mission."

"With all due respect, Sarge, fuck the mission," Taylor shouted, as his voice broke with emotion. "I need to know now."

"Private, you will do as ordered. I promise you we will find out, but we will stay together and continue to work as a squad. Watch Team Bravo, on duty, and when I last checked, still in the U. S. Army," Clayton used his command voice to show he was serious. He was pretty sure that Taylor wouldn't find good news, but he made it his duty to help find his family when the time was right.

Taylor moved off to the edge of the clearing, staring to the south, a firm and determined look on his face. They gathered the gear, studied the maps, and decided to head northeast. There were a couple of small towns just over a few of the nearest mountains. They would head to one of them and find out what was happening.

#

The day was almost over. After walking a few miles, Clayton decided to camp for the night. Once again there would be no fire. The men only ate a few mouthfuls worth of food. It was now time to ration what they had. They didn't know how long they would be out here now. No one was going to be picking them up in two days. They had to make things happen themselves. The survival training had become real survival.

Since there were only five of them now, they would be standing a one man watch. Taylor volunteered to take the middle watch. They didn't plan on getting a lot of sleep that night, anyway.

As the woods became dark, Clayton sat and investigated the shadows of the green forest. Wondering what had happened and what his family were doing back at home on the old farm. He reached into his shirt as worry filled his soul and clasped the pouch he was wearing, thinking about Lori and the kids. He hoped that whatever had happened, hadn't affected them, but didn't feel confident in that hope.

#

The forest is pitch black. Clouds have rolled into the area and obscured the waning gibbous moon that had risen before midnight. It is very dark; nothing but blackness and shadows. Four soldiers lie sleeping in a circle. A fifth is sitting off to the right about ten meters away. The solitary man is Private Mike Taylor. His ruck is beside him and his headlamp wraps around his forehead.

Private Taylor stands, dons his pack and walks towards the edge of the clearing, he looks back at the sleeping figures. None of them stir. It had been a long and tiring day and exhaustion had taken each of the men in the circle. Taylor looks back into the woods and clicks on his headlamp in the red light function and starts walking into the woods. His direction is south. Heading towards Atlanta. His duty now is to find his family. Fuck the mission. Fuck the army.

#

Some hours later, the wood thrush starts his morning routine. Singing his favorite songs. Making the forest sound like a pleasant place, which not long ago had been dark and scary. The sun had just started to light the horizon to the east and visibility was increasing.

Sergeant Sumpson approached Clayton, and gave him a little shake. "Taylor is gone."

Clayton comes awake and looks around. "What?"

"He didn't wake me for the last watch. I woke when I heard the birds start up and he was nowhere to be found. I looked around some and it appears that he headed off to the south. The brush is disturbed going that way. His pack is gone too."

Clayton got up out of his bag and went to the edge of the clearing. A clearly discernible path through the underbrush was heading off to the south. "I guess not knowing was eating at him too much. It's wrong and if we see him again, there will be consequences to his choices, but I'm not going to go after him. I understand his motives. I want to get back to my family just as badly."

"Roger that," Kell Sumpson said. "Let's get packed and ready to go Oscar Mike in twenty minutes guys," he directed at the remains of the squad.

The four men ate some power bars, packed their meager gear and were ready to start another day of humping through the forest. Seeking other people that weren't the enemy. Seeking answers.

CHAPTER 4
THE ATTACK OF THE HILL PEOPLE - THURSDAY, JUNE 7TH

The day remained overcast as the men traveled through the forest. After about an hour of walking, they came upon a forest road. The road headed in the same general direction that they were heading, northeast-ish. Private Taylor had taken the maps with him, so they were going on memory and dead reckoning. The road gave them an easier traveling surface. And roads usually lead to towns, even though this one hadn't had a vehicle on it in several decades.

The men walked in single file with Webber on point. They weren't at full alert, but they were mindful of their surroundings. Clayton was right behind Webber, with Sergeant Sumpson behind him and Private Masvanni taking up slack. Masvanni would check their back trail every so often. So far, it had always been empty, hardly showing that four men had just walked through that area. The birds were quiet in this part of the forest. The silence of the woods was weird and a little unsettling. It seemed that everything had vacated the area.

The men were heading along the road, which was steadily but gradually climbing up the ridge in front of them. The hill continued up on their left. There were several large boulders above them, intermixed with some low, but thick rhododendron bushes. On their right, the hill continued going down into a deep valley. From time to time, they could see a stream moving through the forest at the bottom of the hill. The area below them has several gullies digging into the hillside, each heading off in a different direction.

Thunk! Something hit Clayton's pack. He looked over his shoulder and saw the synthetic feathers of an arrow sticking out of his pack. With shock and surprise in his voice, Clayton shouted to Webber "Someone just shot me with an arrow. Take cover, to the right." Just then a shotgun blast echoed through the forest. It came from Clayton's left, up the hill. He looked in the direction of the shot as he moved off the road, to the right, down the steep hill. He saw that Kell and Masvanni were doing the same.

Another shotgun blast echoed through the forest and he heard Masvanni yell. He couldn't tell if it was the shout of a man who had just got hit, or if it was just surprise that forced it out of him.

"You government people are all gonna die," someone yelled from behind a rock up the hill. "You killed my Lucy and now I'm gonna kill you," the disembodied voice added.

Clayton had taken quick shelter behind a three-foot rock that was just off the road. Another arrow came flying down range to his right. It ricocheted off a tree and hit a large rock, shattering its sharp bladed hunting point. *These guys mean business*, Clayton thought to himself.

Just then, three more shotgun blasts echoed through the woods, each one coming quickly after the other. The sharp crack of a rifle added to the din. They were completely outgunned. It was time to retreat and regroup.

Clayton yelled out, "Head down. Regroup below." He started moving carefully down the steep hill. More shots rang out. He would move a little, take cover, then move again.

Suddenly, more weapons opened up on their left flank. *These guys ARE serious, and it appears they are organized*, Clayton continued in his head.

The orderly retreat became a rout. Clayton slipped on a mossy log and went down hard. He took the brunt of the fall on his right shoulder and a sharp pain shot down his arm. "That's gonna hurt in the morning." Now he was talking to himself out loud.

Clayton sucked up the pain and continued down the hill. He got to the bottom and followed the stream putting distance between himself and the attackers. The shooting had lessened. Every couple of minutes, he would hear some shouting. A shot would ring out and then silence. The sounds started to become muted. The birds started singing around him again. It was tentative at first, but once they became accustomed to him sitting next to a tree under some brush, the birds continued with their day, the battle that had just waged around them already a distant thought.

#

Clayton waited another hour, taking short trips to the north and south, looking for signs of his men. He circled around to where the second ambush had come from. There was a lot of trampled brush, and behind a row of rocks, he found shotgun and 30.06 shell casings. Back down the hill, Clayton came upon more disturbed brush and here he found several blood pools and a trail of trample plants heading back uphill to the west. There was no sign of Webber or his gear. If that blood was his, he had gotten hit, and it looks like he might have been taken too.

Clayton made his way south along the hillside. He avoided the road, cautious in case any attackers still hid nearby. He found more trails, but none of them had blood on them. A hopeful sign. But that was the only sign he found. His men were nowhere to be seen.

After searching the area for more evidence of his men and finding none, Clayton decided to move on. He would continue along the bearing they had been taking. Hoping to come across his men. His squad. His friends.

Clayton let the creek decide his path, moving down hill and mostly north. He would pause and listen for any sign of his men every mile or so. There was nothing. The forest continued through its day. The birds were singing. The sun had crept out for a while as the cloud cover broke up.

What is the mission now, Clayton? he asked himself. *What is happening at home? Are Lori and the kids doing okay? I was supposed to be heading home tomorrow, but instead, I'm a thousand miles away. I have little gear, my uniform has become a target. The world seems to have gone to shit and I have no quick way to get home.*

Watching Clayton, sitting on a log in the middle of the forest, it was easy to see the resolve enter his mind and body. His shoulders became straighter. A grim expression moved across his face and settled there like a piece of stone. "I guess I'll walk home," he said to the forest. "These miles aren't going to walk themselves. If I can find the Trail, I can take it all the way home."

Clayton stood and grabbed his pack. He looked at the hole the arrow had made when the attack began. The arrow had fallen out during his retreat, and he never did find it again as he searched for his lost squad. Clayton noticed, with disappointment, that his axe was no longer strapped to his pack. He had lost that in the confusion too. He swung the pack around and slipped his arms into the straps. There wasn't much in it, but it would start him on his way.

The lone soldier started walking through the forest. The sun was on its way to setting. It had been a long, hard day. The adrenaline rush that the attack had produced had finally receded and he felt shaky and tired. The determination that had now entered him as he thought of his plight was evident in the spring in his step as he started bushwhacking north.

CHAPTER 5
A FOOTPATH IN THE WILDERNESS - FRIDAY, JUNE 8TH

Clayton accepted that he was alone now. His team was gone. Either scattered or dead. He had been walking all night. He bushwhacked at a furious pace as the woods darkened, coming upon a forest road that he began to follow. The road had pointed his nose north for a couple of klicks, then started in a northeasterly course once again as the night wore on. The waning gibbous moon had risen sometime after midnight and helped guide him with its thin light. He didn't dare use his head lamp at first, and after a while he didn't need it. The forest to his right had been getting brighter as the dawn harkened. The wood thrush started his morning routine. His *"ee –o- lay"* echoed through the foggy forest, greeting the morning with cheer, which made Clayton's situation seem all the more hopeless.

As Clayton walked along the road, he saw skillfully laid stone steps coming down the embankment on his right and another set of steps on the other side of the road, going up and continuing into the forest. There was a sign on the left side of the road, saying *Foot Traffic Only* and on a tree behind the sign, there glowed a white strip of paint. Two inches wide and six long. The blaze of the Appalachian Trail.

Memories of twenty-four years ago came flooding back into Clayton's mind. *The A.T. My trail. I found it*, Clayton thought to himself. Clayton sat on the bottom stone step and reached into his shirt again to pull out the pouch he wore there. He opened the pouch and emptied its contents. He caressed the braided locks of hair, smelling the scents of his wife and children. He took the twenty-sided die and rolled it onto the road. When it came to a stop, he picked it up and saw the number 17. "Not a bad roll," Clayton said to the forest. "A good omen if there ever was one."

I'm going to follow this trail home, Clayton thought to himself. Returning the special contents to the pouch, and placing it back inside his shirt, he took the trail to the left. The one that headed north. The one that headed home to his wife and children.

#

As Clayton walked the first couple of miles of what he quickly calculated to be a thousand mile journey, memories of long ago, when he last hiked this part of the trail, came flooding back. It was as if he had been here only a week or two ago, the visions in his mind were so clear. In front of him, he saw a sign that told him he was entering the Blood Mountain Wilderness. Thinking back to his hike, he remembered how that mountain had seriously kicked his ass as he made his way over it, but he had been determined then, and was just as motivated now to conquer it. The resolve came from what awaited him on the other side of that mountain — Neels Gap.

The first resupply stop of his hike long ago. He knew now that wearing his camo uniform had made him a target for others. Everyone was just as confused as he was, the uncertainty of the country was unsettling. He hoped to change his gear, aiming to blend in better. The irony lay in swapping camouflaged attire for something more ordinary.

This time he powered over the mountain, stopping at the stone shelter at the top for a short rest and a look around. From his vantage point atop the rock formation next to the shelter, Clayton could see for miles. All the majestic mountains moving off into the purple distance. Everything seems so calm and peaceful up here. There was no way to tell that all hell had broken loose down in those valleys far off into the distance. He needed to figure out what was going on. He needed to get back home to make sure everything was all right. Never in his forty-three years had he felt so helpless about the situation in front of him. He didn't like the feeling.

Below, the outfitter and hostel stood right in the middle of the trail along a mountain road. As he made his way down, Clayton could catch glimpses of the parking lot and the stone building that was nestled there. All looked quiet here. He didn't see anyone moving about, but he could see that the door to the Mountain Crossings Outfitter was ripped off its hinges and sitting askew against the wall. He did not have a good feeling about this and went into super cautious mode. Slowly, he descended the last hundred meters of trail to the road. Squatting behind some bushes, he surveilled the area for several minutes. He didn't perceive anything from that vantage, so he carefully crossed the road and moved towards the building.

Once again, he listened and watched for movement and sound. The silence and stillness continued. He peeked inside and saw the building had been ransacked and looted. There was ruined gear everywhere, scattered amongst the aisles of the store. There had been a major conflict here.

Entering the building, Clayton made a quick transit of the store. He could see clothes and gear strung about and surmised that he could piece together a kit that wouldn't make him stand out, but it would take some searching.

Clayton didn't spot any new backpacks in the mess, but when he looked up, he saw a line of old and used packs hanging along the wall, high up and out of reach. Each one with a small sign under it. There were all different brands and styles. Mostly old external frames that had clearly seen many miles on somebody's back. Off to the right, there was one that was a little more modern. It was a Kelty, internal frame, about sixty liters or so.

Clayton went over and peered into the darkness of the disheveled store, squinting to read the sign below this pack:

Cleveland Charlie – Thru Hiker – Nine time repeat offender.

The pack didn't look too badly worn and still seemed to be serviceable. "Well, if it was good enough for Cleveland Charlie, it should be good enough for Clayton 'Fictilibus' Collier." He stacked up a few wooden boxes he found and removed the pack from the wall. Opening it, he saw that there was mostly paper stuffed inside, to make it look full, but within the stuffing, he found a cook kit, that included a homemade alcohol stove made from an old cat food can and a nice pot that would work well. Clayton removed the paper and started looking around for more gear that he would need for his journey home.

Clayton's next priority was to find clothes that were not camo. He found a pair of brown convertible pants stuffed into the corner of the room, and after some more searching, he found a black shirt that would do well. A dark gray ball cap with an Under Armor insignia topped off his look. He quickly changed out of his uniform and into the found clothes, immediately feeling better now that he no longer looked like the uniformed enemy that had killed some of his squad. The clothes were comfortable, and he could tell they were good quality. He moved his meager gear from his standard issue survival pack to the old Kelty that Cleveland Charlie had used a long time ago. Clayton looked around some more. His foot kicked a small plastic package. Looking down, he could see it was a Sawyer water filter. Knowing that this device would last longer than the few iodine pills he had left, he placed it in his new pack. He also found a lighter on the counter and a decent rain jacket that was crumpled up in the corner of the room.

Under the counter, he found a full container of rubbing alcohol, and after scrounging in the recycle bin, he found a used coke bottle. He filled the bottle and placed it in one of the side pockets of the pack. He now had fuel for the old stove he had found. His mood was starting to improve.

#

Thud! A noise came from the back room that sounded like a shoe dropping. Clayton made his way down the hallway to the doorway and crouched low. He heard the noise again and knew it was coming from his right just past the doorway. Cautiously, he entered the room, one hand on the handle of his still sheathed knife, the other holding the one trekking pole he'd picked up amongst the destroyed gear.

As he turned to his right, he saw a person standing there with short brown hair, poised over a pile of gear and food. Their back was facing Clayton, so he said calmly, "Hey, how are you doing?" The stranger spun around quickly, her hand going to a four inch fixed blade knife on her belt. "It's okay. I'm friendly." Clayton stated, holding his hands out in front, with the pole's end pointing at the ground. The young woman's brown locks had a choppy look, which she pulled off nicely. She looked at Clayton, with a little fear in her eyes, but also a fierceness that he could sense immediately. "I'm Clayton."

"Gnobbit," she replied,

"Nobbit?" Clayton asked.

"Yes," she said. "G-N-O-B-B-I-T. Kinda like a mix of Gnome and Hobbit, Gnobbit. It's my trail name." She smiled as she said it. She was a little on the short side, but not quite in the category of Halfling. She had a mischievous look about her, that only increased when she grinned at him. She was dressed in all black. The darkness of her clothes contrasted with the lightness of her face and hands. Fic could see chipped black polish on her nails.

"Well, way back a couple decades ago, I hiked the Trail as Fictilibus. You can call me Fic, if you want," Clayton replied. Sharing his trail name out loud again brought back a rush of fond memories from his time on the A.T.

Clayton looked at the pile of stuff at Gnobbit's feet. She had gathered a large amount of freeze-dried food and other sources of calories. "Doing a little resupply?" he asked.

"Yes, I found all this scattered about and a tiny closet in the back had some more stuff. I had to jimmy the lock, but it was easy. I have more than I need right now, so I'm willing to share," she explained.

"My supplies are a little low, so I think I might take you up on that offer. Which way are you heading?" Clayton saw her eyes narrow as he asked the question. A little wariness crept into her voice.

"North. I need to get back home to Pearisburg, Virginia, and find out what the heck happened out there. I was only supposed to be on a three-week hike."

"I'm heading home too. I live a ways north of Pearisburg. My squad and I were down here for some survival training when all of this went down. We had some real shitty things happen, and I have been separated from my guys."

"Squad? Your guys?" Gnobbit's eyes narrowed a little more and a hint of fear entered them. "Are you Army?" she asked, taking a step back and moving her hand to her knife.

"Yes, I am, but I'm not one of the bad guys. Have you seen anything strange dealing with army personnel?" Clayton wanted to put her at ease. He tried to present a relaxed posture, but something didn't feel right.

"That's exactly what a bad guy would say," Gnobbit said. After a second or two of hesitation she added. "Yes, I have. Men dressed in camo and driving one of those drab Hummers are the ones who did this damage. I was hiding up on the hillside while they ransacked the place and took a bunch of stuff. It was scary."

"Those same guys, or ones like them, killed my Lieutenant and another of my squad. I'm not sure who they are, but they are not real army, or they have gone rogue. Also, we were attacked by some locals yesterday which is what split us all up. I think they thought we were the bad guys, and we didn't have the time to explain to them as they were shooting arrows, shotguns and rifles at us. That's why I changed out of my camo when I found these nice hiking clothes lying in the wreckage of the store." Clayton explained. "You know, since we are both headed in the same direction, maybe we should hike together. So we can watch each other's backs. And your skill at finding food seems to be a true asset."

"I think I would like that," the young woman replied. "Speaking of food, I'm a little hungry. I was thinking of checking out the hostel on the other side of the building. Eat a little something and maybe look around to see what is there."

"That sounds like a great idea. I have been walking all night. I'm wiped out. It would be good to get some sleep without having to worry about anyone attacking me. But first, some food."

The pair split the pile of food and put it into their packs. Gnobbit had stashed her pack in a dark corner of the store. After looking around the building one more time to see if there was anything else of use, they went to the door. Clayton stood in the shadows and observed the small parking lot and the road in front of the building. The view looked like a typical afternoon day in the northern Georgia mountains. The clouds had rolled in and it looked like rain was on its way.

They hefted their packs and walked along the building, down some stone steps to the parking lot. They followed a wooden rail fence to a gravel pathway. There were picnic tables under a large tree. Looking up into the tree, Clayton could see dozens, if not hundreds of shoes and boots hanging from the branches. There are many stories about this tree, but Clayton had figured those boots were from hikers who had walked the first thirty-one miles of the trail in the wrong boots and had purchased something that they hoped would work better at the outfitter here. Slinging their rejected footwear up into the tree as a ritual or rite of some kind. Clayton considered it just glorified trash, but it did look cool on a foggy morning, which was what the weather was like the last time he had walked by here, twenty-four years ago.

After the last table, there were stone steps that went down to a green door. Clayton tried the door, and it was locked. The small patio outside the door was surrounded by a short picket fence. Gnobbit dropped her pack, went through the opening in the fence, and walked around the side of the building. Clayton heard the crash of breaking glass as he sat exhausted on the stone steps. The door swung open and there was Gnobbit, smiling her secret smile. "Welcome to Walasi-Yi Inn," she said. "Come on in."

Clayton smiled, grabbed his pack and walked inside the old hostel.

#

The room was dark as they entered. The only light was coming in the three windows to the left. One of the windows had broken glass beneath it. Gnobbit's entry point. Her burglar skills were impressive. The area they were in looked like a living space. There was a mishmash of couches and recliner chairs, a low coffee table, and a few folding chairs. To the right was a cramped bathroom with a toilet and stand-up shower. The back of the room had a small bar, and behind that, a kitchen sink and counter. A passageway on the right led to the sleeping area. It was much darker back there, so Clayton put his head lamp on to explore. The room had several clunky bunk beds all around it. They appeared to be made of 2 x 4s, 2 x 6s, and plywood. Thin mattresses were present on each bed and the upper bunks had ladders built in.

Clayton headed back to the kitchen area and dropped his pack. He was starving. He dug through the new food Gnobbit shared with him and pulled out a nice Mountain House Meal. Chili Mac with Beef. He tried the sink to see if it worked, but no water came out.

Gnobbit was in the living area looking through a bookcase against the wall. "It looks like the water isn't flowing," Clayton stated the obvious. "This building must be on a well. No electricity, no pump working. Luckily, I still have enough water in my canteens. How are you doing for water?"

"I'm good," Gnobbit responded. "I have about a liter and a half."

Clayton pulled out the alcohol stove he had found in the old pack. He saw another can of denatured alcohol on the counter next to the sink when he was looking around and it was still half full. He poured a little into the stove to save the supply he had in his coke bottle and lit it up. A soft blue flame filled the old can. Clayton poured some water into his pot and placed it on the stove.

Gnobbit reached into her pack and pulled out a blue stuff sack. Inside was a small pot with a little stove nestled inside and a small red canister. She screwed the stove on to the canister and fired it up. Her flame was also blue, but it made a low hissing sound that seemed to mean business. "I hope I can get more of this fuel soon. Otherwise, I'll be cooking on a fire for my meals."

"The trail provides," Clayton announced. "You never know when the things you need will just show up. I have seen it happen a hundred times."

"Me too," Gnobbit replied. She sat watching the blue flame lick over the bottom of her pot. Her concentration revealed that she was thinking of something important. "What do you think happened, Fic?" she asked her new hiking partner.

"I really don't know, Gnobbit. We saw what looked like an atomic explosion over Atlanta. What was it? Two days ago, now. Wow, it already seems like a long time ago. So much has happened. If you take that with the addition of the rogue army, it seems like something might have happened to our government. Maybe an overthrow or something. We were completely out of contact with our base, except for an emergency beacon which seems to have stopped working. I remember hearing something on the radio on the way down. That asshole Richard Flaherty was stirring things up again. Whatever is happening, it seems to not only have affected this part of the country, but maybe all over the place. No electricity points to a breakdown in infrastructure and basic services." Clayton reached down to his pack and pulled the beacon out of a side pocket. He turned it on and waited a minute. *Searching ... Searching ... Searching ...* He took the device over to the window and sat it on the sill, hoping that maybe it just needed a better view of the quiet sky.

The water was boiling now. Gnobbit's stove worked a bit better. She had already transferred her hot water into a bag of food, and it was sitting on the counter, finishing up the cook. Clayton did the same with his water and placed his pouch next to Gnobbit's.

He flicked on his headlamp and looked around some more while his meal soaked in the hot water. He wandered over to the bookcase that Gnobbit had been checking out. There were a few dozen paperback books on the shelf. Every genre seemed to be covered. On the third shelf down he saw a long, but slim book with a green cover. *The A.T. Guide* was discernible as his headlamp came to rest on the cover. It was last year's version. *Since Taylor took the maps, this might come in handy along the trail. Let us know what's ahead of us*, he thought. He set it aside and asked Gnobbit. "Do you have a trail guide?"

"Yes," she replied. "I have this year's version of *The A.T. Guide*. I really like it."

"I found an old one over here that I think I will bring along, so we can compare notes along the way as we plan." Clayton set the book on the coffee table and continued looking around.

In the corner he found a covered chest with the words *Hiker Box* on it. He flipped the lid back and looked around inside to see what was there. He found one of those canisters that Gnobbit had used and when he shook it; it seemed to be at least a quarter full. He held it up and showed his light on the can. "The Trail Provides," he announced towards Gnobbit. "It still has some fuel in it. I can bring it along in my pack, just in case. Maybe if we keep finding this stuff, we can share the stove at times. Your stove works a lot better than my little alcohol stove and I'm in the same position as you, as to finding fuel for it."

"Sure," she replied.

The box had a few odds and ends that other hikers had discarded. Some of it was trash, some useless stuff that wouldn't be needed, and a few odds and ends that Clayton didn't feel the need to carry for now. He continued his search of the rooms.

The food was done. Both hikers sat spooning their meal into their mouths. Neither saying anything. Just replenishing calories.

When he was done, he licked off his spoon, folded up his trash, and put his cooking gear away. His eyes had taken on the weight of a thousand tons. "I think I need to get some shut-eye.

If you need me to keep watch or something later, just wake me up." He grabbed his pack and walked into the bunk room. He found a bunk that was in a little alcove, away from the rest of the room. It was even darker back here. He got his bag out and took off his boots. He didn't even bother taking off any clothes. It was warm enough inside, so he just flopped down on top of the bag, and within seconds of closing his eyes, a soft snore escaped his nose. He was already asleep.

#

"Fic, wake up." Clayton could feel his shoulder being softly shaken. The plea to wake up had been a soft whisper. "What's up Gnobbit? You need me to keep watch?" he asked.

"No. There's someone outside. Many someones by the sound of it."

Clayton listened and could hear the tell-tale sound of a Humvee's diesel engine idling out in the parking lot. More than one by the level of sound that was getting through the stone walls. He could also hear men talking and shouting to each other. He quickly got up out of his bunk and slipped his boots on.

He grabbed his sleeping bag and shoved it into his pack. Gnobbit already had her pack beside her.

In the back of the alcove, the bunks had stopped, leaving a small hidey hole that they could use. Clayton grabbed Gnobbit's and his pack and placed them in the back of the space. He ushered Gnobbit into the space and told her, "Just stay there, I'll be back in a second."

She nodded and drew her knife from her belt. Clayton did the same with his knife. He couldn't see shit, so he turned on the red function of his headlamp and moved off to the living room area of the hostel. There was light coming in the windows from the flashlights outside. The beam moved around to and fro and caused shadows to jump up and move around. Clayton turned off his red light and crouched in the doorway. Just then, someone tried to open the door to the hostel. It was locked. Clayton sent a word of thanks to Gnobbit, who had obviously locked the door after Clayton had passed out.

Clayton could hear the men talking to each other and then there was a loud boom as someone, or something, bounced off the thick door. They were breaking in.

Clayton retreated to the alcove and crouched in front of Gnobbit. "They're coming in," he updated her.

"Duh," she whispered back sarcastically.

They heard the barrier give up its last hold on its hinges and the door came crashing down inside the building.

The men stopped talking and came looking. Clayton could see their flashlights scanning over the space. As he watched, the light zeroed in on the bunk room before heading inside. He froze in place and felt Gnobbit do the same.

Only one man came into the bunk room. He shined his light on every bunk as he quickly moved to the end and then back. He even checked the bunks in the alcove, but didn't bother to come back and aim it in their hidey hole.

The light moved out of the room and back to the main space. Both hikers let out a slow, quiet breath that they had been holding. Trying to stay as silent as possible.

"The place is empty," said one of the men.

"Not much here like there was in the store," his companion replied.

"Just following orders. The Regime is now in charge, and they are calling the shots. Personally, I don't think they had to bomb all of those cities, but I guess The Boss thought it was necessary."

"Yeah, that was intense, but this is the way we need it to be. We gotta keep hitting The Resistance hard and fast. Squash it before it takes hold. If they won't give us the power, we need to take it, and take it is what Flaherty did."

Their conversation continued, but they were heading out of the building and their words became garbled and unintelligible. After a few more minutes, the area became quiet again.

The companions remained in place, wanting to be completely sure they were in the clear.

Clayton checked his watch. It was 0430. At 0440, Clayton once again crept out of the hole and into the main room. He moved towards the now open space where the door had been and peeked outside. He saw three Humvees move down the road to the north. He also smelled smoke.

After the Humvees had moved out of sight, Clayton walked up the stone steps and onto the gravel trailway. He could see a flickering light coming from inside the store. Those fuckers had torched it. Seeing the light grow brighter he turned around and moved to the door.

Gnobbit stood in the doorway with both packs. Clayton grabbed his, and slung it on his back. Gnobbit did the same with hers.

They both walked up the stone steps and turned left. Moving under a covered breezeway, they continued along the path. There was an open yard behind the building. More picnic tables and some large trees. The breeze was picking up here, coming down the ridge and blowing through this gap. They moved on quickly into the woods until they came to a small campsite. They hunkered down here and waited for daylight. As they sat near a rock fire ring, a soft rain began to fall. Both hikers pulled out their rain jackets and put them on.

As the adrenaline died down in his body, Clayton could get a more accurate grasp on how his body and mind felt. His body had recharged and repaired itself while he slept. Even his sore shoulder didn't hurt very much. He felt like he could put in a strong hike in the coming day. "Did you sleep at all, Gnobbit?" he asked.

"Yes. I got a few hours. I'm feeling pretty good considering."

"Me too. Are you ready to put in some miles today? Get closer to home?"

"I am," she replied.

The dawn had started to brighten the woods to the east, and the rain continued at a steady patter. Their eyes were well adjusted to the dim light, so they donned their packs and started walking along the now wet trail. Hiking north. Hiking home. As they started their day's walk, Clayton kept thinking about what he had heard. The Regime. The Boss. The Resistance. Flaherty. He needed to learn more.

CHAPTER 6
HIKING NORTH - SATURDAY, JUNE 9TH TO FRIDAY, JUNE 15TH

Clayton and Gnobbit sat on the edge of a three-sided shelter, both nibbling on a power bar. They were both staring in the same direction — straight ahead where a small stream babbled its way down the hillside. The rain continued to fall at a steady rate. Not too hard, but hard enough to soak through even the most expensive rain gear. The surrounding forest dripped and dribbled as they took respite from the constant din of raindrops on their hoods.

They had traveled eleven and a half miles. They were taking it slow. In no hurry. This wasn't a sprint, nor even a marathon. It was an expedition of an unknown length of time and a great distance. If they wanted to ensure they arrived at their destination, they had to try to avoid injury. They had stopped at Bull Gap to fill their water in a nice spring and continued along the ups and downs of the trail. The rain was a constant companion, but the temperature of the air was comfortably warm. The exertion of the trail still had their clothes wet, but with sweat, not rain. The companions had stopped at the turnoff for Whitley Gap Shelter and had a quick breakfast of some odds and ends that each had in their food bags. Clayton had a squashed honeybun and Gnobbit had found a nice poppy seed muffin that she gobbled down like a hungry child.

Onward they had gone. Taking each climb as it came. Not encountering another human at all but seeing and hearing the creatures and birds of the forest who didn't mind the rain at all. They had descended into a gap or two and crossed small forest roads, some old, some still in use, until they had come to Low Gap Shelter. That's where they were now.

It was a little past 1300 as they sat there on the edge of the shelter. Just enough to be out of the rain. Clayton looked around into the shelter, it was of decent size and looked pretty clean. A broom sat propped up in one corner and a shelter log sat in its mailbox-like container attached to the wall. Clayton got up and pulled the log out of the box, then out of a large Ziploc bag.

The shelter log was one of those college composition books with black marble like printing on its covers. It appeared a bit weather worn and tattered around the edges. Flipping through it, Clayton saw that it had many entries. He turned to the last entry.

"June 1st. Just stopping in for a quick bite then moving on. Heading north. Don't know how far. - Signed, Ragged." Clayton read aloud. "No one has been here, or at least signed the log for over a week. I wonder if there are other hikers out here. Doing the same thing we are," he speculated.

"I know it's a little early in the day, but with the rain continuing and us being a bit soaked, maybe we should stay here tonight. It sure would be better than getting rained on out in the woods. I don't think we could push it to the next shelter and the guide doesn't offer a lot of camping options." The brush of the trail so far had thickened up a great deal. Poison ivy was the dominant plant that he could see as they walked along. Clayton was sure they could etch out a place to sleep anywhere along the trail, but finding a ready-made site makes packing up much easier and faster.

"I think that might be a good idea," Gnobbit responded. "My feet are hurting a bit anyway. I think I may be getting a blister on my little toe from all the walking with wet feet. I've only been out here for a few days and I'm still getting my trail legs."

"This is home for the night then," Clayton said. He got up and moved his pack to one side of the shelter. He opened it up and took out his meager gear. Placing his sleeping pad down and his patrol bag on top of it. Gnobbit moved to the other side of the shelter and started her nightly set up as well. She had a two-person tent that she wouldn't need to set up, so she put that aside. Next out was her food bag and cook kit. A small bag of clothes and a stuff sack with odds and ends followed the other gear to the shelter floor. She reached in and pulled out a deflated sleeping pad and a down quilt. She blew up the pad and placed the quilt on the pad. Lastly, she pulled out a blow-up pillow, which was no bigger than a textbook. The set up looked comfortable considering.

\#

They spent the rest of the day lounging around in the shelter. Gnobbit had brought a mass market paperback book from the hostel and had started to read it. Clayton looked through his copy of *The A.T. Guide*. Studying what was ahead and making some calculations on mileage. They had a long way to go and would need to figure out how to resupply along the way. Road crossings were now possibly dangerous places and who knows what the situations were like in the upcoming trail towns.

"So, what's your story, Gnobbit?" Clayton asked as they were lounging in the shelter and the rain drummed a steady rhythm on the green metal roof.

"My real name is Carly. I'm nineteen and just finished my sophomore year at Georgia State University. I'm majoring in Criminal Science. When the semester finished, I hung around at home for about a week or so then headed to Springer Mountain to start hiking north for three weeks. I was hoping to get to the beginning of the Smokies where my family was going to pick me up. When this thing started, my phone died, and I was unable to call home or contact anyone. My family knows I'm out here, but not really where. I can actually walk home using the A.T., because Pearisburg is right next to the trail. So, I guess that is what I'm going to do." She looked over at Clayton to gauge his reaction. He was looking at her with a strange, shiny gleam in his eye.

"My daughter is about your age. I bet your family is as worried about you as I am about her, her brother and their mother. We will get you home. I promise," Clayton vowed.

\#

As the sun was heading towards its setting, which they couldn't see as the sky was still full of clouds and rain, they prepared their meal for the evening. Clayton decided to finish off his last MRE meal. It was Tuscan Beef. He still had one heater left, so he didn't have to fire up his alcohol stove tonight, saving precious fuel. Gnobbit boiled up a pack of ramen, adding some bacon bits to the mix to provide a little protein and to improve the flavor.

They didn't even attempt to make a fire; the woods were soaking wet, the air was a tolerable temperature, and even though they were in a secluded area, they didn't want to take the chance of attracting attention to the smoke and smell of a fire.

Darkness descended on the shelter area, and the two lone hikers rolled into their sleeping gear, letting the night take them. The rain appeared to be letting up, but the forest still dripped and spattered. Clayton was checking his guide one more time with his red light as he heard small snores come from the other side of the shelter. *I think we can do about fifteen miles or so tomorrow*, he thought to himself. He wondered how his family was doing up north in Virginia. Sleep took him after that. A restless slumber, full of scary dreams of people shooting at him and searching for him as he ran along a shady path in a deep wood.

#

Morning dawned with a brightness that had been completely missing the day before. The forest had a freshly washed appearance. The smell of the forest reminded Clayton of laundry on a clothesline. There was still a lot of dampness all around, but the sun would work hard to dry things out throughout the day. The two companions went through their morning routine and were packed and ready to go around 0730.

Clayton took the lead as they left the shelter area and turned right, back onto the trail. The morning's trail was relatively easy. There were no steep climbs or descents. They had filled their bottles at the stream in front of the shelter first thing this morning and were able to top off their water as they needed at the springs and streams along the way. The filter Clayton had found was being put to good use. The gradual climb of the day eventually brought them to another shelter on top of Blue Mountain. The wind was blowing across the mountain top, but they still took the time to stop at the shelter and take a break. When they continued, the trail made its way down the mountain to Unicoi Gap, where a paved road traversed the gap. They carefully came down the trail and sat for a few minutes where they could see the road and check out the scene.

Across the road was a large parking lot. The trail went through the lot before heading up a few stone steps on the other side, where it started to climb the next mountain. They hadn't heard any traffic on the road as they approached. Two cars sat in the parking lot, but they didn't see any people in the area.

Carefully they came down to the road, crossed it, and headed towards the cars. One of the cars was old looking with a generous amount of rust around the fenders. Gnobbit checked the door, and it was unlocked. She did a quick check inside and popped the trunk. The car had nothing that would help them on their journey. The other vehicle, a late model SUV, was locked, but it also appeared to not have anything that they would need or want. It had already come down to survival of the fittest. If Gnobbit could get into something and it contained items that could be put to use, they were going to take it with silent thanks to the *provider* who had no idea they had taken it.

There was a kiosk at the edge of the lot, to the left of the stone steps. Gnobbit spotted a small, blue cooler sitting behind the support of the kiosk. "What's this we have here?" she queried as she changed direction and headed to the billboard that contained information of the trail and general area. She moved past a sign that said: *Free Rides to Franklin, Call Scooter, 828-876-9305.*

Gnobbit opened the cooler and peered inside for a few seconds, then reached in and brought out a can of Coke, a smile crossing her pleasant features. She reached in with her other hand and pulled out a can of some local obscure beer, water dripping off the can and making a clinking sound as it returned to the cooler. "Thirsty?" she asked.

Clayton walked over and took the offered beer. Cracking it open, he replied, "Always." He took the can and drained it in one long series of swallows, it tilted up higher and higher until it was empty. "Ahhhhh," Clayton said with a long sigh, followed by a burp.

Gnobbit laughed and started drinking her refreshment at a more sensible pace. "The ice is melted, and the water is barely cool, but this is the best damn Coke I have had in a long time." She took another long drink and held the can to her forehead, trying to soak in a little of the vague coolness.

They sat for a bit enjoying the day and the trail magic they had discovered, then deposited the empty cans into a trash can on the other side of the kiosk and hefted their packs and continued on.

They started up the steps headed towards Rocky Mountain. They would be re-climbing all the elevation they had just lost coming down Blue Mountain. Around a thousand feet or so. "Well, this mountain ain't gonna climb itself," Clayton announced as he hitched his pack up on his shoulders, tightened his hip belt and continued up the stone and wood steps back into the forest.

The climb was a bit steep in places, but it was manageable. They took their time and kept putting one foot in front of the other. Both had a good sheen of sweat soaking their clothes when they determined that they were nearing the top of the mountain.

#

As they walked along, they started to smell smoke. Wood smoke it was, which probably meant someone up ahead had a fire going. They stopped on the side of the trail to discuss options. They decided to continue slowly, with Clayton in the lead. Ready to retreat or fight if necessary.

The trail curved around to the left with the underbrush thick at the top of the mountain. As they drew closer to what he could tell was an established campsite, he saw the source of the smoke smell. A fire was burning in a stone fire ring. It was going pretty well. With a crack and a pop every couple of seconds along with a shower of sparks that rose up into the air a few feet before disappearing. A man was sitting in front of the fire with his back to the sneaking hikers. He was dressed in a black hoodie fleece and gray pants. The hood was up on his head, leaving his face in the shadows. To his right was a greenish tarp strung between two trees. Under the tarp hung a dark brown hammock.

Clayton continued to approach the man at a slow pace that he considered silent. Gnobbit was right behind him, being even more quiet on her feet. When they were about fifteen meters away, the man spoke without turning in his seat in front of the fire. "Come join the fire. I've been waiting for you," he said. "I hope you are hungry. I have plenty of food and would like to share some with you."

Clayton stood up straight in surprise. He hadn't seen the man turn his eyes to them at all. It is like he had just sensed their presence. He continued walking into the campsite. "I think we will have a visit if it's okay. I'm Fic and this is Gnobbit. We're heading north."

"I'm Brown Shades," he said, finally turning his face toward them. He appeared to be about fifty years old. Had a thick and somewhat long gray beard and was wearing what looked like brown colored sunglasses. "I, too, am heading north. The world has gone to shit, and I need to get back to my car in Damascus. Then, hopefully, I can get back to Pennsylvania, where I live." Brown Shades picked up a stick from a pile he had next to him and placed it on the fire, eliciting another shower of sparks.

"Gnobbit is heading back to Pearisburg, Virginia, and I need to get up to Northern Virginia. A place called Millwood," Clayton said.

"I haven't seen another hiker in four days or so. I was beginning to think I was the only one still out here, but I had a feeling someone would arrive before too long. I wouldn't mind the company on this trek. Do you mind if I join up?" he asked, one of his eyebrows raising in a Spock-like gesture to emphasize the request. "When we get back to my car, I can drive you from there to your destinations. If that is still something that is possible," he offered.

"It would be a pleasure to have you along," Clayton replied as Gnobbit nodded her agreement. "The more the merrier."

"Looks like the beginnings of a Tramily," said Gnobbit.

"Tramily?" Clayton looked at her puzzled. Brown Shades just smiled and waited for her to explain.

"Yes, Tramily. Trail plus Family, Tramily. It's what we call a group of people out here who hike together. That's us."

"Do you have any idea what has happened?" Clayton continued his conversation with the interesting man.

"Not really," Brown Shades replied. "Like I said, I haven't talked to anyone in a while and the last people I talked to down at the outfitters were as clueless as me. I started my hike at Springer Mountain last Sunday. I'm a science teacher at a small high school in P-A. We finished classes on the first of the month. I drove down to Damascus the next day, parked my car, then got a shuttle down to the parking lot at the bottom of the mountain. On Tuesday, I was sleeping in the stone shelter up on Blood Mountain when I was awakened by the bright sky to the south. The next morning, I headed down the mountain to Mountain Crossings at Neels Gap.

"The store had no power, but they were still open. They asked me if I had seen or heard anything and after I mentioned the bright light coming from the Atlanta area, they all grew concerned. After discussing a few likely and unlikely scenarios, I purchased a bunch of food, paying cash, since their registers weren't working, and I headed up here to camp for a few days and think about what to do next."

"Mountain Crossings has been looted or something and when we left there, it was on fire. Some guys dressed in army camo and driving Humvees did the looting and torching. I don't know who they are, but they aren't a legit army. At least not the army I belong to," Clayton shared.

"Hmm, that's interesting. So, you're in the army then, huh?" Brown Shades replied. A serious look reflected in his dark eyeglasses.

"Yes, I am," Clayton said." I have nineteen years in. I will retire next year. My watch group and I were on a survival training mission when all this went down. We lost a couple men to the '*army*' guys," Clayton used air quotes to emphasize the word army. "Then I was separated from the rest when we were attacked by some locals, our uniforms making them think we were the bad guys." Clayton recounted finding new clothes and the conversation he and Gnobbit had overheard in the Hostel. Brown Shades listened intently, nodding here and there.

"I always had a bad feeling about that Flaherty guy," Brown Shades said. "He has been causing trouble in the government for several years now. I wonder if he finally found a way to take over." The two nodded their heads in agreement and uncertainty.

"So, what shall we have for dinner?" Brown Shades moved on to the next subject. "Like I said, I still have a lot of food and if we are moving on, I would like to try to lighten my load a bit. How about some Backcountry Jambalaya?" he suggested.

"That sounds like it would be good." Clayton responded. "Do you need any of the ingredients?"

"No, I have everything we need." Brown Shades said. He went over to his hammock and opened the pack that was sitting underneath the tarp on a piece of black plastic. He removed a very large bag. He reached in again and pulled out a brown stuff sack and brought them both over. From the brown sack, Brown Shades produced a fairly large pot that had a lid to go with it.

He also pulled out a very long-handled spoon. From the other bag, he pulled out a large Ziploc of rice, a pouch of chicken, and a whole summer sausage. He also pulled out a smaller Ziploc that had a mysterious brownish red powder in it.

As he started preparing the meal's ingredients, a sharp gleam came to his eye. He seemed completely at ease and in his element.

The process reminded Clayton of a wizard preparing a most elaborate potion.

The chef poured some water into the pot from a water bottle and placed it in some hot coals that had been moved away from the main fire. The coals were glowing and steam started to come off of the water's surface very quickly. He measured out a few cupfuls of rice and poured it into the water. Next, he opened the pouch of chicken and added that to the pot. He cut up half of the summer sausage with a small knife that he kept around his neck, and he finished it off with two heaping spoonfuls of the brownish red powder. "This is my Bag of Seasons. It has all manner of flavorful things, like gravy mix, taco powder, onion soup and a few other things. I put this stuff in everything," he explained. The concoction was soon steaming and bubbling nicely.

Brown Shades grabbed his green bandana that was through the belt loop of his pants and used it as a potholder to pull the pot out of the fire. They let it sit for a couple minutes, then Brown Shades spooned a good portion into each of the other hiker's pots. They each took a spoonful of the rice and meat dish. Clayton and Gnobbit looked at each other as their eyebrows raised and a smile spread across their faces.

"Yum," Gnobbit interjected.

"I wholeheartedly agree," Clayton added to the praise.

Brown Shades sat back with his own spoonful of the Jambalaya, a delighted smile crossing his face. "I knew you guys were coming," he said mysteriously. "I dreamed about you," he added nonchalantly. Fic looked at him curiously, but said nothing.

When everyone was finished with the main course, they found out Brown Shades wasn't quite done. From his food bag he produced three rectangular, brownies. They had colorful pieces of candy on top. "These are Cosmic Brownies," announced Brown Shades. "I believe they have magical tendencies. At least they taste magical to me."

The three hikers ate their dessert, each relishing the sweet chocolate goodness. "These are pretty good, Brownie," Gnobbit said, shortening Brown Shades' name to fit the occasion.

"My pleasure," he responded. "I still have quite a few of them in my bag."

Clayton and Gnobbit set up their sleeping gear and then headed back to the fire pit. The threesome sat around the fire, relaxing. Putting a log on occasionally, but mainly just staring into the flames. Clayton noticed that as the day darkened, Brown Shades' glasses lightened into regular clear glasses. They were auto-tint eyeglasses.

As they sat enjoying the fire, Brown Shades reached into his pocket and pulled out a small packet of something. He pretended to wave his hands over the brightly burning fire, dropping the packet into the fire. After a few seconds the fire's color turned from a bright yellow, to a striking shade of violet.

"Whoa," Gnobbit exclaimed, "how did you do that?"

"Why, magic of course," replied Brown Shades, smiling and winking at her as he said it. "Actually, the violet was caused by potassium chloride. In this case, salt substitute. My bride — God rest her soul — had me using it instead of the real thing. My blood pressure, you understand," he explained.

"I like the magic explanation better," she giggled. "Can you do other colors?"

"I just might, but not tonight. I think it is time I head to my hammock and get some sleep. If we are hiking again in the morning, I will need to rest up."

Each of the hikers headed to their respective sleeping area. Brown Shades to his hammock, Gnobbit to her tent and Fic to his bivy that he had set up under a bush.

Darkness came to the camp, and with it, the night insects came out to announce their everlasting quest for a mate. Another day on the trail was done.

#

As Clayton quickly drifted off to sleep, his body became very still. As the last remnants of consciousness faded, he started to dream.

The night was very dark, and he sat up looking around. The wind had picked up and made the sparks blow off the dwindling fire. He looked down at his body and he wasn't wearing the clothes he went to sleep in. He had on a chain-mail vest over a padded linen shirt and thick leather pants. His boots went almost to his knees, and he had bracers on his forearms. Belted to his side was a large sword. Next to his sleeping pallet, was a steel helmet with a sigil of a globe with wings sprouting out of its sides.

He looked over at his sleeping companions. They were no longer in a tent or hammock, but had pallets like his on the ground around the fire. Gnobbit was still dressed all in black, but the clothes looked rougher, as though they were homespun. Her top had a deep hood that was raised over her hair, but her delicate features were still visible. Her belt now held a small sword about ten inches long. She stirred in her sleep and the hood pulled back, revealing pointed ears.

Fic looked over at Brown Shades and he now wore a long, brown robe that reached all the way to his feet. Beside his pallet lay a long staff that had a large crystal embedded into its ornate top. The crystal gave off a low blue glow. His beard was still gray, but now hung down almost to his stomach.

The wind blew across the mountain top and rustled the underbrush all around. When the wind abated for a bit, Fic could still hear the rustling. It was coming from the forest right in front of him. He stared into the darkness and saw two red eyes glowing back at him. His hand went to the haft of his blade and a chilling awareness sank in as he looked around. He was surrounded . . . two . . . three . . . four more pairs materialized. A low growl sounded across the clearing. They started moving closer.

The wind blew again and stirred the coals of the dying fire and kindled a small flame. As the brightness grew, Fic could see three men standing above the eyes. The men looked strange. Not men at all, but more like grotesque beasts. If he had to name them, it would have been Goblin or Orc. They were disfigured and huge. Ragged clothes hung on their shoulders, and they had chains in their hands. The chains ran to the red eyes which now became giant wolves. The growl grew louder, and he could see their teeth and the saliva dripping off the large fangs.

He tried to shout to his companions, to wake them, to warn them, but no sound came out of his mouth. The beasts started to advance on him. He drew his sword and tried to shout again. This time a barely audible squeak came from his mouth, but it wasn't loud at all. The monster on the left dropped his chain and the beast came charging at Fic.

He swung his sword with an expert stroke, even though he had never held a sword in his life before. The sword sliced cleanly through the wolf's head. Removing it from the charging body. The body fell to the ground, twitching in agony and the head rolled into the underbrush.

Fic turned once again to warn his new friends and he saw that Gnobbit was no longer in her bed but had disappeared. Brown Shades was rising up from his pallet and grabbing his staff at the same time.

Fic turned to see he was being charged. This time it was two wolves bearing down on him. A flash of purple light came from over his right shoulder and the beasts burst into purple flames; frying them to a crisp instantly. Fic looked back to see Brown Shades standing there and pointing his staff at the attackers, the embedded crystal now glowing brightly.

Movement caught Fic's attention at the edge of the clearing next to the orcish fiends. A small dark figure came running behind the three brutes. Fic saw the flash of a blade as it was whipped across the hamstrings of all three monsters. They let out a scream as they all collapsed to the ground. The last two wolves ran off into the brush, yipping in terror.

There was a great flash. This time from all around and the dead and dying attackers disappeared from sight. Fic stood staring. He heard a voice behind him say, "Beware the Beast of the Apocalypse," and he fell to the ground unconscious.

#

Clayton came awake with a start as the wind whipped across the mountain top. He could hear it ripping along Brown Shades' tarp as it gusted and blew. Everything was as it should be. He was in his bivy, Gnobbit was in her tent and Brown Shades in his hammock, which rocked in the wind. The dream stayed fresh in his mind for several minutes, then started to fade as he fell into an uneasy sleep.

#

When morning came, all was calm. The trio of hikers each came out of their slumber in their own time. Clayton stirred awake to the sounds of Brown Shades stoking the fire to get some water going for coffee. He started packing up his gear and grabbed a power bar for breakfast when Gnobbit climbed out of her tent. They each drank some coffee and talked a little about the day's plan as they let the fire die to embers. "I had the strangest dream last night," Gnobbit said. Clayton looked up at her with a piercing stare and he noticed that Brown Shades was looking intently at her too with a strange expression on his face.

"What was it about?" Clayton asked.

"It's all kinda fuzzy now," Gnobbit said. Then she went on to explain a dream that was weirdly similar to Clayton's.

When she completed her description, Clayton only said, "Yeah, that is kind of strange." Brown Shades looked at the two of them and remained silent. Clayton could tell that his mind was working overtime and wondered if he too had a similar dream. Clayton decided that he wasn't going to say anything just yet about his dream. It was just a coincidence.

#

When all were ready, they stirred the coals, added a bit of water and made sure the fire was out.

Each hefted their pack, snapping the buckles and adjusting the straps. Brown Shades took a large, straight stick that appeared to be made of oak. This was his walking stick. "I call this The Staff," Brown Shades explained. "I have had it many years and have hiked many miles using it to help steady me and move me along."

Looking at The Staff, Clayton was reminded of his dream. Glancing at Gnobbit, he saw her looking curiously at the long stick too. Clayton shook his head to clear it and started walking.

The small Tramily started heading back down the mountain, crossing a forest service road then heading back up Tray Mountain. The day had become rather pleasant. There was a slight breeze that blew up the trail and along the ridge that would cool them while drying a little of their sweat. Large, puffy, white clouds floated along the sky, briefly hiding the sun from time to time, then releasing it to shine once again until the next cloud would arrive.

They took a break at a shelter and refilled their water bottles before continuing on to the next challenge. Here the trail traveled along a ridge top for several miles. The ups and downs were short and gradual, but the day was still tough.

Stopping at Sassafras Gap for lunch, the group each took a little nap, and all felt refreshed for the rest of the day. The last two days had been a little shorter than planned due to the rain and meeting new friends, so today they were going to try to do at least fifteen miles.

When they passed Deep Gap Shelter, they knew that they would be able to finish the planned mileage for the day. It was getting late, and the sun was once again heading towards the mountain horizon when they came to a paved road at Dicks Creek Gap.

"The guide mentions a hostel just a half mile down the road that has resupply. Do you think we should check it out?" Clayton asked.

"I could use a few more items in my food bag. I'm also running low on TP. It would be good to stock up on some so I don't have to resort to using leaves," said Gnobbit. "I'm game to check it out."

"I still have quite a bit of food, but I'm all for checking it out. I've been cooking with the fire the last couple of days to save my fuel, but if we can find another canister or two of that, I wouldn't mind picking it up," Brown Shades added his opinion.

"Let's go then," Clayton said as he started walking down the road. "If we hear any vehicles, we should probably get off the road until we see who it is," he cautioned. His companions nodded their heads in agreement.

After walking on a trail all day, it always seems painful to walk on simple asphalt and today was no exception. All three had a little hobble as they came to the long, uphill driveway that led to the hostel. There was a sign at the beginning of the driveway next to a cluster of mailboxes. *Northern Georgia Hostel and Hiking Center*, it displayed.

Carefully, the three hikers walked up the driveway. They could see the building and it appeared that no one was around. Hanging from the top of the porch was a yellow sign that said: *Welcome Hikers*. The doors were closed and the neon *Open* sign was unlit in the window. At least it didn't appear to have been looted or torched.

Brown Shades walked up to the door and knocked. Clayton cringed internally, but after thinking about it, it couldn't hurt. Unless there was someone inside with a shotgun or worse.

The hikers waited by the door, glancing around the property, when Gnobbit suddenly drew their attention to the window as the curtain nervously twitched back into place. "We're closed," they heard a voice from inside announce.

"We were just wondering if we could get a little resupply. We are running low on food and sundries and need to replenish," Brown Shades explained. "We won't take long and we have money."

"Have you guys seen any army men around?" the disembodied voice asked.

"Yes, but not for several days. We are trying to lie low as we make our way north and home."

The voice fell silent, leaving them in suspense. Just as Gnobbit was getting ready to suggest they leave, a bolt turned in the door and it opened a crack. In the crack they could see a man peeking out at them. From what they could see, he had glasses and a sparse beard. On his head, he wore a green bandana. He opened the door wider and said, "Quick, get in."

The hikers moved inside, still wearing their packs. The room they were in was spacious, with high ceilings, a small kitchen to their right, some tables and benches to their left and a couple sofas further back. The room was dim in the late afternoon light. There was no electricity here either.

"Do you know what is going on?" the man asked.

Each of the three told their stories of how they had come to be on the trail as the world was going insane. Clayton conveniently left out the fact that he was active duty in the army. The guy seemed to be very skittish, so he didn't want to make it worse.

"I'm Bob," he introduced himself. "Mr. Hikes-a-lot when I'm on the trail. I own the place. The army came by and I thought they were going to trash my hostel, but for some reason, they didn't. I don't know why."

"There's definitely something strange going on," Clayton said. "We have been trying to figure it out since it started."

"I have some food and our hiker box has a lot of stuff in it that you can have. Whatever you need, I'll give you," Bob said. "You guys are the first hikers who have come here since last Tuesday. I want to help."

Bob showed them the hiker box and they were able to find quite a bit of food in there. There was also a half roll of toilet paper that Gnobbit took after the other two rolled several handfuls off for themselves. In the bottom of the box, Clayton found a small tarp. "This will work for keeping the rain off my face when I'm in my bivy," he stated, putting the tarp into an outside pocket of his pack.

Bob also had some food and gear in his store. They each took a few Mountain House meals, some ramen and several protein bars. Each of them also took a canister of fuel and Clayton picked up his own Pocket Rocket stove. Clayton offered to pay for the food, but Bob refused to take their money. "I just want to help," was all he would say.

They filled their water bottles from the kitchen sink, thankful that his water was still running. Everyone arranged their new provisions, the success of the resupply making their packs the heaviest they'd been in awhile.

"I would offer to let you stay the night, but I don't think it's safe here," Bob said. "I think the army guys are going to come back. I really think it would be bad if you were here when they do." The man seemed on the verge of tears.

"That's okay, Bob," Clayton said. "We will just head up to the campsite a mile up the trail. We should be fine there."

"I can drive you back to the trail, if we hurry," Bob offered.

"That would be great," Brown Shades replied.

They threw their packs into the back of a pickup truck that was parked around the back of the building and climbed into the crew cab. The ride back to the trail was quick and uneventful. The three hikers climbed out and thanked their host once again.

"Take care," he said. "Be safe."

The truck sped away quickly, making its way back to the safety of the secluded homestead.

The hikers donned their packs and started up the trail. As they moved away from the road, they heard some traffic coming from the opposite direction Bob had just driven. The vehicles sounded large, and diesel powered. They crouched down on the trail and watched the convoy pass. The vehicles were Humvees.

Clayton turned and started walking up the trail. The others followed. In twenty minutes, they came upon a campsite with a few level spots, a small fire ring and a flowing stream nearby. As they were finding their spots, they heard the sound of gunfire coming from far off, in the direction of the Northern Georgia Hostel and Hiking Center. Brown Shades stood and looked in the direction of the shots, a sad expression on his face.

"I hope Bob's okay," Gnobbit said, a worried tone in her voice.

"Me too, Gnobbit. Me too," Clayton replied.

They set up their shelters as the sun's light drained out of the nearby woods. It had been a long day, and the hikers were tired.

They ate a quick cold dinner, finishing the summer sausage on tortillas they had just picked up from the hiker box. They each retired to their sleeping spaces and started the nightly process of repairing the damage that walking all day inflicts on the body.

\#

The following day broke gray and sullen. The ominous feeling of impending rain was all around. The group of three were packed up and fed by 0800. Another day of walking lay ahead of them.

Gnobbit led the way for the first half of the day. The trail had been heading up in elevation for the last few miles, but the climb had been gradual. Gnobbit abruptly stopped and stared at a tree right next to the trail. Clayton hurried to catch up.

Gnobbit was looking at a block of wood nailed to the tree. There was a piece of metal pipe below the block of wood that had grown into the side of the tree. Clayton looked at the small sign. It read: *NC/GA*. They were walking out of Georgia.

"One state down, just a couple more to go," Clayton said as Gnobbit nodded.

Brown Shades caught up to the two hikers. "Ah, North Carolina. I used to live in this state a while back, but I was down by the ocean. North Carolina is a long state. This mountain side is very different from the coastal shore."

The threesome continued on, and the rest of the day was just like any other day on a hike. The forest was darker than usual, with the overcast sky, but the animals still moved and made their noises. Surrounded by the serene woods, they could almost imagine that their world wasn't crumbling around them for a few moments. The day wore on and the miles passed under their feet.

\#

They arrived at Standing Indian Shelter around 1500. Though physically they felt like they could keep going, mentally they were ready to stop for the day. The shelter was typical for the area. There was an extended roof in the front of the three sided shelter and a wooden table in the middle of that space made from thick slabs of wood with large logs as legs. On one side a bench with a back was built between two log supports for the roof.

The three hikers picked spots and unpacked their packs. The rain that had been threatening all day long started to fall.

As the three hikers sat in their shelter, They discovered they all had an interest in the same topic. Gnobbit brought up a scene from *The Lord of the Rings* movie. She hadn't read the books, but had enjoyed all three moves from the trilogy. "There are seven meals in a Hobbit's day," she insisted. "Breakfast, second breakfast, elevensies, luncheon, afternoon tea, dinner and supper."

Brown Shades, who had read the books several times, but had never had the time to see the movies, insisted that Tolkien only mentioned that they eat six meals a day. "Although he mentioned six meals, he never actually listed them," he began. "I think he left it up to the reader to decide what was what."

Clayton, who had read the books as a teenager and had seen all three movies, added his opinion. "I agree with Brown Shades on the book side, but I'm glad the screenwriters put together a list. I was a little surprised that there were seven, but learning about meals like second breakfast and elevensies was interesting."

But as hikers, they all agreed that they would label all their meals the way the Hobbits did. When they actually had the food to eat that many meals, that is.

Darkness came, the hikers slept, and all seemed well in the woods.

#

The morning came, and with it, the rain departed for a time. The hikers stirred, rolled out of their bags, and started the daily chore of stuffing everything they had into a small container that they would carry all day long.

Breakfast today was oatmeal prepared in Brown Shades' pot. They each had grabbed several packets of oatmeal from the hiker box at the Northern Georgia Hostel and each contributed a packet or two. The concoction turned out to be a mixture of cinnamon, apples and peaches, which tasted delightful.

Once all was cleaned up and ready to go, the group headed out of the shelter area and back to the trail.

The first task of the morning was to finish climbing Standing Indian Mountain. As they made their way up the path. – navigating some decent switchbacks, and then negotiating a long steady climb – Brown Shades told them a story.

"Back in the days when the Cherokee still called this place home, a winged monster lived on this mountain, which the tribe called Yunwitsule-nunyi," Brown Shades began, earning the other's rapt attention. There was a large tree that had fallen next to the trail and both Gnobbit and Clayton sat, waiting for Brown Shades to continue. "The monster would swoop down from the skies and steal children. A warrior was sent up the mountain to keep a lookout for the beast. He searched the mountaintop, and eventually found his lair.

"The warrior prayed to the Great Spirit for assistance and his prayers were answered with thunder and lightning which destroyed the monster and its lair. The warrior was so afraid of this sudden, violent burst, he abandoned his post and was turned to stone for his cowardice.

"They say his stone body is still up here somewhere," Brown Shades ended mysteriously. The group continued on. Both Clayton and Gnobbit kept looking into the woods as they moved along the trail, searching for that warrior from long ago.

The hike had modest ups and downs until later in the day when they came to a rather steep jumble of rocks where the trail continued right up the side. As they started up the cliff, they could see the top of a fire tower ahead. They were near the one hundred mile mark of the trail which told them that this was the Albert Mountain Fire Tower.

The crew generated some good sweat getting up that last bit and took a much-earned break. They were close to their goal for the day and still had plenty of daylight left. They dropped their packs and looked up at the tower.

"I wonder if the door is open up there," Gnobbit thought out loud, moving towards the steps and starting up.

Clayton and Brown Shades looked at each other and shrugged their shoulders, moving to follow the little burglar. When they got up to the top of the tower, the door to the shelter-like space was open and Gnobbit was inside looking back to the south, where they had come from.

"Was it unlocked?" Clayton asked Gnobbit.

"It's open now, that is all that matters," she responded with a sly smile on her face.

The space was interesting. There was a walkway all the way around the building. Each wall of the structure had four large, eight paned windows, spanning the full length of the wall. It was basically wall to wall, windows. The rest of the walls were painted white, and the floor was a nice-looking wood flooring. The scenery was breathtaking, offering an unobstructed view stretching for miles in all directions. Each ridge rose beyond the one before it until it faded off into the mists of the day.

They were standing out on the walkway, admiring the grandeur of their view when they heard voices. They looked down into the clearing at the bottom of the tower where their packs lay along a fence. Three hikers came out of the woods from the north. They looked around, saw the packs, then simultaneously looked up to the tower top.

One of the men, short and scruffy-looking, with a good growth of beard and a red Boston Red Sox cap, raised his hand in greeting. The other two went over to where the packs were and dropped their own next to them.

Clayton, Gnobbit and Brown Shades all returned the wave and started down the steps, eager to meet the first new hikers they had seen in two days and wanting to hear their story.

"Hi, I'm Fic," Clayton introduced himself to the three hikers. "This is Gnobbit, and that wizardly looking man is Brown Shades."

"I'm Kudzu. This is Coffeebreak, and that's Grey Goose," he pointed to the other two hikers in turn. The first, Coffeebreak, was at least 6' 3" with broad shoulders and bright, blond hair; the golden stubble on his chin hardly noticeable. Grey Goose had dark brown hair that was almost the exact shade of his hooded eyes. His short beard appeared to be well groomed and trimmed, giving him a stylish look. All three of the men looked to be in their mid-twenties.

Kudzu, would be considered on the shorter side of the height table. His jet black hair was long, down to his shoulders, and as straight as could be. His vivid brown eyes held a deep intelligence. The smile on his face made one want to smile along with him.

"We haven't seen any other hikers in several days. It is sure nice to see y'all," his southern accent was quite thick. "Do y'all know what's goin on?"

"There are a lot of missing pieces, but it appears that the country has been attacked and the army has been corrupted or infiltrated," Clayton began. "That Flaherty guy seems to be involved somehow. Other than that, we aren't quite sure what is going on. We have been avoiding towns and are careful crossing roads, as it seems the enemy is all over the place. Just two nights ago, we saw some at Dicks Creek Gap and heard gunfire shortly after."

"We were in the Smokies when this all went down. We really didn't know anything was amiss until we got to Clingmans Dome and talked to a scared, young ranger who told us what he knew, which wasn't much. At that point, we all decided to keep hiking south, towards home," Kudzu told his story. "We all live in the same town outside of Atlanta, grew up together, and had come out to hike from Hot Springs down to Springer. We are still doing that, but now we have been trying to move faster and further each day. We are worried about our families."

Clayton told them what he had seen in the early morning of June 6th and what they had heard at Mountain Crossings. He warned them to be careful as they got close to Atlanta, explaining that he thought the bright light was an atomic bomb of some sort.

"We still gotta go, no matter what the danger," explained Kudzu. "We need to find our families."

They all sat together under the tall tower, exchanging information about what to expect on the trail and at the road crossings while everyone ate a small snack.

"Be careful at the NOC," said Coffeebreak, using the acronym 'knock' for the well known Nantahala Outdoor Center. "We saw some scary things when we went through there. There was a group of marauders in the parking lot during the day. We saw them attack someone. We were up on the hillside hiding but had a clear view of the bridge and around it. They eventually disappeared; we waited until dark and moved through the area quickly back up the other side."

The southbound trio grabbed their packs and prepared to continue on. The northbound three did the same. They said their goodbyes and wished each other luck, moving back into the woods away from the tower. The groups separated, both a little more knowledgeable about what was ahead, but still not completely sure of what to expect.

#

They walked two more miles and arrived at the Long Branch Shelter, which was empty, of course, with no sign of any usage in the recent past.

Brown Shades put his hammock up just to the right of the shelter, where two perfectly spaced trees offered their support. "My back would rather hang in the air than spend another night sleeping on wood," Brown Shades declared. "I'm much happier after a good night's sleep."

The other two elected to sleep in the shelter in order to make the morning's breakdown a little easier. The shelter had an upper loft, which is where Gnobbit decided to spread out her bag. "I like to have a good vantage point," she explained.

The rest of the evening was routine. Each of the hikers gathered some downed wood from the surrounding forest and Brown Shades had a nice fire going just before dark. After everyone had eaten their chosen dinners, he pulled out a packet of tortillas and some Nutella. He spread the Nutella on the tortillas, folded them in half then placed them on a rock next to the fire. This warmed the chocolate, nutty quesadilla which was pleasantly rewarding to the hikers as Brown Shades passed pieces around to his Tramily. "Gotta have a good dessert after a long day of hiking," he stated, as he took a bite of the sweet concoction.

The wind started to pick up as dark settled on the shelter area. The hikers retired to their sleeping bags. Hoping that the next day would not bring any dangers or unexpected challenges.

#

Just as the forest was starting to brighten into a new day, a drizzle started falling on the shelter. The light tinkling of the drops on the metal roof woke the hikers. Gnobbit, being closer to the roof, was the first to roll out of her sleeping bag. She grabbed her gear and climbed down the ladder to the lower level. She got out her stove and started heating water for tea. While it was heating, she went over to the tree where they had hung their food bags and lowered them all down, bringing them to the shelter.

Clayton took a few moments to get his joints warmed up. It seemed like every single one was stiff as a board. He threw on his rain jacket, grabbed his bag of TP and hobbled like an old man towards the privy. After that chore was done, he got his alcohol stove out and started heating his water for some instant coffee packets he had picked up from the hiker box. He wanted to finish off the denatured alcohol he was carrying before he started using his butane stove.

Brown Shades hadn't stirred in his hammock yet. They would see it move every once in a while, as he shifted around, but he didn't seem ready to get the day started yet.

"Hey Brownie," shouted Gnobbit, "you gonna hike today?"

"I'm working on it," came the reply from the hanging hammock. "It's just so comfortable here."

Soon, he was sitting on the edge of his hammock putting on his boots loosely. He grabbed his cook kit and came over to the shelter to join in the morning ritual. "I think I will have some hot cider this morning. These packets looked like they had been in the box for a long time, but I like the flavor of the cider."

After they each had enjoyed a hot beverage and a light breakfast, they packed everything up and sat in the shelter, looking out at the light rain as it pattered off of the leaves high in the forest and dripped down to the ground. This felt like an all day rain.

Clayton eventually stood and grabbed his pack. "Well ...," he started.

"This trail ain't gonna walk itself," Gnobbit interrupted, finishing his usual mantra for him. She let out a laugh and winked at him.

Clayton smiled back and finished putting on his pack. "I didn't know I was that predictable."

One by one, each of the hikers hefted their gear, placed it on their back, and headed into the woods along the trail. Following the white blazes through the misty forest.

#

The day was a wet walk in the woods. Each hiker just kept putting one foot in front of the other, making miles and trying not to slip on a wet rock or root. There wasn't much talking, just a lot of walking. They had a quick cold lunch at the Moore Creek Campsite when the rain stopped for a few minutes and then they continued on.

The original plan was to camp at a signed campsite after about fifteen miles, but the rain started up again and began to fall harder than before. So, they decided to continue on almost three more miles to the Wayah Bald Shelter, wanting some better cover for what promised to be a wet night.

When they went over the bald before getting to the shelter, a stone tower appeared out of the misty day like a medieval castle of old. They all walked up the stone steps to the observation area, but their view was obstructed. It was as if they were on a stone ship sailing a sea of clouds.

As they arrived at the shelter, the rain was still falling and the light of day was fading. They all changed out of their drenched hiking clothes into something dry and crawled into their sleeping bags to warm their bodies up. It had been a long, wet day, and they were glad the walking part was over for now.

A hot meal improved all of their moods and Brown Shades elected to stay in the shelter for the night. He was just too exhausted to put his hammock up and was the first to be snoring as they all curled in their down and tried to shake off the chill that had been driven into their bones by the constant rain.

#

Morning dawned. The rain was gone. The forest once again had that freshly washed look and when the wind blew, drops would fall about the forest like a small hiccup of a storm. The hikers stirred. The daily routine was starting to become, well, routine. The hikers were up, packed, fed, and ready to go while the sun rose over the mountain to the east. "Yesterday made me sore. It seems like I have an ache in every part of my body, especially my feet and legs," Gnobbit offered.

"Yeah, I'm sore too, but I think it was smart to push on to this shelter. It got us out of the rain and made today's hike a little shorter," Clayton replied. The trio had walked over eighteen miles the day before. Today, they would hike around fifteen to a shelter located only one mile from the river that they would have to cross at a little cluster of buildings referred to as the N.O.C. It stood for the Nantahala Outdoor Center. It straddled the Nantahala River which was a very nice kayaking river. It had even been used for some competition when the Olympics were hosted in Atlanta several years ago.

Nantahala was a Cherokee word meaning *Land of the noonday Sun*. The valley was deep and the climb into and out of the area was steep. The name referred to the fact that when in a valley that deep, the sun can only be seen when it is at its zenith.

This day was a complete contrast from the day before. Where the morning was dark and sullen yesterday, today the sun was out, the birds were singing their morning ritual and the breeze that puffed and wandered through the forest held promise of a good hiking day.

#

That promise was upheld. The day passed by undramatically as they walked along, but, like most days on the trail, there were highlights that stuck out in their minds. The hawk that floated on the wind at the top of the ridge. The sun sending bright rays through a broken cloud as they came to a clearing.

They crossed multiple paved roads as they hiked along, their appearance surprising them each time. No one was riding these remote, mountain thoroughfares — at least not now — so there was no traffic noise to alert them of their presence.

Wesser Bald had its own fire tower. This one was higher than the stone structure from yesterday. The rickety steps went steeply up to the observation platform. Walking up the dozens of steps, which were very widely spaced, made tired leg muscles yell in distress. When the three hikers got to the top, they had a much better view of the spreading landscape. The wind was cutting along the top of the platform, so the group sat below the railing, effectively blocking the wind. They ate a little snack and then looked around some more.

"I believe that little piece of water, near the horizon towards the north is Fontana Lake, where our next major destination lies," Brown Shades stated.

They all looked around. Clayton could see the town of Franklin off to the southeast. He remembered staying there during his hike. The town loved its hikers and catered to them a lot. A bus had picked him and a few other hikers up at a road crossing along the trail and would drop them wherever they wanted to go in town. After having stayed in a cheap motel for the night, the same bus had brought the refreshed hikers back, the driver regaling them with stories of local lore and myth. *I wish we could get a ride to some more food*, Clayton thought. "It is time to resupply," he announced to the other two.

"Yeah, and it sure would be nice to find a shower that worked, even if it's cold," Gnobbit said. "We all have become quite ripe." Lifting her arm and pretending to take a whiff. Screwing up her face into a grimace to display her distaste.

#

They arrived at the A. Rufus Morgan Shelter in the late afternoon. They ate an early dinner, refilled their water bottles, and relaxed as the sun moved towards the western mountain.

They planned to wait until just before dark; head down to the river and carefully work their way across; find some food, if they were lucky; then get out of the valley, returning to the relative safety of the woods. Clayton remembered what Coffeebreak had told them about when his threesome had transited the river. He was going to be very cautious as they approached the bridge that spanned the foamy torrent.

Darkness was approaching. The Tramily was ready. They each had their headlamps strapped to their heads but were going to try to avoid using them unless absolutely necessary.

They continued down the steep path, following the last few switchbacks that took the trail down to the road, which sat quietly waiting for them. To their left, behind a large sign that announced their arrival at the N.O.C., was a small building with a glass front. There was a large sign on the building declaring it the General Store. Across the road was a large wooden building whose sign read *Outfitter S ore*. The 't' missing from the word *Store*. Both buildings looked like they had just barely survived a Black Friday sale. The windows were broken, and the doors were not where they were originally hung. They opted to check out the General Store first.

Carefully, they made their way over to the dark store. So far, the road had been quiet and empty. They stepped inside the building and started looking around. Turning on their red lights to see into the corners. The place had been picked over. It looked like an angry toddler had run up and down the aisles, pulling everything off the shelves as he scurried along.

They were quite lucky in their search. Whoever had done the looting here had been sloppy. They were able to augment their food bags and it looked as though they would have enough to, at least, get to the beginning of the Smokies. They would need more if they wanted to cross that mountain range without going hungry, as opportunities to resupply up there would be sparse.

After they gathered everything useful at the general store, they crossed the road towards the Outfitters, each running across separately, then waiting a couple of beats before the next hiker ran across. They had a strong feeling that someone might be watching them. They had no evidence that this was true, just an overwhelming gut feeling telling them something was amiss.

The Outfitter Store displayed the same tornado as the General Store. They were more or less set for gear at the moment, but Clayton found a nice pair of Darn Tough socks, which he added to his clothes bag. "As we say in the army; you can't have enough socks," he said.

They picked through the rubble, each finding something that they might be able to use. Gnobbit found a long spoon like Brown Shades'. She slipped it into her pack next to her cook kit. Brown Shades found a blow up pillow, like the one Gnobbit had and he tucked that into his pack.

They went over to the restaurant called *The River's Edge*, and looked through the place. It seemed to be less damaged than the other buildings, but it still had been entered. Now it sat silent next to the rushing river as they scavenged through the remnants.

Brown Shades whispered, "Taters." holding up a bag of large russet potatoes. He took three of them and left the rest. He also found an onion and a couple carrots, adding those to his supply as well.

With food bags full and their adrenalin starting to drain out of their muscles, they crossed the footbridge that spanned the river, taking them to the other side.

They followed the trail through a parking lot and across a railroad track. Rising up away from the river, the trail turned where a road ended and headed into the forest. To the right was a cluster of buildings that appeared to be rental cabins. They went over to check it out.

The buildings were nestled within a thick forest. It was hard to see from the trail, offering a good deal of privacy to its usual guests. They dropped their packs on the porch of one of the cabins. *Birch Cabin*, said a sign hung above the door.

Clayton tried the door. It was locked. He looked over at Gnobbit and she was already moving off the porch and heading around the corner of the building. This time there was no sound of breaking glass, but in three minutes, the door unlocked from the other side, revealing a smiling Gnobbit in the entryway.

"The window was unlocked," was all she offered. They came inside and looked around the place with their red head lamps. The cabin had a nice layout. They were in an open living room with a couch and two chairs arranged around a small coffee table. The walls were covered in a nice wood paneling that gave the room a warm feeling. To the right was a decent-sized kitchen. There was a short flight of steps beside the refrigerator that went back to three bedrooms and a bathroom.

The first bedroom had a nice queen-sized bed. Clayton looked at Brown Shades and asked, "Will this be a sufficient alternative to your hammock?"

"It will be just fine," replied Brown Shades, slipping off his pack and setting it beside the bed. They continued along the hall to the next room. This one had a bunk bed with the lower bed being a large double and the upper bed a twin.

"I'll take this one if that's cool," said Gnobbit. Clayton nodded his head, the red light moving up and down the wood panel of that room indicating his approval. She dropped her pack in that room and they passed the bathroom to check out the last room.

This room had two sets of twin bunks, each on one side of the room. "This one will suit me fine for the night," Clayton said, repeating the pack dropping routine the other two had done.

Gnobbit had moved back out of the room and was checking the bathroom. "Hey guys, come here," she spoke in a soft voice. The men came to see what she had found.

When they entered the room, Gnobbit was pointing to a red light that was lit on a small panel connected to the wall. She turned on the faucet in the sink and felt the water. "It's warm," she said in an excited voice. "I'm taking a shower, out you go."

The men exited the room and Gnobbit turned on the shower, starting to pull off her smelly hiking clothes before the door had closed. Five minutes later, while the men were unpacking their packs, she came out of the bathroom wrapped in a large white towel. "Oh my gosh," she whispered. "That was awesome." She was carrying her hiking clothes which were now wet and a little cleaner than before. "I did a little cowboy laundry while I was in there," she added.

She went into her room and Clayton went over to Brown Shade to tell him he could go next. "Don't mind if I do," he said, grabbing his camp clothes and heading to the bathroom.

He too did some laundry as he washed about a week's worth of sweat and dirt off his body. He gave a little salute to Clayton when he came out of the bathroom, indicating it was his turn now.

Clayton went into the bathroom and turned on the water. It was still just as hot as when Gnobbit had turned it on. He looked at the panel with the red light. It had a small label on it that said: *on-demand hot water*. There was some kind of power source around here that was providing electricity to this building. Still, they avoided turning on any of the house lights, for fear of attracting unwanted attention.

After everyone was feeling fresh and all their clothes were hanging on a piece of paracord that Gnobbit had strung across one side of the living room, they sat down at the large butcher-block table in the kitchen and prepared a snack. As they were sitting there, nibbling on their food, they heard approaching vehicles on the road across the river. It sounded like large trucks were coming down the road from the south. For several minutes, they could hear the convoy passing the cluster of buildings of the N.O.C., but they all kept going.

Each of the hikers retired to their rooms and settled in for the night. Clayton was looking at his guide, checking to see how long it would take them to get to the Smokies, when he saw Gnobbit's red light look into his room. "Can I sleep in here? I'm a little creeped out, sleeping in that room all alone," she asked.

"Sure, Gnobbit. Pick a bed," Clayton said, a slight smile on his lips.

"I'll take the top bunk. I like my vantage point, ya know." She threw her bag up on the bunk and climbed up the small ladder. Just as she settled herself, Brown Shade's red light illuminated the room.

"I heard your voices and came to see what was up," he said. He had his quilt in his hand.

"Gnobbit decided to sleep in here," Clayton explained. "We have gotten used to being near each other. Watching each other's backs."

"Room for one more?" Brown Shades asked.

"Of course, sir," was Clayton's reply. Brown Shades placed his quilt on the lower bunk across from Clayton and climbed in.

The room quieted and slowly was replaced with soft snores as the exhausted hikers enjoyed the soft beds of a fine cabin. All was well for now. Clayton cupped his pouch in his hand as he slowly drifted off into slumber.

CHAPTER 7
THE HOME FRONT - FRIDAY, JUNE 15TH

As Clayton and his two companions were waiting for darkness to arrive so they could descend into the N.O.C., Lori Collier was sitting in her darkening kitchen, wondering what had become of her husband. It had been nine days since the war had started. Calling it a war was a stretch. It had been a surprise. It had been fast, and it had been a quick victory for The Regime. Led by one Richard Flaherty. A crazy man that had been causing trouble in the country for several months now. Lori didn't really know a lot, but she had been talking to her neighbors and they had discussed what they did know, and it wasn't good. They had heard that Flaherty, now referred to as The Boss, had his people infiltrate the military and at a pre-planned time, had detonated several nuclear bombs in several large cities throughout the United States. Washington, D.C. definitely. It was reported to be a smoking pile of ash now. New York, Los Angeles, Dallas and Atlanta had been mentioned in the conversations, but no one knew for sure.

The power had been out since the attack and phones weren't working. Army convoys had been driving up and down Route 50, but none of them had come down their road. It looked like a lot of the activity was coming from and going to Mount Weather, but she couldn't be sure. She and the kids had stayed in the farmhouse, not venturing into town or trying to go anyplace else. The small, portable radio had offered no new clues before it had died a slow death. Lori was saving her spare batteries for now, but she would put some in the radio once a day and scan through the band to see if anyone was transmitting. So far, it had produced nothing but static.

Clayton was supposed to be home a week ago. When that didn't happen, she feared the worst, but had a strong feeling that he was okay, and somehow, was making his way home. She couldn't explain the feeling, but she didn't question it.

For now, they had a good amount of food. They always kept a full pantry, canning and drying lots of the produce they grew and harvested throughout the year and this year's garden was already growing and thriving. They had already started expanding the large plot they used to grow every manner of vegetable.

They even had a shed out behind the house that had two large solar panels which led to a solar charger and a small battery bank. The power from the panels kept a small chest freezer running, where they had quite a few pounds of meat being preserved. The power also ran their water pump, so they still had running water for now.

Brittney and Shane were helping with all that needed to be done each day. They had gathered and loaded all the hunting rifles and kept them in a handy place, but so far no one had bothered them.

The back door swung open, and Shane walked into the kitchen. Shane favored his mother in looks, with a dark auburn head of hair, and light blue eyes. There was still a sprinkle of freckles across the bridge of his nose that gave his newly adult face a hint of lingering childhood. He had a shotgun slung over his shoulder. "I just walked the perimeter of the property. All is well at the Collier Homestead," he reported to his mother.

"Great. Did you see anyone over at the Miller place?" she asked. The Millers were their closest neighbor, but they hadn't seen any of them around since the bombs dropped.

"No. It's still all quiet over there. I wonder what happened to them," Shane answered as he placed the shotgun in the gun rack mounted in the hallway just off of the kitchen.

"Where's Brittney?" Lori wondered.

"She was working in the garden. She should be coming in in a few minutes."

Just as he finished the sentence, the kitchen door opened and in walked the subject of their conversation. Her brownish red hair was straight and fell to just over her shoulders. Her eyes tended to be more gray, like her father's. She had a slim, athletic figure. She wore a t-shirt and longish cargo shorts that had smudges of garden dirt on them. She carried a basket full of lettuce and spinach.

"The lettuce is getting ready to bolt, so we need to eat like rabbits for a while," she said. She dumped the greens into a large colander and placed them in the sink, running some water over them to rinse off the garden dirt.

The three family members sat around in the kitchen, preparing a small meal of canned meat, canned green beans and a lettuce and spinach salad.

"Do you think Dad will come home?" Brittney asked her mother.

"If I know your father, that is exactly what he is striving to do right now," Lori started. "He was pretty far away when all this happened, and it doesn't look like traveling the roads is very safe right now. I wouldn't be surprised if he walked all the way home, using that trail he loves so much. He was near its terminus down there in Georgia," Lori said, not knowing that she had just hit the nail directly on the head.

The Collier family, minus one, prepared for bed. They had a good supply of candles, so they each took one to their respective rooms. As they tucked themselves into their comfortable beds, Clayton was doing the same thing in Birch Cabin at the N.O.C.

CHAPTER 8

THE SMOKIES - SATURDAY, JUNE 16TH TO FRIDAY, JUNE 22ND

Light was coming in the windows of the small room where the three hikers slept. They had slept in due to the comfort of the beds and the tiredness of their bodies. Eventually, all were up and each of them took another quick shower to help wake up. They savored the hot water since they weren't sure when the next shower would happen.

Reluctantly, the hikers threw on their packs and left the beautiful, comfortable cabin. They still had a long way to go until they reached their homes, and even though their bodies were craving the simple comforts that the cabin offered, they knew continuing on was the only way to reach their ultimate goal. The trail immediately started climbing as they left the N.O.C. area, and for the next six miles, all they did was climb. The day was pleasant enough; the sky held some clouds that hid the sun from time to time, but the temperature was warm without being hot and there was no sign of rain for now.

They took a nice long break at Sassafras Gap Shelter and ate a warm lunch — summer sausage cooked with real onions and potatoes. Brown Shades performed his chef magic, and the hikers were silent as they shoveled the delicious food into their mouths.

They slept in the Brown Fork Gap Shelter that night and hiked out early the next morning. Now, they were walking along a ridge that overlooked the great Fontana Lake. Steadily losing elevation as the trail headed down towards the dam that held all this water back.

The sun was shining and sparkling off the lake surface, appearing as diamonds through the trees as they continued walking. The trail led to a parking lot at a marina. They came out of the woods, blinking their eyes in the bright, early afternoon sun. They crossed a paved road then continued through a fringe of trees to the parking lot. There was a small building on their right which contained restrooms. After taking advantage of the facilities, they sat in a circle on the other side of the building away from the road and had a discussion.

"I have some food, but I don't think it will be enough to get all the way through the Smokies," Clayton stated.

"Yeah, I'm getting low too," added Gnobbit. Brown Shades nodding his head to indicate the same.

"There's a store at the Fontana Lodge that may have something, but it's two miles along that road we just crossed. There's no guarantee that they would have anything, but we should try to get something more before climbing into those mountains," Clayton declared seriously.

"We could stash our packs somewhere safe and hidden and walk there with just our food bags," Brown Shades suggested. "We can carefully check out the place and approach if it seems safe when it gets dark."

They wandered around the marina for a bit and Gnobbit got inside a small bait shop near the water. She found some canned Spam and a few bags of chips that she divvied out to her hiking partners. "That's a start, I guess," she said.

There was a storage room at the back of the restroom building in between the men's and women's and they stowed their packs there. They grabbed their food bags and their head lamps. They each had their knives and Brown Shades brought along his staff.

They started walking along a typical mountain road — two lanes of blacktop with very little shoulder on each side. It twisted and turned as it made its way through the mountainous area. They had been walking for about thirty minutes when they turned a sharp bend. Up ahead was a fenced-in transformer area with a few poles and transmission lines heading out from it. Across a small driveway was a compact building, and behind that, a large wooden water storage tank. Sitting next to the building was a pickup truck with two men inside. They looked surprised to see them, and quickly fumbled to get out of the vehicle, grabbing long guns as they did so.

The trio had become spread out as they walked along. Clayton was in the lead, with Brown Shades about twenty feet behind him. Gnobbit was about a hundred feet behind them, her pace had slowed on the hard, paved surface.

"Where are you two going?" the first man drawled as he held his shotgun at the ready. He was wearing faded, torn overalls and boots that appeared too large for his feet. His partner had on camo pants and a ratty-looking flannel shirt. On his head was a straw hat that had seen better days.

Clayton looked back behind him and saw only Brown Shades. Gnobbit had disappeared. He tried to play innocent. "We are hikers, out for a couple days. We were just heading to Fontana Lodge to resupply. The phone down at the marina wasn't working." They hadn't even tried the phone, thinking it probably wouldn't be working and not wanting to draw attention to themselves, regardless.

"Well, we can give you a ride. I'm gonna need to take those knives though," he said, raising the shotgun towards Clayton's chest. Knowing that, for now, they had the upper hand, he decided to comply. He removed his knife from its sheath and held it towards the men by the blade. The second guy collected the knives and the food bags they were carrying along with Brown Shades' staff.

"You won't be needin' this," he said, tossing the stick to the side of the road. He put the items in the cab of the truck, grabbing two zip ties from inside. "I'm gonna need to secure you two," he said, showing them the zip ties. He proceeded to tie each man's hands together in front of them. Ushering them to the back of the pickup truck. "I wouldn't try to jump out or anything along the way," he advised. "This road is windy, but we don't have far to go."

It was hard to believe the pickup truck would even start; it looked like it was on its last legs, but start it did, and they continued down the road.

Five minutes later, they took a left turn at a sign that announced they were at Fontana Village Resort. They pulled up into a large parking lot in front of a building that had a sign that said *Wildwood Grill*. There were a number of other vehicles in the parking lot, including a few Humvees.

Straw Hat parked the truck in a space right in front of the building and Clayton noticed that he took the keys and put them up in the visor. He made a note of that fact. They told them to exit the vehicle and escorted them into the building.

"I need to talk to Honcho about you two, so just sit over there at that table and don't be getting any funny ideas," he warned.

Clayton and Brown Shades walked over to the prescribed table and sat down. Over at the next table was a young woman sitting by herself. Her hands were tied too and her long hair fell into her face. She didn't immediately acknowledge their arrival. In fact, she didn't move at all.

Clayton looked around. They were in the main dining room of a large restaurant. There were lots of windows all around, but the door they had come in seemed to be the only exit within view. An armed man stood outside that door. Clayton turned his gaze back to the young woman next to them. "Hey," he quietly spoke to her, "you okay over there?" At first, she remained motionless, but then her head came up and she moved the hair from her face. She appeared to be about twenty-five or so, with wavy, raven black hair and copper brown eyes. Her face was long and slim and below her left eye, a darkening bruise was blooming.

"I'm fine, I guess," she answered. "I was just trying to hike and these pricks took me. They have Yuk too," she added.

"Yuk?" Clayton was puzzled. "Is that another person or maybe a dog or something?"

"Yuk is my Uke. Ya know, Ukulele. A small guitar-like instrument with four strings. I call her Yuk. Those fuckers have her. Have my whole pack, in fact," she explained.

"Well, what these *fuckers* don't know is we have another person out there who didn't get picked up and I bet she is planning something heroic right now as we sit. She is stealthy and can easily outsmart these idiots."

The girl looked up and a gentle smile came to her face, lighting up her eyes with hope. "I'm game to work with you. I saw them put my pack in that room by the kitchen door. When we get the chance, I need to get it back. What's the plan?"

"Well for now, we sit and observe. How long have you been here?" Clayton asked.

"I was picked up this morning. As you can see, I put up a little fight and that asshat, with the assy looking hat, decided to get a little physical after I kicked him in the balls. I have been sitting here for hours. Their leader, someone they call Honcho, came over and asked me some questions, but after that, they just left me alone here."

Brown Shades reached up one hand and placed it on the table. "We will get out of here with little problem. These guys seem a bit unorganized, but they do have guns, so we must be careful."

Clayton looked at Brown Shades in surprise, noticing that he had one hand on the table and the other in his lap. "You are free?" he asked, wonderment in his eyes.

"These things are pretty easy to defeat if you know how. They have weak spots. I had been working at it as we drove down the road, but I didn't want to finish the job until we were alone. Also ...," He lifted his other arm and in it he had another small knife. He reached over and cut Clayton's restraints. He did the same for the young woman. "Just keep your hands together for now, so they don't figure out what we have done." He put his hand back into the loose restraints and gave the appearance of still being bound. "What's your name?" he asked the woman.

"I'm Class Room. Well, my trail name is Class Room. I've been hiking for over a month. Taking my time moving up the trail. I was in no hurry. Or I wasn't until the shit hit the fan. Now I'm just going to try to walk home. I'm from New Jersey. I was in need of food and came looking for some, when these guys found me walking down the road and decided to take me."

They had been sitting at the tables for about an hour now, whispering back and forth while trying to come up with a plan.

The kitchen door swung open, and three men walked over to them. It was Coveralls, another new guy who wore a grease-smudged ball cap, and a large, hulking guy that they knew instinctively was the Honcho. He towered over everyone else and wore camo clothes from head to toe. He was probably about thirty-five or so and his large face was covered in a long, curly beard. He sat at the table across from them.

"I'm Honcho," he confirmed. "So, you say you were out on a hike. Do y'all know what has been going on in the world this past week?" he asked, not expecting an answer. "The government is gone. The army is trying to take over and us here at the dam have decided it was time to take charge. We need some help in our work and that's where you come into the picture. You will be working for us now."

The three hikers stared at him and then Brown Shades said, "What manner of work do you mean, sir?"

"Whatever I need, old man. Cooking, cleaning, breaking rocks if I feel the need. You are mine now."

"We're … yours?" Clayton asked, looking intently into the big man's face.

"You got that right. I say jump, you ask how high. Anything you need to do, *anything*, won't be done without my permission first." He stood and hulked over them to show his strength and dominance. "Y'all just sit tight here for a while until I think of something for you to do." The three men disappeared back into the kitchen.

#

Darkness had settled into the village resort and the three sat where they had been left. They were going to try to escape as soon as it was fully dark and the men had gone to sleep. They had seen about ten other men in the nearby area, but hadn't noticed any women.

The man armed with a shotgun continued to block their only escape route. As he stood looking out towards the parking lot, there was a sound like a low whistle that came from his left. He looked towards the noise, and from his right, a large, oak stick came swinging out of the dark and connected solidly with his head. It sounded like a baseball bat hitting a watermelon. The man dropped straight down to the ground as if his legs had disappeared. He was out cold.

Gnobbit walked into view holding Brown Shade's staff and peered into the dark restaurant. "We're over here, Gnobbit," whispered Clayton.

She leaned over and lifted the shotgun from the unconscious man's shoulder where he had slung the weapon. She opened the door and walked over to the trio. "Hi," she said. "Nice night for a hike, huh?" She had an accomplished smile on her face.

"I had a feeling we would be seeing you again soon. I'm glad it was this soon," Clayton said, returning her smile. "Let's get out of here. I have a plan, follow me." He slipped off the tie wrap that Brown Shades had cut and let it fall to the floor. The other two followed suit and moved to the door where Gnobbit waited. Gnobbit handed the Remington 870 to Clayton who checked the chamber for a round and peeked into the magazine, seeing at least two rounds there. He held it at the ready.

Gnobbit handed The Staff to Brown Shades. "I believe you lost this, sir," she said as Brown Shades took the long stick with a bow.

"Wait," Class Room said. "I need to get my pack. To get Yuk." She shot a worried glance over to the closet beside the kitchen door. "It's in that closet over there."

"I'll help you," Gnobbit said and started over to the closet. "I'm Gnobbit," she introduced herself softly.

"Class Room," the hiker responded as she reached out her hand in the form of a fist to Gnobbit, who bopped it with her fist. They went over to the closet, and Gnobbit had the flimsy lock defeated in less than a minute. Class Room reached in and grabbed her belongings. Clayton could see the ukulele strapped to the pack as she threw it on her back and the two women joined the men.

Slowly and quietly, Clayton opened the door and exited the restaurant with the others close behind. "Follow me," he said.

He walked fast to the old pickup truck they had arrived in. Went to the driver's side and opened the unlocked door. He flipped down the visor and the keys fell into his ready hand. The others smiled in the dark and started getting into the truck. The old Ford Ranger had two bucket seats and a long bed. As Clayton slid into the driver's seat, Class Room threw her pack into the back of the truck and joined Clayton in the cabin as Brown Shades and Gnobbit climbed into the back of the truck.

Clayton started the jalopy and shifted quickly into reverse, keeping the headlights off for now. As they started driving towards the exit to the village, a man came out of the restaurant and shouted when he realized what was happening. He started running towards the quickening truck. He reached the back of the vehicle and grabbed onto the tailgate, pulling himself up onto the bumper.

Brown Shades stood in the bed of the truck and held his staff ready. He poked the guy in the chest, trying to knock him off. The man reared back some, but he kept his grip. The old man changed his aim and swung the other end of the staff towards the man, slamming the side of the man's head with the heavier edge of the long oak stick. The man dropped as fast as the first man, rolling loosely across the parking lot as the truck started gaining speed. "I think I might have to rename this staff Thorin Oaken Club," he said with a smile.

Clayton figured it was time to turn on the lights and when he did so, they saw another man standing in the middle of the road. This man had a shotgun of his own and he was trying to level it towards the truck. He aimed at the approaching truck but was blinded by the sudden glare of the headlights, throwing his aim low and causing his shot to hit straight into the grill instead of the windshield.

Clayton pointed his new shotgun out the side window, steadying it on the side-view mirror. He pulled the trigger, sending a hail of buckshot towards the armed man. The shot went wide, but it made the man decide to get out of the way, and as the truck moved past him it clipped his right leg sending him sprawling. Clayton sped off, leaving the men and the village behind them as they headed up the same road they had come down a few hours ago. The twisty road challenged Clayton's driving skills, but he was able to handle the sudden turns and safely got them back to the marina. He drove straight to the restroom where they had hidden their packs. Brown Shades and Gnobbit jumped out of the truck bed as soon as it had slowed enough and ran to the back storage room to grab the packs. They were back at the truck, throwing the bags into the bed and climbing in right as Clayton finished turning the truck around to face the exit.

As the truck started back out from the marina road, Clayton noticed steam coming from under the rusty hood. At the end of the parking lot, Clayton followed a sign pointing the way to the dam. The lake spread out on his right.

They drove down the road and onto the dam. The steam was increasing its escape from under the hood and the engine was now making a funny sound. "Just a little more, old truck," Clayton urged the struggling beater. They finished crossing the huge dam, passed a small picnic area and came to a parking lot. The white blazes started up the mountain at this point, turning off the road. Directly ahead, a yellow gate blocked the way of vehicles.

They came to a stop and that was all that the truck could deliver. The engine coughed a few times then grew silent. The *tick, tick, tick* of the cooling engine and the accompanying hiss of the escaping steam were the last words of the wounded vehicle.

They all grabbed their packs and started up the dark trail. Conveniently, the guys had left their knives in between the two bucket seats. Clayton grabbed them and sheathed his, handing the other to Brown Shades who did the same.

They didn't dare turn on their head lamps yet. It was a dark night, with no sign of the moon in the sky full of stars. They made their way clumsily at first, until their eyes started to adjust to the darkness. Once they could make out the trail as a slightly lighter track in between the trees' shadows, they were able to quicken their pace. In the distance, they could hear vehicles arriving at the parking lot down below. They heard a few shouts and saw some lights flash back and forth for a while, but they never seemed to get any closer. In fact, they started to fade until there was nothing to hear except the slamming of a car door and one beep of a horn.

After Clayton was more comfortable with the distance between the hikers and the parking lot, he called for a halt, and they assessed what had happened. "Is anyone hit or hurt?" Clayton asked first.

"I'm not, but did you see Brownie slam that guy on the back of the truck?" Gnobbit asked excitedly. "That guy is kinda hit *and* hurt."

"I am unhurt," was all Brown Shades said.

Class Room also checked in as being okay. They sat in the middle of the trail, inspecting their gear, making sure nothing had been lost in the excitement of the night. Gnobbit took two almost empty food bags she had stuffed into her pack and handed them back to Clayton and Brown Shades. "These were in the bed of the truck," she said. "I kept mine attached to my belt during the excitement, but they are no fuller than they were before since that resupply mission was a bit of a failure." Everyone resituated their gear, and then they were on their way again.

\#

The time was approaching midnight when they arrived at a sign that said, *Birch Spring Gap*. There was a rail along the side of the trail for tying horses, and down some stone steps, a path ran past a spring then along a few tent sites. They quickly set up their sleeping shelters and tried to get some rest.

Clayton decided that a watch would be necessary. He discussed the idea with the group, and all agreed to help out. As the others nestled into their quilts and sleeping bags, Clayton sat on a stump in the dark, with the shotgun laying across his lap. Even though the day had been the longest they had traveled so far, along with the excitement of being captured and escaping, Clayton still felt very much awake. He wasn't ready to sleep just yet. Staring down the trail where they had come, he heard nothing but the night noises as the stars moved above him. Clayton's attention was alerted when he saw some movement to his left, where the others were sleeping. It was Class Room. She raised her hand to acknowledge him seeing her then slowly approached in the dark. "I'll watch for a couple hours so you can get some sleep. I sure can't sleep much. Still too hyped up from the chase."

Clayton smiled tiredly at her and held up the shotgun, "Do you know how to handle one of these?"

"I was a regional trap shooter champion when I was in the 4H club as a teenager," she replied. "I can handle an 870."

She took the shotgun and Clayton threw her a slow, tired salute. "I stand relieved," he said and headed to his bivy. He crawled into his bag and was asleep within a few seconds. The tiredness had finally caught him.

Class Room continued the watch of the dark, silent trail. The unease of her earlier capture kept her alert and sharp-eyed for the entirety of her shift. Brown Shades relieved her in the early hours just before sunrise. He kept the shotgun that she offered, but also had his trusty staff nearby. When it was Gnobbit's turn, she too, kept both weapons ready.

#

The morning arrived safely, along with a thick fog. The dark forest lightened slightly into a white veil. The hikers arose from their slumber and gathered around a cold fire pit next to Brown Shades' hammock. "Let's see what we have for supplies. Our plan didn't quite go the way we wanted on that expedition, but we are going to have to make do with what we have until we can find more," Clayton started. He dumped his food bag on the ground next to the fire ring. The others grabbed their bags and did the same. Brown Shades still had the most to offer, but all around, the pickings were slim for fueling four hikers who were about to walk over seventy miles to the other side of this popular, but remote National Park.

"If we ration carefully, this food should last about three days, maybe," Brown Shades calculated. "Hopefully we find something more by then."

They divided up the food, so each had an equal share to do with as they saw fit. Everyone understood that they had to be careful with how much they ate each day, but that they shouldn't starve themselves. At least not yet. That might come later. Right now, they needed fuel to get the day started. None of them had slept much during their night of excitement, their hyped up feelings lingering even after they felt confident that the lazy locals hadn't chased them up into the mountains.

Clayton unloaded the shotgun counting how many shells they had left. The plug had been removed from the 870 giving the magazine full capacity of four shells. There had been one in the chamber when they relieved the man of his weapon, but Clayton had sent its contents towards the man in the road, leaving them with four shells. He reloaded the weapon and made it ready.

They each ate a power bar for breakfast and a cup of a warm beverage. As they were sitting around the fire ring, Gnobbit asked Class Room, "So, how did you become Class Room?"

"I just got back from doing a year in the Peace Corps. I was stationed in Paraguay and one of my duties was to help teach the children in the village music. When I started my hike, I was hanging out with a few other late starters, we were talking about what we do and I was describing the conditions we had to endure in Paraguay and what our classroom was like. A guy named Spider started calling me Class Room and, as a lot of Trail Names go, it stuck," Class Room explained.

"Ah, a fellow educator," Brown Shades stated. "I teach science up in P-A. Welcome to the Tramily."

Each of the others explained what their name meant to them and how it came about. Every name usually had some kind of story connected to it.

Clayton had been given Fictilibus long ago when he was doing his thru-hike. When he started his hike, all of his gear was mostly brown. Some things were light brown, others were a clay colored brown, some dark brown. Clayton and a few other hikers were sitting around the fire early in the hike and one of the women in the group had taken Latin in college. She was saying that Clayton blended into the clay embankment he was sitting in front of, then spoke the Latin word for clay, *Fictilibus*. The fact that his name was Clayton and he used Clay as a nickname at times, made it even more appropriate.

That became his name, and he accepted it as it was different and a little mysterious. When his hike had ended, he still kept that name to use whenever he was on the trail. He liked it. The longer they stayed out here, the more he thought of himself as Fic and the less he considered himself Clayton.

Gnobbit explained how she got her trail name. It was a nickname she had as a young girl. Her cousin had tagged her with the moniker. She was short and stealthy and they shared a love for *The Lord of the Rings* story. Gnobbit's parents also had a few gnome statues out in the front yard that she would always play with. The cousin smashed the two together and gave her the name. Gnobbit decided it was a good enough name to hike with when she set out.

Brown Shades looked out through his clear eyeglasses that had been a dark shade of brown just yesterday. "These glasses I wear are photo-sensitive. When the sun is out, they darken to a brown color. On the first day of my hike, I was matching pace with an older woman who was out for a couple of days. We spent the day passing and leapfrogging each other and ended up at the same camp for the first night. The day had been sunny with large puffy clouds blocking the sun every so often. One time, I would see her and my glasses would be clear; the next, they might be darkened by the bright sun. At camp, she asked me about my glasses and after my explanation, she bestowed me with the trail name Brown Shades."

After their insightful story telling, it was time to put some more distance between Honcho and his men. They started their day's hike by continuing up to the top of the ridge.

#

Once they completed the climb up to Doe Knob, the ascent became less severe. There were still a lot of ups and downs, but they weren't as long and not too steep. They decided to end the day at a little over eleven miles at the Spence Field Shelter.

This shelter was fairly large with space for at least twelve sleepers. The area in front of the shelter was covered and there was a stone fireplace within the shelter itself. They had enough Mountain House diners left for each of them to have one final one and the conversation was comical as Gnobbit tried to trade her Beef Stew for Brown Shades' Beef Stroganoff. As Brown Shades hesitated to commit to the deal, Gnobbit revealed something she had been saving for a special occasion. "How about I sweeten the deal, Brownie," she said as she placed a slightly smooshed Cosmic Brownie on top of her trade.

"That will tip the scale," Brown Shades said, grabbing the brownie and placing it in his hoodie pocket. The deal was made and the trade complete.

After the meal was done, the Tramily sat around the small fire that Brown Shades had kindled in the fireplace and Class Room detached Yuk from its strappings on her pack.

She plucked a few chords, checking the tune, then started playing a song. It wasn't familiar to any of the hikers, and she sang no words along with it, but it was soothing and put the group at ease. The music itself seemed to have a magic that eased their aches and left them feeling refreshed.

"That's a cool little guitar you have there," Gnobbit admired her instrument. "I think it would be nice to learn how to play it."

"It's a ukulele and its name is Yuk," Class Room replied. "And I will gladly teach you," she added, smiling at the younger woman who was lying on the upper level of the two tier sleeping platform of the shelter.

The Tramily of four relaxed around the comfort of the fire, taking a few moments to clear their minds of the worry about the quickly diminishing food supply. They still had a long way to go and the days ahead looked as though they might be accompanied with hunger pangs.

#

It rained a little overnight, giving the morning a dank, wet chill. The hikers went through their morning routine slowly. Trying to shake off the chill of the morning, they prolonged changing out of their dry, warm clothes and into their somewhat nasty, sweat-dampened, hiking clothes. Gnobbit hefted her pack, swinging it onto her back and said, "Well, this trail ain't gonna hike itself." She winked and smiled at Fic and started out in the lead.

Fic smiled back at her and hefted his own pack. The shotgun was tied to his shoulder strap. He could keep his hands free, but still be able to ready the weapon, if the need arose.

Today they planned to get to Clingmans Dome. There they hoped to find some food, but the danger of a possible public place was something they were worried about. Caution would be key. They didn't want another Honcho episode.

#

The cold, foggy day drained the hikers of the energy they had received from their meager breakfast. Lunch was just as sparse and when they arrived at Double Spring Gap Shelter, they knew they were done for the day, a few miles short of their goal.

Changing back into their dry clothes, they made a nice fire in the shelter fireplace. They had their third small meal of the day. The rationing was going well, but their energy level was low because of the lack of calories. They had about two days of food left.

Tomorrow, they would wake early and cover the last three miles to the summit, arriving sometime near daybreak. There was a small gift shop that sat on the access path that they wanted to check out.

The wind had picked up as evening approached, which blew the fog away, but stole their heat as it swept into the shelter. Everyone was in their quilts on the sleeping platform early, hoping to prevent themselves from shivering and burning extra calories they couldn't afford to lose.

#

After a quiet night the hikers all started stirring around 0400 and were on the trail before 0500. The climb was steady, but not too strenuous. They moved along with head lamps for a while, then without them as the morning started lightening the forest and the trail. They arrived at the paved walkway as the sun had already started its journey across the sky and observed the area. All was quiet. They dropped their packs and Fic and Gnobbit headed down the pathway to check out the gift shop. Fic carried the shotgun and Gnobbit had found her own piece of oak as they had walked along yesterday. It wasn't as large as Brown Shades', but it still had a heft, and she liked the feel of it in her hands.

The sky was mostly clear, with a section of mackerel sky to the east. The early sun tinted the clouds an orangish red that was striking. "Let's check out the tower," suggested Class Room. "I bet we can see pretty far from there."

"This is the highest point on the trail," stated Brown Shades. "We are at 6658 feet in elevation."

Class Room looked over at Brown Shades with admiration, "You do know a lot of stuff, Professor." She smiled as she said it.

"As a fellow educator, I'm sure you understand the reward of passing on the things you know. Increasing other's knowledge and skills. It feels good to give out the information."

Class Room nodded her head in agreement and turned towards the walkway. "Come on, wise sage. Let's check this thing out."

They followed the spiraling ramp that took them up to the covered Clingman's Dome observation platform which offered a 360 degree view. The two companions walked around looking where they had been, and where they still had to go. The view was perfect. The sun was shining across the land and they could see fog and mist laying in the low valleys far below. The green forest seemed to go on forever; one ridge after the other, spreading out and getting bluer as they grew farther away. Below them were numerous dead trees that reached up from the ground like skeletal fingers.

When Class Room and Brown Shades returned to the packs, Fic and Gnobbit were returning from their search. "We found a few things," Gnobbit said, tossing a bag of chips and pretzels at the other two. "There was no one around." She also had a couple bottles of water that they shared amongst themselves, topping off their water containers. They ate a small breakfast and enjoyed the chips and pretzels the two had found.

#

Another day of walking was before them. As they followed the trail, they started noticing dug up areas next to the path. It appeared that someone had gone through the underbrush and duff with a hoe or small shovel.

After noticing the disturbed soil, they were all a bit more aware of their surroundings while they continued their trek. As they came around a bend, they saw another area where the ground had been torn up and heard a series of grunting sounds. Slowing, the group started looking around, trying to find the source of the sounds. Gnobbit was on point and had the shotgun on her shoulder, which Fic had given her when she volunteered to walk at the front of the group. She unslung it and held it at the ready, continuing slowly down the trail. Brown Shades was behind her and held his staff in both hands, carrying it at port arms. Class Room came next, and she walked along looking to the left and the right. Fic took up the rear position.

Suddenly, a squeal sounded from the left of Fic and the brush started rustling. A large hog came bursting out of the bush and ran straight for Fic. He pulled his knife, but knew it was going to take more than this five-inch blade to handle this pig. The wild hog was a dark brown color with a rough, scraggly fur sticking up on its hide. Its large head pointed straight at Fic, four-inch tusks bursting out of its mouth, dripping with saliva.

Fic stood at the ready and waited for the hog to arrive. As it neared him, he stepped to the right and swung the base of his knife down to the pig's head. He hit the beast at the back of his skull, but it appeared to have no effect. The boar flicked its head and its tusks slid along Fic's leg. He felt a sharp pain in his calf and rolled to the right as fast as he could.

The pig ran past him and slowed down, working to turn and have another run. As he did so, a shot rang out. The dirt to the rear of the boar exploded up into the air and the pig squealed a hurt scream. It turned to its left and headed down the hill at a fast clip.

"I think I hit it," said Gnobbit excitedly. She came up to Fic and looked at his leg. "I guess he hit you too." She bent down to observe his injury. Fic's pant leg had a good rip in it and the skin underneath was also a bit ripped. It wasn't too deep, but it was about four inches long. Fic hissed in pain as she probed the gash. "I thought you were a big, strong soldier," she chided him.

"It hurts like a bitch," Fic answered. "Thanks for taking the shot. I don't think I could have gotten clear if it had charged me again."

The group gathered around the injured Tramily member and worked to clean and bandage the wound using Fic's first aid kit. They poured some alcohol that Fic still had for his stove and squirted on some antibiotic cream before putting on a few butterfly bandages and then wrapping it tightly with some gauze.

They got ready to go and continued down the trail. Fic had a nice limp, but it didn't slow him down too much. His main concern was infection. This was a dirty life and wild hogs were known for dirty tusks. Keeping it clean and bandaged was going to be a priority. He needed his legs to get home. Gnobbit handed him her walking stick, which he accepted gladly. She walked away with the shotgun at the ready, leading the way.

#

The rest of the day went a bit slowly. They let Fic set the pace. He found that once he got moving, the pain of the gash subsided some and he could keep a decent speed, but when they stopped for a break, his leg would stiffen up and it would take a few hundred meters for it to loosen up again.

They descended rather steeply to Newfound Gap, the trail rising at the end to come onto the road. Across the way was a large parking lot with an old stone monument in one corner. This usually busy tourist area was completely empty. Unless the road was closed due to weather, this place usually had at least a few cars parked in the spaces.

They crossed the lot, passing a sign that said they were standing on the North Carolina-Tennessee border. "So, are we done with North Carolina?" Gnobbit asked.

"No," Brown Shades answered. "We have been traversing the border for the last three days. As soon as we got up on the ridge, we have been walking the line. We will continue to do that until after we pass Erwin."

Brown Shades gestured to his right. "That stone structure over there is called the Rockefeller Memorial. It's where FDR dedicated the park back in 1940. This is usually a popular place."

The party checked out the stone building and the restrooms. There was nothing to be found except more toilet paper, which they all took a share of, of course.

The trail became rather tame for the next half mile or so. "Tourist Friendly," Gnobbit called it. Soon though, the trail was back to being a serious hiking trail.

#

They arrived at the Icewater Spring Shelter when the sun was heading over the ridge to the west. After another small dinner,

Fic assessed their supplies. One day's food and three shotgun shells was the tally.

The group spread out in the shelter. Class Room and Gnobbit placed their sleeping gear on the upper level. Gnobbit lounged on her pad, looking through the shelter's register and writing a few notes from time to time. Brown Shades and Fic set their bags up on the lower level off to one side. Fic didn't want to be climbing up the short ladder or jumping down to the ground. His leg was doing okay, but the pain was still present and every once in a while, a sharp jolt would run up his leg from the gash. He rummaged through his first aid kit and found a couple Motrin, fondly referred to as Vitamin I on the trail for its chemical name of ibuprofen. Fic's sleep was restless; each time he moved, pain would remind him of his close call with the feral beasts that roam these hills — descendants of escaped domestic pigs that the mountain people brought to this land long ago.

#

The birds started singing and the sky started to lighten. The front of the shelter had a magnificent view. Facing east, it was promising a beautiful sunrise. There were a few clouds in the sky — fluffy and scattered — adding to the beauty of the view and acting as places to catch the vibrant colors of the dawn.

Fic gingerly crawled out of his sleeping bag. His leg was throbbing, so he had gotten all the sleep he was going to. He walked out of the shelter area, picking up the shotgun that had been sitting propped at his head on the edge of the sleeping platform.

The covered area in front of the shelter, with its table and a few bench-like features around the edge, was still dark. As Fic came to the edge, he saw two rabbits feeding on the grass of the lawn-like area in front of the shelter. Fic slowly and quietly chambered a round into the 870's action. Brought the weapon to aim and fired. The bunnies had been far apart, so he couldn't get both with one shot, and he didn't want to use up all the shells, so he was happy when the rabbit to the left flew into the air from the impact and fell to the ground, already dead.

Fic walked over to the fallen rabbit as shouts of surprise and alarm came from the building. He bent and picked up the somewhat mangled animal and turned to the shelter. The others were at the edge of the covered area, sticks and staffs at the ready. "I got him," he said, smiling. The shelter residents looked at Fic incredulously, before letting out a breath. Gnobbit smiled at his feat, Class Room looked jangled at being awoken in such an abrupt way, and Brown Shades stood with his hand on his staff, already planning a recipe for the acquired protein, mumbling ingredients to himself.

Shooting a rabbit with double aught buckshot will not only do the job of ending the animal's life, but it will start the tenderizing process too. There was still plenty of meat, but the nine large pellets of the shell had done some damage.

Fic walked back to the shelter and placed the rabbit on the table. "I appreciate this guy being here for us and thank him for giving his life so we could go on," he said respectfully.

"It looks like it's time for some rabbit stew," Brown Shades said with a large grin.

Fic cleaned and skinned the rabbit and cut the meat into pieces. They started boiling some water and added the meat, sprinkling in a few spoonfuls of the brown powder from Brown Shades' Bag of Seasons. He still had one small potato in his bag, which he cut up into tiny pieces and added to the pot. Class Room walked around the lawn, admiring the gorgeous sunrise that had delivered on its promise, painting the sky with bright red and orange. She found some wild onion growing near the woods and picked some to add to the pot.

The stew boiled away, the smell emanating from the pot making their stomachs announce their hunger. Once thoroughly cooked, each hiker had a steaming pot of very watery rabbit stew to savor.

"Red sky in the morning, sailors take warning," Brown Shades said softly, as he stared out at the bright sunrise.

Fic took stock of their essential supplies again. They still had a day's worth of food, maybe a little more now if there was any leftover meat. Only two shotgun shells remained after the morning's hunt.

#

Friday had greeted them with another beautiful sunrise. Yesterday was a painful blur to Fic. They had walked over twenty miles. His leg had throbbed the entire way, but he had still managed to go the farthest they'd gone in one day since starting this trek. They had also eaten the last of their food by dinner time. Their bags were now empty, with the exception of some seasonings and maybe an odd tea bag or packet of mayo. It wasn't anything that would do much good.

They were almost done with the Smoky Mountains. They had been walking steadily downhill since early in the morning. The environment around them was changing. Where the higher elevations had been dense with pine trees, now their surroundings had transformed into maple, oak, and sassafras, with mayapple growing along the forest floor. The poison ivy was back too. They had done it. Hungry and a little hurt, but they had made it through the Great Smoky Mountains.

They were heading back toward rural civilization, where the possibility of getting food was more promising than before.

#

The noon sun was shining down on the hiking party as they passed a black box with green writing — intended for hikers to deposit half of their backcountry permit as they entered the park going south — that marked the end of the Smokies. Just ahead was a paved road. The trail followed the road as it crossed the Pigeon River, then continued to go under Interstate 40. Until this point, the group hadn't heard any indication that there was traffic passing by on the usually busy highway, but just as they neared the underpass, they heard vehicles approaching. They hurried to get out of sight under the road. A convoy of trucks passed over them, neither stopping or slowing, they clearly had places to get to.

The party waited until the sound of the trucks had stopped, then they quickly moved along the road until they saw a long flight of stone steps with a metal railing running up the side heading back into the woods. They ran up the steps, Fic bringing up the rear, hobbling on his injured leg.

His leg was already hurting a bit less today. Class Room had noticed that the wound looked as though it was starting to heal when she'd changed his bandage. She had doused it once again with alcohol and antibiotic cream and wrapped it up with new gauze and tape.

The trail followed the edge of the ridge until it came to a gravel road that was smaller than the others they had just traveled on. They started walking up the hill away from the trail. The Standing Bear Farm Hostel was about two tenths of a mile away.

They continued up the road until they could see a cluster of brown buildings across a dainty, babbling stream. They came to a building where an old man sat on a small porch, where an old man napped in a rocking chair, one leg propped up on the railing. A long, gray beard flowed from his face and shoulder-length, dark gray hair sprouted from under a black ball cap. Around his mouth his beard had been stained a brownish color from constant cigarette smoking. On a small table next to the man was a large ashtray with a pack of Marlboros sitting next to it.

Fic cleared his throat and one eye opened on the man's face. The other eye blinked open, he lowered his foot and stood with a start, coughing into his hand. His gaze scanned the hiking party before landing on Fic, noticing the shotgun resting benignly in the crock of his arm.

The man's eyes darted from Fic's weapon to a shotgun that was standing in the corner of the porch by the door. He looked back at the group and said quietly, "Nuts." Then followed up with, "Well, hey. How y'all doing today?"

"We are doing pretty good, but we are kind of hungry. Do you have any resupply for sale?" Fic asked. He lowered the shotgun further, trying to show that they meant him no harm.

"I have a lot of food, over in the whatsaname … the pantry store. You are welcome to some. I'm the only one here. Name's

Kent, I'm the caretaker. I haven't had anyone here in the past three days or so. We work on the honor system here, you keep track of what you take and pay when you leave. I'm running a special since it's the end of the world or something. Five bucks for a bunk and use of the facilities, although the electricity is out, so the shower will be cold, but the water is running. Also, you can take half off all the food you take," Kent explained to the party.

"Thanks, Kent, we may just take you up on that deal," Fic replied.

The party talked amongst themselves and decided that a shower may be nice, even if it is a cold one. They all still had some cash but were running low on that, too.

"We are staying the night," announced Brown Shades, strolling right into the bunkhouse. Kent went to follow him and grabbed the sitting shotgun. He took it inside and set it next to the first bed in the bunkhouse.

"With all the commotion, I have to be careful of who comes around. The, whatsaname, army was here a few days ago, but they didn't do anything bad. Even though something ain't right about them. I was surprised because I have been hearing things. I think they, whatsaname, cut me some slack, since I'm dying. I have lung cancer." The group looked at Kent, shocked at his bluntness. "It's cool," he said. "It's the smokes. I couldn't quit before and now that it's too late, I don't see the need to."

Kent walked through the bunkhouse as the others entered and selected their bunk for the night. There were eight bunk beds in the room, so everyone had their own lower bunk. Except for Gnobbit, who threw her pack up on a top bunk by the door and climbed up to start unpacking — she needed her vantage point.

They all settled in and then Kent showed them around the farm. There were several buildings in the compound. Each building had its own function. Right outside the bunkhouse was the kitchen. It contained a couple of long tables, a sink, stove, and microwave.

Past the kitchen was another building that held the shower area and beyond that was yet another building that had a set of sinks and a dryer. The sinks were where they washed clothes. The old fashioned way, with a washboard.

Outside was a large fire pit, and across the way, stairs led up to a fifth building. This room was what the famished hikers had been anticipating most — the store. The walls were lined with every manner of hiking food: rice and pasta packets, freeze-dried meals, ramen, tuna, packets of chicken and plenty more filled the shelves.

The group eagerly picked something to eat right away. After their quick snack break, they started selecting items to refill their empty food bags. The prices were decent, and with the discount, they would be able to afford the cost of a night in a bed and some resupply. Class Room noticed that most of the food was beyond its expiration date, but they weren't worried about that at this point. These details, which once seemed like hard and fast rules that needed to be adhered to, felt trivial when food was scarce and the state of the country was uncertain.

They ate a hearty dinner, refilling their calorie banks that had become depleted over the last few days, and got a fire going in the big fire pit. Kent asked if they were willing to do some work to earn another 25% discount on the food and the whole group volunteered to help.

For the next hour, they cleaned up the place, cut some firewood and completed the chores that Kent needed help with. Afterward, they all sat by the fire, chatting sporadically and planning the next day's hike. Brown Shades reached into his pocket and pulled out a small bag of white powder. He dramatically passed his hands over the flames and the yellow fire turned a bright green. Everyone oohed and awed and Gnobbit was quite excited. "What did you use for that bit of magic, Brownie?" she asked.

"Green comes from borax. I had found some under the sink in the kitchen of Birch Cabin and have been carrying it since then. I was waiting for a comfortable time to try it out; tonight seemed like the perfect opportunity," Brown Shades explained.

Class Room decided to bring out Yuk while they continued to convene by the fire. She would strum for a bit, then play a short sample of a song — some recognizable, some unique. As she played, the party felt the music flow through them and the magic soothed them. Having full stomachs helped a lot, too. After strumming out a few songs, she started showing Gnobbit a chord, then would have her try it on Yuk — the teaching had begun.

Kent stood over by the bunkhouse, smoking one of his Marlboros, his shotgun next to his chair and his foot up in its usual position on the rail of the small porch.

Fic looked around at the companions he had gathered so far on his trek. He was reminded of his dream and could so easily imagine a Thief, a Mage, and a Bard surrounding him — a slightly wounded Warrior — as they refilled their energy bars. He considered the games his son always played and jokingly thought to himself that an Elf Ranger and a Dwarf Cleric were all they needed to complete their party.

#

Fic is sitting in a rustic cabin. There is a bright fire burning in a large fireplace on the far side of the room. Music is playing somewhere; it has a mysterious sound. Something that could be felt and seen and smelt, not just heard. It brought a strange sense of wellbeing to his body.

He looked at his clothes and he was once again dressed as a fantasy warrior. Looking around, he sees the raven hair and face of Class Room. She is the one creating the music. It isn't a ukulele in her hands, but some sort of mandolin or lute type instrument. She looks up at him and smiles. Her dazzling brown eyes are sincere and seem to shine in the firelight. She is dressed in rough linen and woven wool. The clothes look to be of fine design and the style suited her perfectly.

Next to her sits Brown Shades, looking like a wise mage. He is listening to the music and is humming along. His large wizard's staff leans against the wall near the fire.

Gnobbit is laying on a cot to the right of the fire. Dressed in her dark thieves' clothes. She appears to be dozing, a soft smile on her face.

Suddenly, there is a loud knock on the thick oak door. The music stops and Gnobbit opens her eyes and sits up. Brown Shades looks at Fic and nods his head.

Being the closest to the door, Fic stands up and walks to the opening. A large beam is barring the entrance. He lifts the beam and leans it against the wall, reaches for the clever, wooden latching system, and pulls the portal open.

Before him stand two men. One is short, dark and bearded. He wears ornate armor and a kilt adorned with straps of metal and leather. A large axe is strapped to his belt. The other is tall. Very tall. His delicate features seem to glow in the night. A mustache adorns his handsome face and pointed ears that resemble Gnobbit's show through his bright, white hair. He is dressed all in green leather. A bow is strapped to his back and a quiver of arrows are on his shoulder.

Both men smile at Fic as if they know him. Fic starts to smile back and a cough rings out.

Fic startles awake in his bed in the bunkhouse at the Standing Bear. Kent is coughing in his sleep a few bunks away. The dream starts to fade from his memory, but the tune that Class Room played still rings in his ears.

Eventually, Fic returns to the land of slumber and the rest of the night is spent mending his wounded and half-starved body.

CHAPTER 9
TOWN VISITS - SATURDAY, JUNE 23RD TO FRIDAY, JUNE 29TH

The next morning, the party of four arose to the sound of a rooster out in the yard somewhere. Fic was up and out of bed first, heading straight to the kitchen to get some breakfast started on the gas stove. Kent had given them some fresh eggs, and Fic fried two of them in the large cast iron skillet that was sitting on the counter. He added some bacon bits to the mix and a slice of cheese. His mouth watered as he watched the eggs bubble and sizzle. The other three hikers were lured out of their bunks by the aroma that protruded into the odor of the bunkhouse and drew them to the kitchen building.

Each building had its own peculiar smell. Most were a little unsavory, but each was unique. The bunkhouse had the slight odor of urine. The kitchen had an odd smell near the sink, kind of swampy or mildewy. The shower and the laundry rooms each had a different grade of damp smell. These interesting notes gave the farm an interesting aura. This place was legendary to the hikers of the trail. It had been around for several years and most hikers who came through had a story to tell about Standing Bear.

The foursome sat around the table in the kitchen-like room eating their breakfast and trading small talk. Gnobbit started absentmindedly humming a tune. The tune sounded a lot like the song that Class Room was playing in Fic's dream. Slowly, each of the three turn their heads towards Gnobbit with strange looks on their faces. "What's that song you are humming, Gnobbit?" Class Room asked with a slightly curious expression on her face.

"Oh, nothing," Gnobbit replied. "Just something that came to me as I was sitting here eating." She continued with her breakfast, heedless to the continued stares each were giving her. Eventually, the other three hikers went back to scarfing down their food. No one mentioned anything else about the song.

Fic heard Brown Shades mumble under his breath, thinking no one could hear, "*A dwarf and an elf. Together.*" Fic smiled at Brown Shades but said nothing.

The breakfast was fantastic, and all the hikers felt refreshed and ready to get moving. Cold showers had helped to enliven the foursome as well, their freshly cleaned bodies ready to regather all the sweat and dirt awaiting them on their journey. They packed up and went to settle with Kent.

"You guys really helped me out here. I do appreciate it," he began. "I'll tell you what, just give me what you can spare, but make sure you keep something for up the trail. The ATMs ain't working and credit cards are useless pieces of plastic. Cash is king for now."

Each of the hikers gave all that they computed. Everyone still had some cash left, but no one had much. They thanked Kent for his hospitality and gave their best wishes. Class Room and Gnobbit both gave him a little hug which he seemed to appreciate a lot.

#

The morning started with a climb up Snowbird Mountain. It was a steady ascent of around 2500 feet spread out over four and a half miles. They arrived at a weird-looking tower, huffing and puffing, and Fic called for a break.

The tower was a round roof sitting on top of a square building. The roof was offset from the square structure to create a porch-like overhang in front. Coming from the roof was a funnel looking antenna that resembled a smokestack. The site was surrounded by a wooden rail fence displaying multiple *No Trespassing* signs.

They came up to the fence and dropped their packs. Gnobbit stretched her muscles, relishing in the brief absence of her heavy pack. As she rolled her neck to the left, she noticed a man sitting in a grassy area. A large, black pack sat beside him, and he was cooking a meal on his stove.

The man appeared short and stout, and his hair was dark, curly and long. His dark beard covered his face, obscuring his mouth. He killed the flame in his stove, stirred what was inside his pot and pulled it off the burner. Just then, he noticed the hikers who were staring over at him. He looked at each of them raptly for a few seconds, then a smile broke on his hairy face. "Hallo," he greeted them. "Welcome to Snowbird Mountain. I'm just having a little second breakfast here. Climbing up that mountain made me hungry. I bet youse are the Party of Four." He spoke in a brogue that revealed he was not originally from this continent.

He put the pot on the ground and came over to the other hikers. He had large boots on, which made his feet look out of proportion to the rest of his short, thick body. His clothes were rough and wooly looking, mostly of a brownish color. Instead of pants, he wore a kilt. It wasn't of a bright plaid pattern but was a dark brown and had pockets. Around his neck, he wore a large, ornately carved, Celtic cross that had been made from a piece of wood. "I'm Rodent Whisperer," he introduced himself. "Does anyone ken what is going on in this country?"

The group introduced themselves all around and told Rodent Whisperer what they knew, what they suspected, and what they had heard. Once the group was done comparing notes, Rodent Whisperer continued, "I have been hiking north. I was behind youse guys up in the Smokies. I kept seeing your shelter register entries, Gnobbit," he said, looking over at the young girl and giving her a wink. "You write a nice journal. I had decided to try and catch you all up. I decided to bypass that last hostel, and I guess I did catch you up and then passed you late yesterday. The registers are where I first saw Gnobbit referring to your Tramily as the Party of Four. I'm hoping we can change it to Party of Five." A pleasant smile broke across his face. He looked hopefully at the party.

"Of course, you can join us. How far up do you need to go?" Fic affirmed and inquired.

"I dinnae ken at the moment. I'm over here on a six-month travel visa. I'm from Scotland, if you hadn't noticed. I was planning on hiking the whole thing, but times have changed, and therefore, so do plans. I'm really not sure if it is even possible to fly out of the country now." A worried look crossed his face, but was gone quickly, replaced with a stern stubbornness.

"How are you doing in the food category?" Brown Shades asked.

"I'm doing alright. My pack has a lot of space and I have been stocking up on as much food as I can carry when the opportunity presents itself. I was able to sneak into the general store at Fontana Village in the middle of the night, while those crazy bastards were sleeping. They had appeared a little frazzled when I was observing them from the bush. Did youse have anything to do with that?" He looked around at the group, respect showing in his dark eyes.

"We might have," Brown Shades replied, his own twinkle in his eye shining back.

They joined Rodent Whisperer as he ate his second breakfast, snacking on whatever was handy in their food bags. Some clouds started rolling in as they finished up and the freshly-formed party of five continued down the trail.

"I guess if we keep adding people to our party, we should just use the Tramily name of The Party," Gnobbit suggested.

"That sounds perfect," Rodent Whisperer agreed. The others nodded and smiled. Trying the official group name on their lips. The Party. The irony of this optimistic name during these dangerous times was not lost on them. But it was definitely a celebratory occasion when they came across a new companion, instead of the numerous malicious people that seemed to be trying to keep them from getting back home.

#

The Party traveled another ten miles as the clouds in the sky became thicker and darker. Rain was heading to the mountains of North Carolina and Tennessee.

Roaring Fork Shelter was a long log structure. Smaller than the shelters in the Smokies, but big enough for The Party. Brown Shades was happy to go back to his hammock for the night, erecting it between two trees that were near the shelter. The rest of the group spread out inside the shelter. After gathering some wood, Rodent Whisperer pulled out the hand axe that he kept strapped to the side of his pack. He used it to process the wood into easily burnable pieces. Working with Brown Shades, they had a nice fire going as the forest darkened.

As the flames grew, Brown Shades asked Rodent Whisperer, "Where in Scotland are you from?"

"Edinburgh," was his reply, the r rolling off his tongue in his brogue.

"Ah, I attended a conference there a few years ago. Magnificent city with a deep, enthralling history. I didn't have a lot of time then to sightsee, and would love to go back one day. Perhaps, when we can travel again, I can come over and you can show me around."

"That would be nice. I always enjoy sharing my homeland with others," Rodent Whisperer replied. "It 'tis a bonnie country and there is plenty to see in the city and the surrounding highlands."

A light drizzle started to fall around the hikers while they sat around the fire. As the drizzle became a light rain, then a heavier shower, they retreated to the shelter to stay dry, and the rain doused the fire with its watery drops. Class Room asked the new party member, "How did you become the Rodent Whisperer?"

"It was a funny thing," began Rodent Whisperer. "On the third night of this hike, we were all staying in the shelter at Gooch Gap. I was set up in the shelter on one side and as we were trying to sleep, the mice had come out to play. I started talking to them and they seemed to sit and listen to what I was saying. After a while, the mice went away and didn't bother us the rest of the night. The group were impressed with my mouse wrangling skills and named me Rodent Whisperer. I liked it and adopted it as my trail name."

Each member of The Party told their origin story and talked about all the adventures they had experienced so far on this strange hike, including their encounter with the wild boar.

"I saw you were limping a little as we hiked today, Fic," Rodent Whisperer remarked. "Is that from the pig?"

"Yes. When I was charged, I couldn't quite get out of the way of his tusks, and he opened me up some. It has been getting better, but the soreness comes and goes as we walk." Fic replied.

"I'm kind of a healer in my village. I serve the old gods and sometimes they work through me," Rodent Whisperer said mysteriously. "Have you ever heard of Reiki?"

"I have," said Fic. "Isn't it like channeling some universal energy and passing it through a person to help heal and comfort them?"

"That is almost exactly what it is. I'm surprised you know."

"My wife has studied a lot of the holistic arts. I remember her researching Reiki for a couple of months."

"If you like, I could check out your wound, and maybe help you out some."

"Go for it, honorable cleric," Fic smiled at the Scot and lifted his leg to pull up his pants past the wound.

Rodent Whisperer removed his bandage and checked out the wound. He massaged around the area and then placed his hands on either side of the gash, an intense look on his face. To Fic, it seemed as if the area around the wound heated up some. The pain began to subside. He didn't know if it was his imagination or if true power was being wielded through Rodent Whisperer's hands. The healer continued this way for about ten minutes. When he was done, he put some more antibiotic ointment on the wound and re-bandaged it.

They settled into a comfortable silence in the dark shelter. Brown Shades retired to his hammock. The hanging structure swayed back and forth as the Mage found his comfort; then it was still. One by one, the hikers retired to their sleeping bags and quilts, and within minutes, the snoring of exhausted hikers flowed through the shelter.

#

The Party was sitting at Deer Park Mountain Shelter. The day was late, and the sun was heading towards the edge of the mountain to the west. They had walked almost fifteen miles today. Fic's leg felt surprisingly good throughout the day. He could hardly tell that he had a large wound on his calf anymore. They had left early and made good time, getting to camp in the early afternoon. They all rested in the shelter, Brown Shades even putting up his hammock to catch a few *z's* before the next challenge was to begin. In three more miles, the trail was going to go through its first town. All the other towns they had passed so far had been away from the trail, some by quite a few miles, but this one was different. It would be hard to avoid the town because they would have to use roads to do that, and the roads were not safe.

They had decided to cross through it in the dark of night, to try to avoid detection and being taken prisoner again. They didn't know what to expect, but they were going to take every precaution they could. Their weapons were either rudimentary or low on ammo, so getting through with the utmost stealth was the goal. With about an hour's worth of daylight left, they slung their packs and moved out of the shelter area. They had rested enough and ate a good meal before heading out. After they walked off the stiffness that seemed to always afflict their bodies when they stopped moving, they felt good.

The trail moved steadily downhill with darkness descending onto The Party as they approached the French Broad River valley and the small town of Hot Springs. As they moved along the ridge, they would come to an opening in the forest every once in a while. They could see where the town was, but it was almost completely devoid of light. The young crescent moon was approaching the western horizon and provided little light. They would use their red head lamps from time to time, but mostly just relied on their night vision to see the trail. They could see some lights sparsely around the town and noticed several large bonfires here and there, but there were no streetlights or any sources of illumination coming from most of the houses.

They hunkered down about a hundred meters up the hill from where the trail entered town and waited for the village to go to sleep. A short time after the moon set, they continued down the last of the trail and came to a road with a parking lot next to it. To their left, was the remains of a house that was recently burned to the ground. "That's where the Laughing Heart Hostel was," Fic said. "It looks like someone wanted it gone."

They went over to the charred hulk and checked it out. The long, low building was no more; it had completely burned. It appeared that no firemen even attempted to douse the conflagration. As they checked out the remains, they saw that the large stone and wood lodge behind the hostel had also been torched.

They moved on. The trail joined the road here and continued downhill through the town. They passed the Smoky Mountain Diner; it was dark and empty. Next to it was a Dollar General; its windows had been smashed, and the door was ajar. They decided to check it out. It was a mess inside, but they were all able to grab a few things that hadn't been destroyed or ruined to supplement their food bags.

The group continued through the very small heart of downtown. They passed the Welcome Center — which didn't appear very welcoming — and the post office which was also a burned-out shell. They looked into the outfitters and the tavern. Everything was dark and quiet. Not a soul was around.

They crossed a small bridge over a creek and continued towards the railroad tracks. They could see light up ahead and hear the low rumble of generators.

The Party carefully moved along the side of the street. Seeing a vacant fruit stand on their right, they veered toward it to keep to the shadows. As they approached a bend, they saw a row of cars. They had been parked end to end across the road where the bridge spanned the river below. Light shone down the road towards the hikers and all around the bridge area. They could see men dressed in military uniforms moving around on the other side of the barricade. They couldn't go much further without walking into the middle of what was, most assuredly, the enemy. They would need to find another way around. They moved towards the noise, carefully staying in the cover of a few small buildings along the road and a row of high hedges. Up ahead, on the right, was a white sign with green lettering. In the darkness they could just make out that it said:

Hot Springs Resort and Spa.
Campground, open all year.
Canoe and Kayak rentals, see camp host.

They followed the gravel road that led into the dark campground. They quickly came to the check-in booth, and noticed a few dim lights in the cabins in front of them. The flicker of a flashlight could be seen far off within the cluster of cabins and tents, illuminating a person walking through the campground. "This camp is occupied," Rodent Whisperer softly spoke to Fic.

"It must be where those guys on the bridge are sleeping," replied Fic. The campground as a whole appeared to be settled down for the night. There weren't very many lights, and they couldn't tell if there were guards posted.

"We have to go the other way, anyway," whispered Gnobbit. Holding up a copy of the resort map she had picked up at the check-in booth. The map included the campground, spa buildings, and boat rental area. The resort spanned a large area along the river on both sides of the main road. "The boat rental is back across the road and up towards the spa area."

They retraced their steps back towards the road and huddled next to the fruit stand to get their bearings. There was an opening in the split-rail fence at the corner of the property that led to a crosswalk. They crossed the road, out of sight of the men at the bridge.

There was a line of trees next to the railroad tracks and a gravel road leading to a large building. They paralleled the road on the grassy berm and came to the spa building; a small sign pointed the way to the boat rental area.

There were about twenty kayaks and fifteen canoes stacked next to the river. They found two canoes and lifted them, taking them to the water's edge. Gnobbit came over with four paddles in her arms. Handing one to Fic and two to Rodent Whisperer. "Here ya go, RW," she said.

Rodent Whisperer handed one of the paddles to Brown Shades. "You're with me, Professor," he said, dumping his pack into the canoe on the left.

Gnobbit went with Fic while Class Room got into the middle of Rodent Whisperer's canoe.

"The plan is to get across the river before the bridge then go around the bridge back to the trail. It looks like there is a road on the other side," Fic relayed to the others.

They pushed off and headed out into the dark river. It was completely black out there. The moon was gone, and clouds had rolled in. The overcast filled the sky, lowering the ceiling quite a bit. The water bubbled and churned merrily. The current was swift here. They could hear the sound of rapids on the other side of the bridge.

The hikers with the paddles started pulling to get across, but it became clear quite quickly that the current wasn't going to make this an easy task. They were being pushed towards the bridge.

Everyone realized at the same time that they weren't going to make the other shore so easily and the plan adjusted immediately to a silent pass under the bridge.

As they approached the upstream side of the bridge, they stopped actively paddling and just steered the canoes. None of the barricade guards appeared to be looking down at the river. Most of the activity was at the two ends of the bridge and the lights were only shining towards the roads on either side, leaving the churning river dark to the night sky. The canoes entered the even darker shadow of the bridge and passed under their enemies.

The current propelled them to the other side, the sound of the rapids churning loudly in their ears. Gnobbit could see a slight glimmer of white water up ahead. She pointed it out to Fic, and he signaled that they needed to paddle and make the other shore before those rapids.

Everyone dug in. They passed through a modest example of what was ahead and pushed harder. Twenty meters from the white line of rapids, both canoes made it to the shore next to each other. There was a small sandy area, and they quickly jumped out and pulled the canoes on to the bank of the river. They had made it.

They hid the canoes in the brush and bushwhacked to the trail, which was just beyond some thick reeds. They made their way along the water before navigating long switchbacks that climbed 2000 feet and led them away from the river and small town. The Party hiked throughout the night to put some distance between the corrupt soldiers and themselves. Just after midnight, they came to a clearing that had space for several tents and multiple trees that were perfect for hanging a hammock. A large fire ring dominated the center of the campsite and there were even a couple logs and rocks that worked as crude seats.

They set up their sleeping spots for the night in silence and immediately rolled into their sleeping bags to try to sleep. It had been an extremely long and stressful day. They had hiked the length of a marathon today — their longest day so far — but they had made it through a trail town and had avoided being spotted or captured.

"I'll take the first watch," Rodent Whisperer said. "I was well rested when you found me and am still a little excited from the canoe ride. I'm not a fan of water."

Fic handed him the shotgun and threw a soft salute his way. "I'll relieve you in a few hours," he said.

Town days used to be something hikers looked forward to, Fic thought to himself as he slid into his bag and zipped his bivy shut. *Now it's get in and get out without any trouble. This world had become really fucked up.* He rolled over in his sleeping bag and fell asleep quickly.

The crickets sang their song and an owl called out a warning, alerting others of the strangers in their woods as the camp settled into an uneasy slumber. In a few more days, they would have to do this all over again as they descended upon Erwin, Tennessee; the next town the trail traversed through.

#

The rain had started at about noon. It had been steady for the last five hours, slowly soaking into everyone's rain gear. The Party was wet and miserable. They had hiked over eighteen miles so far, and they still had several miles to go until the next shelter. The day was darkening prematurely due to the rain and thick overcast.

They crossed a small dirt road and could see a light coming from the window of a cabin that they could just make out in the forest. They stood talking; wondering how that cabin had power and if there was anyone there.

From the other side of the road, a voice said, "That's my cabin." They looked over to where the voice had come from, surprise on all of their faces. Before them stood a rugged man in a long poncho. Next to him sat a large fluffy dog. Its fur was wet from the rain, but it didn't look uncomfortable. "You all look like a bunch of drowned rats. You should come visit with me for a spell. I have a nice fire going and I also have food," he offered. "And beer," he added. The man had chin-length blond hair that faded to gray, which he continuously had to brush behind his ears to keep out of his face. His beard was of medium length and matched his head. He was of a stocky build, and he moved his body easily, with an interesting agility. He walked up to them, the dog keeping pace at his knee, its tail wagging slowly, and motioned for them to follow. He was wearing a long poncho that covered his large bulk. The bill of a ball cap protruded from the hood of his rain gear.

"I'm Paul. Paul Thomas and this here is Copper," he pointed to the dog. "Welcome to my mountain."

The vote was unanimous to head to the cabin, and they followed the man to his abode.

As they approached the building, they were now sure that electric light was coming out of the window. "Do you have electricity, sir?" asked Brown Shades.

"I do. It is provided by the sun. I have a clearing behind the cabin, and I have an array of a thousand watts that provides me with all the power I need. Except when the weather is like this, but I have a hefty battery bank, which can last a couple of days."

They entered the cabin, removed their packs and rain gear, and went to sit around the roaring fire that was burning in a large cast iron wood stove. The dog shook off, spraying the guests, but no one minded; they all felt like doing the same thing. Paul removed his poncho and they saw he had his own shotgun strapped to his chest on a one point sling, unnoticeable under his rain gear. He grabbed an old towel and helped dry the large Goldendoodle's thick fur.

The hikers were ready to change out of their wet gear and into their dry camp clothes.

"I have plenty of hot water. The bathroom is down that hallway," he pointed out.

"Ladies first," Brown Shades offered to the two women, who promptly gathered their stuff, heading down the hallway. Class Room headed in first, while Gnobbit arranged her clothes and awaited her turn.

The cabin had an interesting decor. There were odds and ends all over the place. Not quite in the hoarder category, but they could tell Paul liked to collect things. In the kitchen area, there were no less than fifteen cast iron skillets of several sizes. On the shelves, Fic counted three old coffee grinders, two cheese graters, two flour sifters, at least a dozen spatulas of various sizes and styles and other utensils and gadgets. Each couch or chair had a hand-knitted Afghan blanket and in the corner of the living room, there was an ancient stereo system with an actual turntable. Next to the turntable was a large collection of vinyl records.

Paul started gathering various meats, cheeses, and other ingredients from his refrigerator and pantry and started to make a meal that would warm them all up. On the menu this evening: mac and cheese made from scratch, with chicken and ham mixed in. Just thinking about it made everyone's mouth water with anticipation.

Paul pulled out several brown bottles with no labels, "I make my own beer. This is an amber ale that I call *Rust Belt Ale*. If you are thirsty, this will do the trick."

Everyone popped a cap, except for Rodent Whisperer, and the murmurs of approval came from all around.

As Paul prepared dinner, The Party each took their turn taking a quick shower and putting on dry clothes. The front porch was screened in, and that area became the make-shift laundry drying room. Fic ran a piece of paracord from two of the posts, and damp, dripping hiking clothes started growing on it like a vine. After each shower, another set of clothes grew there. The hikers comfortably spread out and relished in the comfort of the indoors. Feeling safe and getting warm. It raised everyone's spirits by several degrees.

Class Room and Gnobbit sat by the stereo and started looking through the albums. They found one that looked interesting and put it on the turntable. Gnobbit fired up the power and put the needle on the turning disk. Soft sounds of blues music came flowing out of the speakers. Everyone was content. Class Room pulled out Yuk, and started strumming along with the music, matching the melody perfectly.

Copper had become quite attached to Gnobbit, following her everywhere she went. Gnobbit returned the affection by giving the big dog lots of scratches behind her ears and rubbing her tummy when she rolled over onto her back.

The rain continued to fall, and The Party sat in the cabin, enjoying the evening. The woods grew dark, and the wind picked up some. Everyone was so happy to not have to be out in that weather. "I take each day as it is given," Fic said to Paul, "but leaving this day outside, while we're inside — safe, warm, and dry — is nice every once in a while."

After the meal, Paul showed them his extra room. The large space had two sets of bunk beds placed in an L shape in one corner and a small dresser up against the opposite wall. "Most of you guys can sleep here. That large couch in the living room is also pretty comfy. Sometimes I just sleep there instead of heading to my own cold room. The stove keeps that room pretty toasty on nights like this," Paul said.

Gnobbit moved to the bed on the right; throwing her quilt up on the top bunk. Class Room was below her. Brown Shades across from Class Room and Rodent Whisperer put his stuff on the other top bunk. Fic claimed the couch. He also planned on taking the first watch. Even though everything felt safe, there were still dangerous people out there. Possibly looking for them.

After everyone was content with their bed choice, they all returned to the warm living room and talked about what was happening in the country.

"I have a ham radio down in the basement and I have been trying to find out what has been going on. I haven't left this mountain since everything went down. More than three weeks. I'm self-sustainable here, but eventually, I will need to find more supplies," Paul started. "It seems that guy, Richard Flaherty, aka The Boss, has created quite a stir in this country and the world. He is the leader of some paramilitary group called The Regime. They infiltrated a lot of areas, including the military and some government. I heard some guy spreading a conspiracy about how he might be some kind of alien sent here to cause havoc. Maybe preparing the way for some alien invasion." Paul laughed to himself, then continued more seriously. "He somehow got his hands on several nuclear bombs and executed a coordinated attack on the United States. Setting off the devices in at least a dozen large cities. Taking out so much infrastructure, that a very large portion of the country is now without electricity, cell service, and so many other things. He has caused mass chaos throughout the nation. Washington DC is ashes, the president unaccounted for, but presumed dead at this time.

"There is a large resistance that sprung up when he started making trouble, made up of people like you and me, who just want things to calm down, but refuse to be subject to that asshole's Regime. They have been helping me and I have been helping them."

Fic told Paul the goals of The Party and where each of them needed to go. "We will certainly help The Resistance wherever we can. They seem to have the same ideals as us."

"I'll give you directions to a guy I have been talking to in Erwin. He may be able to help you out when you skirt that town," Paul offered. "His name is Charlie."

"That would be great," Fic smiled. "Any help we can get is appreciated."

Paul's beers were very tasty; he kept pulling more out of the fridge and even went down to his basement to restock the refrigerator after a while. Rodent Whisperer was the only one who opted for the iced tea that Paul offered as an alternative to the beer. Soon everyone was yawning. Gnobbit and Class Room retired first, quickly followed by Brown Shades. Rodent Whisperer drained his glass, ice cubes tinkling at the bottom — a luxury that none of The Party had been able to enjoy for some time. He stood, thanked Paul for his hospitality and headed to the last bunk in the bedroom.

Fic and Paul finished their last beers at the same time and Paul took his leave to his small room at the other end of the hall. Fic checked the action of the shotgun, placed it on the floor beside him, then lay back on the couch, pulling his sleeping bag next to him. It was warm enough inside that he didn't need to get inside the bag.

He soon fell asleep to the muffled sounds of the large logs cracking and popping in the wood stove. Copper lay on her bed next to the couch. She would maintain the watch for the night; warning of anyone approaching this remote cabin in the woods.

#

The rain had appeared to stop during the night, but it was falling again as the hikers came out of their room, rubbing the night's grub out of their eyes. Paul had been up for a while and was cooking bacon and eggs in two large cast iron skillets. A delicious smell wafted through the cabin. A large pot of coffee was percolating on the stove — another antique of Paul's that still functioned perfectly. Everyone feasted.

The Party was all sitting around the long butcher block kitchen table, feeling full and content. "Ya know, a zero day might be perfect for today," Paul said. "That rain looks like it will be around all day. I have plenty of food here and I even have some to spare, if you need to resupply."

It took barely two minutes for everyone to agree that it was time for a day without hiking. Or, more precisely, hiking zero miles — hence the name zero day. They had been hiking every day for about three weeks straight. Their bodies were getting stronger each day, but the wear and tear was still taking its toll. Even though delaying the trek would put them a little behind in their quest to get home, they needed to keep their bodies capable of hiking those remaining miles.

The rest of the day was spent cleaning the rest of their clothes, repairing their gear, and adding some food that Paul offered them to their supply. They listened to music the whole day; sampling the eclectic collection that Paul had gathered from old record stores, yard sales, and flea markets. Every once and a while, Class Room would play a song or two. Her voice was like silk, and she was very talented. Gnobbit even performed her first song; one that Class Room had taught her when they sat together the last few days. The music, both from the old turntable and from Yuk, soothed all the hikers' souls. Even Paul had a content smile as he listened to the hikers sing their songs.

Paul came up to Fic as he was cleaning the shotgun and held out his hand — there were five shells in his palm. "I don't have a lot of ammo to spare, but you can have these. It is a mishmash of shot sizes, but all 12 gauge," Paul offered.

Fic took the shells, put three of them in the magazine and the other two in the belt pouch of his pack. They now had seven shells, much better than the two they had when they discovered this sanctuary in the woods. "I really appreciate this, Paul," Fic said. "We have a long way to go and who knows what dangers await us. Having some fire power makes me feel a lot better. We won't forget your hospitality and kindness."

They passed the day relaxing and eating and relaxing some more. Everyone took a nap during the day; it was glorious and decadent.

After another fine dinner and a few more beers, the hikers relaxed around the wood stove. Paul brought out an old VCR player and a stack of movies on VHS. They watched *Caddyshack*, laughing at the old, tired jokes of Chevy Chase and Bill Murray.

As darkness fell and the movie ended, the hikers of The Party retired to their respective bunks and spent another night safe, warm, and dry.

It was nice to take this break, but already Fic could feel an antsiness that wanted him to keep walking — back to his family up north, back home.

#

Morning found the rain gone. Fic tightened the straps on his pack. Everything was ready to go. He was ready to go. The rest of The Party was all packed up too. It was time to get back on trail. After another large breakfast, they took their leave of Paul.

Gnobbit had started calling him Elrond in honor of the leader of the mystical redoubt in the mountains called Rivendell from *The Lord of the Rings* trilogy. The cabin seemed to have a magical feel, and Paul appeared to like the reference. "Bye, Elrond. We are forever in your debt." She stood on her tiptoes and gave him a kiss on his bearded cheek. He blushed a little and gave her a hug.

Paul said to Fic, "I contacted Charlie yesterday with the ham radio. He said to meet him at dusk in two days at the old Uncle Johnny's Hostel; it's right next to the trail as you come down from the ridge. He'll be waiting at the back of the property where there is a pavilion for hammocks."

"Roger that," replied Fic.

The others each said their goodbye to the humble mountain man. They thanked him for his hospitality and genuinely hoped they could return to visit with the stranger-turned-friend and his furry companion after all the mayhem ended.

They walked back to the trail and continued north. Paul and Copper stood on the road where he had walked them back to the trail. Copper let out a farewell bark as they started up a rise and turned a corner in the trail. The Party faded into the still dripping forest.

#

Unlike the past two days, this day was spectacular. The sun was shining with only a few perfect fair weather clouds floating towards the east like large sailing ships in the sky. As they walked along, Class Room and Rodent Whisperer started discussing the intricacies of soccer — or football, as Rodent Whisperer referred to it. Both loved the sport and Rodent Whisperer was a pretty good midfielder in his younger days. Class Room had been a sharp forward, with many goals to her credit. Their conversation became rather heated as they discussed the last World Cup when Scotland had defeated Paraguay to advance in the tournament. The sports debate continued as the group conquered the biggest climb of the day to the top of Bald Mountain.

The wind at the top was whipping across the bald, stealing the heat from the hikers. They arrived at the shelter about five hundred feet below the top. Fic had wanted to get back on track, so he had encouraged everyone to hike another long day after their lazy, decadent zero. Everyone was feeling good, and they completed the twenty-five miles with no problems. Fic also wanted to make sure they made their rendezvous with this Charlie guy that Paul had arranged for them.

The shelter was long and had two levels. The Party picked their spaces and set up their beds. Brown Shades walked off and circled the shelter to find some useful trees. He found two that would suffice, was set up quickly, and back at the table for dinner.

The fire in the pit in front of the shelter was a comfort after the grueling winds of the bald. Another long day walking north was complete.

#

The Wood Thrush announced his agenda of the day as the forest lightened with the approaching dawn. Fic sat up in the shelter and looked out into the morning. They needed to hike the seventeen miles to Erwin by dusk, timing their arrival with darkness. They wanted to make sure they didn't miss Charlie at the hostel.

The day's hike was uneventful, and they found themselves losing elevation again as they approached the Nolichucky River. As the trail wrapped around a ridge, a view opened up to the northwest. They could see the streets of Erwin off in the distance. They wouldn't have to walk through the center of town, like they did in Hot Springs, but the settled area was still close. This time they could see some lights in the windows of the houses in the town. Another difference from Hot Springs.

Dusk had settled on the area when The Party came to another road after what felt like a never-ending succession of switchbacks taking them down the mountain. A waxing gibbous moon hung in the sky behind them, providing a trace amount of guiding light.

The trail turned left onto the road and headed towards a bridge that spanned the river. Straight ahead was Uncle Johnny's Hostel.

They approached the cluster of buildings and passed into the shadow of the covered porch. They followed a pea gravel path around the side of the main building and saw several small buildings beyond in a yard-like area. At the back of the yard, a shadowy pavilion stood in silence.

The Party moved to the pavilion and gathered into a circle, looking around silently in the darkening yard.

"Hello," said a voice in the shadows. "You guys are right on time. I'm guessing you are the ones known as The Party." A large man moved out of the shadows.

"I'm Charlie."

#

Charlie was a big man. His girth was great and his stature on the tall side. He wore a ball cap with an emblem of an orange football helmet. The symbol of the Cleveland Browns. His face was full, a little on the chubby side, and he wore wire-rim glasses. There was a scruff of beard on his face, but it was sparse as if it was still deciding if it was a beard or just several days' growth. "Follow me," he said softly.

Charlie walked across the yard towards the road. They passed through an opening in the tall privacy fence and then continued along it, keeping in the shadows.

At the end of the short gravel parking lot they were skirting, there was a patch of grass, then a very small cabin. Charlie led The Party to the brown, dilapidated structure. He unlocked the green door and stepped inside, motioning for them to follow.

When everyone was in the dark cabin, Charlie shut the door and struck his lighter. He found a tealight candle on a table next to a window which was shuttered and curtained. He lit the candle and returned it to the table. As the flame of the candle started drinking the melted wax, its flame grew larger, dimly revealing the decor of the tiny cabin. There was a twin bed at the far end, under another darkened window. A couch and easy chair were arranged in the remaining space. Next to a table was a kitchen sink and a compact refrigerator and stove.

The group dropped their packs and spread out on the various sitting arrangements. Rodent Whisperer sitting cross-legged on the floor. Charlie opened a cabinet and pulled out a half gallon bottle of Old Crow. He grabbed a handful of small solo cups and poured seven measures of whiskey. He passed it around to the sitting hikers. Everyone took one, except Rodent Whisperer, who shook his head and said, "No thanks."

Charlie grabbed a chair at the kitchen table, facing it towards his guests, and sat down. "Paul estimated your arrival accurately. I had only been waiting for about fifteen minutes. I'm Cleveland Charlie and I'm here to help you on your trek. The Resistance is growing, and we can use all the help we can get."

"*The* Cleveland Charlie?" Fic asked. "The nine-time repeat offender of the A.T.?" Fic was a little awestruck as he checked the old man out, a smile coming to his face.

"Ten now," corrected Charlie. "I did one more after donating that pack to Mountain Crossings, but that was the last one. My knees finally told me enough is enough, so I found a different way to serve the trail. I now help hikers along the way with advice and such. I know a lot about the trail."

"Does that pack look familiar?" Fic asked, pointing to the pack he had been wearing since Mountain Crossings, way back in Georgia.

"Why, that is old Phobos," Charlie replied. "I thought it looked familiar. What happened to your old pack?" A quizzical look changed his expression.

"It was the wrong color," Fic said a little evasively. "I needed something that would blend in a little better and would be durable, and yours had proven results. I actually saved it, because while we were there sleeping in the hostel, some of those fake army guys came and torched the building. It would have burned with all the other scattered gear and broken shelves."

"Ah, the fake army guys. Those are Flaherty's men. Most of them are real army, just gone rogue and are supporting and fighting for The Boss. They are making our job a lot harder to do," Charlie explained.

"So, is Phobos a name for your pack?" Fic asked.

"Yes," Charlie said laughing. "I used to name all my packs. I named that one Phobos after the Greek god Ares' son. It means fear. There is a saying out here on the trail, when we are trying to find the best way to lighten our load, that 'you carry your fears.' This usually leads to you carrying too much 'just in case.' Since I was carrying that pack, the name felt right. It reminded me to think about what I put in there. The only piece of gear that weighs nothing is the stuff you leave behind. I would ask myself: 'do I need this or does my fear want it?' If I couldn't answer the first part of the question with a 'yes,' it stayed behind."

They spent the next hour telling their stories and hearing Charlie's own tale. The Resistance had started before the bombs dropped and was growing fast. The people didn't want this kind of leadership and they were going to fight it as long as they could.

"I have some food to spare. MREs we stole from Flaherty's rogue soldiers, or as we have started calling them, the Flarmy. I'm sorry that I don't have much more." Charlie pulled out a box from under the table. "Take what you need, leave what you don't."

The group started looking through the box. Taking a few items and adding them to their food bags.

Charlie reached into his pocket and pulled out two shells, twelve-gauge slugs. He handed them to Fic. "For your 870"

Fic took the shells and put them in his pocket. "Thanks," he said. "We need all we can get; this is our only firearm for now."

"I was wondering if you guys want to help out The Resistance?" Charlie continued with a rise in his voice. "We have been using the trail, just like you guys, to move information up and down. Spreading the word, moving supplies where the Flarmy can't see them. We got our own Ho-Chi-Minh trail here in Tennessee. Our courier hasn't returned from a trip north and we need to send an important message up to the Greasy Creek Hostel about twenty-four miles north along the trail. If you wouldn't mind delivering it, I'm sure they would appreciate it and also help you along like I'm doing. They are one of The Resistance's safe houses."

"It would be a pleasure to do our part," replied Fic. It would be good to have a side-quest to think about. That way the long distance that still remained between him and his family — his primary quest — wouldn't keep nagging him each step he took north.

"Luckily, the bridge over the Nolichucky River isn't blockaded like in Hot Springs, so you just need to cross it and re-enter the woods. I'll walk with you a bit. It's a little over four miles to a nice shelter up the ridge. With the moon, you should be able to make your way there without too much problem."

Everyone readied their packs, and after Charlie checked outside, they exited the small building and walked back towards the Hostel and then the bridge. Their packs were pretty full now, with all the help they had been getting lately. Fic knew the food wouldn't last long, but it was good to know they wouldn't have to worry about being hungry for a few days at least.

The dark river was moving swiftly below the bridge as The Party crossed it quickly, trying to physically will themselves invisible to any watching eyes. The trail then dove into a tree-covered path, hiding their presence.

Charlie paused at a railroad crossing and said, "This is as far as I go. You guys be careful and godspeed to you." He fist bumped each of the hikers in turn. Bopping Fic last. "I can tell that you seem to be the leader of this troop. I'm guessing you have some kind of leadership skills from ... your job?" Charlie's questioning look and raised eyebrows clearly indicated that he wanted Fic to fill in that blank where the pause was.

"I'm active duty army," Fic admitted. "I was on a training mission with my men when all of this went down. If there are rogue army betraying their oath and country, I didn't know about it beforehand. This all took us by surprise, and I lost my men. Two were killed by the Flarmy, as you call them, and I was separated from the rest after some locals attacked us, thinking we were Flarmy, and using the tried-and-true method of shooting first and asking questions later. I didn't stick around to answer their questions, and I, unfortunately, don't know the status of my men. We were scattered without a rendezvous plan.

"I try to keep that part of me on the down low. I'm just trying to get home to my family now. The army is secondary until I complete that mission. Especially if I am not in on the rogue army's plans."

"It's all good," replied Charlie. "We all have something that we need to keep private. God knows I sure do."

The Party all nodded at Charlie, turned, and walked up the trail on the other side of the tracks, the newest members of The Resistance heading out on their first official mission.

#

The moon was approaching the western mountain when they arrived at the shelter. Everyone was tired from another long day, so they all spread out in the shelter and went to sleep straight away. Fic lay there on his sleeping pad, his eyes growing heavy, thinking about Lori and the kids. *How were they doing? Were they having any problems? Were they still thinking about me, hoping that I would be home soon?* As sleep took him, his dreams tried to answer some of those questions.

CHAPTER 10
THE HOME FRONT II - THURSDAY, JUNE 28TH

While Fic was heading towards Erwin, Lori, Shane, and Brittney sat in the living room. Across from them sat a young man. His name was Jim Henry, and he lived about a half a mile away. Lori knew his parents. He was a year older than Shane. Even with him sitting down, it was clear he was a lanky guy. His sandy brown hair was sticking up in numerous cow licks — something Lori remembered he had always had since he was a young boy. He was dressed in camo hunting clothes and was wearing a sidearm. An AR-15 was next to his chair, leaning at the ready. "I really could use y'all's help in patrolling the area," he was saying. "My boys and I plan on keeping the area safe from those rogue army units and that takes manpower."

"I'll help," Shane said excitedly. Lori looked over at him with a sharp glare, she didn't like his excitement. This was real danger, not some video game shoot-'em-up.

"I'll be the decider of that. I need more information," Lori said. Shane gave her his own defiant look.

"Well ma'am, we're just trying to keep the area safe," he repeated. "We patrol from the mountain to the river and from the highway up our road about three miles. We check out anything we find that is suspicious and take care of problems we find."

"How do you take care of them?" she asked.

"Whatever it takes," he said, looking over at his AR-15, then back at Lori. "We will give y'all food for helping out. It's the least we can do." His smile was a little off-putting. He had slightly crooked teeth and his grin was expansive, but it didn't reach his eyes. He actually looked a little creepy.

"We would keep Shane well protected. We all protect each other. His shooting skills would be an asset. We also try to take game when we are out on patrol. We have been keeping everyone fed," he continued his pitch.

"Mom, I really want to do this," Shane said. His voice almost on the whiney side, but not quite yet.

"I'll help too," said Brittney. "I'm actually a better shot than Shane." She winked at her brother, who smirked and shook his head in the negative. She was right, but his ego wouldn't let him admit it to an outsider.

Jim moved his gaze to Brittney, and that creepy smile broke out on his face again. "That would be nice. We can use any help that is offered. I'll even put you two together, if that is what you want."

Now both kids were looking at their mother. She sighed, "Alright. We have to man the home front until your father gets back. A little more venison wouldn't be bad either. Our garden is doing pretty good, so I can do some trading of our veggies for other things that we are running low on. We need flour and some chicken feed, if you come across some. We have eggs, spinach, lettuce, some strawberries and some of our tomatoes are almost done." Starting this barter process was Lori's way of letting the children know that she was allowing them to join the Blue Mountain Patrol, as Jim was calling it.

"We have some handguns, but if you can bring your own long guns or a shotgun, it would help a lot," Jim said.

"When can we start?" Shane asked, the excitement was betrayed in the pitch of his voice.

"You can come on patrol with me tonight," he replied. "We leave at dusk."

Lori looked at her two kids and wondered if this is what Clay would do. She immediately answered herself that he would. She was certain of it.

She sent her thoughts out into space to try to find her husband. *Was he making his way back?* She thought for a moment and then nodded her head. She was certain of it.

CHAPTER 11
THE RESISTANCE - FRIDAY, JUNE 29TH TO WEDNESDAY, JULY
4TH

The Party was on the move again. The exhausted hikers had slept in until the forest was well lit, and the birds had started their daily singing. Now, they were continuing the climb that they had started last night after meeting Cleveland Charlie.

Their side-quest was still taking them along their route home, but they would have to walk off the trail about half a mile to get to the Greasy Creek Hostel, where they would deliver the large manilla envelope Fic had secured in his pack. It felt good to have the diversion of this mission to keep them going, while also letting them help The Resistance. He didn't know what had happened to his army. Was it still the service he knew, or something that hat rotted into an outfit he didn't want to be a part of? Whatever had happened, it had completely shaken up his life. Before leaving home at the beginning of this month, everything had been going according to plan: finish the last year of his career, retire from the army, and then find something else to do. He was still young; there were plenty of things to do to keep him busy and interested. Now, everything was chaotic. The future was foggy at best.

The dream Fic had last night was still with him. The details had already started to fade from his memory, but the feeling of it remained. This one was different from the recent vivid dreams he'd had lately. He had been at home, sitting in the living room with Lori and the kids. They were discussing something, but he no longer remembered what it was about. The dream had jumped around after that. They would be out in a garden pulling weeds, then out hunting — but the hunting was different. It was like he was hunting something other than a deer, rabbit, or turkey. It felt like the tension he experienced when he had hunted men back in Iraq and Afghanistan. It left him unsettled. The emotional response to the dream made him tense, affecting his movements as he navigated the trail. His tone of voice was curt when responding to his companions as his mind kept wandering back to the nightmare.

#

Early on in the day's hike, they came to an open, grassy area called Beauty Spot. They paused briefly to enjoy the grand views all around. In front of them, they could see the ridge continuing to rise. In the distance was a whale shaped mountain whose top was covered in pine trees. Something about it felt dark and mysterious. The lower surrounding peaks had a mixture of hardwoods, but the dark green hemlock and red spruce made the mountaintop look ominous. The mountain was called Unaka, and before long, the trail would bring them right to its peak.

As the day passed noon, the hikers were all ready to stop for some lunch. The day had become quite hot and humid, and the shade of the spruce forest, which grew closer with every step, looked like the perfect spot for a rest.

They entered the deep, cooling shade of the forest and found a nice clearing. Everyone dropped their packs and dug out some food. They sat in a loose circle, eating food out of Ziploc bags and wrappers.

Gnobbit asked to see Rodent Whisperer's axe and he happily handed it to her handle first. She hefted the item in her hands, checking its balance and the sharpness of the blade. "I bet I can sink this blade in that dead tree over there," she said pointing the axe in the direction of an old pine that had lost the top half of its trunk; all the bark had fallen off to lie on the forest floor around it.

"Feel free to give it a try, lass. It is a sturdy tool and will be able to handle the jolt when you miss," he roared a hearty laugh.

Gnobbit took aim and swung her arm back. Shooting it forward and releasing the axe at the precise moment. *Thunk!* The axe landed directly in the middle of the dead tree.

Everyone laughed and clapped at the spectacle. Gnobbit took a bow before retrieving the weapon and handing it back to Rodent Whisperer, who nodded his admiration as he grabbed the handle.

As everyone enjoyed their lunch, Fic thought he had seen something move in the forest out of the corner of his eye. When he looked over, there was nothing there but the dark spaces between the spruce trees and the underbrush. It happened again a couple minutes later and Fic was starting to wonder if it was the uneasiness of his dream that was making him paranoid, when Brown Shades softly interrupted the lunch conversation to say, "I think we have a visitor." Fic, relieved that someone else had noticed the movement, nodded his confirmation. Everyone became subtly alert, not showing that they were preparing for action.

Fic checked the location of his shotgun. It leaned against his pack, which sat against the tree he was sitting under. It was less than an arm's length from him. He scanned the forest, looking for the movement that wasn't his imagination.

From the opposite direction of everyone's focused attention, a soft step sounded and a very tall, very green man stood between two of the dark trees. His skin wasn't green, but all of his clothes were of one shade of green or another. Even his hiking sandals had a green tint to them. The man's height was striking. At least six and a half feet. He wore a hat made of green leather. His shirt and pants were both a dark green and so were his socks, which he wasn't wearing, but were hung off of the side of his pack, drying. He wore a backpack, of which the main color was — wait for it — green. In his hands he held a rough-looking bow that had an arrow nocked in the string. He held the bow at the ready. Not drawing or aiming, but a second was all it would take to do both.

"Hello," said Brown Shades in his teacher's voice. "That's a nice bow you have there."

"Thanks," the man said. "I made it myself. Just a couple days ago. It seems a man needs to go armed in these woods nowadays."

"Come join our circle," Fic said. "Do you need any food?"

"I will join you. I have plenty of food, but I'm starting to tire of the same thing. Maybe we can do a trade."

"That's a definite possibility," said Gnobbit. "Do you like MRE's? We have a good supply of them and I'm already ready for something different." She turned up her nose at the tan pouch she was holding in her hand.

The green man joined The Party and sat amongst them. He pulled out some interesting-looking bars that were in a beeswax wrapping. They looked homemade.

"I made a crap ton of this pemmican. It's good, but eating it all the time gets old. I've never had an MRE. Would you like to trade for some of my pemmican?" he asked Gnobbit. "I'm Finn," he introduced himself, smiling at Gnobbit as he offered his beeswax wrapped food.

She smiled back, taking the food and passing her MRE to the striking man. "Gnobbit," she said. Her gaze lingered on him for several seconds after the transaction was complete. He seemed distracted by her too, but only for a second.

Everyone else introduced themselves and they started doing the age old trail tradition of trading information. Which way are you heading? (North) Have you seen anything strange or had any problems? (Yes, to both) What is your plan? (Keep heading North) Do you want to join our group? (Of course).

With that, Finn became the sixth member of The Party. The towering, light-footed bow wielder instantly gave Fic the impression of a noble elf. They were a decent raiding party now. All the skills and fantastical races seemed to be represented. The Elf Ranger had made The Party complete.

Finn was in his early twenties, with long blond hair. Ultra bright. Like platinum. His mustache matched his hair and turned at the ends of his mouth and proceeded down his chin. His green clothes and gear contrasted well with his bright, golden head.

"I'm a college student majoring in Adventure Education at UNC," Finn told his story. "I was spending the summer living in the woods. My plan was to walk several miles along the trail, then head into the wilds, away from the blazes and practice my bush craft: living off the land, hunting, making primitive fire and shelters. I'd just finished a foraging class last semester and wanted to take all my new skills into the real world by gathering wild edibles to supplement my diet. My ultimate goal was to just live as naturally as I could. I had just begun about a week before the war started and I hadn't even known it had happened. I'd been in a pretty remote place, but I met a couple of guys when I crossed the trail again who were heading home to Atlanta, and they told me what was going on.

"After trying to go into a town to resupply, I was chased by some army men. I was able to lose them, but I became more cautious after that and have been spending more time up in the mountains, slowly making my way north. I'm from West Virginia, so I just figured I could either walk back to my car way back in Georgia and expose myself on the roadways driving home or just keep heading north. Living off the forest as I go. Staying out of sight and out of mind.

"I made my bow and a few arrows to help supplement my food, but after the encounter with the army guys, I thought I might need something for personal protection."

"Yes. It definitely feels more comfortable having something. We were lucky to come across this shotgun and The Resistance has helped with providing some ammo," Fic said.

Fic told Finn about The Resistance and all that they knew about The Regime and The Boss, Flaherty.

"I'm all in on helping with The Resistance. This 'boss' guy needs to go. I would like to help with that," Finn said.

Lunch was done, and they had some more miles to walk today. They wanted to be able to get to the hostel early tomorrow. Once they delivered their package, they would then figure out how far to go from there.

Everyone gathered their gear and continued down the trail. The day continued to be sunny and warm, but down in the green tunnel of the trail, the heat was tempered some. The humidity still had a way of soaking them through like they were a sponge, but as long as everyone continued to drink water, they would all be fine.

After coming off the enchanting mountain they stopped at a shelter for a rest and gave their backs a break from carrying their packs. After that respite, they decided to continue on four and a half more miles to a campsite next to a spring that was listed in *The A.T. Guide.*

#

They arrived at their destination an hour before sunset. As they moved through the area, they could tell it was an old, abandoned apple orchard. The trees had been left to their own devices many decades ago; they were gnarled, crooked, and unpruned. Some had large hollow spaces in their trunks and looked as though they'd fall over with the slightest gust of wind. The Party dodged rotting apples that littered the path that ran through the orchard and into the woods. When they made it to the edge of the forest, they saw several huge boulders. To the left of the boulders, was a pipe jutting out of the rocks. Water flowed from the pipe — cold, clear, fresh, spring water.

The Party spread out around the spring and the grassy area around the trees. There was a small fire pit at the edge of the woods and the group gathered there after settling their gear, made a modest fire and cooked their dinners.

The light of the sun left the sky, and the only light source was the flickering, yellow flames of the fire. Class Room pulled out Yuk and started playing a melody. Finn started humming to the tune and then singing, but he wasn't singing real words. Or at least not words that they could understand. They seemed to be a different language, but a language that only Finn knew. It was soothing and hypnotic and everyone listening started to feel a deep comforting relief. When the song was over, everyone felt energized but relaxed. It was another magical moment on the trail.

"I think I dreamed of you," Gnobbit said to Finn when the song was done. The others nodded their heads at Gnobbit, but no one said anything.

Finn looked at Gnobbit and said, "I think I dreamt of you too. Weird, isn't it?"

Fic started to wonder if they were somehow sharing the same dreams. He shook his head to clear the thought, but it kept coming back as the night wore on. The group either feared the prospect of them all having the same dreams or had just started to accept it as a normal part of their world now. Fic didn't know what to think.

Soon, the flames became coals, and the coals turned to ash as the fire consumed the fuel it had been fed, signaling to the hikers that it was time for bed. Finn was a hammock hanger too. He and Brown Shades were the last to fall asleep. They had hung their hammocks near each other, and Brown Shades kept bombarding Finn with question after question about his classes.

"I wish these survival classes had been available back when I was in college. How very intriguing. I gained a large chunk of my knowledge of the outdoors from Boy Scouts."

"Boy Scouts is where my love of the outdoors first evolved, as well." Finn revealed.

They talked softly for a while until the conversation ran out, and sleep came to all The Party.

#

The morning was warm, but an overcast had rolled in during the night. The Party packed up and hit the trail. It was less than three miles to the forest road that would lead to the Greasy Creek. When they arrived at the gap where the road lay, they turned off the trail at a sign and followed the old lane down to a house that sat at the very end of a long driveway. There was a sign in the yard of a piece of land that had two large buildings built on the hillside. The house was gray and long, with a covered porch along the whole front of the house. Behind the house was another gray building. The sign said: *Greasy Creek Friendly*. Fic smiled at the use of the word friendly instead of hostel, which sounded a lot like hostile. The owners of this inn must have a really positive attitude.

As The Party walked up to the house, two dogs came from behind the building. Their panting faces made them look like they were smiling, and their tails were wagging wildly. The black lab in the back gave a short welcoming bark. Or maybe it was an announcement of their presence to the owners, because the door to the house opened and a woman walked out.

Her graying, brunette hair was in a bun on the top of her head. She wore a large sweater — even though the day was pleasantly warm — with a flour-dusted apron over top. "Welcome to Greasy Creek," she said, lifting her hand to point the way. "The bunkhouse is over there. You can set your stuff in there for a spell and come talk in the kitchen. I'm Silvia."

The Party dropped their gear as instructed, then walked back to the house entering at the rear where the kitchen was. The room was spacious, with a large table at one end where they all sat. Silvia put a plate of cookies in the middle of the group. "Help yourself. I'm sure you are all a little hungry." The group each took a cookie and started munching.

Fic took the large envelope he had fished out of his pack and slid it across the table to Silvia. "Cleveland Charlie sends his regards," he said. "This is for you."

She took the envelope and placed it on the counter by the hallway. "Thanks," she said. "This is some important stuff. How's Charlie doing?"

"Pretty good as far as we could tell. We didn't get to spend a lot of time with him. He helped us out, and we returned the favor for The Resistance," Fic replied.

"This will be very helpful," Silvia said. "We all need to work together to get rid of this craziness. I know it's early in the day, but y'all must stay here for the night. I have lots of food and can actually use a little help around here for the day. We can arrange a little work-for-stay and I can feed y'all."

After a short conference, they decided to stay and help for the day and head out early the next morning. The Party settled into a comfortable rhythm, helping Silvia clean up the house and then helping to move a load of firewood from a dumped pile to a nice stack next to the house. In the meantime, Silvia cooked a large lunch. When the food was ready and the chores at a stopping point, everyone sat around the table, talking about the things they had seen and done the last couple of weeks. The conversation was light and happy. *The country might have gone to shit, but this group was doing okay*, Fic thought.

Fic struggled with the feeling that only hiking three miles for the day was time wasted, but tried to remind himself of the importance of being able to relax and recover. And a short day, or what the hikers called a Nero, was better than a Zero mile day. At least they had made some progress on getting closer to home.

#

After lunch, the group was hanging around in the kitchen, when the door opened, and a man walked in with a shotgun slung over his shoulder and a handful of fresh game in his right hand. It looked like a rabbit and two squirrels. He had a head of thick, curly hair that added a few inches to his perceived height. A pair of glasses framed the middle of his face and below them was a coarse beard that went as far down as his hair went up. There was a good amount of gray in his otherwise black beard. He looked at the group and a smile broke on his face. "Ahh, visitors," he said.

"Hikers who are heading north. Trying to get home. They came from Charlie." Her pointed look at the new man conveyed more information than those three sentences and the man gave a knowing nod and once again looked at the group.

"I hope you are hungry. We have some good meat to cook for tonight's dinner. You guys are staying, right?" he asked, holding up the game he still held in hand.

"That's Gizmo," Silvia introduced the man. "He helps out around here."

Gizmo had been staying at the Greasy Creek for a little over a year now. The year before, he was a hiker. He had hiked this far and had sprained his ankle on the trail right before the turnoff. He had limped down the old forest road to the hostel, healed, started helping out, and never left. He was a handy guy who could fix most things and since he had been there, he had fixed her leaking roof, changed out the water pump in her old Ford and helped remodel the bathroom in the bunkhouse.

Silvia got to work on the rabbit and squirrels and the hikers helped by setting the table and gathering fresh vegetables from the garden. Dinner was a lavish affair. Stewed game with potatoes and freshly picked green beans all cooked on a large wood burning stove. It was a good down home meal.

In front of the house, down the hill a little, were a couple of picnic tables and a good-sized fire pit. Gizmo started a fire as the light of the day was leaving the area and the comrades relaxed by the flickering flames, talking and making S'mores. Silvia had provided the ingredients. The Party recognized that this was a special occasion. Things like marshmallows and chocolate were hard to come by.

#

Everyone slept in the bunkhouse that night. The two dogs patrolled the area and would let their owners know if anything was amiss. Before he turned in, Fic sat in the kitchen with Silvia, drinking a cup of tea that she had made for him.

"I have another mission for you, if you are game," she looked at Fic hopefully.

"As long as it is a mission that takes us further north," he replied.

"It does. The next link in The Resistance chain along the trail is the Boots Off Hostel up in Hampton, Tennessee. I have a small package that needs to be delivered." She didn't mention what was in the package and Fic didn't inquire.

"We'll do it," he said.

She handed him a wrapped box about four inches square. On top of the box, she placed a miniature statue of a gnome. "Take this along too. Give it to Jimbo at Boots Off. It will let him know that you come from us."

Fic picked up the small statue of the bearded little man with a red hat and blue robe. *Gnobbit is gonna love this*, he thought.

#

"Whoa, this is cool," said Gnobbit excitedly. "I want to be the one to carry it to Boots Off."

"It's all yours." Fic said. "Just make sure you don't lose it along the way. It's our ticket into the hostel."

Silvia had stacked a load of resupply food on the kitchen table when she fed them breakfast, telling the hikers to take what they needed. Everyone had filled their food bags. The day of rest had done everyone good and they were ready to put some more miles in. They thanked Silvia and Gizmo for their hospitality and company, then made their way back to familiar ground

The morning was spent ascending Roan High Knob. They were back over 6000 feet, and the air took on a crisp coldness as they passed the summit and stopped for lunch at the shelter.

The rest of the day had them descending the mountain and then crossing two long balds. The open grassy areas made them feel a little exposed, but there was no traffic on the road at Carvers Gap. The views from these balds were spectacular, but they moved along quickly until they were out of sight of the road. They would be able to see a person from pretty far off on the open grassy areas if someone was up there, which meant they could be seen too. They could also see where the trail was heading from at least two miles away.

They passed another shelter that was right on the trail, then turned off the path at a sign that announced they had reached Overmountain Shelter. This shelter was a large barn with some grass fields surrounding it that could sleep a large group of people.

As they approached the shelter, two men came out of the barn and watched them approach. They were scruffy looking, and both wore jeans and T-shirts.

"Hello," said Fic. "Is there room for six more in the barn?" Fic asked, knowing the barn could sleep about twenty people. More if the weather was bad.

"Well, I'm sure there is," said the guy on the left. He had short, choppy hair and the makings of a scruffy beard. He seemed to be in his early twenties. "We been stayin' here for a few days. There's too much trouble down in town. Lots of people were shot. We come from the town of Roan Mountain, Tennessee. We had to get out quickly and only had a little food. You guys got any food to spare?" he finished with a hopeful look in his eye.

"I think we can spare some food," said Fic. "We don't have a lot and have been moving north fairly fast, but we can help you out some."

A girl came walking out of the barn. She was maybe sixteen and looked like she had just woken up from a nap. "Hey y'all," she said, raising her hand in a shy wave. "I'm Dotti."

"Ah, yeah. I'm Scott and this here is Dubba. He don't talk much," Scott said.

The group introduced themselves one by one as they grabbed their food bags and found some things they could donate to the three refugees from town. A nice pile of food grew between the hikers.

"This should hold you over for a while. If you need more and can't go home, you might want to hike to the Greasy Creek Friendly and see if Silvia can help you out. She is always looking for help at the place and seems to still be well supplied," Fic explained.

"We might just do that," Scott said. "Thanks for the food. We do appreciate it."

The Party entered the barn and walked up to the second floor. The threesome had spread out in the shelter. Their gear was scattered around, and it definitely looked like they had been living there for a little while. They gathered their stuff and made room for the other hikers. Their equipment looked serviceable enough but appeared old and heavy and most likely purchased at the nearest Walmart. It was doing the trick and that was all that mattered.

After looking around some, the hikers picked their spots for the night. Finn decided to hang his hammock in the woods right behind the barn. He was always more comfortable in his hammock and in the woods. Brown Shades decided to stay in the barn, hanging his hammock between some large beams on the lower level which was open on one side.

After setting up, they all had a good dinner and then hung out enjoying the cool evening breeze. It had been another long day — about seventeen and a half miles — and everyone was tired and sore after climbing the mountains and balds during the day.

There were several lengths of rope hanging from the rafters and Fic decided that they should hang their food bags to keep them away from the mice that surely lived in this barn too.

Scott, Dubba, and Dotti had kept to themselves, but did contribute to the conversation in the evening. They seemed to be quite hungry when they made their dinners of the donated food.

Darkness arrived, and The Party retired to their sleeping setups for the night.

#

Fic came awake. It was very dark in the barn, but the nearly full moon was shining up above and its light was coming through the cracks in the walls and roof. He tried to orient himself through the haze of disrupted sleep, certain he had been awoken by a noise in the night. A shaft of moonbeam ran across the hanging rope in the middle of the loft. He looked at the rope where their food bags were hanging, and was alarmed to see that the bags appeared to be gone.

Fic got up quickly and grabbed his head lamp. He went over to the rope and confirmed that their food bags were no longer hanging where they had left them. He pointed his light over to where the others were sleeping and noticed that the threesome were also gone.

"Son-of-a bitch," he whispered as he went to wake the others.

Luckily, his shotgun was still resting next to his sleeping mat where it had been when he fell asleep. He shoved his feet into his boots, tying them loosely, placed the headlamp on his forehead and swooped up his shotgun, jacking a shell into the chamber.

The hikers that had been sleeping in the barn came together in a circle. Brown Shades came up from the lower level, fixing his glasses over his sleepy eyes. "Brownie and Class Room, stay here and guard the gear. They may still be in the area," Fic instructed the two hikers. "RW and Gnobbit, come with me."

Everyone grabbed their head lamps and weapons. Fic led the way down the stairs to the lower level. His light beamed across the open area and fixed on a green object. It was Finn coming in from the woods behind the barn. He had his bow in his hands and an arrow nocked. "Trouble?" he asked. "I saw the threesome heading out a few minutes ago and was wondering."

"It looks like they took our food. All of it," Fic answered.

"Follow me. I know which way they went," Finn said.

The four hikers followed the path that went back to the trail. They tracked the easily seen footsteps the threesome had made through the dewy, long grass of the field. The moon made the tracks stand out.

They got to the forest canopy, and the trail was harder to see. Finn kneeled down at the sign that pointed to the shelter and surveyed the ground. "It looks like they headed south. These tracks here look like the girl's slim sneakers. Let's go."

They had started out with white head lamps, when they started following the trail south. Once they were certain they were on the right trail, they went to red, and then turned the lights off all together, hoping for an element of surprise when they came across the thieves.

The moon was shining into the early July woods, and they could see pretty well. The light dappled between the leaves, shifting to and fro as a light breeze moved the branches of the trees. This created moving shadows on the forest floor. It was enchanting and scary at the same time.

After about fifteen minutes of fast, dark walking, they saw a light moving up ahead. The threesome was still using their flashlights to move along. The chasers quieted their steps as much as they could and continued to close on the moving light.

When they could make out the person carrying the light, they matched their pace and followed at a distance, waiting for a chance to catch the thieves off guard.

They were close enough to hear a few words of conversation from the three. It sounded like Dotti needed to stop for a rest. Scott kept telling her they would be able to stop in a minute. He told her there was a shelter just up ahead.

The pursuers gave each other a nod in the dark. A plan had come to each of them naturally. After a few whispered instructions, the four chasers closed in on the three runners.

Scott, Dotti, and silent Dubba came to the shelter and dropped their packs. They all sat on the edge of the shelter, panting a little, their heads looking down at the ground.

Fic walked into the clearing around the shelter, his shotgun in the crook of his arm. "I think you might have accidentally taken something of ours," he said, keeping the shotgun pointed at the ground, but ready to move it quickly.

The three thieves jumped like a snake had been thrown in their laps. Dubba let out a high-pitched scream. He jumped back into the shelter as he came to his feet.

"We didn't take anything," Scott tried to lie. Fic just stared at him, saying nothing.

"He has a gun," Dotti pointed out the obvious.

"But if we rush him —" Scott revealed a half-baked plan.

"I wouldn't do that if I were you," Fic warned. "I can't remember exactly what shell I have in the chamber. It could be a slug. Maybe some buck shot or even bird shot, but no matter what it is, it would hurt a lot if I had to shoot you."

As he said this, Finn moved into the clearing, his bow drawn and pointing at Scott's chest. Rodent Whisperer moved in on the other side of Fic, his axe in his hand and at the ready. Gnobbit came from behind the shelter, her stick in her hand.

"Just give us our food bags. You can still keep what we gave you earlier. This isn't the way to navigate this crazy reality we are experiencing. I know you might have become desperate, but that doesn't give you permission to take other people's stuff without permission. It may just get you killed nowadays" Fic lectured.

The scared threesome opened their packs and pulled out the food bags they had taken from the rope. They placed them in a small pile at the corner of the shelter edge. Rodent Whisperer sheathed his axe and grabbed all the food bags, handing a few to Gnobbit. "We were just so hungry," said Dotti. "We had run out of food a few days ago and ... we were just so hungry," she repeated.

"Now I'm gonna have to ask you to gear up and head south. Just keep going until I can't see you anymore. I wish you the best of luck, but I hope you learned a lesson here," Fic said.

The threesome did as they were instructed and started walking away from the shelter. Fic nodded to the others, and they quickly started heading back to the Overmountain Shelter.

#

They arrived back at the shelter in about forty minutes. They had gone farther than they realized on their chase through the moon-dappled woods. They found Brown Shades standing guard outside the barn with his staff at the ready. He smiled when he saw they were all carrying food bags. "I see you found them," he said. "Any trouble?"

"Not really," replied Fic. "We caught up to them, confronted them and they saw the wisdom of giving the bags back. Hopefully, they won't try that again."

"I guess we are going to have to start standing a watch even out here in the boonies," Fic suggested.

"Yep," Gnobbit said, a snarky look on her face. "Can't trust anyone nowadays."

"I'll keep watch for a couple hours," said Finn, walking back to his hammock.

"It'll be light in a few hours," said Fic. "None of us are probably going to get much sleep. We can get an early start to the next camp."

The Party went back up to the loft of the barn and rested for an hour. They were all packed, fed, and ready to go when the sun started to lighten the field.

As they ascended Little Hump Mountain, the sun rose in front of them. Promising a bright and warm day on the trail.

#

The trail ran over a lot of open mountain tops with bald grassy summits. As they crossed the two Hump Mountains the feeling of exposure made them walk faster in the high visibility areas. After summiting, the trail went downhill for several miles and re-entered the forest. On their way down, they had passed a sign that indicated they were leaving North Carolina for the last time. They were in Tennessee for good now — no more walking the border. At the bottom of that mountain was a highway. They could hear traffic as they approached, and they slowed their speed as they got closer. Gnobbit snuck up to the road to take a look and returned quickly with news of what she had seen. "That traffic is all military. It seems to be a pretty long convoy. Trucks, personnel carriers, hummers," she informed the group.

They all snuck closer and waited for a lull in the traffic. When the road grew quiet, they made their move and crossed the road at a trot, heading up the incline on the other side. In a minute, they were back in the woods, climbing away from the road.

#

In the late afternoon, they approached Mountaineer Shelter, their home for the night. The shelter was impressive. It had an overhang, which covered the front of the building, and a thin table built into the front wall, which also provided a third sleeping area as a loft. The main part of the shelter had two sleeping platforms just like in the Smokies, only smaller

The Party found their places as usual and settled in for the night. Gnobbit bedded down on the top floor; Fic, Rodent Whisperer, and Class Room took the middle platform; and Finn and Brown Shades hung their hammocks in front of the shelter. They stood a watch during the night again, keeping vigilant and alert. Their experience from last night and the significant number of enemies they witnessed passing by made them realize they needed to constantly be on guard.

#

The night passed uneventfully, and in the morning, they were on the move.

The sky was overcast most of the day and that tempered the heat, but the humidity seemed to have risen. They stopped for lunch in the Moreland Gap Shelter and then came to Laurel Falls. The falls were impressive, and the trail traveled next to the stream for a while along cliffs that rose up from the water.

Evening was approaching when they arrived at Laurel Fork Shelter. The shelter had stone walls and a wooden roof. The ground dwellers found their spots, and the hammock sleepers found their trees.

Dinner was their last decent meal apiece. Their food bags were almost empty again. They still had odds and ends that could nourish them for a couple more days if needed, but it was time to find more meals to carry. Giving up what they did to the three hungry thieves cut their rations short earlier than planned.

They didn't make a fire because they were pretty close to the town of Hampton. Their current side-quest ended tomorrow on the outskirts of the town, near the large lake named Watauga.

Today was July 3rd, Fic realized that tomorrow would mark being away from his family for a full month now. He could see the full moon rising over the mountain behind the clouds. The moon had been full when they had started their training. A complete turning of the moon had passed.

As they sat in the shelter, staring at the dark fire ring in front of the shelter, they could hear bangs and pops off in the distance. At first, they thought they might be fireworks — an early celebration of the Fourth of July. Some remnants of what the country used to be; parades and barbecues with hot dogs, baked beans and potato salad. But they soon realized that it was the sound of a firefight. Automatic weapons and single shot rifles. Explosions every once in a while. They didn't know what they would find in the morning, but they would proceed with caution as they climbed the last mountain before the highway that heads into Hampton Tennessee. Boots Off Hostel was just off that road.

#

Fic sat watching the forest grow lighter by the minute. He had stood the last watch of a quiet night. The firefight had slowed down then quit after a while and The Party had tried to get some sleep, but their efforts were in vain. The shelter wasn't ideal. There were a lot of bugs in the area due to the close proximity to the water, and after hearing some noises under the wooden platform floor of the shelter, Fic had discovered a large spider living under there. It seemed to be a little aggressive, but mostly left them alone. Everyone was ready to get away from this shelter, so they ate a quick breakfast and headed up that last climb before getting to the hostel.

The trail made its way up the mountain using several switchbacks, which eased the climb. The overcast from last night was now lower and signaling some oncoming precipitation. Before they got to the highest point on the mountain, the rain started to fall. It was a slow, steady rain that felt like it was going to last all day.

#

In three hours, they had hiked almost seven miles and were approaching their destination. As they got to a gravel road that connected to the paved US 321, they saw a sign that turned them left up the gravel way.

They followed the direction of the sign, passing a few more signs that pointed the way until they turned on to a long driveway that went uphill. As they approached, they saw that several cars and trucks had been parked across the driveway as a sort of barricade. There was a man on the other side of the cars with a scoped rifle in his hands. He drew a bead on them as they walked up the driveway.

"Gnobbit, do you have that gnome handy?" He looked over at his short companion who was walking beside him.

"Yep. Right here. I moved it to my front pocket for this very purpose," she replied.

She pulled the small statue from her pocket and held it up in her hand for the man to see.

The man behind the barricade zeroed in on what she was holding, then moved his head back from the scope, taking in the whole group. He stared at them keenly, trying to see if he recognized them or not.

"Silvia sent us," Fic said. "From the Greasy Creek."

The man lifted his rifle and motioned for them to come forward and head to the side of the barricade where they could more easily get by the line of cars.

Fic noticed, as they walked up the last of the driveway, that there were a lot of shell casings scattered about and some broken vehicle glass. There was even what appeared to be a pool of blood amongst the weapon refuse.

When they had passed the cars, he saw even more casings on this side of the barricade. The man slung his rifle and came over to them.

"I'm Fic." He proceeded to introduce his five companions.

"Jimbo," was the guy's response. He was a broad man. A short brown beard grew on his face, well-trimmed and neat. He wore jeans and a camo rain jacket. High cowboy boots covered his feet.

"We have a package for you," Fic explained. "It looks like you had some excitement here last night," he said, pointing at the spent shell casings laying on the ground.

"The bad guys, who are just locals that have joined the Regime army, tried to penetrate our defenses last night," Jimbo replied. "They didn't get too far. Did you see that blood trail to the right as you came up the drive? We hit at least one of them and took no casualties ourselves. They ended up retreating, but we think they will be trying again soon."

Jimbo had a small walkie talkie on his belt. It was one of those inexpensive sets that only reach short distances. He called to announce the visitor and to ask for someone to come relieve him. A scratchy voice replied in the affirmative.

They started walking up the long driveway, and noticed another man walking down the driveway wearing a brown rain jacket that had numerous duct tape patches on it. He had a shotgun slung over his shoulder.

"This is The Party," he said to the man. "They come from the Greasy Creek."

The man nodded at the group and touched his dripping ball cap in a brief salute, "I'm Sobo. Welcome to Boots Off."

He continued on and took up the position that Jimbo had just vacated; keeping his eyes down the road and scanning the nearby woods from time to time.

The group came to a house that had a covered area in the back. Inside were a couple of picnic tables and a small kitchen area with plenty of shelving and storage.

They dropped their packs and Fic opened his to pull out the small package. He handed it to Jimbo.

"Thanks," said Jimbo. "I have been waiting for this for a while." He placed the small box beside him on the bench. "Our courier system is still working out its bugs and these damn rogue army are causing all kinds of problems for us."

"We are glad to help," said Fic. "We probably wouldn't have made it this far if it wasn't for The Resistance. We are trying to get to Damascus where Brown Shades has a car. Hopefully, we will be able to get everyone where they need to go with that, but it seems the roads have a lot of Flarmy traffic on them, so the plan is still being worked out," he used Cleveland Charlie's word for the enemy.

"Yeah. Driving on the highways is beaucoup risky. The Regime travel it extensively and are well armed. They stop everyone they find. Most don't get to continue on. They are either taken prisoner or worse. They have been working very hard to quash The Resistance, but we just keep on growing."

Suddenly, the thought of getting off trail and traveling by car the rest of the way home excited Fic. The difference is amazing between moving at two and a half miles per hour and sixty or more miles per hour. What takes them a week to walk, can be covered in a few hours.

If he could be home by this time next week or sooner, he would be able to be with his family. Protecting them and figuring out what happened to his army and how he would help fix it. Being back near his unit would make it easier to determine what had happened and if there were still good soldiers out there who would work with him to set things right. There had to be other good soldiers like himself and his squad.

Thinking of his squad, he wondered what had become of them. Were they still out there, doing what he was doing? Were they captured — or worse — killed? Laying in some ravine in the middle of the woods in Georgia? Leaving his men had been hard, but at that time, he had seen no other choice. Weaponless and marked as a rogue army soldier, he had to change the mission and find a way home.

"You guys hungry?" Jimbo asked, snapping Fic out of his thoughts. "We still have a good amount of food. When this all started, we went into town and picked up all we could fit into the trucks. We can last several weeks here without having to leave the grounds."

"Aye, we could eat," Rodent Whisperer said. "Also, if we could resupply, that would be fantastic. We still have some cash, but if there is anything else we could do to earn the food, we will do that too."

"We may have a few things to do here, but members of The Resistance get taken care of. In fact, your payment will most likely be another delivery. This time to Damascus."

"It would be our pleasure," replied Fic.

They had a good lunch in the kitchen area and Jimbo showed them the bunkhouse, cabins, and camping area in the woods. They decided that spending the night here would be smart, then they would head out very early in the morning to get away from the road before daylight. The first part of hiking near the lake would be open and exposed. Hopefully the rain will have stopped by then.

Jimbo's radio squawked. "I have a movement at the bottom of the hill," Sobo's voice came out of the walkie. Jimbo grabbed his rifle and rain jacket and started heading to the barricade.

"How can we help?" Fic asked.

"Grab your shotgun and come along. Do any of you have other firearms?" Jimbo asked.

The others shook their heads, showing that they only had their staffs, axe and knives.

"I have my bow, with only three arrows, but I'm coming along, anyway," said Finn.

"I have another shotgun and a 45 handgun. If anyone wants to grab those, we could use the help."

"I'll take the shotgun," Class Room said, moving to the corner where Jimbo pointed, picking it up and checking the chamber.

Rodent Whisperer took the handgun and all the hikers headed into the still falling rain, down to the barricade. Brown Shades and Gnobbit each carrying their staff.

They approached the cars and saw Sobo crouching and looking down the driveway. At the bottom of the hill was a Humvee, parked across the way and idling its engine. They had come back for more. This time in the middle of the day.

The hikers lined up along the cars, weapons at the ready. Whoever was in the Humvee was just sitting there. It looked like there were at least three people in the vehicle.

"I'm gonna head into the woods here and try to circle around some. Maybe get behind them," Finn said.

"I'll come with you," Gnobbit said. "I'm a quiet stalker."

Finn nodded, and the two faded into the wet forest to the left of the barricade.

The three soldiers got out of the vehicle and moved behind it. They all had firearms.

One of the soldiers took out a white handkerchief and waved it over his head. "Can I approach?" he shouted from next to the Humvee.

"Come on up," Jimbo shouted down the hill. "Unarmed."

The man slowly walked up the driveway, his arms out to the side, showing he was unarmed.

When he got close to the cars, Jimbo said, "That's far enough, Kirk. What do you want?"

"Well Jimbo, by the authority of the Regime army of Hampton we are gonna need you all to surrender and give up your weapons. The Commander wants you to join up with us or there will be more trouble. He's mighty pissed that you shot Doug last night."

"Is that who we hit?" Jimbo said, laughing. "That idiot never could figure out when to put his head down. I'll tell you what, since you are now firmly on the private property of the Boot's Off Militia, I'm gonna have to ask you to surrender and give up your weapons. We don't want you to join up though. You can go back to your Commander and tell him to go fuck himself. I think it's pretty funny that Larry is calling himself a Commander. From a grocery store owner to Commander in just a few weeks of all hell breaking loose. You have ten seconds to get back to your Humvee, make like a tree and get out of here." He had a big smile on his face, enjoying his mangling of the old saying. Kirk looked back at his guys then up the hillside as if he was searching for something, but the pained look on his face revealed that he wasn't seeing anything that he wanted.

Just then, there was a shout from up on the hillside. The forest was thick up that way, so they couldn't see anything. Another shout turned into a scream and a shot rang out from up in the woods.

Kirk looked startled, and he took a few steps back. His arm reached into the small of his back and drew a handgun from his waistband.

Class Room screamed, "Gun!" Pointed her shotgun at the man and fired. The shot hit him square in the chest and he went down, his 9mm pistol skittering on the gravel driveway.

More shouting came from up on the hillside and the men down at the bottom of the driveway started shooting up towards the group. They all took cover under the barricade.

Jimbo aimed his rifle at the Humvee and took a couple of well-aimed shots. He shot the tires, but they were self-sealing, so nothing really changed. The soldiers would shoot every couple of minutes, then hide down behind the vehicle.

"Kirk," one of the guys shouted to his leader. "What should we do, Kirk?" There was real fear in his voice.

Class Room had sat down behind the barricade. She had dropped the shotgun and was crouched hugging her knees. She appeared to be in shock. Fic bent down next to her and put his hand on her shoulder. "You did good," he said. "If you hadn't reacted so fast, who knows which of us might have been hit. Take a breath and just stay low. We will handle this," he tried to reassure her.

Just then a groan came from in front of the barricade. Fic peeked over the cars and saw Kirk moving around, clutching his chest. He had a flak jacket on. It must have taken the brunt of Class Rooms shot. He was still alive.

Fic jumped over the barricade and grabbed Kirk. Lifted him in a fireman's carry then climbed back over the cars. He laid him on the ground and Rodent Whisperer assessed his wounds. Some shot had hit flesh, but most had been stopped by his vest. He was a lucky man, but not very smart. Unarmed means unarmed.

"Okay, Kirk, take a deep breath. You're alive. For now. You need to tell your men to lay down their arms or you won't be alive for much longer," Fic instructed the wounded man.

Fear entered the man's eyes at the steel cold look that Fic gave him. He yelled down the hill, "Johnny. Derrick. Stand down. Cease fire. Lay down your arms."

Jimbo watched through the scope as the men did as instructed. He had them walk up the driveway with their hands up. When they got close, Rodent Whisperer and Brown Shades came out and checked them for any hidden weapons.

Just then, they saw Finn and Gnobbit come down the hill next to the Humvee. They checked out the vehicle before walking up the driveway.

"They had a guy coming through the woods, trying to do the same thing we were doing. Luckily, Gnobbit saw him first. I put an arrow in his leg and Gnobbit put him to sleep with that wicked stick of hers." Gnobbit was smiling. She had her stick in one hand and a rifle in the other. The spoils of war.

"We tied him up with his own belt and shoelaces. He is up on the hillside. Still alive, but probably in quite a bit of pain," Finn said.

The Party and Boots Off Militia brought the men up to the hostel area. They locked Johnny and Derrick in one of the small cabins and left Gnobbit to guard the door. Finn and Rodent Whisperer went back up the hillside and escorted a wobbly and stunned soldier from up on the hill. Jimbo moved the Humvee up to the edge of the barricade. Adding its bulk to the barrier.

Rodent Whisperer checked both men out. Fic handed him the first aid kit he had found in the Humvee. "No sense using our own supplies on these guys," Fic said.

When the wounded men were all taken care of, they were brought to the same small cabin — now a holding cell — and then the group gathered together to discuss their next move.

"I'm not sure how long it will take for the *Commander* to come looking for his men and vehicle. More trouble might be on the way. It might get a little messy," Jimbo said, smirking at the word "commander".

"We are here to help as long as you need us," said Fic.

"The parcel I have for you really needs to be delivered as soon as possible to Damascus. This might turn into a prolonged siege as we are well supplied and have good defenses. You could be stuck here several days until those idiots from town figure out that they need to leave us alone. I think it might be a better idea if you head back into the woods tonight or you might not be able to leave at all," Jimbo continued.

"Don't you need our firepower?" Fic asked.

"My neighbor has been helping when needed. He is just beyond the fence at the end of the property. We have a gate between us. Hank and his three sons have been watching that side of the perimeter. In fact, I'm surprised that he hasn't already shown up."

As if on cue, a freckled faced young man came walking from the direction of the fence with a rifle on his shoulder and a handgun holstered on his hip. "You guys alright here?" he asked. "We heard shots and went on the alert at our place. Dad thought I better come check."

"We are all good, Jerry. We have a few prisoners now. Kirk and his idiot cousins," Jimbo explained. "We will probably bargain them away with Larry, so he leaves us alone, but it might get a little hairy later."

He introduced Jerry to The Party and fists were bumped all around. "They are going to be heading out soon on their next mission, so I may need you and your brothers help later if Larry comes looking."

"Roger that," said Jerry. "We'll be ready and on channel 14."

He headed back towards the fence in the still falling rain.

It was settled then. They would head out on their next side-quest. It would keep them heading north and get them away from the escalating hostilities. The next several minutes had the hikers getting their gear together.

Jimbo gave them several days' worth of food for their bags. He let Gnobbit keep the rifle and gave her a couple rounds of ammo to go with it. He gave Fic a few more rounds for the shotgun. Finn was handed five hunting arrows with sharp, steel hunting broadheads. The Party was becoming an armed squad. Lastly, Jimbo handed Fic another large manilla envelope full of papers: their next mission. "Deliver this to Crazy Carl at the Broken Fiddle Hostel in Damascus," he instructed. He also placed a baby's boot on the envelope. "This will be your identification pass, telling Carl that you come from us." Gnobbit picked up the boot and put it in the top of her pack.

Rodent Whisperer returned the handgun and would carry Gnobbit's rifle. She was happy with her stick for now. "I need to figure out a name for this beauty," she said to herself as she admired her walking stick. She had already started to carve impressive little designs into the wood.

Their packs were heavy and fully laden with their gear and food. "I have an idea," Jimbo said, pulling out the keys to the Humvee. "Everybody pile into the hummer. Put your packs on top and squeeze in."

It was a tight squeeze as the six hikers piled into the large Humvee with Jimbo behind the wheel. "I'll be back in a few," he said to Sobo. He put the vehicle into reverse and then headed down the driveway to the small, paved road.

"We will have to skirt the town using Swimming Pool Road, but I think this rain will be keeping everyone indoors. Besides, they are used to these hummers driving around. We will hide in plain sight," Jimbo explained.

They made it around town and up another road until they came to a stop sign. Jimbo followed a sign that pointed the way to Wilbur Dam, and pulled over at a trailhead. The familiar white blaze was on a tree showing the way of the trail back into the woods.

The Party exited the vehicle, grabbed their packs, and started heading into the woods. The rain continued to fall. Fic turned to Jimbo and shook his hand. "Thanks for everything. We will get this parcel to Damascus. Also, happy Fourth of July," he said with a smile.

Jimbo smiled and shook his head. "Thank you for your help. Without you guys, that encounter might have gone very differently. Some fucking Independence Day, huh?"

They still had a few hours of daylight left, but the water-laden sky was already making it feel like evening. They had almost ten miles to go before they would reach the shelter they were hoping to get to, but there was another shelter only five miles away.

Jimbo watched until the hikers disappeared into the forest. He wished them the best, hoping they would all get back to where they needed to be. His thoughts turned back to his next ordeal. What to do with Kirk and his cousins?

He put the Humvee in gear and headed back to the Boots Off Militia compound. Spitting wet gravel from the back of the tires that had taken hits today, but continued to do their job just fine.

The Party slowly made their way up the mountain beside the huge lake. When they were a couple miles away, they heard the sounds of another firefight which no longer sounded like fireworks at all.

#

It was dark when The Party made their goal and walked down the short trail to the Iron Mountain Shelter. Everyone was tired and wet. They moved about their chores like robots. Spreading their bags and pads in the shelter and putting up the hammocks. Changing out of their wet clothes, the hikers had a quick hot dinner and retreated to their down. Exhaustion took all of them quickly. There was no watch set.

CHAPTER 12
DECISIONS - THURSDAY, JULY 5TH TO TUESDAY, JULY 10TH

The rain stopped sometime during the night and the sun rose to a bright sky that had lots of fair weather clouds. The day's hike was uneventful. They crossed two empty roads and walked through a couple cow fields. After one gate, they encountered a herd of cows standing directly on the trail. There were mothers and their calves. The young ones would approach the hikers as they came by as if they were expecting something, then they would shy away and head back to the protection of their mothers. In another field, small butterflies that were sitting in the low bushes would fly up and envelop the hikers as they walked by. It was an enchanting part of the day where they could sense the magic of the area. They kept the day's mileage at a reasonable level since they were all still feeling the effects of the encounter and distance traveled of the day before. The long days were becoming easier to do, however. Each of the hikers now had strong hiker legs. Even though everyone experienced daily aches and pains, and would get a little stiff when they sat for a while, the night's rest would usually regenerate them and they would be ready for another long day. Fic liked this, as each long day got them closer to Brown Shade's car and possibly a quick dash home.

They arrived at Abingdon shelter in the afternoon and set up. Dinner was hot and delicious, and they even decided to make a small fire in the evening. As they lounged around, Gnobbit pulled something out of her pocket and let it drop into the fire as she moved her hand over the yellow flames. This time the flames turned blue. She looked proudly over at Brown Shades and said, "I can do it too, mister Mage."

He smiled at her and nodded his head. "Very good young Padawan. I'm betting you used hand sanitizer for that little trick."

Gnobbit nodded and smiled back. "Yep. Just like you told me it would. I wonder what color we can change it to next time."

The Party discussed the next day's plan. They would be heading into a town where the trail ran right through the middle. Plan A was to find Brown Shades' car, find some gas and head north on Route 81. Brown Shades would drop off Gnobbit, then Fic, then Finn, before heading to New Jersey to drop off Class Room. Rodent Whisperer was planning on keeping him company the whole way, and would figure out what to do next at the end of their journey. It would be a risky venture given what they had seen and what others had told them about the Flarmy patrolling the highways and stopping people, but they would give it a try anyway and hope for the best. They really hadn't discussed Plan B just yet.

They cleaned and made ready their weapons as best they could. They now had two firearms and some ammunition, a bow with several arrows, two attack sticks and an axe. Of course, everyone also had their own knife of varying sizes. Not as powerful as they wanted, but better than what they started out with.

They stood watch that night; each hiker taking a few hours to ensure the others could sleep in peace.

#

The next morning dawned a little cloudy, but the heat had risen during the night. It was promising to be a warm day. They had ten miles to get to the edge of Damascus. Brown Shades' car was on the other side of the small town, near Laurel Creek. They were going to get down near the town in the cover of the forest and see what was going on. From there they would plan their next step.

The walk was not too bad. Everyone was hot and sweaty when they lost the last bit of elevation before the town. Just a few miles out, they came to a sign saying they were leaving

Tennessee and entering Virginia. The trail through Virginia is around 550 miles. Fic's home was about 520 of that up the state. He had already walked around 500 or so since starting this journey, and he was still only halfway there. Hopefully, this next half would be done in a few hours instead of a month.

They sat in the woods, observing through the trees. Looking for soldiers or other people or any sign of trouble. This part of the town was quiet. They didn't see any people or vehicles on the roads or around the houses within their view.

Gnobbit and Finn snuck down to where the trail dumps onto the streets of Damascus and reported back that they were empty.

The Party continued on. Fic and Rodent Whisperer were at the front with their weapons drawn and Finn walked drag, with his bow in his hands and an arrow nocked.

The trail traversed the middle of the street into town. They passed under a sign that was a popular photo op for A.T. hikers who had made it this far. A small, slim park paralleled the road. At the end of the park was a large, red caboose at an intersection where another street came into the town.

This is where the group paused as they assessed what they had just come across — a literal wall of cars. They weren't just parked next to each other to make a barricade like at Boots Off and Hot Springs, but they were stacked on top of each other. Some kind of wrecker or crane must have been used to move the vehicles into a pile.

That explained why there wasn't any town traffic that they could see. The barrier completely blocked access to all cars.

But it also didn't appear that anyone had been blocked inside the town. Either it was deserted before the barrier went up, or everyone was staying inside.

They crossed a small bridge and walked the three blocks to where Brown Shades had parked his car. They would have to figure out how to get through or around that barricade, but they were still feeling confident as they made their way to the parking lot.

They turned the corner and were greeted with an empty lot. As they stared at the vacant square of asphalt, the barricade came back into their mind's eye.

"Shit," Brown Shades said, disheartened.

They back tracked to the barricade and Brown Shades pulled out his key fob that he had been keeping in his belt pouch in a Ziploc bag. He pressed the lock button three times. They heard a muffled double beep coming from their right.

Brown Shades repeated the button press until they were standing in front of his vehicle.

It was not only on the bottom of the makeshift wall, but also completely flattened by the weight of the other cars. They wouldn't be driving anywhere in that car.

The Party huddled near the red caboose, the time had come to discuss Plan B. Everyone felt down and defeated. Brown Shades kept staring at his car, crushed and abused, sitting at the bottom of that pile. He looked absolutely heartbroken and near tears.

They decided that they had to do the only thing possible now — keep walking. But first, they had a mission to complete.

Fic and the others started off towards the Broken Fiddle Hostel. The deserted streets were all that they saw. The empty silence created an eerie atmosphere in the town.

They crossed the creek on a bridge and looked ahead to where the main street turned to the right, the trail following along with it. According to Fic's guide, the Broken Fiddle was right at that turn.

As they crossed that street, they saw that another wall of cars blocked the road about two blocks up. This place had become a fortress, but where were the inhabitants?

The hostel was a long one-story house. On the front porch hung a sign that announced the name. Attached to the sign and swinging in the slight breeze was an actual fiddle, with its neck broken. They went to the porch and looked into the window of the green door.

They saw no one. Fic tried the door, confirming it was locked. He knocked a few times and waited. Nothing changed.

The Party spread out, walking around the structure to see if there were other entrances. They found a large, covered area at the back of the house inside a fenced in backyard.

Fic checked the back door and was going to knock, but discovered it was unlocked.

Gingerly, he opened the door and entered the kitchen area, the other's following him inside. "Hello?" When only silence greeted him, he went further into the building and kept calling softly, trying to find someone. The building was empty.

"Look what I found on the table over there," Class Room said, holding up a piece of paper.

She handed the paper to Fic. It was a photocopy of a hand-drawn sign.

Wanted: *A group of terrorists calling themselves The Party. Wanted for the killing of two officers in The Regime army. Considered armed and dangerous. Reward for information in their capture. Punishment for those who harbor them.*

Under that was an even cruder drawing of six people. Presumably their likeness — it was hard to tell.

Fic stared at the paper. *Where did this come from and how did it get here ahead of their progress?*

"The Regime army left it outside the barricades," a voice said from the corner of the room. The Party startled and spotted a solemn-looking woman standing next to an open closet. Apparently, the building wasn't vacant after all.

Fic held up the sign, smiling, "So, are you going for reward or punishment?"

"Punishment, of course," she replied, smiling back.

"We are looking for Crazy Carl. We have a package for him from Jimbo down at Boots Off," Fic said.

"Carl's dead. Killed yesterday by the soldiers that dumped all those leaflets of your wanted poster. I'm Cindy, Carl's girlfriend." She had no emotion as she said this awful revelation. She was still in shock from the death of her boyfriend.

"The army men had come to the barricades demanding to talk to someone in charge," Cindy explained. "The town had come together as a group that decided to resist the invasion of this Flaherty guy, isolating the town with the barricades. No one person was in charge, the Mayor had disappeared shortly after the war started, but Carl had been one that the townspeople had come to respect, so he and another hostel owner had decided to go see what the soldiers wanted.

"They had shown them the wanted paper and demanded that they give you up, saying you were wanted for murder. I'm not sure why they thought you would be here. Maybe they don't know you are walking, or they are overestimating your daily mileage.

"The conversation grew heated, and the leader of the soldiers had drawn his pistol and shot Carl point blank in the face. Carl and Joe had gone out unarmed in good faith and Carl got shot for it.

"Those who were watching from the barricades were armed and had opened fire on the soldiers who retreated to their vehicles and drove away.

"Carl lasted about an hour before he died. A lot of the community that had been living behind the barriers became afraid of another attack, so they decided to leave town and head into the hills for a spell. The rest are hiding in their houses hoping it blows over.

"I don't think anyone would turn you in here, but you might want to get back into the woods," Cindy continued. "Be careful at all the road crossings and don't trust anyone you meet that is wearing a uniform. The trail might be over 2000 miles long, but it is only four feet wide. If they really want to find you on the trail, a road crossing will probably be where they will set up their ambush."

The Party sat in silence, disturbed by what they had just heard. This was serious, and now they would have to continue up the trail as wanted criminals. They hoped that they could outdistance the people who were looking for them. They hadn't even killed anyone, which was adding to their confusion. What had happened after they left Jimbo and his militia? Were the shots they had heard as they climbed the mountain by the lake coming from Boots Off? So many questions.

It was still early in the day, but they understood that the sooner they got out of this deadly town, the better. Fic handed Cindy the envelope and the baby boot. "I guess this goes to you then," he said.

Cindy took the envelope and put it on the kitchen table, "I have some food, but not much else. Take what you need."

#

The Party headed out of the building and continued down the road. They had to climb over yet another car barricade to exit the town. "It looks like they used every car in the town to make these walls," Gnobbit observed.

After following the Creeper Bike Trail for a few hundred meters, the trail headed back into the woods and up a hillside. They considered using the Creeper Trail for a while to move faster, but it ran next to a road, so they decided not to chance being seen out in the open. Into the woods they walked.

As the day was getting late, the hikers started their last climb before the shelter. They ascended about a thousand feet and counted nineteen switchbacks to get up to the top. They'd gone another ten miles after leaving their mission location.

Exhausted, they finally rolled into the shelter area and started their nightly routine. They would stand the watch once again. As wanted criminals — even if they were innocent of what they were being accused of — they had to be extra careful. Two people would stay up together. They would keep each other company and also increase their vigilance.

#

The next two days were nothing but walking. They needed to get as many miles as they could between them and the soldiers down in Hampton. They would wake early, before the sun was up, quickly eat and break down camp, then hike all day long until they would stumble into a shelter area to set up, eat, and then try to get some sleep. They continued to keep the watch every night. Two hikers sitting together in the dark with their two firearms, occasionally talking quietly, but mostly keeping quiet and listening to the night sounds. Finn and Gnobbit always stood a watch together. The others traded off on their partners, depending on who was tired and who was alert.

After an almost twenty mile day that included the Damascus stop, they did twenty-four miles the next day to Wise Shelter. The highlight of that day was climbing up 2000 feet to Whitetop Mountain. As they topped the mountain, the wind whipped across it in a crazy torrent. They were in the clouds as they crossed an open area and the mist just moved past in small streams. The day after was a twenty mile day to Trimpi Shelter. The Party had entered the Grayson Highlands and the excitement of this day was seeing the wild ponies that inhabit the area. The semi-tame ponies would come up to the hikers to see if they had any apples or other food. They would lick the arms and legs of the hikers, tasting the salt on their skin. It was nice to see these beautiful wild animals in this enchanting environment. It almost made them forget the trouble they were in. Almost.

Each time they would come to a road crossing, no matter how small the road was, they would pause and Gnobbit or Finn — sometimes both — would sneak forward to scope out the crossing. If it was clear, the group would hurry across and get back into the woods as fast as they could. Caution was the key.

The weather stayed pleasant those two days. It didn't get too hot because an overcast sky kept the July sun from beating down on the hikers. There were a few short rain showers, which helped cool down the hikers as they moved along at the fastest pace they could manage.

After hiking almost sixty-five miles in three days, their bodies were starting to feel the pain of the wear and tear. They needed to find a place to rest that was safe and out of sight. Maybe even a distance away from the trail.

Class Room had been exceptionally quiet the last couple of days. She didn't want to handle either of the weapons anymore and would sit off by herself whenever they took a break. Gnobbit tried to talk to her, but she would just tell her that everything was fine. Fic could tell that she was anything but fine. The fight at Boots Off was still weighing heavily on her mind. Even though what she had done was right and had kept the rest of them from being wounded or worse, she was still having trouble coming to terms with shooting a human.

As The Party lay exhausted in the Trimpi Shelter, Fic looked at his guide. Trying to find a place they could safely rest for the good part of a day. *Maybe we can take a break at the Settlers Museum*, Fic thought. *We could do another 18.6 tomorrow, then take a break for a day or so at the farm.* The Settlers Museum was a working farm that had been there since the 1890s. Maybe they had even planted some crops that they could take advantage of.

The farm would be close to a road, so they would have to be careful, but their bodies needed a rest.

#

The following day, The Party continued north on the trail. Fic noticed that Gnobbit and Finn had started to walk together a lot. Talking softly and making each other laugh. He felt that a deeper relationship was developing in the pair. Maybe even something romantic. Fic decided to walk with Class Room for a while. He talked to her a bit to judge her mood and then worked towards mentioning the slump she was going through. "Class Room, I can tell what happened at Boots Off is weighing heavily on your mind and I know there is little I can say that will help, but I'm going to try, anyway. When I was deployed over in Afghanistan, we all went through stuff like this after any kind of engagement. It was hard, but we had the knowledge that we were there to do a job and that job was super hard sometimes," Fic started.

"This situation we are in now, is a lot like that. Our job now is to get all of us home, safe and sound. What you did was not only necessary, but heroic. You were the one who saw Kirk's treachery first, and you were the one who did what you had to do. You took him down, and luckily, you didn't kill him. Your quick thinking and action kept the rest of us from getting wounded," Fic looked over at Class Room. A single tear ran down her cheek.

"I just keep seeing that guy get blown over when my shot hit him. It's not the same as shooting clay pigeons. I think a little of me died when I saw him hit the ground," Class Room said. "I agree with everything you said, but I just can't shake the dread I feel now whenever I even look at the weapons. I'm afraid I may be useless if we have to do this again."

"That's just fine," Fic answered. "From now on, you don't need to worry about shooting. You can help in other ways. I know we have been hiking hard these last few days, and you haven't played Yuk in a while. Maybe when we get settled at this farm tonight, you can pull her out and play a little for us. We all feel better when you play your music."

"I think I will do that," Class Room replied. "It always makes me feel better too when I play Yuk." She flashed Fic a smile that he hadn't seen in several days. "Thanks, Fic. This really helped."

"No problem. Just remember that all of us are here to help in whatever way we can," Fic assured her.

#

The sun had come out and was shining through the forest, lighting misty beams of light and giving the forest a mystical look. It was midday. They were approaching VA 16. They knew they were getting close because they could hear the traffic on the road. It didn't seem like a lot of traffic, but it was the most they encountered since leaving Damascus.

The scout team went ahead as the others waited in the woods. Gnobbit came back fairly quickly. "The shelter is just up ahead. It is out of sight of the road, and no one is around. We can take a break up there. They have a shower in the back."

The hikers moved up to the shelter. Finn came back reporting the road and the visitor center parking lot as empty for now.

They each took turns taking a quick cold shower and washing out some socks and underwear, which they attached to their pack to dry. Fic sat at the edge of the shelter with his shotgun, keeping an eye towards where the road was. A few times they heard something drive down the road, but nothing stopped or paused. The road came all the way up to the shelter, but Finn had reported that there was a closed gate at the end of the parking lot.

When everyone was feeling a little fresher, they prepared to move on. Just then, they heard another vehicle coming down the road. This one pulled into the visitor center and came to a stop in the parking lot. They could hear its diesel engine idling in the lot. After a few minutes, it turned off.

Fic looked over at Finn, who nodded and started to head towards the parking lot, his bow at the ready. Fic motioned the others to get their gear and get behind the shelter. "Stay out of sight for now but be ready to come up," he advised. He set his pack with the others and, readying his shotgun, turned towards the road.

Carefully, he moved up the road where Finn had disappeared. He had a feeling that if anything happened, a bow might not be the best weapon to counter an attack.

He saw Finn hiding behind a bush and looking towards the lot. He made a soft sound to get Finn's attention and let him know he was coming up. He joined Finn and followed his gaze to see a Humvee parked in the lot. Two men were inside, dressed in military camo. They appeared to be eating lunch.

As they sat there, observing, one of the guys got out of the vehicle and started walking towards a large, green dumpster at the end of the lot. He didn't appear to be armed or on any kind of alert, but he was heading right towards them.

The two spies remained calm and motionless as the man walked up to the dumpster, opened the lid, and then threw his trash away. The country was all fucked up, but this guy was doing his part to keep this new America clean. The absurdity of it all made Fic want to laugh, but the urge quickly vanished as the man walked around the dumpster, getting even closer to them, and then stopped.

He unzipped his fly and exhaled a long sigh as he emptied his bladder on the bushes behind the dumpster. He finished, zipped up, and started back towards the hummer. Fic breathed a silent sigh of relief. Adrenaline coursed through his body, and he started to shake a little.

The man re-entered the Humvee, and it started up again. The driver put the vehicle in gear and headed out of the parking lot, turning left towards Marion, Virginia.

Finn looked at Fic with a relieved expression on his face and let out his own sigh. They slowly backed out of their hiding place and headed back to the shelter. That was enough excitement for now.

#

A few hours later, The Party came to a sign that pointed to the right, indicating the Settlers Museum was one tenth of a mile off the trail. They followed that trail and came to an open area where there were several old, unpainted buildings. In the middle of them all was a white two story farmhouse. They sat, observing the area for movement or people or anything that would raise an alarm. Nothing stirred but the bugs and some birds. Finn and Gnobbit did their usual scouting mission and reported back that the place was deserted. The Party advanced towards the farm carefully and made their way to the farmhouse.

The door to the farmhouse was locked, but Gnobbit was inside quickly with her skills. The Party checked out the building. There were a few bedrooms on the second floor, a rustic kitchen, and a living room with a couple couches. They found places to set up, and relaxed a little. They decided to all stay in the living room, using the couches and sleeping on the floor. Being close together seemed like the best way to stay safe, instead of spreading out all over the house. If anything bad happened, they could always use the second floor as the high ground in a defensive position.

Fic and Rodent Whisperer took a walk to explore the deserted grounds. They found a large cornfield that was still growing, but it was too early to have any edible ears. Out by the road was an old schoolhouse that was part of the museum grounds. They went inside and found a treasure trove of food and other supplies that are normally kept there for hikers. They gathered a bunch of food, a mostly full canister of fuel, and an assortment of other items that the hikers were in need of before returning to the farmhouse. Everyone looked through the cache of food and supplies, sorting it and dividing it up amongst themselves.

Dinner was a happy affair, the discovery of new food options instantly improving everyone's mood. They rewarded themselves after four hard days of hiking with an extra portion each.

The Party decided they would rest here tomorrow for the whole day, in order to give their bodies some time to recover from the extensive miles they had just put in.

They didn't think they were far enough away from that wanted poster, but each day they were a little further north.

As darkness came to the farmstead, The Party sat around the living room and Class Room brought out Yuk, playing softly as the other hikers sat and listened. Finn sang when she played a song he recognized. Gnobbit joined in, and the duet was a perfect medley of their two voices. The mellow music made everyone feel relaxed and content. Her music definitely had a magical quality that helped them feel better.

Fic could tell that playing made Class Room feel better too. The bags that had been under her eyes the last few days seemed to disappear and she was smiling as they finished the last song.

Brown Shades had searched through the house with Gnobbit and Finn earlier and had found a fifth of bourbon in one of the kitchen cabinets. The Party passed it around as they were sitting in the living room. Each of the hikers would take a quick nip and then pass it on to the next hiker. When it came around to Rodent Whisperer, he just passed it on to the next person with a smile. No one said anything, they now understood that Rodent Whisperer wasn't a drinker, and no one tried to pressure him or even ask him about it.

"I haven't had a drink in two years," Rodent Whisperer volunteered. "Before that, I was very close to killing myself. I'm an addict and an alcoholic. Heroin was my drug of choice. I was in pretty bad shape. One day I reached rock bottom. Living on the streets of Edinburgh, sleeping under an overpass. Not eating any food, just looking for my next hit. One day I was thinking of robbing an old lady I saw come out of the bank and realized I needed to change the way I was living, or I wasn't going to be living much longer."

"I quit cold turkey that day. The next month was a blur filled with pain, and puking, but I came out on the other side sober. I got a job and then a place to stay and started saving up for this hike. I had wanted to hike for a long time, but my habit had made that unattainable until I quit ruining my body."

Gnobbit had tears running down her cheeks. She went over to Rodent Whisperer and gave him a hug. "We won't drink around you if it bothers you at all," she said.

"That's okay," he responded. "It has no power over me anymore. I still remember its soothing properties when used in moderation. You all are welcome to imbibe as you wish."

Everyone else came over and hugged the large, dark Scotsman. There were tears all around.

#

The next morning dawned like a typical midsummer day in southern Virginia. The promise of a hot, sticky day was clear.

Fic walked out onto the porch of the farmhouse. A cup of steaming coffee in his hand. Today was going to be a do-nothing day. Gnobbit and Finn were on the porch, sitting next to each other on the top step of the stairs. Gnobbit had stood the last watch of the night, supposedly relieving Finn.

Fic looked at the pair. "Good morning you two," he said smiling. "Did you ever go to bed Finn?"

"No. We started talking when Gnobbit relieved me and before we knew it, the sun was coming up. It was a good conversation," he said, grinning at Gnobbit.

She looked back at him in an interesting way. *Something's brewing here*, Fic thought to himself. "There's coffee in the kitchen. Brown Shades has been finding all kinds of goodies. This is real coffee. Not instant. Class Room is cooking pancakes and summer sausage for breakfast."

"Yum, I'm hungry," said Gnobbit. She stood up and looked at Finn. "So, after breakfast?" she asked, her eyebrows raising in a questioning manner.

"That sounds like a plan," replied Finn, smiling at her again.

Gnobbit went into the farmhouse and Finn stood beside Fic. As he stood, it seemed to Fic that he just kept getting higher and higher, his lofty form still a shock.

"We are going to go for a walk around the grounds after breakfast," he explained to Fic. "Check out the buildings and see what's around."

"Make sure you take either the shotgun or rifle," Fic replied. "And have fun," he added with a wink.

After breakfast, Fic, Brown Shades and Class Room were sitting on the porch enjoying another cup of coffee when the pair of scouts came out of the house. "We will be back in about an hour," Finn said. Gnobbit had the shotgun over her shoulder. Finn had his bow.

Watching the tallest member of The Party walking beside the shortest made a smile come to the observers' faces. "Now there's a cute couple," said Class Room, watching the two young hikers walk towards the barn that was across a courtyard in front of the house. They noticed that just before the couple turned a corner by a building, Finn reached out and took Gnobbit's hand. Everyone on the porch looked at each other and laughed.

When Gnobbit and Finn hadn't returned in two hours, Fic and Rodent Whisperer went out looking for them. They circled around the property, searching for any indication of where the two hikers might have been. When they got to the road, they walked along it towards the old schoolhouse, ready to move off if they heard anything coming.

The two seekers arrived at the schoolhouse and still hadn't seen any sign of the two scouts. As they sat and discussed their next move, they saw Finn and Gnobbit come fast walking down the road towards Fic and Rodent Whisperer. They had baskets of vegetables in their hands. "We found some stuff," Gnobbit said, a large grin on her face.

"I see that," replied Fic. "Can we help?"

They divided up the freshly picked vegetables between the four of them and started walking back to the farmhouse. "Where did you find these?" Fic asked.

"There is a house just around the corner that has a very large garden," Finn explained. "We liberated some ripe ones. No one seemed to be around. The garden looked like it hadn't been tended to or weeded in several weeks," continued Finn. "If we didn't take them, they would probably be starting to rot soon."

They returned to the farmhouse to everyone's delight and the rest of the day was spent relaxing and snacking on things that they had found in the schoolhouse or around the grounds.

Finn and Gnobbit withdrew to a corner, away from the rest of the group, giggling and whispering, oblivious to everyone's knowing smiles.

"Trail love," Fic said softly to Class Room. She nodded her agreement and gave him a wink.

Class Room picked up Yuk and started strumming a soft tune. Fic sat listening. Thinking about his family back home. Wondering if Lori and the kids were doing okay or if they were dealing with the rogue Flarmy. Were they in danger? So many questions and so many miles to go before he could find out.

That night they cooked up some vegetables and made a salad with the rest. It felt great to eat fresh produce instead of dry stuff, reconstituted with water. Everyone sat around after dinner and just vegetated. There was no fire to stare at, but the setting sun put on a beautiful show as it moved behind the mountain to the west. Lighting up the sky in bright reds and oranges before fading to purple then black. "Red sky at night, sailor's delight," Brown Shades chanted in a soft voice.

They slept as they had the night before — all in the same room with a watch set on the porch. The night passed quietly, and The Party slept peacefully.

CHAPTER 13
HOME FRONT III - TUESDAY, JULY 10TH

Shane sat in front of a roaring campfire, staring into its flames; a tired look on his face. He wore a camo hunting shirt and brown pants. A blue bandana was tied round his left bicep over the sleeve of his shirt. The bandana was the insignia of the Blue Mountain Patrol, of which Shane was a member. His sister was too, but she had started to split her time patrolling with tending the garden. Tonight, she was at home.

Shane had teamed up with Jim and his cousin Chester on this patrol. They had been out for two nights now. This morning, Chester had shot a deer that was standing at the edge of a field, as they walked a trail that circled one of the properties that they were protecting. The gutted and skinned deer hung from a tree behind their tents. They would have to get the meat back to the house tomorrow and get it processed and preserved quickly. Hunting in the middle of a hot July made saving the meat a priority.

"What's your sister doing tonight, Shane?" Jim asked, his creepy grin looking over the fire at Shane. "I sure do like when she comes out on patrol with us."

Shane was growing tired of Jim's obsession with his sister. He had shown an uncomfortable amount of attention to her ever since they had joined the Patrol. "She is tending the garden today," he said tersely. "You do know she isn't interested in you, right?"

"I know that, but a girl can change her mind. I'm a good guy. She'll figure that out one day," Jim pleaded his case. "I won't wait around forever though," he added.

Shane just looked at him. He knew she was never going to become interested in any kind of relationship with Jim. That was part of why she started cutting down her patrol times to work at home. She had confided in Shane that she really didn't like him hitting on her all the time. Shane didn't like it either.

Being in the Blue Mountain Patrol had proved worthwhile so far. It gave him something important to do and working on the patrol increased his family's food supply. They would always be on the lookout for wild game to add to the pot, and would also spend time fishing when they could, adding a variety of protein to the table.

Their patrol route covered a large perimeter of their operational area. After heading south towards the highway, they would check on three of the homesteads along the road, then make their way towards the river. They'd patrol along the river and check on four more of the homeowners up that way. When they reached their northern border, their patrol would circle back around and head home, checking the last five houses along their route.

It felt good to help the community. They were keeping everyone safe from the marauding bands that seemed to be cropping up in the area. Their organization and possession of weapons made the thieves go elsewhere, looking for easier prey.

So far, the army had not come into their area either, but they had seen them traveling up and down Route 50 every day.

From time to time, the Blue Mountain Patrol would venture north and west of their usual operational area, but the river had been their eastern border so far. Except for one time, when Shane got curious and ventured past the river and up the mountain alone to see what was up at his dad's base. He'd had a feeling that something concerning was going on at Mount Weather.

When he had observed the military post, he'd noticed that the army trucks seemed to be going to and from there at all hours, which wasn't common for this area prior to the attacks. It appeared to be a significant location for whatever project these army people were working on. He didn't think these soldiers were the same army that his father belonged to. He had the feeling that they were part of Flaherty's army.

The news of the attacks and the takeover of the government and armed forces by Richard Flaherty and his Regime had been passed amongst the families who were under the protection of the Patrol. A lot of what had happened and why was still unknown, but they had come to realize that avoiding the men dressed in the camo uniforms and driving the military vehicles was the smart thing to do for now. They had been lucky that they hadn't been bothered by the rogue army yet, and they wanted to keep it that way.

Shane didn't really like patrolling with Jim and Chester, but that was how the rotation had worked out for the week. Jim wasn't only creepy; he had a mean streak and sometimes he seemed to get alarmingly power hungry. It was clear some families feared him, and Shane was sure he was doing cruel things from time to time with the power he now had as the leader of the Patrol.

Chester wasn't as bad as his cousin, but he usually followed Jim's lead. He was a couple years younger than Jim and looked up to him. He was a good shot with the rifle as the deer hanging behind them professed, but he just seemed to be a little slow on the pickup for most things. Chester was on the heavy side and not very tall. He had a strange laugh that was starting to grate on Shane's nerves.

Jim pulled out a jar of moonshine that he had picked up at the last farm they had visited. The man who made the liquor had given it to The Patrol in exchange for some dried venison they had been carrying. He took a swig and sprayed some of it into the fire. The fire flared bright for a few seconds from the high proof liquid, then returned to its normal height.

Jim laughed and did it again. Shane just stared at him. He'd realized pretty quickly that Jim's leadership skills left a lot to be desired. Jim passed the jar to his cousin, who tried to repeat the trick with mixed results. Shane took his turn with the jar, only taking a small sip to warm his insides and relax his mind. The last two days hadn't been hard, but he was ready to get back to the farm for a couple of days and take a break until the next rotation started.

The fire died down and the men bedded down in their tents for the night. Shane lay in his sleeping bag, wondering when his father was going to get home. He was beginning to lose hope. It had been over a month since he left on his training mission just before the war. He knew that he was far away and hoped that he was still out there somewhere, trying to get back to Millwood. Trying to get home to his family.

CHAPTER 14
GNOBBIT AND FINN - WEDNESDAY, JULY 11TH TO SATURDAY,
JULY 21ST

The morning dawned, promising one of those hazy, hot and humid days. The Party was packed and ready to go before the sun had crept over the mountain to their east. They left the farmstead and walked back to the trail.

They took one last look through the hiker boxes that sat in the old schoolhouse. Each hiker grabbed whatever caught their eye, not minding a little extra weight on their backs in exchange for a few luxury items they found. Gnobbit found a six-pack of coke in the corner. Each hiker accepted a warm can of sweet energy to carry up the next mountain or two and enjoy after they were back in the woods.

They carefully crossed the road and moved quickly into the open field that led back into the woods. Soon they were back under the morning shade of the trees and moving along comfortably.

After a couple miles, they came to another road. Just beyond was Interstate 81. They could hear intermittent traffic on the large highway, but this area appeared vacant.

They crouched in the high bushes about a hundred meters away while Gnobbit and Finn did their thing.

When they reported back Gnobbit said, "There are a couple of gas stations, an old motel, and a restaurant called The Barn. The trail follows this road for a while, then another that goes under the Interstate. It's pretty exposed, so we need to be careful."

The Party didn't follow the trail in the open, but stayed at the forest's edge, keeping a buffer of high bushes between them and the road. As they approached the large red building called The Barn, they heard a vehicle coming down the highway. The sound changed as it slowed to exit the highway.

The land rose where they were walking to meet the parking lot of the restaurant and they huddled there, listening to the vehicle approach. Finn crawled up to the edge of the berm and peered out between two bushes.

The Humvee exited the highway and turned towards the road they were following. The crackle of gravel under the vehicle's tires announced that it was pulling into the parking lot of the restaurant. It parked in front of a low flight of wooden steps and a uniformed man got out and walked into the building.

Finn came back to the huddled party and relayed what he had seen. "He is alone," he added. As they sat there a loud, long scream came from the restaurant and then some yelling that was indecipherable.

"We need to help," Class Room said, a worried look in her eyes. "That asshole is the cause of that scream, I'll bet."

The Party quickly moved up the berm and across the parking lot. There were large windows all around the building, and the lot was large and open, so the thought of sneaking towards the restaurant was abandoned and they resorted to a fast charge to get inside.

Fic was in front with the shotgun and Finn was right behind him. Rodent Whisperer was next with the rifle and the two staff wielders followed behind him. Class Room came last — no weapon in her hand, but a determined look on her face.

They burst into the dining area and across some tables, near the kitchen door, the uniformed man stood over a frightened brunette woman. The source of the scream.

The man was turned away from the others and was so intent on trying to overpower the woman, that he didn't hear them come clamoring in. She had seen them and a look that pleaded for help gave the man a clue that something was happening behind him.

He turned his head to his right to see Fic's shotgun leveled at his head. He had a knife in his hand which is what he was using to convince this young woman his intentions were bad. A look of surprise was painted on his face.

"Get the fuck away from that woman," Fic ordered. Of course, the man did not obey.

The uniformed man grabbed the woman and put his arm around her neck. Pulling her close and moving the knife to her neck. "Fuck you," he replied.

"You seriously want to do this?" Fic asked the man. "You are not going to get away. You are going to pay for this. One way or the other. I promise you that any harm you bring to that woman will be inflicted on you tenfold. Don't be stupid."

As the man stood there looking at the weapons pointed at him, recognition came into his face. The rapid transition of his expressions was a sight to see. He went from determined, to surprised, to determined again, but Fic thought he also saw some fear in there too.

"You are that Party we've been looking for," he said, moving his gaze down to his holster where a pistol sat encased. He had run out of hands to draw weapons with, and they watched as several ideas played out in his head.

As the stalemate continued, the kitchen door behind the man slowly and silently started to open. A stick of brown wood, about four feet long, came whirling out of the kitchen and bounced off the guy's head. He moved away stunned, not expecting someone to flank him, and released the woman, who ran towards Fic and his crew. Out came Gnobbit, ready to swing her staff again. Class Room rushed out behind her, a cast-iron skillet in her hand. She wound up with all of her strength and swung the pan around, connecting squarely with the man's face. Down he went. The knife clattering to the ground.

Class Room approached the man and removed the pistol from its holster, placing it in the small of her back. She had an angry, wrathful look on her face. She raised her arm as if she was thinking of using the skillet one more time for good measure but refrained when she saw that the guy was out cold.

Everyone looked at each other with the same thought in their eyes, *What do we do now?*

"Thank you so much," the brunette said. "That creep has been coming here for a week now. He has made me uneasy since day one, and today, he's proven my instincts correct. If y'all hadn't shown up —" she trailed off, shuddering at the thought of what could have happened.

Fic tied the man up with some rope that the woman gave him, and Rodent Whisperer checked him out quickly to determine the extent of his injuries. He was still unconscious and bleeding from a cut on his head, but he would probably be okay after his concussion healed.

They gathered in the dining room to talk to the woman and decide their next move.

"I'm Flo," the woman said. "My parents own this place and we have been trying to keep the kitchen going as best we could with our generator, but we are pretty much out of food. I was just here today to do some cleaning and then I was going to close up and head home.

"This asshole came in and realized that I was alone. You saw what was going on when you came in. I'm so thankful that you did," she abruptly changed the subject, "Are y'all hungry? I have enough to make you some sandwiches."

She got up and headed to the kitchen after everyone nodded in the affirmative. The man started to stir, she paused, wound up, and kicked him in the stomach. A loud groan escaped his mouth as he lay helpless. She continued walking and disappeared into the kitchen.

She was back in a minute with rolls, lunch meat, tomatoes, lettuce and cheeses. Everyone gathered around the spread and made their own sandwiches. They were delicious.

The Party still didn't know what to do about the soldier that was lying on the floor in the corner. Evidently, they still hadn't outwalked the wanted poster yet because the guy had recognized them when they came in.

The soldier started to stir again, and Fic figured it was time to have a talk with him. He walked over to the man who had moved up to a sitting position. He was looking at the group with a hostile glare. When Fic crouched down next to the man, he drew back fearfully as if Fic was going to cut his throat. "I know who you murdering scum are and you will not get away this time," he spat out angrily.

"We haven't killed anyone … *yet*," Fic said with a stern look. "We are just trying to get home in this mess, and we can't have you fucking that up."

"Can I have a word with you, sir," Flo asked Fic. They went into the kitchen to talk.

"I don't think his people know he is here. He has always been with another guy when he has come in here before. He also mentioned something about sneaking away from the base, which is the Econo Lodge in Marion about eight miles away. If he disappears, I don't think they will know to come here to find him," Flo explained.

"I guess he comes with us then," Fic decided. He went back out into the dining room and discussed his plan with the others. After some back and forth, they decided to bring him along long enough to get him far away from his Humvee and his base. If he behaved, they could release him several miles up the trail. They would use the Humvee to get past the interstate, then dump it somewhere where it wouldn't be found too fast. Flo had mentioned that there were lots of checkpoints on the roads where it would be too risky to get through them in a commandeered Humvee.

They got ready to go. Getting the man on his feet, Fic said, "You are coming with us. If you are good, we will release you when we feel safe. If you give us any trouble, we will put a bullet in you and leave you for the forest animals. Understood?" The look of fear was back on the man's face.

They kept the man's hands tightly bound in front of him, but his feet were free. Fic tied a piece of the rope around his waist and held the other end as a sort of leash. If he tried anything, a sharp tug on the rope should bring him down.

They all piled into the Humvee and sat the man in the back between Rodent Whisperer and Fic. Finn drove with Gnobbit and Class Room up front. Brown Shades sat in the back cargo area with the packs.

They said goodbye to Flo and thanked her for the food. She thanked them repeatedly for saving her and blessed them continuously.

Finn drove the vehicle down the road that went under the interstate, and they followed it another mile or so until they saw the trail coming out of the woods, crossing the road, and continuing along the edge of a field until it re-entered the forest. There was a small parking lot where the trail emerged from the woods. Beyond the lot the land sloped down towards a small creek. They parked the Humvee at the edge of the lot, grabbed all of their gear, then pushed the vehicle over the edge, letting it careen off of a couple trees until it came to a stop at the bottom of the hill. Its camouflaged coloring helped to blend it into the forest.

The Party continued on the trail, making their way back into the cover of the forest. The soldier walked slowly at first, but a few nudges from Gnobbit's staff had him keeping the pace better. "I think I will name my staff, Pain," said Gnobbit.

"*Dolor* is the Latin word for pain," Brown Shades informed her.

"Dolores it is then," she said, adding her own little twist to the name with a smile.

The Party made their way along the field, moving at the quick pace they had become accustomed to when they needed to make some miles before they slept.

Bringing this guy along had just complicated their trek to a great degree. Fic just hoped it wasn't a bad decision to do so.

The rest of the day's hike went as usual. The trail moved through forest and field, their backdrop switching from shaded oaks and maples to grazing cows. In the afternoon, they arrived at the Knot Maul Branch Shelter. The thick rhododendron hid the shelter until the last thirty feet. It was a typical shelter with only one level and room for about eight sleepers. Someone had written *Darth* on top of the word *Knot* in Sharpie on the sign announcing the name of the shelter. May the force be with them.

The prisoner, whose name was Tucker as evidenced by the name tape on his camo uniform, had been well behaved throughout the day's hike. He kept silent as they walked along and showed no signs of any heroic plans being cooked up in his head.

"You'll sleep against that back wall. We don't have any pads or a sleeping bag for you, but being a soldier, I'm sure you can tough it out," Fic directed the man. Tucker nodded his head and moved to the back of the shelter. The rest of the ground sleepers put their sleeping pads with their heads facing out of the shelter, effectively blocking the man in. If he tried to get by the sleeping hikers, he risked the chance of waking the others. Fic also tied his legs for the night.

"What about if I gotta piss?" Tucker asked.

"Just let me know and we will handle it. Together," Fic answered.

The hammock sleepers put their hammocks next to the shelter on some good trees. The Party sat down to make their dinners. They gave Tucker a bit of their food. He had to walk too, so he needed at least some energy. Keeping him a bit hungry and slightly weak was insurance against escape attempts though, so he only was given the smallest ration.

Yuk played in the approaching darkness, an attempt to calm the frayed nerves of the group after finding themselves unwanted babysitters of an unsettling prisoner. Two hikers stood the watch when everyone turned in. One would keep their eyes out into the forest and the other would watch Tucker. They were still too close to Marion to let him go.

Class Room mostly ignored the man. When she did point her attention in his direction, a hate-filled scowl would cross her face. She did not like this man or the fact that they had to remain in his company. If they hadn't come when they did, who knows if Flo would even be alive still. She had kept the man's pistol. Tucked into her pants all day long and now under her sleeping pad near her head. In this moment, with this vile man in their camp, she felt safer having the weapon than not having it. The shock and dread she had felt when she had shot the soldier back at Boots Off had faded to a dull feeling that she had come to terms with. If she was faced with another situation where she had to protect her Tramily, she was mostly sure that she would be able to do it now without hesitation. The hate she was feeling for this scum was making it easier. Witnessing his violent behavior, had broken her reluctance to carry a weapon. The anger she felt when she imagined not getting to Flo's rescue in time boiled within her.

#

The night passed uneventfully, and Tucker behaved himself. In the morning, Fic took him along on his leash and let him into the privy while he stood watch outside with the door slightly ajar.

After a scant breakfast, The Party plus one packed up and started walking again. After some early ups and downs, they started a long, slow climb. The forest became a field, and they could see far below from the ridge top. The view was interesting. From their vantage point, they could see a huge bowl formed by a circle of mountains to their northeast. "That's called *God's Thumbprint*," Brown Shades informed them. "Created by the collapse of massive underground limestone caverns long ago. Inside is the highest mountain valley in the state of Virginia. It is very fertile farmland."

Around lunchtime they came to a stone shelter sitting at the top of the open ridge. The shelter was a long rectangle with a door at one end and windows along the walls. It wasn't the typical shelter as it had four walls. A table and some wooden bunk beds filled the inside.

They ate lunch then moved on. As they walked along, Tucker in front with his leash in Fic's hand, Fic tried to talk to him. He asked him about his background and how he ended up as part of the rogue army. Tucker wouldn't talk at first, but after a couple of hours he started sharing some details. What he said gave Fic a little more information about what was going on.

"I was a reservist, doing my time at the Virginia National Guard Armory down in Gate City," Tucker began. "I was living in Abingdon and working as a clerk in a hunting store when I wasn't drilling. I have been following and supporting Richard Flaherty for a long time now. He is a pretty smart guy and he knows how to get power. When the shit went down, I took the initiative and seized a bunch of weapons. I was able to contact some of his people and joined up when I found a nearby outfit. I was rewarded with a promotion and was living in the Econo Lodge in Marion where we have set up." He seemed proud of his accomplishments.

Fic asked him a few more questions but grew weary of his arrogant attitude. He decided he preferred a quiet prisoner.

The end of the day brought them to Jenkins Shelter. The trail had steadily moved off the ridge during the last part of the hike and the shelter was next to a nice stream at the bottom of the valley.

The shelter was a replica of yesterday's and they set up in the same formation as before, preparing for another night of switching off guard duty.

\#

Fic had discretely discussed the next steps of dealing with Tucker with the others. They decided that he would be released today after they had walked to a remote area away from roads.

The morning started out with a climb back up onto a ridge. Once they were up on the ridge and moving along, Fic stopped and faced Tucker. The soldier was a sorry sight. The long days of hiking and the scant food he was given had taken the desired toll.

Fic untied his hands and removed the rope from his waist. "You're free," he said. "If I ever see you again, that bullet will find you."

The man stared at Fic for a good ten seconds before he realized that he was no longer tied to the man. He looked around and Fic pointed to the way they had just come. "That way," he ordered.

The man started walking. As he passed Class Room who was at the end of the line, he looked at her and smacked his lips in a kissing gesture. "I'll see ya later, honey," he said slyly. She was the only one who heard it.

Her look became steel, and she touched the butt of the pistol in her waistband. "You better hope not," she replied. Daggers shot out of her eyes and into the back of the departing soldier. After a few seconds, he started to jog, then run until he had moved below the ridgeline and out of sight.

"I sure hope that is the last we see of him," Fic said, before turning and walking north away from where Tucker had been lost from sight.

They felt a need to move fast and go far today. Fic kept telling himself that releasing the soldier had been a good idea. *We don't have to guard him. We don't have to feed him. He seemed to be ambivalent to the whole Regime situation.* After telling Fic how great Flaherty was, he changed his tune with a new story. He told Fic that he was just swept up in the wave of rebellion when the army went rogue. Going with the flow to stay alive. He had seen what was happening to those that resisted the takeover. If you weren't with them, you were against them, and a bullet was your prize. No matter which story was true, Fic had developed a strong dislike for Tucker. He hoped the guy was heading back to his unit, and wasn't going to try to come after him and The Party.

Their one challenge of the day was coming out of the woods near Interstate 77 and needing to walk over it this time instead of under. When they first came to the highway, they passed a small store that sat at a bend. It had been burned to the ground.

Nothing was left but a black, ash filled square next to the road. They moved fast to get over the Interstate and back to the cover of the woods. Nothing moved around them as they quickly walked across the bridge.

They arrived at Jenny Knob Shelter in the late afternoon. Everyone felt worn out from the twenty-three miles they'd accomplished today. They made a small fire to soak in the power of the flames and ate their dinners in silence. Gnobbit and Finn were talking about their college classes, comparing what they were taking and what they wanted to take — if there was ever another semester to go back to. Gnobbit decided to set up her tent near Finn's hammock out beside the shelter.

Darkness came, and the hikers retired to their sleeping pads and hammocks.

#

It was about 0200. Class Room lay in her sleeping bag staring up at the roof of the shelter. She had to pee. She pushed the bag back and crawled out to the edge of the shelter. She slipped on her shoes, grabbed her headlamp, her toilet kit and the pistol, then headed towards the privy, which sat at the end of a path over a rise, out of sight of the shelter. She nodded to Brown Shades, who was on watch as she passed him sitting at the table.

She entered the dilapidated structure and did her business. Once finished, she exited the privy and turned to head back to the shelter. A hand came out of the darkness from beside the outhouse and pressed against her mouth. Another wrapped around her waist and started moving her into the woods. "I told you I would see you again, bitch," a voice said in the darkness.

Class Rooms red head lamp fell off her forehead to the ground. Her arms were pinned to her sides and couldn't move. Fear wasn't rising in her gut. Anger was. *Tucker had followed them*, was all she could think.

The man shifted his arm to get a better grip, but that was enough for her to get one hand free, she reached behind her to the pistol in her waistband and drew the weapon. She raised her arm up with the pistol, placed the muzzle of the pistol up against the man's jaw and pulled the trigger. The blast spattered blood against the side of her face and hair, and the man released his hold on her mouth and waist. He fell to the ground without a sound. She turned and put two more bullets into his body, not caring that he was already dead. She stood there pointing the weapon at the dead man dressed in a camo uniform.

Brown Shades came running over with his headlamp on white and the shotgun at the ready. He shined the light on the prone man. The name Tucker was clearly displayed on the body's shirt.

The rest of the group came running over, head lamps shooting beams all around. Fic came slowly up to Class Room and reached his hand up to cover the pistol still aimed at the dead man. "Nice shot," he said softly. "I'll take your weapon if that's okay." She let him take it with a sigh. She didn't look freaked out. She looked mad and determined. She looked fierce.

"That fucker tried to take me," she said. "He had whispered to me as he left, that he would see me again. I guess he followed us all day, waiting for his chance. My damn bladder almost did me in. Luckily, I take Kevin with me everywhere now."

"Kevin?" Fic asked.

She pointed to the pistol. "Kevin," she said. I named him after my big brother. He was always my protection growing up. He died last year. His essence is now in this pistol, protecting me still.

"Works for me," Fic said. "May he continue to protect you. You have come a long way."

They all went back to their beds, leaving Tucker lying dead in the woods behind the privy. They would deal with him in the daylight.

Shaken, Gnobbit told Finn that she didn't want to be in her tent alone and he climbed in with her. Class Room told Brown Shades she would relieve him now. She wouldn't be able to sleep much the rest of the night. The adrenaline was still flowing through her body and would be for some time.

"I'll keep you company," Fic said. "I'm pretty jazzed up too."

The camp grew quiet. Fic threw a couple small logs on the fire coals and in a few minutes, small flames started licking up and making the shadows nearby dance and flicker.

Fic had warned him not to come back. He paid the price for not listening.

#

Morning came, and the hikers arose to meet the day. Fic sat at the table drinking a cup of instant coffee. Gnobbit's tent zipped open, and Finn unfolded himself from the small two-person tent. Gnobbit came out next. The couple approached the table and sat close together, Finn placed a comforting arm around Gnobbit's shoulder that he left there for the duration of breakfast. Fic gave them a reassuring smile, glad that Gnobbit felt safe with Finn, The trail brought people together, even in the most dire situations.

Fic was in no hurry to deal with Tucker. He had threatened to leave him for the forest animals when he had first become their prisoner, but he was rethinking that promise. They didn't have a shovel, but some sort of preparation needed to be done to his body. More of a sanitary reason than a compassionate one. He didn't give a fuck about Tucker. The man had been let go, and warned to not come back, but he had still followed them. He got what he deserved. For Flo and for what he was planning to do with Class Room. The world was a better place without him.

After breakfast, they moved Tucker's body further back behind the privy and a little down a hillside. The area didn't appear to be used by the hikers much. There was a good supply of rocks at the bottom of the hill in a small gully, so they moved him down there and piled the rocks on him to form one of those graves they make in old westerns. It may keep the critters off, but Fic didn't really care. Once this current world condition resolved itself, then he could think about retrieving the body. Thinking of this reminded him that Lieutenant Pierce and Corporal McAfee were still in their graves up on a mountain in

Georgia. He also wondered about the status of his other men from the squad? All that seemed like a thousand years ago already. So much had happened in this one week training exercise that had grown to more than a month of traveling along a now dangerous trail. This was true survival. Not something that can be simulated in the woods over a few days. Him and the other members of The Party were pretty good at it.

They packed up and continued along the great Appalachian Trail. Pearisburg was now within two days' walk from here. Hopefully, they would be able to find Gnobbit's family when they got there.

"Where do you live in Pearisburg?" Fic asked Gnobbit as they slowly climbed up the next ridge.

"My Mom's house is on the southwest corner of town. About three or four blocks from Main Street. We will be able to get to it from Cross Avenue, which the trail crosses. It will be most of a mile to her house from the trail on the road."

#

During the day, they came to a sign that announced the Dismal Falls only three tenths of a mile down a side trail. After a short discussion, they decided to go check out the falls. The day was warm, and everyone was thinking that washing their clothes along with their bodies might be a good and refreshing idea. They had felt a subdued sense of relief when they left Jenny Knob Shelter and Tucker's body. At least they knew that Tucker or his men weren't actively chasing them now, but they also realized that the wanted poster was a little more accurate now.

They walked down the trail and could hear the falls. The roar of the cascade grew louder and louder as they approached. They passed through a small grove of white pine and came to the creek. The water swirled around large rocks and tumbled down the steep sides of the falls. The Party dropped their packs and found a nice pool of water about three feet deep. They all refreshed themselves for the next hour, then wrung out the water, put their shoes back on and continued down the trail.

They arrived at Wapiti Shelter in the early afternoon and decided to call it a day. The next shelter was another ten miles up the trail and they were still only a day's hike from Pearisburg. They would be able to get to Gnobbit's house by tomorrow afternoon.

They set up in and around the shelter. Gnobbit set up her tent next to the shelter and Finn didn't even bother to hang his hammock. They would be sharing sleeping space again tonight.

Rodent Whisperer started gathering wood and the others joined in. Finn held an impromptu training session on the kinds of natural resources that make the best tinder and kindling. He broke out his fire making kit and everyone tried their hand at getting an ember going. Rodent Whisperer was the lucky worker to get the hot, smoking coal that was able to produce a nice flame. As the fire started crackling, Finn took out his bow and everyone tried their hand at shooting some blunt arrows he had made at a makeshift target he set up next to a tree away from the shelter. Class Room and Gnobbit won the competition, with Fic placing a close third. As the forest darkened and the fire spit its sparks, Yuk came out and Class Room restored their strength and stamina with her soft, comforting music.

#

The next morning was foggy and misty. The visibility was only about fifty meters or so and the air had taken on a cool, clammy feel. The Party packed up and started walking.

They walked for a few hours before stopping for a break at a clearing next to the trail that had some nice fallen trees to sit on. They were the perfect height and there was room for everyone. Brown Shades felt something wriggling in his hair and pulled a small inch worm off of his head. He looked at it and mumbled some Latin name to himself then he tossed it into the woods next to the trees.

Fic saw something dangling from the brim of his hat. He took it off and there were three of the little critters attached to it. After that, each of the hikers found a few of the harmless but creepy larvae on their person. Either in their hair, or on their pack. Rodent Whisperer even picked several off of his kilt where they had hitch-hiked a ride.

As they continued on, they kept seeing more and more hanging from the trees on slender invisible silk threads. They were everywhere. When they stopped and listened, the sound of the creatures eating the leaves all around made a disgusting smacking noise. Soon they all noticed little brown and green dots of a liquid-like substance all over the leaves of the bushes and trees. "That's their feces," Brown Shades nonchalantly pointed out. The group — excluding Brown Shades who would stop and admire the worms every so often — were feeling creeped out and nauseated by the infestation around them, but they persevered, knowing their destination was on the other side.

Eventually the inchworm invasion subsided. Their numbers grew less and less until they had walked out of their zone. They spent at least fifteen minutes picking the critters off of their clothes, pack and bodies until they couldn't see any more. They were pretty sure that they would keep finding them hidden somewhere in their gear for the next few days.

#

They saw a sign for Angel's Rest Rock, next to a small trail that led to the edge of a cliff. Gnobbit convinced them all to come out and have a look. The sun had burned off the mist and fog and visibility was now several dozen miles. Far down in the valley, they could see a river snaking its way along. Next to that was the small town of Pearisburg, Virginia. "See that large parking lot in the middle?" Gnobbit asked. "Follow the road on the right. That goes right to my house. I think I can make it out, just barely."

They returned to the trail and started to head down, losing elevation as the trail approached the road that led to town. They reached the road and checked the area for soldiers. It seemed all clear.

They started carefully heading down the road, which continued to serpentine downhill as it made its way into town. They stuck close to the edge, ready to retreat into the woods if they heard anything coming. Gnobbit led them down several streets, navigating the area with ease. They could see people walking near Main Street, but the pedestrians paid them no mind or didn't see them. The last house on the lane was Gnobbit's. It was a small two-story house with a large yard. Blue shutters framed windows on the front and the siding was painted a dull yellow.

Gnobbit dropped her pack and ran to the front door. She opened the screen and tried to turn the knob. It was locked. She knocked a few times. When no one came, she looked over at a potted plant hanging on the porch. She went over and picked up a rock that was in the pot with the flowers. It wasn't actually a rock, but a key safe. She retrieved the key and opened the door.

Gnobbit entered the house, calling out to her mother and brother. No one answered.

The rest of The Party came into the house and dropped their packs. Finn had carried Gnobbit's gear inside.

Gnobbit searched the house. "They're not here now, but it looks like they had been here not too long ago. There are recently dirtied dishes in the sink and the coffee pot still had some cold coffee in it. Maybe they went into town for something," Gnobbit speculated.

They all gathered in the living room and sat down. The first thing they noticed was that the town had electricity. Gnobbit opened the refrigerator, and the light came on showing an almost empty box. There was some juice and condiments on the fridge door, a few eggs and a couple containers that looked like they held leftovers, and some veggies in the drawer.

When darkness arrived, they decided to send out a scout team to see what was up. Gnobbit led the way with Finn and Fic behind her. They only brought Kevin the handgun, because they didn't want to draw attention with a shotgun or rifle.

They slowly walked towards Main Street. When they reached the business center of the town, they turned right and walked down the sidewalk. They passed a closed gas station which was across the street and a block later a Post Office that had suffered an extensive fire. It wasn't burned to the ground, but they were pretty sure no mail was flowing through that building.

When they reached the Rite Aid — also closed — they crossed the street and headed back the way they had come. They could see a few people walking around, but Gnobbit didn't recognize anyone, and the people seemed to be avoiding them.

They got back to where they had started and decided to check out the Food Lion and other shops in the large parking lot. As they were walking down the long grassy area before the asphalt lot, they heard a vehicle coming down the road. They moved behind a small storage trailer that was parked at the back of the lot and watched the Humvee drive slowly down the street. It didn't slow or turn to where they were. It just continued down the street on a slow patrol.

They quickly crossed the parking lot and went to look inside the windows of the grocery store. It was closed, of course. They were walking along the front when a young woman came out of the store next to the Food Lion. She started when she saw them, almost turning back into the store she had just exited. "Susan," Gnobbit said excitedly. "It's me Carly."

"Carly? Oh my gosh it is you. How are you? Did you just get into town? Have you seen your mother? She is so worried about you," Susan said very quickly, not waiting for any answers. She held Gnobbit's hand in hers moving it up and down with each question.

Gnobbit gave her a quick version of where she had been and how she got here, then asked, "Where is my mother? I was at the house, and no one was there. Not her, not Billy. No one."

"They may be on a work party. The army is in control here and they treat us horribly, making us work for them," Susan explained. "You guys need to be careful. There is a curfew. I was trying to get home myself; I lost track of time."

They all quickly made their way back. Susan lived a block away in a small house also on the corner. She lived alone. "I've got some food I can bring over tomorrow morning. I'll see you then. Stay low and don't let the army see you."

"Thanks Susan," Gnobbit said. "We really appreciate it."

The three scouts headed back to the house and told the others what they had found out. They ate a meager meal and settled on the couches and floor. Finn and Gnobbit went up to her room for the night. They had become inseparable.

#

Fic was in a cabin again. Dressed in his warrior clothes once more. This was a different cabin. Large and roomy, with a warm glow that spread to every corner. A large fire was burning in the huge stone fireplace and candles were lit in sconces all around the main room of the cabin. A large, wooden table occupied the center of the room and sitting all around it were Fic's friends and companions. At the head of the table sat Gnobbit. She wasn't wearing her usual black, rough clothing, but had on a fine felt jacket that was still black but trimmed in gold thread. A delicate tiara sat on her head, blending well with her short hair above her pointed ears. Beside her sat the noble elf, Finn. His green clothes also looked a grade above the normal tanned and dyed leather he wore when Warrior Fic first encountered the elf. But back then he hadn't known the elf's name. He too wore a small crown of golden woven vines with silver leaves spaced evenly throughout. Smiles were pasted on each of their faces.

The table was full of food. A wonderful feast had been prepared. A celebration was taking place. Along the sides of the table, the rest of The Party were seated. Next to Finn, sat Rodent Whisperer, the mighty dwarf. His bushy beard held bits and pieces of food. He was happily devouring a huge turkey leg that had been pulled off the very large turkey that dominated the laid out food. Next to Gnobbit, sat Class Room. Her lute in her hands, softly strumming a pleasant tune that made everyone feel content.

Brown Shades sat sipping a very large mug of what appeared to be a dark beer or ale. He raised his flagon towards the head of the table and shouted, "Huzzah," to the happy couple. "May your days together always be a delight." He chugged the beverage and let out a loud burp. The others clapped their approval.

An empty chair sat next to Class Room and Fic came around and sat there. Reaching for a large roll and buttering it with the cool crock of butter that sat on the table. He took a bite and felt as if he had gone to heaven. The roll was still warm, and the butter had a richness he hadn't tasted in a long time.

The feast seemed to last a long time. Each of the others stood and made a speech. All devoted to their admiration of both Gnobbit and Finn. When it was Fic's turn, he stood and didn't know what to say. He looked at the two at the head of the table. No words came.

Gnobbit rose and came to where Fic was standing. She reached up, placing both hands on the side of his head and pulled him towards her. She gave him a long kiss on his cheek and whispered, "Thank you for getting me home. I don't think I would have made it without you. Also, thank you for bringing me Finn." She winked and kissed him again. Turning, she returned to her seat at the head of the table.

Just then, a dog came padding out from the darkened room that was off to the left in the cabin. Fic looked closely at the canine and noticed it wasn't a dog at all, but a fox.

The scene faded and Fic turned restlessly. He didn't wake up but fell into a deeper sleep until morning came to the house on the lane.

#

An interesting, dreamy night was followed by a gray morning. Rain was once again in the forecast. The hikers arose from their sleeping spaces and started an unfamiliar morning routine. Being inside, with electricity and running water, had become foreign to them.

"I had the strangest dream last night," said Rodent Whisperer. "I was a dwarf, and we were at a celebration of the happy couple here."

Fic stared at him for several seconds and suddenly Brown Shades said, "I think I had the same dream."

Fic shifted his gaze to Brown Shades, when Gnobbit, Finn and Class Room all chimed in at the same time that they too had a very similar dream. Finally, Fic too admitted that he had a number of dreams in which they were all fantasy characters and it seemed that the dreams had a way of foreseeing the future.

They spent the next thirty minutes talking about the dreams that they all had over the last several weeks and how they all seemed to be the same dream, although with minor differences for each person. "I dreamed of you two showing up," said Brown Shades with a nod. "A warrior and a thief," he added, winking at Gnobbit, who smiled back.

Everyone was amazed and a little freaked out by what was happening. Were they psychically connected somehow? No one could explain how this was happening.

#

Shortly before seven, a soft knock on the door found Susan. She was carrying a large tray covered with a towel. They let her in and she set the tray on the kitchen table. When she removed the cloth, they saw quite a breakfast spread before them. Eggs, pancakes, sausage, juice, toast, the works. "I have a pretty extensive pantry. The fresh eggs come from the Libby's place. They still have a bunch of chickens," she said to Gnobbit, who nodded in understanding.

"Thank you so much. Are you sure you can spare all this?" Gnobbit asked.

"I have a lot," she responded.

The Party sat around the large kitchen table and ate a wonderful meal — an echo of the shared dream. As they ate, Susan told them about what had happened here in Pearisburg when the war came and went.

"Basically, the power had gone out on June 6th along with all communications, and two days later, a long line of military vehicles had entered the town and basically took over. They said they were here to help with the transition to the new leadership of The Regime, led by Richard Flaherty — or The Boss, as we're forced to call him — and we were now under their *protection*.

By protection they meant they could harass us and order us around, and for some, it meant a bullet in the brain.

"We quickly realized that resistance was futile. At least for now. About two weeks later, when we were now under the thumb of Colonel Branson and his goons, we started hearing about The Resistance. Some of us have been helping when we can, but we have to be careful.

"The army have settled into a routine and think they have pacified us. They turned on the electricity, but there are still no communications in or out and no TV. Blake Speers had a ham radio set up in his basement that hasn't been found yet. He had to move the antenna into the woods and put it up in a tree to avoid discovery. We have been in contact with Resistance fighters.

"Your mother and brother have been working over at the Celanese Plant across the river. I'm not sure what they are doing there, but I don't think it is making filters for cigarettes anymore. They usually are picked up in a large truck in the morning and come back a couple days later. Tired looking and a little scared. They don't talk about what they were doing, they seem like they are afraid to.

"It's still dangerous to stay here. If you guys stick around, it is only a matter of time before the army notices you. And I just realized that you guys must be The Party. The soldiers were talking about you about a week ago but hadn't said much since then. Did you really kill two soldiers?"

After assuring her that the wanted poster was a lie and explaining what had happened in Hampton, Susan seemed satisfied with their story. They left out the part about Tucker. It seemed like the prudent thing to do.

The hikers sat talking about what they should do next. It seemed that the six of them shouldn't be seen together as a group, because that might stir some ideas that they are the badly drawn figures on the wanted poster that must have made its way here.

"I need to find my mother and brother," Gnobbit said. "You guys should continue on. Try to get home. I'm home now and my journey is over. I would never have made it without your help." She looked at the other members of The Party. Tears were welling in her eyes and this started a round of hugging.

"I'm staying with you," Finn said matter-of-factly, looking down at Gnobbit from his high height.

She looked up into his eyes and nodded her head. "But what about your family?" she asked.

"You're my family now. Eventually, I may get back to see what is up, but there's no hurry. My family, as it is, probably hasn't noticed that I never came back from college. We aren't really close."

"You are going to have to be careful," Susan warned. "You kind of stand out here. Your height alone will make people notice you. That hair is a beacon to the others to check you out."

Gnobbit went into the pantry next to the kitchen and brought out several cans of food and some rice and beans. "I know this shit is heavy, but you need to re-supply. Take it all."

The hikers gathered all of their gear and prepared to leave. They would wait until darkness. The less they are seen, the better it will be.

Susan left to go to work at her little store next to the Food Lion. "Stay low, be safe and good luck," she said to The Party as she left with the tray of empty plates and bowls.

Gnobbit hugged her and closed the door behind her. She turned to the others and said, "Now we wait for dark."

#

At around 1600 a large open truck came rumbling down the street. Stopping from time to time along the way until it pulled up next to Gnobbit's house. Two figures climbed down from the back of the truck and walked to the porch.

Gnobbit stood at the front of the group who tried to be as unthreatening as possible to avoid alarming the woman and teenage boy who came walking through the door.

"Mom," Gnobbit said to the woman.

"Carly!" the woman responded. She dropped her small backpack and ran to her daughter. The boy came along behind, a surprised smile on his face. He saw the others standing behind his sister and a look of alarm, then one of understanding came across his face. He went to add his arms to the hug that was taking place in front of him. "How did you get here?" Her mother asked after pulling back and looking at her daughter with tears of joy in her eyes.

"I walked," she replied.

#

When the reunion had calmed down some. Gnobbit's mother was introduced to The Party. "This is my mom, June," Gnobbit said. "And my brother, Kip." Hands were shook all around along with a few hugs. Kip was so happy to see his sister, that he just stood over by the table as silent tears ran down his face. "I missed you so much," he said, his voice catching. "I thought you were maybe dead."

Gnobbit reached up and gave him a kiss on the cheek. "Naw," she said. "There's no way I wasn't gonna get home. I had a lot of help, but I would have done it alone if I had to."

Gnobbit sat at the kitchen table and told her family the story of her hike. The bombs she saw, meeting Fic and the others, the obstacles along the way. Finally, she laid her hand on Finn's who was sitting beside her. "Finn is thinking of staying here for a while," she explained to her Mom.

June smiled and put her hand on the couple's clasped hands. "You are welcome here Finn. Is that your real name or some trail name?" she asked.

"Well, sorta both," he said. "My name is Marty Findley. People have been calling me Finn pretty much my whole life. I intend to help out here wherever I can."

"Your name is Marty?" Gnobbit asked, smiling at her new beau.

"Yes, Carly, it is," he smiled back. "That's weird, but I guess I can get used to saying it. You can still just call me Finn."

"I'm still Gnobbit. This experience has changed me so much, I don't feel like Carly anymore."

After they discussed what they were planning to do, June went back into her pantry and came out with even more food, and she insisted they take it. "We can get more food around here. Take it all." June started handing cans and boxes of food to the hikers. They each took some with grateful thanks.

After shoving as much food as they could into their packs, they waited for the sun to set. Fic was starting to get antsy. They had relaxed most of the day, and now he was ready to get walking again. He still had many miles to go to be reunited with his family. Seeing Gnobbit returned home, made him all the more anxious to get to his home.

When the street was dark enough, the four hikers stood on the porch, ready to go.

Fic walked over to Gnobbit. Smiling down at her, "I am really gonna miss you, Gnobbit." She threw her arms around him, hugging him tight as tears fell from her eyes.

"Me too, Fic," she replied.

"When this is over, we will be back to see how you are doing," Fic said.

"Okay, I'm gonna hold you to that," Gnobbit said.

Fic reached his hand out to shake with Finn, pulling him into a hug. "Take care, son. It was good having you along for a while. Take good care of each other."

"I will. I'm really looking forward to getting to know Carly and her family."

After everyone said their goodbyes, they headed down the street where they had come in and walked back to the trail. The road was empty, the forest dark. When they got back to the trail they turned right and reentered the woods. After about a mile, they came to a short road walk. This was the area of the factory where June and Kip had been working. They moved as fast as they could to get past the factory, which had numerous lights glowing and seemed to be bustling with activity. They got past it without attracting any attention and got back into the darkness of the woods.

Everyone was energized by the experiences of the day and ready to walk a few miles in the dark. There was no moon and the rain that had fallen during the day while they were inside was threatening to return.

It was close to midnight when they walked into the Rice Field Shelter at the top of the ridge on the edge of a grassy field. The four hikers all set up quickly in the shelter and fell asleep instantly.

#

For the next three days, the four hikers did nothing more than the normal hiker routine. The monotony of walking, eating and sleeping consumed their days. They made the miles they needed to, to get up the trail, exhausted at the end of each day. Nothing out of the ordinary happened. The road crossings were quiet and peaceful, the terrain was negotiated. The hikers walked on. A mountain would be climbed, and the next one would show itself in front of them. They continued to put one foot in front of the other.

They did sixteen miles the first day and twenty-one the next. After the third day of another sixteen miles, they found themselves at Pickle Branch Shelter. The uneventful days and lack of dangerous encounters had started to make this feel like just a regular long-distance hike. The day before, the hikers had stood in awe, looking up into the expansive limbs of the Keffer Oak; sitting right next to the trail with a small sign announcing its title. They had even stopped off at the Audie Murphy Memorial to pay their respects to the most decorated World War II vet, who had died near there in a plane crash decades ago. They saw no army soldiers trying to find them. The only thing that set this apart from an ordinary hike was that they didn't see any other hikers. It was as if they had the whole trail to themselves. Alone in the mountains to fend for themselves.

#

It was a Friday morning. The sky threatened rain as they walked up the blue-blazed trail that ran from the shelter, back to the A.T.

The trail had a steady climb up the next ridge. There were lots of switchbacks to get up onto the mountain, then a steady rise in elevation as they walked the crest. Near the top was the first of the Virginia Triple Crown — Dragon's Tooth — a spire of rock rising up into the sky at the top of the ridge. As the hikers checked out the formation, a light drizzle started to fall.

They realized the challenge of a technical trail as they descended from the pinnacle. The trail had become a vertical rock climb that required everyone to use four limbs to negotiate the rocky, steep pathway. When they finally got to the bottom, they came to a road. A small sign pointed up the way to the Four Pines Hostel.

They had only walked about seven or eight miles so far that day, but they decided to head up to the hostel to see if there was a hiker box they could hopefully find some food in.

They quickly walked up the quiet country road. The hostel was actually a homestead of an eccentric old man who liked to give his hiker guests good-natured jests. As they walked up the driveway to the buildings, the old man came out of his house with a shotgun cradled under his arm. "You guys hikers?" he asked, his bushy eyebrows moving up and down with each word. His mouth was lost in a bushy gray beard.

"Yes, we are," replied Fic. "We were just wondering if we could look through your hiker box for some food. It's been really hard to find food for sale and we are starting to run a little low."

"You're welcome to take a look, but I'm not sure there is much in it. The hostel is around back in the large garage. If you are looking for a bed tonight, I'm still open for business. Donation based of course."

They walked up to the garage/hostel and went inside. There was a large table to their right as they entered, and beyond that a small bathroom. Next to the table was a mishmash of assorted sofas and chairs. The rest of the building was taken up by several bunk beds built from two by eight boards and plywood. Basic and rough, but under a roof and out of the still falling light rain.

They found the hiker box and rummaged through it. The proprietor was right; the pickings were slim. They did find a few items to take, but it probably wasn't enough to get them to Daleville, the next town they would walk through.

As they sat inside, discussing whether to continue on or stay here for the night, the old man came walking into the building. He no longer had his shotgun, but an old dog followed him inside.

"I'm Kyle," the man said. "This is my place. Have you decided to spend the night?"

"Yes, we were thinking of doing just that, but we are all pretty low on cash and haven't had any way to replenish our wallets as we have been moving north in this chaotic world," Fic explained.

"I'm not so much worried about money. This is a time to help each other out. Are you going all the way? Still?" Kyle asked.

"No, not all the way. We are all just trying to get home. I live in Northern Virginia, Brown Shades here is from Pennsylvania, Class Room next to him is from New Jersey, and Rodent Whisperer there is from Scotland. We haven't figured out how he is going to get home yet," Fic had pointed to each hiker as he introduced them. They each nodded as he stated their goals.

"I'll tell you what, we have a couple chickens we just butchered. My wife, Lilly, was thinking of frying them all up today. We will gladly feed you. We'll figure out payment later. I have a few chores that might even get you some real hiker food instead of the pickings you just went through."

The promise of a fresh, home cooked chicken dinner sealed the deal for The Party. "Aye, we will definitely accept that offer," said Rodent Whisperer. "It will be good to do something besides walking all day. This short day is earned, I say." He looked to Kyle to receive a job to do. "What can I do to earn that keep?"

Kyle had a number of chores to do around the farm. The four hikers were each given something to do that wouldn't get them too wet outside and would earn them a nice meal and a dry place to sleep for the night.

They each claimed a bunk and set up their sleeping bags. Lilly served them a feast that had them sitting around the fire that Kyle had made outside the hostel, feeling content for the time being. The rain had stopped while they ate dinner inside. The surrounding farm dripped, and trickles of water ran down the hill, but nothing was coming out of the sky for now.

Yuk came out and filled the air with soft tunes that melted into the air above the crackling fire.

"This was a good idea," Brown Shades said. "I do miss Gnobbit and Finn though." Everyone nodded their agreement. This was the first time their group shrank instead of growing. They were still The Party, just slightly smaller.

Class Room had been a little different since leaving Pearisburg. Actually, her transition had happened after Tucker's death. She had hardened. Killing him had helped her get over her slump from shooting Kirk. The anger she had felt as he had grabbed her, knowing the evil that resided within this man, had made it easier to accept her role of ending his life. She was at peace with her current situation. No longer afraid to defend herself or protect others. Kevin still accompanied her in her waistband. Never leaving her side.

#

They slept well in the hostel as the rain returned during the night. By morning, it had stopped, and the day dawned bright and fresh.

Kyle brought a box of hiker food that he had kept in his house for times when hikers had empty food bags. They filled their food bags with the provided food.

"Your work yesterday was payment enough for your stay," Kyle said. "Keep your heads low and stay safe."

They thanked Kyle and Lilly for the great hospitality and headed back to the trail.

#

The first part of the day was very easy. They moved fast and came to a large parking lot where the trail crossed a road. They were approaching McAfee Knob. A famous place on the trail where a lot of people get their photo taken on a rock outcropping that looks precarious.

When they walked through the parking lot, they noticed that a couple cars were in the spaces. They wondered if they would finally see some other hikers on the trail today and if it would be a safe encounter if they did.

They crossed the road and started up the climb that led to the overlook. The day was getting hotter, and they were pretty soaked with sweat when they reached the top. They hadn't seen anyone on the way up, but when they walked out to the overlook, there were three women sitting at the rocks. They looked surprised to see hikers with backpacks and they stared at them and the weapons they were carrying.

Fic tried not to look threatening. Lowering the shotgun and smiling towards the women. "Hello," he said. The others with him smiled and nodded themselves.

The women relaxed a little seeing their friendliness and seeing Class Room with them helped even more. They approached the women and began to talk with them.

They didn't reveal a lot about themselves, just that they were heading north. The women had come from Daleville. They said that things were fairly normal there. The army did come through every couple of days, but they were mostly leaving them alone. The electricity was usually on and the stores were open during the day.

Fic told them that they planned on hiking into town tomorrow and the women told them to come to the small convenience store at the gas station across the street from the Howard Johnson and next to the Pizza Hut. They would be able to help them out with some food and other treats.

The Party thanked them profusely and started to head out.

"Wait," one of the women said, "can I take your picture on the overhang?"

"Sure," all the hikers said together.

They stood on the edge of the rock ledge and the woman took their picture from across the cliff. She showed them the picture and asked for their email addresses, so she could send it to them.

"You have Internet?" Class Room asked hopefully.

"Well, not at the moment, but we are hoping that things will get back to normal before too long," she said. "I'm Carol, by the way. This is Lisa, and that's Britney."

"My daughter's name is Brittney," Fic said, a little sadness crept into his voice. "She's up in Northern Virginia. I'm hoping to get back there as soon as I can."

They wrote down their email addresses for the women and prepared to leave.

"We'll see you tomorrow," Carol said, smiling at the hikers who had just walked into her life.

They walked along the ridge next to the last part of the Triple Crown — Tinker Cliffs. The drop-off was impressive as the trail ran next to the edge. When the trail turned away from the cliffs, it started to head downhill. They walked a couple more miles and arrived at the Lambert Meadows Shelter. This would be their home for the night.

Brown Shades hung his hammock down by the creek and the other three slept in the shelter. As darkness came to the campsite after dinner, they talked about what the town visit would be like tomorrow. Were things starting to get back to normal again, where people could go out on day hikes and take pictures? The stores will be open. Too bad their cash supply was still rather low.

Meeting another Brittney out here brought thoughts of home back into Fic's mind. He wondered how his daughter was doing, how his wife and son were holding up, and if their farmhouse was still a safe place.

CHAPTER 15
HOME FRONT IV - SATURDAY, JULY 21ST

Brittney was driving a quad down a dirt driveway. A white farmhouse could be seen at the end of the lane. A large red barn, its paint faded and peeling, was off to her right. On the other side of the house was a small unpainted shed. A large amount of smoke was rising into the air behind the building.

A hunting rifle was slung over her shoulders across her chest. She was on patrol alone — the way she had come to prefer. This was the homestead of Jules McCreary. She was an older woman, her husband long dead, and any children grown and moved on. The farm hadn't been planted in several seasons, and the fields had become fallow and weed strewn.

The quad pulled into the courtyard between the house and other buildings and came to a stop. The smoke from the fire was very black; she wondered what kind of trash Mrs. McCreary was burning over by the shed. Brittney turned off the quad and dismounted. She went to the front door of the house and knocked. There was no answer.

Her patrols for the last few days involved slowly driving from one house to the next, checking on the residents and seeing if there was anything that could be donated to the cause or traded for something else. It kept the inhabitants in touch and made sure no one was going hungry or having any trouble.

Her brother was doing the same thing in a different area. She hadn't seen him for about three days now. Lately, they had been doing this to avoid patrolling with Jim and his minions. She had compared notes with Shane and come to the conclusion that something wasn't quite right with the Blue Mountain Patrol. At least under the leadership of Jim. It seemed that the benevolent assistance they had been providing to the local residents had warped into something else. Almost like a protection racket. It seemed that Jim was starting to demand more from the people he was protecting. His closest followers had started to follow his lead and it seemed that whenever she pulled into a homestead, a look of fear passed across the neighbors' faces before they realized it was her. She wondered what that meant.

When no one answered the door, she went over to check out the fire. It had to have been set not too long ago. When she walked around the shed, she was hit with an intense and foul odor. The smell of burning rubber, mixed with something else. Something like burned meat hit her hard. As she checked out the fire, she saw that it was tires that were on fire.

The thick black smoke curled out of the bright orange flames. Lingering above the pit before rising up into the air and being swept away by the wind. There was something below the tires. She couldn't quite make out what it was. She circled around the fire and on the other side she saw something that froze her blood. A hand, old and wrinkled, stuck out from under the tires. That looked like Mrs. McCreary's hand.

Brittney shrunk back from the fire, un-slinging her rifle and making sure there was a round in the chamber. She looked around the courtyard for any signs of another person. That old woman didn't get under those burning tires all alone.

When she looked at the courtyard carefully, she saw an extra set of tire prints like the ones she had made coming into the area. Someone on a quad had been here not too long ago.

She went to check the door and found it unlocked. When she went inside, she saw that the place had been ransacked. The kitchen was a mess, the cabinets contents strewn all about. The pantry looked as if it had been raided. Brittney felt tears come to her eyes. The Patrol had failed to do the one thing they had pledged to do. They had failed to protect the residents of their little valley next to the river. Someone had breached their perimeter and attacked one of their own.

Brittney jumped onto her quad, fired it up, and sped down the driveway. She needed to tell her mother and brother what she had found.

CHAPTER 16
PUSHING NORTH - SUNDAY, JULY 22ND TO THURSDAY, JULY 26TH

Morning brought more fog and a light mist for a few hours. It burned off quickly as the four hikers traversed the last ten miles to town. Approaching with caution as usual, they heard a bit of traffic on the road before the noise faded away into the distance. They moved through the last line of trees and high grass. Across the highway and to their right was the red roof of the GB gas station. Further on was the red roof of the Pizza Hut. They hurried across Route 220 to the gas station. It was getting close to lunchtime, so everyone was more hungry than usual. They could smell the smoking meat as they approached the building which started their saliva flowing. It smelled divine.

They put their packs down around the corner of the building, just past the source of the delicious smell, and went inside the open store. The bell tingled as they entered. In front of them was a large meat counter. It was mostly empty, except for a few items in the case. The shelves of the store were also quite bare.

Carol was behind the counter. She smiled at them, but the smile had a strange, strained flavor to it that put Fic on his guard.

She greeted the hikers and told them to come over to the register. She seemed a bit nervous. Something had changed.

"Are you okay, Carol?" Fic asked, concern in his voice.

"I'm fine. Just a little on edge," Carol began. "After we left the Knob yesterday, we were discussing your plight on our way back to the car and we figured out who you were. Since there were only four of you, we were skeptical at first, but after thinking about what you said about your trek, we realized that you were the notorious Party that we had been warned about.

They say you guys are mad killers out in the mountains, who come into towns, kill a bunch of residents, and then steal all that you can." Tears were welling in her eyes, but her expression also appeared fierce. Fic noticed that a handgun was sitting on the counter in front of Carol. He made a note but didn't mention it.

"Those stories are a little embellished I would say," Brown Shades said, looking at Carol in the eye with a serious expression. "We have been harassed by the Flarmy all the way from Georgia, but anything we did was to defend ourselves or those with us. We are not murderers, and we don't kill residents."

"I felt that way yesterday, but we have just become a little leery of things now. I still want to help you guys, but you will need to get moving soon. If The Regime comes through on a patrol, they might be quicker to figure out who you are, and they certainly do believe the wanted posters. I smoked up some brisket this morning, in preparation for your arrival. I can make everyone a foot long sandwich, with some cheese and onion. To go, of course. I don't have a lot more, but you can take whatever you need that you find in the aisles."

"We want to pay you," said Class Room. "We don't have a lot of cash, but we want to give you what we can."

"You guys still have a long way to go," said Carol. "I have your email addresses. I will send you each an email with an IOU, well actually a, You Owe Me, and we can settle up when this calms down, and things get back to normal."

"Deal," Fic said. "We really appreciate this, and I assure you, we are good people, just trying to get home, and your help will get us there."

The Party filled their food bags. Each time they restocked, they extended their range just a little further. Of course, they would be looking for food in just a few more days, because they don't carry a lot — just enough to get them a few more days down the trail.

They all put their freshly wrapped foot long sandwiches in the top of their bags and thanked Carol profusely. They wrote down Carol's addresses too, both email and actual location of the station so they could get in touch with her when everything was back to normal again. Whatever that may mean now.

The Party threw their packs on and walked back to where the trail headed into the trees on their side of the road. The trail started to climb as soon as it left the road. After crossing under Interstate 81, the Lee Highway, and one other road, they were back in the forest and slowly gaining elevation.

When they reached the top of Fullhardt Knob, they stopped at the shelter there and ate half of their sandwiches, saving the rest for later. Rodent Whisperer had planned to do that too, but his sandwich was gone before he knew it. He smacked his lips and rubbed his stomach, smiling pleasantly and feeling satisfied. "Ahh," he said with a long sigh, "that was some tidy scran." Smacking his lips once more.

After eating, they continued along the ridge crest for a few miles. Following its slight ups and downs, then heading down into a valley and following that until they arrived at Wilson Creek Shelter.

For a very long time during this trek, the shelters had been vacant and lonely when they rolled into camp each night. It had been quite a while since they had encountered another hiker — either out on the trail, at a shelter, or in or near town. When they walked up to this shelter, however, they could tell it was occupied.

Half the shelter was full of someone's strewn out gear. An orange sleeping pad had a blue bag laying on it and behind that was a gray pack. There was a clothesline strewn across the front of the shelter and several pieces of laundry hung to dry. There was no hiker around to claim the gear.

The hikers turned and looked into the woods. All they saw was the late afternoon sun dappling its green beams to and fro as a slight breeze filtered through the forest.

They dropped their packs and casually walked around the camp, looking for some sign of a hiker in the area.

They were sitting around the picnic table when a man came walking up from the hillside with three water bottles in his hand. He was startled when he saw them and froze in his tracks. He was of medium height, with a full red beard of substantial length. He looked to be wearing nothing but his long underwear. An old red ball cap sat on his head, slightly askew. The hat had a brim that was full of holes, and the plastic support showed through in several places.

The hikers watched the man as they could plainly see options running around in his head. It looked like several were offered and rejected before he decided to just finish what he was doing.

"Hello," he said. "I haven't seen another hiker in weeks. I'm Ragged."

The others smiled at the hiker and invited him to the table. "I think I remember seeing your entries in the shelter log way back in Georgia. Have you been in front of us all this time?" Fic asked.

"I guess so. My trek has been an interesting one. I've been mostly avoiding everyone and every place. I do my resupply at night, sometimes without my benefactors knowing until later," he smiled. "I've become tired of hiking, and I decided to spend several days just not walking. I've been here almost a week now."

The conversation drifted from topic to topic as they told stories and passed information back and forth. Ragged had been gathering wood for days, so they started a nice fire and Yuk made her appearance as they all lazed around the fire, telling their tales and actually feeling revitalized for a while.

The calm, peaceful, music and stimulating conversation momentarily distracted Fic from the constantly repeating questions in his mind of his family's situation. But the respite was short-lived. Tomorrow would be another day of walking. Danger still waited out there, and as they had found out in Daleville, they still hadn't out walked their wanted poster. In fact, the stories had become larger and even more untrue. Would they ever get far enough away from Boots Off to breathe a little easier?

These thoughts filled Fic's head as everyone headed to their sleeping positions for the night.

#

The next morning, The Party was all set to go. They asked Ragged if he wanted to join them as they headed north, but he declined.

"I'm just gonna hang out here for a couple more days. My knee has been bothering me a lot and sitting around and not hiking has made it feel a lot better the last couple of days," he told them. They wished him well and headed out from the shelter area and back onto the trail.

#

The next four days were a blur. They continued the best they could as the miles went by and the sun made its journey across the sky. Trekking through humid heat, rain — both heavy and light — and sporadic wind as the forest moved to the whims of the Mother's nature.

Hunger set in as their food bags became more and more empty along with their stomachs. Climbing each mountain became a chore and their rest periods became longer and more frequent.

#

The party was taking a break. Each of the hikers was eating a little snack from their almost empty food bags. They were in a small clearing next to the trail. Large oak trees surrounded them. A cardinal alighted on a long branch of one of the oaks and started singing. It would fly to another tree and sing a few notes, then fly to another branch on another tree. It seemed to be checking them out as they sat in the clearing, completely circling them as it moved from tree to tree. It gave one final high-pitched chirp and flew off towards the north.

The break was over, and the hikers stowed their food bags, hefted their packs, and continued down the trail. The terrain had been easy so far this morning, but now they started a long, slow climb back up onto the ridge. There were switchbacks every so often and Fic was in the lead. As he turned a corner, the trail ran a long straight way before turning again. He had an excellent view of the path for several hundred meters. Sitting up ahead — in the middle of the trail — was a fox. The fox's fur was a dark reddish color. His feet and tip of the tail were black. He sat looking curiously at The Party as they slowly made their way up the mountain.

Fic stopped and stared curiously at the fox. It was clearly following their progress. Fic turned around to the group who had also come to a stop behind him and said, "Check out that fox." He turned around to point at the animal, but the trail was empty. Fic drew his gaze up and down the mountain to reacquire the fox, but it had disappeared. Just as mysteriously as it has appeared.

"What fox?" asked Brown Shades, looking over his shoulder and up the way.

"There was a fox sitting right on the trail, looking at us," Fic replied.

"If you say so," answered Brown Shades.

#

The Party eventually reached the top of the mountain. There was a clearing at the top that had been used as a campsite for several years. A large fire ring dominated the middle of the clearing. Arranged around the fire were long trunks of trees that sat in front of massive rocks, both serving as rudimentary seats. Sitting on one rock, was a young man. A pack sat on the ground beside him, an open book in his hands as he watched the hikers approach, a neutral expression on his face.

Fic approached the fellow hiker and waved a greeting. "Hi, I'm Fic," he said. The young man nodded in return, a slight smile tugged at the corner of his mouth. As the other members of the party finished the climb up the mountain and entered the clearing, Fic would introduce them to the youth. He would nod and smile but remained silent.

Each of The Party dropped their packs and got comfortable. Digging into their food bags, looking for any last remnants to eat.

The curious, smiling stranger reached into his pack and removed a large Ziploc bag full of food: candy, crackers, beef sticks and cheese. All sorts of appetizing snacks. "Here, have some food," he said, laying the bag on the ground in front of the hikers. "I'm Kitsune. I was wondering when you would arrive," he said, smiling at the group. "I want to join your Party."

CHAPTER 17
BLUE MOUNTAIN PATROL - THURSDAY, JULY 26TH

Jim Henry sat in a pickup truck on a small dirt road with trees lining both sides. Beside him sat Steve Dury, one of the Blue Mountain Patrol members. Steve had a worried look on his face. Almost as if he was feeling nauseous.

"I don't know, Jim," said Steve. "I don't think we should be doing these things to those people. We were supposed to be helping them, not killing them."

"Shut your damn mouth, Steve," Jim yelled in the man's face. "We do a lot of hard work here and deserve some 'French Benefits.' It's not my fault some of them try to resist our demands." The fact that he mangled the phrase was not noticed by either man.

"This isn't what I signed up for, Jim. I was perfectly happy helping the people of this valley. Yeah, the power did go to my head for a bit, but I think we took it too far. This ain't right." Steve's voice was shaky now and he seemed to be on the edge of tears.

"Well, I'll tell you what, Steve, you better stay in line and keep your mouth shut or you just might find out what the smell of burning tires is like up close," Jim threatened.

"I ain't gonna say anything, Jim, but we gotta be more careful or this is gonna come back and bite us in the ass," Steve said as he looked out the truck's window and down the lane.

CHAPTER 18
WAYNESBORO - SATURDAY, JULY 28TH TO SUNDAY, JULY 29TH

The Party walked up the last incline of the path before the road. Fic, in the lead, could see a guardrail at the top of the climb. High grass grew on each side of the trail and the sun was shining brightly on the green blades of grass and the contrasting dark brown dirt of the trail. Fic came to the guardrail and stepped over.

Behind him was Brown Shades, his staff ticking on the hard packed dirt and his glasses their darkest shade in the bright sunlight. He too came to the guardrail, looked up and down the road, then stepped over, just as Fic had.

Next in line was Rodent Whisperer. His large boots stood out as he walked up the trail. Above the boots were bare hairy legs and above that a brown kilt wrapped around his waist. His large, wooden cross swung back and forth. He stood at the guardrail and waited for the hiker behind him.

Class Room's face smiled out of her long black hair. Her brown eyes sparkled as she playfully knocked away the hand Rodent Whisperer offered to help her step over. "I got it, you old dwarf," she said with a laugh, lightly stepping her long legs over the rail and moving to the right. Rodent Whisperer smiled back at her and followed her over the barrier.

Last came the agile form of Kitsune, the newest member of The Party. His light brown skin glowed in the sunlight. A knitted cap with fox ears covered his short-cropped, tightly curled black hair. He had a small pack. A toy fox, like the ones that dogs play with, that have no filling, was attached to his pack. The long tail swung back and forth as he walked along. A short Katana knife was in a sheath on his belt. The top of a small mass-market paperback could be seen poking out of his back pocket. Kitsune came to the guardrail and stood looking at the other members of his new group. His slight smile said that he was happy to be with this crew. He had watched them a lot before joining them two days ago. Moving around them in the forest as he figured out who they were and what their quest was.

He stepped over the guardrail then looked back down the trail. No one was there. No one was on the road either. The place was completely deserted. It was hard to believe that they were at the gates of a very popular national park. One that saw millions of visitors a year. The great Shenandoah National Park. A mountainous, forested land, spanning over a hundred miles. There was a twisty, turny road that ran the length of the park. Skyline Drive was its name. The trail ran alongside this road, crossing it many times.

Smiling at The Party in front of him, he started to follow them. All was clear. Kitsune thought about Gnobbit and Finn, the group's prior scouts. Even though he hadn't met these two, he still felt like he knew them as the others had told him many stories from their travels before meeting him, mentioning Gnobbit's and Finn's exploits along the way. Kitsune had taken over their role of scouting road crossings. He seemed to be just as stealthy as the short thief and the tall elf.

The trail followed the road for a bit, and they came to a small parking lot with a welcome kiosk. The Party gathered on the grass next to the information sign. They each had a bit of food that Kitsune had provided when he joined them. He had a huge zip-lock bag full of an assortment of different food that he had "discovered" along the way before meeting The Party. He had distributed it to the others with relish, enjoying the laughs of delight when someone would exclaim in surprise and glee when they saw something that they had been craving. They had all pretty much been craving everything though. Food had become scarce along the trail. The whole area seemed to be vacant of people and a lot of them had taken all they could before leaving. They could still find some things that had been forgotten or left behind, but it had been a while since they had eaten a large hearty meal. Kitsune's gift had been perfect, but they continued to ration what they had as they moved north along the trail.

Now, The Party was trying to decide if they should continue along the trail, or head into the small town of Waynesboro, Virginia, just a few miles to the west. Fic knew from his guide that it was about three and a half miles to the edge of town. They didn't know what they would find there, but after each of them had checked their food bags and found them lacking, they all voted to try heading into town to see what they could find.

They had only walked about five miles so far in the day, but this detour was necessary. Their bellies insisted.

They crossed the road and bushwhacked down a short hillside to the road to town. Across the way was an old, abandoned gas station. It looked like it had been that way for some time. Well before the fall. They all picked around the buildings anyway, finding nothing useful.

Each continued towards town separately, after satisfying their curiosity. Walking along the shoulder, getting spread out along the way. Kitsune was still in the rear and after a while the twists and turns dropped him out of sight of the others.

The day had become hot as they moved along the road. They made their way to the edge of town. No cars came past them. They couldn't hear any vehicles on the roads nearby. Most notably absent was any traffic on I-64, which they had crossed under as they started heading towards town.

As Fic walked along, a cardinal came flying past. It appeared to be on a mission. It would dip down by each of the hikers as it passed them, as if it was checking on them. It disappeared ahead of them around the next bend in the road.

About an hour later, they came to a single story building that had an old Pepsi sign at one end of the building. Fic walked up on the porch of the building and looked into the glass doors. It was dark inside, but he saw that the doors weren't locked. Well, they weren't locked anymore. Someone had taken a crowbar to the lock and pried the doors open. He went to the side of the building and waited for the others to catch up.

Kitsune was the last to arrive. It looked like he had been hiking hard or even jogging a little and sweat was running down his smooth face. He quietly mentioned something about a cat hole when Fic questioned him with his eyebrows.

Fic let everyone know what he had seen so far, and they decided to check the place out. They went inside and looked around in the cool darkness. The building was a small store, but the shelves were bare. They found a few minor items, dividing them up amongst themselves and realizing they still needed more. They didn't know if they would find any food while they were in the park, so they each wanted several days' worth if they could find it.

Brown Shades checked a tiny office at the back of the store and found that there was a dead body lying on the floor next to the cluttered desk. The stench hit him like a sledgehammer as he opened the door. He only stayed long enough to verify that there was just one dead body back there and nothing else of value. He shut the door quickly and went and told the others of his findings.

They all exited the building and gathered outside to share what they had found.

Kitsune didn't seem surprised at Brown Shades' discovery. He mentioned that he had been to this town before and he remembered that there was an outfitter just up ahead and after that, a Speedway grocery store, suggesting they check there next.

They moved along and quickly came to the outfitter store. The houses had become more numerous and closer to the road as they got to the edge of town. The entire area seemed too empty. Nothing moved, but the tree's leaves in the warm, steady breeze moving from the west into their faces. They repeated the search process at the outfitter store. "If you see any wool socks, I need to replace at least one pair if I can," Rodent Whisperer mentioned.

"I could use a fresh shirt," said Fic. "This one has quite a few miles on it and quite a few gallons of sweat too. I have had this since Georgia, it is time to put it to rest. It's never had a really good washing.

It surprised them that there was quite a bit of gear in the looted store. They had found the door off its hinges, and everything scattered inside, but a lot of product was still there and even though it had been thrown about, it was just what they needed. Each of the hikers were able to find the clothing items they wanted to change out, so they could continue on with their journey. They even found some power bars in one corner of the building, under a jumble of clothes racks and scattered and destroyed gear.

They gathered outside the building before moving on. "At least we didn't find another dead body in this place," Brown Shades said thankfully.

Wanting to find some more food, The Party continued along Main Street. They came to an intersection with dark streetlights. Not a soul was seen. The only sound was a few birds and a light breeze running down the street, tossing a random piece of trash to and fro. Fic was expecting to see a tumbleweed roll down the road and hear a red-tailed hawk call, but the blue jays yelling at each other in a nearby small stand of trees was all he heard. Across the street and on the right was a Speedway gas station. The Party spread out as they crossed and approached the store, moving at a quick pace and looking back and forth to see if anyone was around. They advanced on the store behind the pumps and tried the door. It was locked. "I sure wish Gnobbit was still with us," Fic said, rattling the locked door, missing her burglar skills.

"I think there might be a door around back," Kitsune said. "Maybe it isn't locked." He went around the corner of the building and disappeared from view of the others. In two minutes, he was standing on the other side of the glass door and turning the bolt that was keeping the others out.

"You got skills, kid," Rodent Whisperer commented, moving past the young man and heading down one of the dark aisles. This store seemed more intact than the others they had visited. There wasn't a lot of food on the shelves, but each of the hikers found a few things that were still sitting on the shelves or lying on the floor.

The mood grew a little light as Class Room bartered with Fic, trying to trade a pack of ramen she had found for some pork rinds that Fic had picked up from the floor in the back corner.

The trade complete, the hikers once again departed the dark, quiet building and gathered in the parking lot off to the side.

"Where do you think all the people are?" asked Brown Shades to the group. No one had an answer, and they went about loading their latest take into their food bags inside their packs.

#

As they sat in the parking lot, trying to decide if they should continue or head back to the trail, Kitsune caught some movement out of the corner of his eye. He looked up towards an overpass that crossed above the one they were on. He thought he saw something short, but fast, move back away from the far side of the guardrail. He kept staring and saw it again. "There is someone here," he whispered to the others.

Everyone became instantly alert. Reaching for their weapons first, and their packs second. They all looked to where Kitsune focused his gaze.

"I see something there by that large white building," Class Room stated. "It looks like a kid," she commented, hefting her pack and moving towards the overpass.

The others followed. Each hiker checked their weapons, but didn't wield them just yet.

The Party crossed the street at the overpass and walked along the front of the building. They moved along until they came to an intersection. "There he is," Fic said with surprise, as he pointed to the left. He had seen a short person running across the street and into the yard of a house that had tall hedges on its perimeter. They picked up their pace, trying to catch another glimpse of this elusive person. Fic hoped that they were still paralleling the runner, but he had lost sight of him again.

They came to the next street and they all saw the short person crossing the street and then disappearing into a yard. "It seems this kid is purposely waiting for us and intentionally being spotted," Brown Shades stated. "I think he is trying to lead us somewhere."

"Let's follow him then," said Fic. "But keep alert. This could be a trap. In fact, I'm starting to get a little spooked."

"There's a river up ahead. If this kid is heading that way, the bridge is the easiest way across the water," Kitsune said.

The Party approached the bridge, at the ready and constantly checking their surroundings. There was a small, landscaped area near the river. It had some small trees with some large bushes in front. Standing next to the trees was a kid.

The kid was dressed in dirty jeans and a faded orange tee shirt. A small leather jacket covered the shirt. A brown cowboy had sat atop their head. Large brown eyes looked out over a long, thin nose, liberally covered in freckles.

The kid started walking towards The Party, and took off the hat, a long spill of red hair tumbled out.

She shook her mane and smiled at the Party, looking at her surprised.

"Hi, I'm Daisy," the girl said. "I'm sorry it looked like I was runnin' from you. I just had to make sure you were good people before I revealed myself. What's your names?" she asked forwardly.

"Why … you are a lass," said Rodent Whisperer, stating the obvious. "You are rather sleek and quick running about."

Fic took a closer look at the girl. She was about ten years old, maybe a little older. Her hair and clothes looked like they needed some washing, but his clothes were just as dirty, if not more so. He couldn't remember when his last shower had been. He noticed that she had a holster on her belt which looked like it held a small revolver. Daisy's hand rested on the grip. Not threateningly, more of a comfortable afterthought.

"Are you alone, Daisy?" he asked, unconsciously looking around for others.

"Yep, ever since my Pa died, I been on my own. I got plenty of food and stuff," she said, a slight catch in her voice as she mentioned her father. "I'm livin' over in the Kroger right now. Like I said, lots of food. Y'all are welcome to come visit for a spell."

"That would be nice," said Class Room, looking at Fic and raising her eyebrows with an expression that would bear no disagreement as she protectively put her hand on Daisy's shoulder.

"Yes, let's check out your place for a bit. We might just decide to stay in town tonight. It is starting to get late. Our detour into town took longer than expected and the next shelter is still eight miles from Rockfish Gap. We have been pushing hard for about a week now, and I think it is time for a short day," Fic said. "By the way, where is everyone?"

"The army took 'em," Daisy replied. "A bunch of buses came in one day about a month after the bombs went off and the power went out. Most of the people had left, fearing the fallout from the bombs. They made everyone who was still around get on. Pa had me hide in the cellar of our cousin's house, while he went out to try and find Aunt Missy and the boys who had gone out looking for supplies and hadn't come back. Failin' that mission, he eventually hid somewhere too. After dark, he came back and got me and we took off into the nearby woods for a few days," her story continued.

"We watched from up on the mountain as buses kept comin' into town, and from time to time, we would hear gunshots and one gigantic explosion. Then, a whole bunch of smoke started risin' from different neighborhoods in town. After a few days, the buses stopped comin' and there was no one left. We were startin' to get hungry because we had lit out so fast and didn't have a lot of stuff, so we snuck back down into town. There were no people around and we saw that our cousin's house and about three more on the same street had burned to the ground. We found that we could set up camp in the Kroger, and that's what we did. There wasn't a lot of food in the storefront, but we found quite a bit that we could eat in the back warehouse."

Now, Daisy's voice got a little deeper and quieter as she continued telling The Party how her Pa had started feeling sick. "He kept complainin' about his arm being numb and his jaw was hurtin'," Daisy said. "One mornin', I went to wake him, and he wasn't there anymore. I mean he was there, but his spirit was gone. I guess he had died durin' the night, and I didn't even get to say goodbye." At this point, Daisy stopped talking and a tear spilled out of her left eye.

Class Room went over to Daisy and gave her a hug. "I'm so sorry you had to experience that, darling. Life has become quite hopeless since the bombs."

"I buried him over across the road in the Smith's backyard. That was as far as I could move him. He ain't too deep, but nothin' has bothered his resting place so far," Daisy stated nonchalantly, the tear on her cheek already dried and forgotten. "Life has always been hard, and it made me and Pa hard. His heart just couldn't take it all I guess."

Everyone stood looking at the young girl, a sadness permeated the group as she finished her story.

Fic cleared his throat and attempted to change the subject. "Okay, show us your home, Daisy," Fic said to the girl. "I'm starting to get hungry, and we can share what we found so far today."

"Follow me, I'll feed y'all," Daisy replied.

Daisy turned and started for the bridge over the swift flowing water of the South River, leading the way to the large grocery store she now called home. The others followed behind, stringing out into a long single file line.

Daisy guided them through an open park before taking a shortcut across an empty parking lot, until they could see the large squat building with the blue Kroger sign on it. It looked inviting and forbidding at the same time.

Daisy continued past the side with the main doors and walked along the windowless brick building to the back. They turned the corner and saw two blue dumpsters that were pushed together; one of them was in front of a brown, metal door. Daisy went up to the one dumpster and gave it a push. It moved out of the way, giving access to the brown door.

She pulled a screwdriver out of her pocket and pried the door open a crack. She pulled the door all the way open and walked into the dark, cool loading dock of the grocery store.

They walked past the loading area, which had a lot of boxes strewn about — some stacked neatly, some broken and spilling their contents, some laying empty by the doors.

Daisy moved into the warehouse and led the group over to a small area that had long stacks of boxes that created a sectioned off space inside. There they found two cots with sleeping bags on them, separated by a nightstand, a desk stacked with boxes of food and a large cooler sitting in the corner of the makeshift room. Next to the cooler was a small table with a propane stove on it. Several cans of propane were in a box next to the table. Beside the box sat a brown, beat up backpack that had seen better days.

"Does anyone want a pop?" she asked, opening the cooler and reaching inside, pulling out a Coke. "It ain't cold, but it still tastes good."

Everyone helped themselves to a can and the next few minutes were silent except for the sound of pop tops and swallowing.

"Ahhhh," said Rodent Whisperer, "that truly hit the spot. Thanks, lassie."

"You're welcome," Daisy responded. "I still have quite a bit stashed away."

The Party dropped their packs and found places to sit comfortably, while Daisy lit a small propane lantern. She went over to a couple of the boxes next to the wall and picked out some bags of snacks. She placed them on the table and told the hikers to help themselves.

"So, where did you get the peashooter, Daisy?" Fic asked.

"It was my Pa's," she replied. "When he passed, it became mine. I know how to shoot it too. Killed a couple river rats just the other day. I'm kinda low on ammo though."

She pulled the small revolver from its holster and presented it to Fic grip first. Fic took the weapon and gave it a look. It appeared old, but well cared for. It was a snub nose 38. He noted that it was fully loaded and ready to go. He handed it back to the girl.

"That's a nice little piece," Fic said.

Daisy re-holstered the weapon and continued her story.

"Since Pa has gone, I been lookin' for my cousins. My Aunt Missy and her two boys, Joey and Davey. That's whose house I hid in which is now ashes. I'm pretty sure they got taken on the buses, but I been seein' signs of other people around. I haven't seen anyone, but I see they been there — a box opened that had been closed before; bikes and stuff moved or missin'. Someone is around, I just need to find them.

"When we came to this store, we thought it would be empty. It had been a while since the bombs and the store closed after a couple days, sayin' they were all out. What we found when we broke in, was a nice stash in this very warehouse. I guess the manager or whatever was lookin' out for himself, but he got taken away, so we claimed it when we found it," she stopped to take a breath.

"So do you know why everyone got taken away?" Brown Shades asked, looking with interest at the girl and her story.

"Not a clue, but they all went towards the interstate, so they coulda been taken anywhere up or down state," she replied.

"I'm pretty good at takin' care of myself," she continued. "Pa taught me a lot of skills. I can hunt and fish and we always had a good garden at home. We live up in Luray and had been visitin' my Aunt Missy when the bombs came. I been doin' all right here, but this food won't last forever, and I don't know if my kin are ever gonna come back." Her voice caught a little, but she had a stern look and no other tears streaked her dusty face.

"We can take you home," Class Room said, not even bothering to check with the others who were all nodding their heads in agreement. "You can join our Party. Is that where your Ma is?"

"I don't have a Ma. She died when I was born. It's just been me and Pa since … ever. I'll think about your offer, but other than a mostly empty house, there's nothin' or no one up there for me to go back to," Daisy replied.

\#

Daisy took the group for a tour of the building. They exited the warehouse area to the main shopping area. Thin light streamed through the windows at the front of the building. The store was a mess, litter strewn about everywhere. A lot of it was empty boxes that once held food and other grocery items. They explored the whole store and even found a few forgotten items that were here and there in the building.

After that adventure, they all came back to the small room and sat together again.

"If it's okay, we would like to spend the night here with you," Fic stated.

"Sure," Daisy replied. "We got plenty of room."

The group spread out, and each found a place to set up their sleeping arrangements. Kitsune found a perfect place to hang his hammock between two of the steel pillars that supported the warehouse roof. After securing his sleeping spot, Kitsune lounged in his hammock, getting in a few minutes of reading before having to move on to their next chore. Brown Shades, setting up his own hammock nearby, had noticed that the young man appeared to be quite an avid reader. "I see you are rarely without a book in your hands whenever we have any down time. What are you reading now?" Brown Shades asked him.

"Yeah," replied Kitsune. "I get my love of reading from both of my parents and my grandma. This one is about a group of rabbits that live on a down. They have many adventures and must travel far to achieve their goals. Sort of like us," he laughed and turned the page, licking his finger before doing so.

"I know this book and have read it myself. A fine specimen of literature. We must compare our bibliographies some time."

Daisy started looking through the boxes again, taking out a can here and a box there. She took everything over to the stove area and picked up a large pot that was next to the table. She started opening cans and boxes and put everything into the pot. She added some water from a canteen that was in the cooler and lit the flame on the stove.

"I'm makin' Everything Stew," she said. "Pa taught me how to make it. I just pick stuff that might taste good together and heat it up. Usually it's pretty tasty."

The hikers looked at the concoction; the smell emitting from it as it started to warm up was surprisingly appetizing. It looked like chili, canned chicken, some sort of pasta, green beans and a few other powders and spices that were not easily identified. Brown Shades added a few large pinches of his special spices to the mix, nodding his head after taking a taste.

Daisy announced the stew was done and everyone spooned some into their pots. Silence reigned as the hikers concentrated on filling their bellies. "That was amazing!" exclaimed Rodent Whisperer.

Kitsune got up and went to fill his pot again, licking his lips as he did. Everyone followed his lead and, in a few minutes, the big pot was empty. Satiated, everyone lounged around lazily.

#

The day was done, and the light was leaving the store. The Party sat around the lantern and told stories about the adventures they had so far. Daisy was interested in the fact that they had walked all the way from Georgia. "I always wanted to take a hike on that trail," Daisy said. "I've been to the park a lot and have walked on the trail there, but I've never done a lot of nights out on a hike."

"We can probably get you all geared up if you decide to come with us. We checked out the outfitters on our way here and there is still a lot of gear strewn about in the store," Class Room said, hoping she would decide to come with them.

Daisy was still a little reluctant to commit to coming with them. She changed the subject and asked them to tell her more about what had happened in Damascus.

Eventually, the other hikers wandered to their sleeping bags, and the lantern was set low. Only Fic and Kitsune remained.

They talked in low voices about the next few day's plans. Once Daisy decided what to do, they would gear up and continue north. Fic was anxious to get back to his family, and Kitsune didn't really talk too much about why he was out there and what he had been doing before they had met him.

To Fic, he was still a bit of a mystery. Waiting for them in that clearing as if he was expecting them. Seeming to know things that he shouldn't know. It was as if he could move around the map quickly, checking things out, and then bring that information back to them. There had already been quite a few times when he had been away from the group for a while, usually behind, but when he would catch up, he would seem to know what was ahead of them.

He had been hiking south when they met him, but he quickly decided to pivot north in order to join them. Fic didn't know if he had family or even where he was from. The boy was a quiet, closed book.

He definitely was helpful to have around. He was always polite and willing to do the extra work that comes easy to a seventeen-year-old.

Fic decided he wanted to know more about this boy. "So Kitsune, where do you come from?" Fic started his quest for answers.

"I was born in Maryland, and grew up there, but I finished high school a year early and have been kind of wandering around for a while. I had decided to take a gap year before college and I wanted to explore the area. I like to be in the woods. I feel at home there. My folks are still up in Maryland — I'm eager to get back to them but I have a strong sense that they are okay for right now. I was out on a camping trip when the bombs fell. For a while I tried to get back home, but the closer I got to DC, the worse it got. I decided to head south for a while to maybe find someone to travel with and I found you guys."

This was the most Fic had ever heard the boy talk. He wanted to know more, "That is a cool hat you wear, with the fox ears. Is there a story behind it?"

"My Memom, uh, my Grandma, made it for me. She has always connected a fox to me, she saw one staring at her through the hospital window right after I was born. The toy fox I hang on my pack, my mother gave to me. I had one like it as a baby and would carry it everywhere. I lost it long ago. Before I headed out into the woods, my mother gave me this replacement as a good luck charm. I also have a strong connection to certain birds, especially cardinals. When I was a child, every time I played out in the yard, several bright cardinals would perch on the trees nearby and call out to me. Singing their distinctive song and seeming to serenade me. It is one of my fondest childhood memories."

Fic's eyebrows went up when he mentioned cardinals. He recalled the memory of all the cardinals that have seemed to visit them a lot lately. It started right before they met Kitsune. "Did you see that cardinal today that seemed to swoop down on each of us as we walked the road to town?" Fic asked.

"Yes, I saw it," replied Kitsune. "Interesting, isn't it?" he added with a slight smile.

Kitsune looked at Fic for a good ten seconds, saying nothing, just looking at him with his deep brown eyes.

Finally, he spoke, "My father used to tell me a story. It was about a fox named Kitsune, who had the ability to shape-shift into human form. In my father's story, he was a hero who was a guardian, and friend to others. Doing good deeds and protecting his friends from evil demons. I always loved that story, and along with it, foxes. It's why my trail name is what it is. Foxes are cool."

Fic looked back at Kitsune, more excitement coming into his face. "Ya know, just before we met you, we had a weird encounter. First with a cardinal, and then I saw a fox up ahead on the trail, staring at us. No one else saw it, so they only sorta believe me, but I assure you, I *did* see one," Fic said.

"I believe you," said Kitsune, that same slight smile moving onto his face. "I hope we see it again."

Silence grew between the two. The lantern sputtered a bit, signaling the tanks near emptiness. Fic reached over and killed the flame. "I guess I'm off to bed. See you in the morning," Fic said.

Both men retired to their sleeping bags. Fic was sleeping at the foot of the two cots, which Daisy and Class Room were occupying. Rodent Whisperer was sleeping just outside the boxed room, his snores echoed through the warehouse like a small buzzing saw. Brown Shades was in his hammock, wrapped in his large brown quilt. Soft snores came from his hanging bed as it swung slightly back and forth with the slow rise and fall of his breathing.

Kitsune went to his hammock, which was a good ten meters away from the others, except for Brown Shades. He sat on the hammock sideways, his favorite way to recline while in camp. He stared out into the dark warehouse, slowly sipping from a long water bottle every few minutes. He seemed to be waiting for something.

Soon, Kitsune could hear another low snore coming from the boxed-in room. Fic had joined the realm of the sleeping. All the hikers were usually pretty quick to fall asleep, especially if the day's hike had been long. If they were hungry, slumber helped them forget about their empty bellies for a time. The last several days had taken their toll. Their full bellies had made falling asleep even easier.

Kitsune took one last sip of water and placed the bottle next to his pack. He stood and walked towards the front of the store. Moonlight was coming in through the windows. A full moon on a clear night.

The young man walked to the doors and checked them. As he had discovered earlier when they were exploring the store, the one door opened easily. He pushed it open and went outside.

The night sounds hit Kitsune with a welcoming wave of crickets, katydids, and a few night birds. A bat fluttered above him, jerking back and forth, looking for its next bit of dinner.

Kitsune walked to the road and crossed the street. Disappearing into the yard of a large house.

One minute later, a large fox came out the other side of the yard, heading south, away from where Kitsune had entered the woodsy yard, as if it had been spooked out.

The fox trotted lightly down the middle of the dark street. He sniffed the air and after two blocks, turned west and continued down the middle of that street.

After a few more turns and sniffs the fox came to a row of burned houses. It was evident that no one exerted any effort to control or extinguish the fires. The houses were almost all burned to a pile of ash and twisted pipes.

The fox thoroughly sniffed around one of the houses, which wasn't completely destroyed. After seeming to find something it had been looking for, it started trotting down the road again, following a scent.

The fox came to the end of a road that crossed the street and stopped at a long, red brick building.

After another check of a scent on the ground, the fox turned right and started walking along the length of the long building. When the building stopped, he turned left and walked along the fence of a pair of tennis courts. Behind the courts was a football field. He traversed the length of the field along a hill that ran above, and came to a squat red brick sign. The animal stared at a sign as if he could read the words, *Fishburne Military School, Est 1879.*

The fox's nose diligently worked once more and he looked at the building behind the sign. In one of the windows on the second floor, he saw a flickering light. It appeared to be a candle or maybe a small fire. The fox approached the building.

After sniffing around the multiple doors to the building and seeming to find none easily opened, he went around the side of the building. There he saw one of the windows on the second floor — above a small, brick porch — was slightly open with a rock holding it from closing all the way. He sniffed one last time and then started down the road next to the school, heading towards the Kroger. After walking down the middle of Main Street, the fox veered right, entered the yard of one of the houses and disappeared from sight.

Ten minutes later, a dark form enters the store, walks to the back, and enters the warehouse area. It is Kitsune. He finds his hammock in the dark and slips inside. Within minutes, a small, quiet snore emitted from the hammock.

#

Morning came to the warehouse as a faint glimmer of a gray dawn. The clear night had given way to a cloudy morning and there was rain in the air. Each of the hikers had become particularly attuned to the weather and they would make bets on what time the precipitation would start and how long it would last. Brown Shades almost always got it right within a few minutes or so.

The Party had a mishmash of breakfast foods from the things they had scavenged the day before. Ranging from peanut butter on a rice cake, to a few crumbled pop tarts, to a medley of junk that was a sorry excuse for a first meal of the day. Though, after the last of the crumbs were finished, they all still seemed satisfied with what they had picked out of their food bags.

Daisy pointed to a row of boxes against the wall in the warehouse, "Y'all can fill your food bags if ya want."

"Have you decided to come with us?" Class Room asked the girl, giving her a stern look of concern. "I really think you should. We can help you get back to your family."

Daisy returned Class Room's look and said, "I really need to find out about my Aunt Missy and my cousins. I been worryin' about them a lot since Pa passed. Maybe we can do some lookin' around some. Like I said, someone is definitely here. Maybe it's Aunt Missy and the boys."

Kitsune looked over at Fic and said, "I have a few ideas of places to look around town. Maybe someone is holed up somewhere, just like Daisy is here."

"You said you have been here before," Fic responded. "Where should we look first?"

"There is a Military School up on 11th Street just a few blocks over. We can start there," Kitsune said.

"Sounds like as good a place to start as any," said Brown Shades.

The Party placed their now full packs in a corner of the warehouse, keeping their weapons and some water and snacks. They all headed out of the store, closing the door firmly and pushing the dumpster back in front of the door.

Kitsune turned towards Main Street with Daisy next to him. "So have you ever been to Fishburne," she asked.

"Yes, I have," he replied, "Quite recently, actually." That slight smile was starting to become a repeat visitor to his face. It looked good on him.

The hikers walked the few blocks and arrived at the football field. "Let's check this building first," said Kitsune, pointing to the building that a clever fox had been checking out not six hours ago.

They broke off into pairs and started checking the multiple doors, finding none open.

Kitsune was teamed up with Rodent Whisperer and they tried the door around the corner from the others. The door had a small, brick porch above it and Kitsune pointed out the slightly ajar window. The porch had some architectural brickwork that could provide a foothold and Kitsune sprung up on a railing and vaulted up onto the foothold like a parkour expert. He reached up to the top of the porch and vaulted once again. He was on the roof.

Kitsune looked down at an astonished Rodent Whisperer and told him to get the others and he would come down and open the door below, before disappearing into the building.

Rodent Whisperer gathered the others, and when they returned, Kitsune was standing at the now opened door. "This man is an acrobat," Rodent Whisperer stated, a look of awe still on his face. "You have to teach me some of those moves sometime, Kit."

The Party entered the building and Kitsune pointed up the stairs, "I think I smelled smoke up there."

The Party cautiously headed up the staircase, spread out two to a step, and entered a long hallway with doors on each side. Slowly, they worked their way down the hallway, opening a door and checking inside, weapons at the ready, but not brandished.

At the third door on the left, they found the lock engaged. As they were fiddling with the doorknob, they heard a noise from within. It was the sound of a shotgun pumping a round into the chamber. The Party scattered back to the last room quickly, getting out of the hallway as fast as they could.

"Aunt Missy!" Daisy yelled as Class Room pulled her into the room.

As Fic, the last to get into the room, was moving through the doorway, he heard a muffled voice say, "Daisy?" The voice sounded young — a boy.

Fic stopped at the doorway and shouted, "Daisy's here. Do you know her?" He held his shotgun at the ready, but it was pointed low.

"I'm here!" yelled Daisy, who had come back behind Fic. "Is that you, Joey?"

"Yeah," the boy replied. "Who's that with you?"

"Friends," she responded.

They heard a bolt turn, and the door swung open. Out walked a boy of about twelve years. A large pump shotgun in his hands. He was tall for his age and wiry. "Boy, it sure is good to see you," he said to Daisy. "I thought you and your Pa had been taken away on those buses. My Ma and Davey were taken. I was too, but I was able to sneak away when we took a break. I made my way back here and went home. When I found my house in ashes, I holed up here. I had crawled into the basement and found my Pa's old Remington and some shells. It is a little singed, and I'm really surprised the ammo didn't cook off, but it was far from the worst of the damage," he told his story.

The boy looked at the group of people around him. Checking each face in the dim light of the hallway and moving to the next when he saw no one he knew. "Where's your Pa?" he asked his cousin.

"He passed," Daisy replied in a soft whisper. "I think his heart gave out. I buried him across the street from the Kroger in the Smith's backyard." Her voice caught a little again and a look of sorrow came to her face, but then faded back into a hardness that spoke of courage and fight.

Joey went over to his cousin, slinging his shotgun and gave her a hug. "I'm so sorry, cuz," he said. "Uncle Ned was a good man. I will miss him. Have you been all alone since then?"

"Yeah. I been livin' in the Kroger, in the back. We found a lot of food stashed back there, so we set up camp. Pa died a few days ago." Her voice stayed hard and clear this time. It seemed she was not comfortable freely showing her grief to the others.

"Do you know where they were taking you, son," Fic asked Joey.

"I'm not completely sure, but I did hear a couple of the soldiers say something about Mount Weather or something. I never heard of the place," Joey replied.

"I have," said Fic. "I used to work there. It is a pretty important place for the Military and the Administration. Do you have any idea why they were taking you there?" he asked the boy.

"Naw," was his response.

"That's about a two hour drive from here and very close to where I'm trying to get to. I'm trying to get back to my family, who live just off the mountain from Mount Weather, near the river.

"I was stuck down in Georgia doing some survival training with the army, when the bombs fell. I have been trying to get back ever since. I've picked up some friends along the way," Fic said, motioning to the rest of The Party.

The boy's eyes tightened when Fic mentioned the army. "Army?" he said, reaching for the strap of his shotgun, but just leaving it there at the ready.

"I know what you are implying," Fic said, placing his hands out in front of him in a placating gesture. "I'm one of the good guys. The ones you saw who took everyone away are part of some rebellion that started when the bombs dropped. These traitors killed a few of my men. As far as I'm concerned, my contract with the army is on hold until I find my family and find out what is happening to our government. It seems Mount Weather is a part of it," Fic continued. "Our mission there was pretty secret, but I can tell you that the place is a large underground base, where important people can go to stay safe in times like these. If the enemy has access to that base, I have no idea what that tells us about the rest of the government."

Joey, accepting Fic's explanation, took the group into the room he had been holed up in and showed them around. He too had been resourceful in setting up his hidey-hole. There was a large brick fireplace at one end of the long room. Joey had set up around that. The remains of a recent fire showed in the fireplace with a pot set off to the side on an improvised tripod. A sleeping bag was spread out to the side and a green Kelty backpack was next to it. Beside that was a box of food and a gallon jug of water.

"Good setup," said Daisy. "My room is better though," she added with a little twinkle in her eye. The cousin's camaraderie was evident, and they appeared to enjoy teasing each other occasionally.

"You'll have to show it to me," he replied. "I was just fixin' to go check out the Kroger, anyway. My food box is getting low."

"Why don't you bring your stuff and stay with me," Daisy said to Joey. She looked over at Class Room, who had a worried look on her face. "I have decided to stay here, Class Room. I appreciate the offer to join you guys, but I think I need to stay here with Joey and help him find his Ma and brother."

"If they are at Mount Weather, that is where we are heading," Fic said to the two kids. "Maybe we can help you find them."

The two tweens looked at each other for a bit and then walked off to the corner of the room to have a quiet discussion. The private conversation went on for a few minutes as The Party tried not to listen to what they were saying. Kitsune and Rodent Whisper decided to take a look around the building. Fic, Brown Shades and Class Room spoke together in soft voices, already starting to plan how they would gear up the young cousins.

Daisy and Joey came back to the group. "We'll come with ya'll," Daisy announced. "Joey wants to find his Ma and Davey and doesn't think they are comin' back here."

The group reconvened and gathered Joey's things, helping him load his pack.

The Party, now numbering seven, exited the building at the same door they had entered. They wanted to check out some of the stores on the way back through Main Street and started navigating in that direction. They turned east and walked towards the football field on Federal Street. As they passed the field, Fic noticed that it looked like it had been used not too long ago, and not for a football game. There were tire tracks on the field and places that looked like something had been corralled there. It was all tamped down, the grass was browner, and there was trash strewn about everywhere. He made a note of it as they walked away from the school grounds.

#

On Main Street, they searched a couple of the small stores along the way. Class Room found a lighter in one store. Hers was getting low, so she was happy to replace it. Kitsune retrieved a book from an otherwise empty shelf and added it to his ever changing personal library, leaving the novel he'd just finished behind in its place. Rodent Whisperer added a bit of rope to his pack that was under the counter of another store. He liked having rope handy just in case.

As they were turning onto the street where the Kroger was, they all heard a low rumble. The sound of an engine going through its gears as it climbed an incline, heading towards them. It sounded like a diesel.

The roar got closer and louder and as they were standing on the corner on a red brick sidewalk, they saw something come over the rise, a long way down Main Street. It was a bus.

"Quickly!" Fic said, "Let's get out of sight."

Everyone ran down to the next block, coming up alongside an antique shop. They saw the bus come out of one of the side streets and pull to the curb at the school, next to the football field.

Men in army uniforms got off the bus and walked around the area. As The Party watched, more people started exiting the bus and were directed down the hill into the football field. The torn up field made sense to Fic now — they had been holding people there, preparing them for transport to Mount Weather for some unknown reason.

"Follow me," said Daisy. She started across the street to a small driveway between two buildings. The Party followed her as she made her way behind the right structure to avoid being seen by the men on the bus. She headed back to the street after going through a couple of backyards and they came out across the street from the grocery store, right by the door where they had been entering.

They ran to the dumpsters and pushed the one blocking their entrance aside. Daisy opened the door again with her trusty screwdriver and they were all safely inside within a couple of seconds.

"Who do you think those people were and why are they back?" Joey asked.

"I don't know," replied Fic, "but we are going to find out."

#

"I'm gonna go out and see if I can sneak in close to the field," said Kitsune quietly.

"I'll go with you," replied Fic.

"No, I don't think that is a good idea," Kitsune said with a bit of authority. "I'm pretty stealthy and I should be able to get a good look at what's going on by myself. Less people out there, less to be discovered and maybe captured."

"Okay," replied Fic, "but if you aren't back in an hour, I'm coming after you." He had a worried look on his face but knew Kitsune had a point. The boy was good at surveillance. He always seemed to have intel on what is ahead of them when they are approaching danger.

Kitsune checked his Katana, and Fic offered him his shotgun. "Do you want to take this, just in case," Fic asked the boy.

"No, I don't intend on being seen," Kitsune said. "At least not recognized as someone they want to catch," he added cryptically.

This time, Kitsune left the building by the large brown door, pushing the dumpster back in front of the door to protect those within.

Kitsune crossed the street and entered the alley, he followed it about halfway down, turned right into a well-wooded yard, and disappeared behind a large hedge.

Two blocks away, the football field was bustling. There were about thirty people all gathered in a cluster at the fifty yard line. The group themselves looked like an older set of people, with several young children that looked more like the adults' grandchildren than their kids. A few of the people were coughing and one seemed to be about to fall over, looking flush with fever. About thirty feet away from them, a cluster of five soldiers gathered in a circle, discussing their plans. As the soldiers talked, a cardinal flew over the field. Circling around twice, swooping down next to the people as if checking them out closely, and then landing on the ground about ten feet away from the soldiers.

The bird pecked at the ground once or twice before cocking its head in the direction of the men as if it was listening in on their conversation.

"Okay, Corporal," a man with Sergeant stripes said to a rather portly man whose uniform was wrinkled and whose chin was in need of a shave. "Process these rejects quickly, so we can get back to Weather. This empty town gives me the creeps. Always feels like someone is watching us, even though we most likely got all of them."

"Roger that, Sarge," the disheveled-looking man replied. "Let's go guys," he said to the two privates next to him.

The three men went over to the group of old, sick people. The cardinal jumped into the air, flapped its wings a couple times and glided back to the ground near the crowd of people. Corporal Disheveled looked at the clipboard in his hand and started calling names. Each time he said a name, a person in the group would hold up a hand or say "yes" or "here." He continued until he had finished the list — each person present and accounted for.

An old woman at the edge of the crowd near the soldiers asked the Corporal, "What are we supposed to do now? Some of our houses have been burned. Where do we get food? Where —"

"Listen, lady," the Corporal cut the woman off. "Just find a place to stay and work together to find food. We aren't your babysitters, but you need to take care of these kids until their parents get back. Maybe if you do a good job, we will send you some supplies. As it is, we are leaving you a couple cases of MREs. Y'all are too weak to do the work at Weather, so you are rejected. We don't have a lot of use for you." The Corporal turned and went back to the other two soldiers.

"All present, Sarge," he reported to the Sergeant.

"Very well," the Sargent replied. He turned to the other man, who had the bars of a Second Lieutenant on his collar. "Shall I send them off?" he asked the leader of the group.

"I will address them first," the Lieutenant said. He walked over to the crowd and cleared his throat.

"People of Waynesboro, we have brought you back here because we don't need you right now. We will be checking on you and may need you again if our mission changes. Our leader is making a lot of changes in this country, and you need to realize that we are here to stay and will be calling the shots. If we say jump, you only need to start jumping. We will determine if it is high enough. You can't jump high enough, so here you are. You are actually lucky we brought you back at all." He paused here and looked up at the school buildings and around the field. His eyes focused on the cardinal that was standing there looking right back at the uniformed man. The bird realized that the Lieutenant was staring at him, so it took flight and circled around the crowd to the other side of where the man was addressing the sickly people.

" If your house is no longer there, go find another place to stay. You are all in charge of taking care of these children. You can go now," the Lieutenant waved his hand at them dismissively.

The cardinal took flight, but this time, it kept circling around the field, getting higher and higher into the sky. Looking down as the small, sad cluster of people started to spread out from the field. Some stayed together in groups, others went off in ones and twos to check to see if they still had a house or if they needed to find something new. The five soldiers returned to the bus, started it up, and drove back to Main Street, turning left and heading back to the interstate

After a few more circles, the cardinal flew off towards the river, disappearing from view.

#

Fic was standing at the brown door, opened several inches, so that he could look at the alley across the street. Suddenly, he sees Kitsune enter the alley from one of the yards, turn, and head toward the store. Fic looks at his watch, only forty minutes have passed since the boy headed out on his mission. Kitsune approaches the building and steps up to Fic.

Fic whispered, "What did you find out?"

"A lot," Kitsune replied. "Let's go inside to discuss it."

The two men head back to the small room and gather everyone around. Kitsune relates what he had found out. His details about the conversation surprised and worried Fic. "How close did you get to these people?" he asked the boy.

"I was pretty close," he replied, "but they were talking loud, and I was well hidden." His sly smile was back.

"Do you think your mother was possibly in that group, Joey?" Kitsune asked the boy.

"Well, she isn't really old and was pretty healthy, so from what you said about the shape of the people, I'm not very confident," Joey said.

"Let's go talk to some of those people and find out," Fic said.

"I'm comin'," said Daisy, as Joey stood up and started walking towards the door.

"Okay, young lady," replied Fic. "Me, Kitsune, and you two can go. The rest of you can start getting ready to leave. If that bus decides to come back or drive down that road back to the trail, we might want to be back in the woods."

The four walkers headed out of the grocery store and back down the alley. They walked through the yards until they came to Joey's neighborhood. He showed them his mostly burned house and they took a look around. As they were walking in the front, the door of the still intact house across the street from Joey's opened, and the same old woman who had asked the soldiers questions came out onto the porch.

"Joey?" the woman asked. "Is that you?" She started down the steps of her porch and approached the foursome.

"Hi, Mrs. McHenry," said Joey. "Have you seen my Ma and Davey? Did they come back with you on the bus?" he asked with a worried look on his face.

"Oh Joey, it is so good to see you. Have you been hiding here since we were taken away?" she asked. "You and your little cousin?"

"Yeah," Joey replied. "I snuck away when the bus took a break and made my way back here. Daisy has been here the whole time. She and her Pa hid up in the woods." He suddenly remembered that his Uncle Ned was no longer with them, and a sad look came to his eye.

"Her Pa passed a few days ago," he added. Now the woman was the one with a sad look.

"I'm so sorry, honey," she said to Daisy, who nodded her head and looked down the street. "I'm also sorry for you, Joey. Your mother and brother are still at that horrible place they took us to. They were forcing us to work for them. Hard, manual labor. They deemed the ones who came back with me too weak, either too young or too old, to do the work."

"What kind of work are they doing, ma'am," Fic asked the woman.

She looked at him and his shotgun and a little wariness went into her gaze. "Who are you, sir?" she asked him.

"I'm Clayton," he replied. "We are traveling north on the Appalachian Trail and are trying to get back to the area of Mount Weather. That is where my family is. We met Daisy yesterday and found Joey just this morning. We are trying to help them find their kin."

She seemed satisfied with his explanation and continued on, "They are doing a lot of manual digging down in that wretched base. Making us do it. Enlarging the place or something. A few people have already been killed or died from their cruelty and abuse. And Mount Weather isn't the only place they sent the residents of this town. I saw several of the buses heading south and west as we were taken north. They spread us out all over. Luckily, your family was on the same bus as me, Joey."

"So is my Ma and Davey okay?" asked Joey. "When did you see them last?"

"I saw your brother just before we got on the bus to come back," the woman said. "He was in a work group that was moving from the rooms they were keeping us in, to the digging area. He didn't look too happy, but he was still healthy and not sick. I haven't seen your Ma in over a week."

Joey turned to Fic and said, "When do we leave Fic? I need to find them."

"We can go as soon as you two are ready," Fic replied.

Daisy nodded her head and said, "I'll need some gear though. I have a small backpack and my sleepin' bag and such, but I'm not ready to do any long term walkin'."

"We can check out that outfitter that we searched on the way here," said Kitsune. "I think I remember seeing gear that might come in handy."

Daisy turned to Mrs. McHenry and said, "We will be leavin' some food in the back of the Kroger. Just go in the door by the blue dumpsters. It is all in the corner in a little room-like area constructed out of cardboard boxes."

"Thank you, my girl," Mrs. McHenry said. "They didn't leave us with much and who knows if they will give us more."

"Take care of yourselves," Fic said. "We wish we could help more, but we need to keep moving up the trail if they are coming here to find workers. I wonder how my family is dealing with this, being so close to Mount Weather."

The four members of The Party made their way back to the other three hikers who were packing their gear at the grocery store and re-entered the building.

They updated the rest of the group about their conversation with Mrs. McHenry and everyone started to gather their gear.

They packed up Daisy's things, and she hefted her brown backpack that was now very much stuffed to the brim. They all took as much food as they could carry. There was still a good amount left over for the remaining townspeople whenever they decided to come and get it.

The Party filed out of the dark warehouse, and pushed the dumpster in front of the door.

Daisy took Joey over to her father's grave and they paid their respects, while the others waited at the edge of the yard. "We gotta go rescue Aunt Missy," Daisy said to the long pile of packed earth that had a small wooden cross at one end. "We'll see ya later, Pa," she added.

They walked back to Main Street, turned right, crossed the river, and started out of town.

At Rockfish Gap Outfitters, they found gear for both tweens' loadouts. Daisy's brown pack was too small, but they found a medium-sized pack stuffed into the corner that would be a good replacement. It was a Deuter women's pack. A maroon color that had a small silk flower pinned to the side. The flower was a Daisy.

"Well, this pack certainly has been waiting here for you," said Class Room with a smile as she helped Daisy pack it up with her old gear and some new stuff she had found in the mess throughout the store.

Class Room lifted the pack, checking its weight, nodded her head and held it for Daisy to slip onto her back. At first the pack seemed to dwarf the ten-year-old girl, but as she buckled it up and adjusted the straps, it seemed to work for her.

Joey's pack was already of a decent size and appeared to be well worn and an older model. "This was my Pa's pack from when he hiked the trail," he said. "It worked for him on the A.T., so it will work for me."

He added the few things that he still needed for some long distance hiking, and at last, the group of hikers were ready to continue down the road towards the park. Off they went in single file, spreading out along the side of the road. Kitsune in the lead this time and Fic bringing up the drag position.

The hikers moved along at a good pace, not worrying about any buses for now, just trying to get under cover of the trees; to the white blazes guiding them north towards their respective goals. Every step bringing them closer to family, to home, to desperately needed answers.

#

About an hour later, The Party was back at the parking lot they had sat in the day before. It seemed like it had been so long since they were on the trail, but it had only been a little over twenty-four hours. It was just after noon and the day had become hot and humid. They could see storm clouds far off in the west, but heading their way.

The hikers entered the forest and started the process of making miles. Since they had started quite late, they were only trying to make the first shelter. It was about seven miles away and the trail was fairly easy at first. The experienced hikers didn't want to put too much on their newest members mileage wise; the kids needed to develop their trail legs. Class Room and Kitsune were walking along at the front of the group. Kitsune took out two candy bars and offered one to Class Room. She took the package of sweetness and said, "Thanks. I noticed that Kitsune is the Japanese word for fox, so I was wondering if you spoke the language."

"I do," replied Kitsune. "My grandmother is Japanese and she and my father taught me to speak in a conversational way. I'm not fluent, but I can hold a conversation if I need to."

"I know a little, myself," replied Class Room. "My roommate in college was from Japan, she taught me several words and phrases and we would practice together after doing our homework. We also had a few phrases we used as a secret code when we were out together.

As they walked along, Class Room would try a phrase or two on Kitsune and he would translate her words or offer a better pronunciation of the language. The miles passed quickly as the pair became immersed in their lesson, loving the nostalgia that the language brought them both.

#

They arrived at Calf Mountain Shelter at around 1700. Kitsune and then Fic had set an easy pace as the rest of The Party monitored how the cousins were handling the hike. As they entered the shelter area and dropped their packs, the kids looked tired but invigorated. Joey seemed to enjoy himself immensely, and Daisy kept talking about her new pack, which she had named, Flower.

It had become routine for the group to break off around the campsite and set up their gear. Kitsune and Brown Shades preferred to sleep in their hammocks nearby. Rodent Whisperer still carried a tent that he would put up from time to time. The kids, Fic, and Class Room opted for the shelter. Picking their spots and claiming them with a pad and bag.

After everyone was set up, they all wandered in the nearby forest and picked up wood for a fire. Brown Shades started the fire and had it crackling and spitting up sparks in no time. He secretly added one of his special packets of powder to make the flames turn several different colors to the delight of the tweens. "I found that packet in the outfitter store. It contains several different chemicals that change the color of the flames," Brown Shades said, an amused look on his face. "Here I was creating my *potions* with household items and these things have been around all along."

They ate dinner in silence and then spent some time sitting around the fire. Class Room sat braiding Daisy's long hair as they laughed together, a close bond had already formed between the two. As everyone spent time enjoying the warmth of both the flames and the companionship, Kitsune and Joey found that they had a common interest in anime. They chattered enthusiastically, comparing how many episodes they'd seen of their most loved shows before Joey shyly pulled a worn notebook out of his pack. "Can I show you some drawings I made of my favorite characters?" Joey asked, a slight blush on his cheeks.

"Of course, I'd love to see your sketches, Joey," Kitsune answered encouragingly.

Joey, basking in the attention, flipped through his notebook and eventually ended up passing it around for everyone else to see too.

The surrounding forest grew darker until all that could be seen was the hikers within the circle of light that the fire provided. The night noises of a summer evening sung and moved about.

One by one, the hikers moved to their beds until it was just Brown Shades and Fic left. Fic realized that he was usually the last to hit the sack each night. He wasn't sure why. Whether it was a sense of duty to protect those with him or his worry that his family was somehow in danger. He didn't know.

"So, what do you think is happening at your old workplace, Fic?" Brown Shades asked him.

"I really don't know, Brown Shades," replied Fic. "Something seems to be going on there and it is a continuity of operations site. I would have thought if this attack was nationwide, that the President and some of his cabinet would have evacuated to Mount Weather. Continuing to run the country and fight that asshole Richard Flaherty from there," Fic mused.

"It seems like it's the enemy who is doing this and if they have possession of that place, then I have pretty much lost hope for the legal government. They must have been dug in deep, and were ready to go when the bombs dropped."

"Yes, I agree," Brown Shades said. "We could be walking into one hell of a hornet's nest, but I'm willing to be by your side. Even though I hope to get back to my home eventually, I am committed to helping you find your family, just like we did with Gnobbit."

"I appreciate that," Fic said. "We only have about a hundred and fifty miles or so to go. After all this way, that seems like almost nothing. If we can keep moving at a decent pace, we can be there in maybe a week and a half."

"Have you had any more of those strange dreams?" Brown Shades asked Fic.

"No," Fic replied. "Not since that last one down in Pearisburg."

"Yeah, me neither," Brown Shades replied. "Well, time for bed for me," Brown Shades said. "Maybe we'll have one tonight." He winked at Fic, getting up and heading to the shelter.

Fic sat at the fire for a while thinking about Brown Shades use of the word "we'll," like it was now a natural thing to all have the same dreams together.

Fic poked the burning logs around in the fire pit to tamp the fire down for the night. As he was doing so, the rain that had been threatening all day long started to fall. He continued to sit by the fire for a short time as the rain gained momentum. The fire began hissing as the drops made their way through the forest canopy and started to get him wet. He stirred the ashes one more time, breaking up the larger coals and then headed to the shelter.

He lay in his sleeping bag, staring into the darkness of the shelter as the rain danced on the metal roof. His hand reached under his shirt and clasped the necklace he wore there. The leather pouch with the trinkets and locks of his wife and children's hair weaved into a braid brought him comfort. He thought of his wife Lori, his daughter, Brittney and his son, Shane. He wondered if they were alright. He hoped that whatever was going on in Mount Weather hadn't affected them. As sleep came to him, his mind stayed with his family.

CHAPTER 19
HOME FRONT V - SUNDAY, JULY 29TH

Lori lay in her bed as the darkness filled the room. Rain pattered on the roof of the house. Usually a calming influence on her, but tonight she felt uneasy. Brittney was in her room, hopefully sleeping. She heard a key turn in the kitchen door, which opened and closed, and Shane softly called to the house, "I'm home."

He had been on patrol with one of the other guys from the Blue Mountain Patrol. She had heard the quad pull up and drop him off about ten minutes ago, but he must have done something out in the barn before coming inside.

The last few days had been hard. She sent out a wish for Clayton to hurry home. She had such a strong feeling that he was getting close. She had no idea why she thought this as she hadn't heard anything since the day he left for his training exercise in Georgia. Still the feeling was strong.

Things were getting unsteady in the area. The activity going to and from the mountain — most likely to Clayton's workplace, Mount Weather — had increased a lot lately. Buses traveled along Highway 50 very frequently. She had no idea who was on the buses, but it didn't seem good.

So far, whoever occupied that base had left them alone. They didn't know why. The BMP, as the kids referred to their group now, had ramped up their patrols, but had reduced the area of operations after several incidents started to attract attention. Someone had suggested that it was that rogue army that was doing the killings, but no one knew for sure.

Something bad was happening in the area. They had discovered three more people in the nearby properties since Brittney had found Mrs. McCreary in that burning pile of tires.

This person or group of people were preying on people who were alone, usually older and usually — more or less — helpless. It didn't seem like the person was robbing the people they found. They just seemed to be killing them for the sake of it. Sometimes there was torture involved, either to gather some kind of information or just someone's sick idea of fun. A few days would go by, then a new body would be found. Sometimes the culprits burned the bodies, but usually halfheartedly, without much success in eliminating any evidence. Sometimes, they were left in staged displays. Maybe sending a warning or something that, so far, she didn't understand. It made everyone snappy and on edge.

Lori got up and went downstairs to the kitchen, carrying a lantern that had been by her bedside. She entered the kitchen and there sat Shane, her seventeen-year-old son. Dressed in dark jeans and a black tee shirt. A blue armband, the mark of the BMP on his right arm. He was eating an apple.

"How was your patrol, Shane," she asked the young man.

"Good," he said between bites. "Quiet," he added. "There was a lot of traffic along the highway tonight. Steve had counted about thirty vehicles."

"So, you were on patrol with Steve, huh?" Lori asked. "How is his mother doing? I heard she had the summer flu the other day."

"He didn't mention her," Shane replied. "He did seem to be distracted tonight though. Like he had a lot on his mind."

"Did you try to talk to him about it?" Lori asked.

"Nah," Shane said. "We don't talk about that stuff out there."

"What do you talk about?"

"Things."

"Things?"

"Yep."

Lori sighed and went over to the jug of water on the counter and poured herself a glass. She was starting to regret letting her kids get involved. A couple of the guys in the group seemed to be getting used to having power and this power might have been starting to corrupt them as it always does.

With the recent unsolved murders, her apprehension had grown by leaps and bounds. When one or both of them were out on patrol, she didn't sleep until they were home safe.

"I'm gonna head back up to bed," she told her son. "Don't forget to check the chickens in the morning if you are heading out early."

"I'm off for a day or so, but I'll check them out," he replied. "Good night, Ma."

Lori went back up the stairs to her bedroom, crawled back into bed and doused the lantern. She lay staring up at the dark ceiling and listening to the house make its small creaks and cracks. She reached for the necklace she had around her neck. The necklace had a small crescent moon shaped charm. She squeezed it and thought of Clayton. He had given her the necklace before his first deployment. The family had a ritual during the kids' early years when Clayton was gone for several weeks or months at a time on deployment. Clayton would tell the kids to always look at the moon when he was away, and they were missing each other. "I'll look at the moon too, every night," he told them. "If we are both looking at the same thing, we can feel like we are together."

Lori quickly falls into an uneasy sleep, she starts to dream.

She sees her husband, Clayton, hiking down a trail. He turns to her and smiles. He is dressed as an ancient warrior, with armor and a large sword. Behind him is a tree with a long stripe of white paint. As he stands there, other people start passing him on the trail. First, a wise-looking Wizard, dressed in a brown robe, holding a long staff with a large crystal on the top. Next is a short, squat Dwarf. He holds a large axe balanced on his shoulder. A vibrant woman comes next. She has a lute in her hands and plays a short melody on the instrument, humming to the tune as she moves out of sight. Two young hobbits pass her view next. A male and a female, both with large hairy feet. They are holding hands and hurrying to catch the others. Last to pass her sight is a large red fox, with black feet and a black tipped tail. The fox looks back at her before it moves out of sight behind Clayton, her warrior husband.

"We will be there soon," the fox says to Lori, shocking her at its ability to speak.

"After the moon is full again. Look for us," the fox added before turning and disappearing from view.

Lori rolls over and her sleep deepens as the house continues to creak and crack.

CHAPTER 20
SHENANDOAH - MONDAY, JULY 30TH TO THURSDAY, AUGUST 2ND

The rain that had started yesterday evening continued off and on all through the night. In the morning, the rain continued still, and it didn't look like it was going to stop very soon.

The Party slowly started their day, everyone came into the shelter to cook or eat their breakfast. After an hour or two of taking their time, they decided that they needed to get moving up the trail. It wasn't going to walk itself.

The cousins pulled out their brand-new Frogg Toggs rain jackets and donned them before they headed out. The jackets were XLs, so their small legs sticking out of the long jackets was a funny sight. Everyone else's gear was starting to look tired. Everything had a dingy, dirty appearance, but all the equipment was still working fine. That's just what the trail does to the things that are carried day after day.

They continued on, heading north through the park. The day before, they had only crossed Skyline Drive twice. Today, they would cross it five times.

Each time they came to the road, Kitsune would scout ahead to check that the coast was clear. Each time he would report back that the crossing was empty, and no one was around. They would swiftly cross and get back into the safety and concealment of the woods.

The goal was to hike another thirteen miles today. That mileage was an easy slog for the veteran hikers, but they were still figuring out how the cousins could handle the miles with the weight they were carrying. The kids seemed to have boundless energy. They were still excited about hiking with The Party and the chance of finding and rescuing Joey's mother and brother. They seemed to have no problem keeping up with the others. When they took breaks, Brown Shades would quiz them on some of the plants, trees, insects and animals they would see. In his element, the old professor would regale them with data and information that they found fascinating. The lessons made the day go by faster.

Around lunch time, they came to Loft Mountain Campground. The trail circles around the campground, and before it continues on, there is a short side trail to a general store. As they walked around, they couldn't see any trailers or RVs in any of the campsites. Just like everything else in the area, it was deserted.

They took the trail to the store to check it out. It seemed to be intact but was locked up tight. Each of the hikers tried to find a way in, but no one wanted to take a crowbar to the door — not that they had a crowbar to use anyway. They decided that they were all well enough supplied because of Daisy's help so there was no need to break the door.

Instead, they went to the picnic tables next to the store and made some lunch. The rain had stopped for now, so they dug out their food bags and ate a meal.

Daisy finished eating, picked up some of the trash that was generated by the meal, and went to take it to a dumpster she had noticed on the other side of the building. As she walked up to the bear-proof sliding door and went to open it, a bear came walking towards her from the other side of the dumpster.

Both Daisy and the bear started in surprise. Daisy yelled out, and slowly turned to look how far away the others were; her heart pounding as she realized they were still fifty feet away. She looked back, the bear stood frozen in place staring at her. Cautiously, she started backing away from the animal, saying, "Hey bear!"

The others had heard her yell and started towards her. When the bear saw the others approaching, she turned and swiftly disappeared around the building's corner.

Daisy spun around and ran back to the others. She jumped into Fic's arms, shaking like a leaf in a heavy gale. She had experienced quite a scare. "I got ya, girl," Fic said. "It was probably just looking for an easy meal. Not a lot of *pic-a-nic baskets* around, with there being no tourists or campers," he said, imitating the cartoon character, Yogi Bear.

Daisy stepped back to the ground and looked over to where the bear had disappeared. "That was a big one," she said with a shaky voice. "I think I peed myself a little." Everyone laughed and looked to where the bear had left the scene.

Brown Shades repeated the rhyming reminder "If it's black, fight back. If it's brown, lay down. Luckily there are no grizzlies in this part of the country. You did good, Daisy. The bear probably smelled our food, their sense of smell is 2100 times better than a humans."

The Party packed up their food bags and headed back to the trail. The rise and fall of the path was relatively easy as the day continued on. They were up on the ridge, just riding its waves.

#

The sun was starting to head for the horizon when they took the trail that led to Blackrock Hut. They were in the park proper now and their crossing of the highway every few miles was a routine they had perfected

The Hut was down a short trail off of the ridge. Arriving at the shelter was just the first step. Now, the camp chores began: finding and setting up sleep spots; gathering wood for a fire; starting the fire; assessing their food supplies in order to plan a meal for the evening.

The large stone fireplace in front of the shelter was a camper's dream. There was a good space to make an easy fire, a sturdy grate to place a pot, and even a swinging arm with a hook on it where a pot would simmer quickly.

They all decided to cook over the fire in order to conserve fuel for their stoves. The meal of choice: another one of Daisy's Pa's special stews. Rodent Whisperer's pot was the biggest, so they each found something to contribute and added it to the recipe, along with some water. Once the fire had created some good coals, they gathered them together and put the pot on to cook.

The conversation while they waited for their dinner to finish was about the bear and when they were going to see more. "Shenandoah has a lot of bears," Fic said. "They are somewhat used to humans and know that wherever we go, possible food is available. The sad thing is when a bear does get fed, either intentionally or accidentally, they usually will be removed from the area or sadly, put down," Fic preached. "It is probably a good thing that there aren't any people around to throw their trash around. Healthier for the bear."

The Everything Stew was deemed done and the hikers grabbed their spoons and scooped out a portion to eat. Everyone gave the concoction the thumbs up. Soon the pot was empty, and everyone's belly was full. They cleaned up the dinner dishes and everyone gathered their food bags.

The shelter had a nice bear box nearby. It was a large metal rectangle, with two heavy doors. To open the doors, one needed to insert their fingers into a slot and push a lever. Everyone put their food in the box and Class Room latched the doors.

The fire started to die down as the forest grew dark.

Daisy and Joey both wielded poker sticks, using them to fiddle with the fire and make it burn more efficiently. They would add a stick from time to time until there were no more in the pile.

The hikers relaxed by the fire. Kitsune sat close to the flames, using the dim firelight to read his ever-present novel. Class Room mindlessly strummed Yuk as she listened to Rodent Whisperer rehash the bear encounter with the kids, who embellished the details with each retelling. Brown Shades swung in his hammock nearby, occasionally interjecting a fun fact into the conversation before only snores could be heard coming from his direction. If an outsider observed their campsite, they would see a spirited group of people, talking and laughing as though they were just out on an exciting camping trip, not trying to find their missing kin during a nuclear war and an overthrown government.

Fic sat on his sleeping bag, watching the cousins talk and poke the fire. He switched on his red headlamp and looked down at *The A.T. Guide* that had been with him since Georgia. The book looked like it had been through a lot: tattered and torn. He felt a little tattered and torn himself. Thinking back at all he had been through since that June morning when he had kissed his wife goodbye and headed south with his watch team.

For now, it seemed that they had moved out of the range of the people who were trying to catch them in southern Virginia. This area seemed to be devoid of people. They were getting close to his destination. Fic would find his family, and after he made sure they were okay, he would figure out what was going on in Mount Weather. He knew all the ins and outs of the secret base, and maybe his key card still would let him in.

Fic looked up at the cousins at the fire. They had stirred all of the coals into a slowly smoking trickle and were coming into the shelter to get into their sleeping bags.

He put the guide into the pocket of his pack and slipped into his bag too.

The night sounds took over the forest as The Party spent yet another night as outsiders in the woods of the Appalachian Trail.

#

During the night, Fic was awakened by the sounds of snuffling coming from the direction of the bear-proof storage box. He quickly flashed his headlamp at the box and there were two large eyes glowing back at him. Behind the two large eyes were four small ones. A mamma and her two babies were looking for their goodies. After a quick second or two, the eyes blinked out and the bears scrambled away. Fic was thankful that they had that box; fighting the rogue army and unfriendly townspeople was one thing, competing with nature in this way would be a hard setback.

Morning came and the camp stirred. The hikers were reluctant to part from their warm wrappings as yesterday's hot, muggy day had turned into a slight cold snap. Warm puffy jackets became the uniform of the morning, while they waited for warmth to find them. Joey stoked up a small fire and everyone huddled around for a while. Feeding it little sticks to keep the flames going, but not making too much of a blaze.

Soon, everyone was packed and ready to put in the day's work. Fic was last to leave the hut area and he checked to make sure no one had left any gear behind. Fic turned to the trail and felt a crisp breeze on his face. Today may be a good day to hike. Cool enough to dry their sweat quickly, but not too cold to chill their bodies.

The miles moved by rather quickly at first. The day finally warmed up some, but it looked like more rain was on the way. Along with the cooler temperatures, it might be a little more challenging than it had been lately. The threat of hypothermia was always present, but more so when the temperatures dip and the wind picks up.

After a quick cold lunch at one of the road crossings, the rain started to fall, just as they started back up the trail. The Party continued in silence, letting the rain do the talking as they kept slogging along the trail. The rain grew heavier, creating a muddy stream where the trail once was and soaking all the hikers to the bone. Rain gear is nice, but nothing is truly waterproof, at least nothing that wants to breathe. Since they had kept moving to keep warm during the day, they completed the thirteen miles to the next shelter by 1500.

Everyone but Kitsune wanted to set up in the large shelter. He was still happy to hang his hammock in between two nearby trees in the rainy forest. The Party members were all shivering as they set about putting down their pads and bags and getting out of their drenched clothes and into something dry.

Everyone huddled in their sleeping bags, their legs and waist covered as they sat and replenished their calories. They each made something quick and warm, hoping to ease the deep chill that wracked their bodies.

The kids had done really well again today, even with the adverse weather. Fic thought they might try a longer day tomorrow. There was a small campground a little under twenty miles up the trail and the next hut was just a bit further on from that. They would see how the day goes and keep their options open.

No one bothered trying to make a fire on this soggy night. The wet wood would never catch, even if anyone were motivated enough to leave the comfort of their down quilts.

Darkness came to the shelter and the hikers slept.

#

Morning dawned bright and warm. It was amazing how the weather changed up on the mountain. Everyone was in a much better mood, and after a quick breakfast, they were ready to go. The path was covered in puddles and water still flowed down the trail in some places, but as the day wore on, the rain from the last two days was burned back into steam.

Today's trek had a steep climb. Everyone was glad for the workout and found themselves soaking wet, yet again, when they reached the top — this time from sweat instead of heavy rain. They ate lunch at a small picnic area next to the road. As they were sitting there with all of their gear spread out around their packs, they heard a vehicle coming along the twisty road. Everyone quickly grabbed any gear that was around them and headed into the cover of the forest.

Fic sat at the edge of the trees and watched the road. They heard the sound of a vehicle engine far off, but nothing came into view for several minutes. Finally, a dusty blue pickup truck — at least twenty years old — turned one of the twists in the road and came lumbering by. Shifting through the few gears it had as it climbed up the incline of the road.

The truck passed the picnic area and continued on, moving out of sight as it rounded another bend in the road.

"It looked like an older gentleman was driving the truck," said Fic. "He had a long white beard and wore a large cowboy hat."

After that small bit of excitement, everyone put their gear back properly in their packs and moved on to tackle the five miles they still had to go. They had made good time in the morning but lunch was a little late because everyone had felt good and wanted to keep walking.

The Party arrived at the small campground as the sun was starting to head towards the horizon. They picked a campsite along the edge and set up. Everyone had to use their sleeping structures at this site, since there was no shelter. Rodent Whisperer decided to lay his sleeping bag out in the open — what he called cowboy camping — as the day had been fresh and warm and it looked like the good weather was going to continue throughout the night.

They ate a meal and were sitting around a small fire as darkness fell in the quiet camp. They heard an owl hoot in a nearby tree. Right after it was answered by another hoot from a few trees over. The Party sat in wonder as a large family of owls came flying into the trees of the campground and called to each other as if they were planning the night's hunt. From what Fic could see, it seemed like the parents were teaching their brood how to go about it.

Eventually the owl family moved back into the nearby woods and their calls faded from the campground.

While Class Room slept in her tent, Kitsune and Brown Shades hung in their hammocks. The cousins were sharing a two-person tent that they had found in the outfitters; Joey carried the tent and fly and Daisy carried the poles and stakes. They hadn't erected it yet and were fine with forging the overhead cover after the long day of hiking, so they joined Rodent Whisperer. Fic also decided to join the three and sleep around the campsite's fire ring under the open sky.

They fanned out around the fire and settled into their bags, talking softly around the fire. Daisy and Joey had done very well today, keeping pace with the others and not showing any fatigue other than the normal stiffness after a break. They were swiftly adjusting to being on the trail and walking all day long. Young people are often resilient and adapt quickly to challenging situations; these two were no exception. They were proud of their almost twenty mile day.

"I can't believe we hiked that far today," said Daisy. "Before today, I'd never walked more than a few miles at a time. Now we've hiked almost fifty miles in the last three days!"

Joey nodded his agreement as he massaged his calf muscles and his feet. "I still don't have any blisters," he bragged as Daisy was nursing one that had developed on her little toe. She looked up at him and stuck out her tongue as he smiled back.

The fire reduced itself to ashes and the darkness became complete on the top of the mountains of Shenandoah. Each of the hikers hunkered down in their bags and as one of the owls hooted its question one last time, the only answer was soft snores.

#

The morning sun reflected off the dew that coated the grass around the cowboy sleepers. They all had a little coating of wetness on their bags but were still mostly dry themselves.

The camp came awake, and everyone was up and moving about as the day brightened. Everyone was sitting around the table drinking coffee or snacking on a honeybun or crumbled pop tart, when they heard the pickup's groaning engine come into range again. They all froze as the vehicle got closer to the campsite. They were hoping that it would pass the campground and continue on, but to their horror, it turned into the camp and pulled up alongside the office building that was close to the road. It was the same pickup from yesterday.

Fic looked at the others and saw their alarm. He told Brown Shades to come with him as he went to meet the guy and motioned for the others to start getting ready to go. He had a strong feeling that the man was harmless and could possibly be helpful. The two tweens started gathering their gear and stowing it, while the two adults went to strike Class Room's tent and pack their gear. Fic realized that Kitsune wasn't present. He had been up with them earlier, and he hadn't seen him walk off anywhere.

He motioned to Brown Shades, and they started walking to the pickup truck. They had left the shotgun and the staff back at the campsite to keep the man at ease. As he walked along the campground road, he saw Kitsune up at the edge of the forest. He waved to Fic and motioned with his hands that he would circle around the edge and keep an eye on them. Fic nodded his head and kept walking, quietly telling Brown Shades what he had just seen.

They approached the pickup truck. The man — the same one Fic had seen the day before — was looking into the bed of his truck as he moved stuff around and didn't even notice them approaching.

"Hello, good sir," Brown Shades said to let the guy know they had arrived.

"Aaah!" the man yelled as he appeared to jump out of his skin. "Where the hell did you guys come from?" he asked, looking frightened and a bit mad at being snuck up on.

"We are traveling the Appalachian Trail, heading north. We spent the night in this fine campground. Are you the caretaker here?" Brown Shades made an educated guess.

"I am," the old man answered. "Though there's just me here. No campers. Except for you two of course. I just went down the mountain yesterday to get some supplies. I was able to find some and after what I saw, I knew I just needed to get back up here. There is some bad stuff going on down in the valley."

The man appeared to be somewhere north of seventy, and his long gray beard reached down to the top of his chest. Under his cowboy hat, his dark gray hair fell to his shoulders. The wrinkles on his face were deep and abundant and his skin showed obvious signs of being exposed to a lot of wind and sun through the years. His eyes were a deep, dark blue. From a few feet away, the pupils blended in with the dark iris making them look larger.

The man reached into his shirt pocket and pulled out a pack of Marlboros. He tapped a smoke out, grabbed it with his lips and offered his pack to the two men. The hikers declined the offer, and he lit up, took a long pull, and let it out.

"I'm gonna have to quit these coffin nails soon, since not too many seem to be around anymore. In Virginia, no less." He noticed the men watching him and introduced himself.

"I'm Monty," he said, reaching out his hand to the two men.

Fic and Brown Shades shook Monty's hand in turn as they introduced themselves. "So y'all say you are hiking?" Monty asked. "Where's your gear?"

"There are actually seven of us," Fic replied. "Our friends are over at one of the sites near the trail. We had a long day and came to the campground near dusk, so we decided to bed down here. Do you need us to pay for the night?"

"Nah, that's not necessary," Monty replied. "If you help me unload my truck, I'll consider us even," he added with a twinkle in his dark eyes.

The two men commenced to move several boxes from the bed of the truck to the small office. Placing the load in a back room behind the main counter.

"Do you guys have enough food?" Monty asked. "This load will last me a while, but if you are in need, I can spare some."

"I don't think that will be necessary," replied Fic. "We got a good resupply in Waynesboro, and I think it will get us through the park. Hopefully, after that, we can find some more. It's getting pretty scarce near the trail and all the people seem to be gone from the area."

"Yeah, I noticed that too. I been up here since about a month before the bombs fell. I was planning on working the whole summer up here. After the war happened, a lot of people came through at first, trying to get somewhere else. Some stayed a night or two, others just moved on. Eventually less and less people would come through and I haven't seen anyone for about two weeks now, except you two."

"Do you want to meet the rest of our party?" Brown Shades asked.

"Sure," replied Monty.

As they turned to head to the campsite, a cardinal flew past them and circled the three men. After a few circuits, it flew off back the way it had come.

The men arrived back at the camp where the others were packing up. Brown Shades introduced Monty to The Party and everyone greeted Monty with a smile and kind word.

"You guys are quite a group," Monty said. "I see you have means to protect yourself," eyeing the weapons that each of the hikers carried.

Kitsune arrived back at the group, and he too was introduced. Everyone joined in the conversation and answered Monty's questions as he talked to the hikers.

"Your adventures have been outstanding," Monty said. "And here I am, hiding away up on the mountain. I feel I need to be here, though. How many shells you got for those shotguns?" he asked Fic.

"Not too many," Fic replied. I had about six double ought buck, and Joey brought along five of his own shells, so eleven."

"I think I can help you out a little," Monty said. "Wait here." The old man scampered off to his office and came back a few minutes later with a box of 25 double ought buck shells. "Here you go," he said, handing the box to Fic. "I have several boxes for my old Remington, but I can easily spare one box. You guys are heading into danger, I'm pretty sure. On my last re-supply, I went north and had to turn back when a group of men had a blockade near the park entrance on the road that heads into Luray. They all had weapons and most of them were pointed at me. I quickly made a U-turn and got out of there, but I heard a few shots as I took off. You need to be careful when you get up that way. They may still be there."

"Thanks for the shells, we can definitely use them," Fic said. "A shotgun is pretty useless once you run out of ammo."

The hikers talked with Monty for a while until everyone was ready to go, and then they said goodbye and headed back to the trail.

#

The day was very pleasant. The sun would come out from behind a large cloud and shine through the forest for a few minutes, then go back behind another cloud, making the forest a few shades darker for the next several minutes. This kept the temperature at a somewhat comfortable level, but everyone was still sweating when they came to the turnoff for the Big Meadows Wayside. Even though they could stretch their food for several more days, it was worth the short walk to see if anything could be found at the wayside.

The side trail led down to Skyline Drive and they carefully walked along it for a few hundred meters before coming to the buildings of the wayside. There was a small two-pump gas station in front of the combined restaurant and store. Unlike the camp store they had seen at Loft Mountain, this one had been breached and the doors were hanging open.

The Party entered the building and started searching. A few bags of chips and a package of donuts were found and stuffed into a food bag, but the place had been thoroughly picked over.

Daisy let out a happy squeal and came out of the kitchen with a large can of blackberries. They opened the can right there and everyone spooned out a portion as they passed around the sweet treat.

"Yum," Daisy giggled with glee.

Class Room went back into the kitchen and after some intensive searching, she found some canned meat and some rice in a box that would make a decent meal. She decided to cook it up right away since their stomachs were hinting that it was lunch time. The Party wandered back outside and sat around some picnic tables while they ate the meal Class Room put together for them. As they finished, they spread out on the grass and enjoyed the mild weather while they relaxed. Kitsune had his nose buried in a book, as usual. Rodent Whisperer pulled out a deck of cards and started teaching the kids how to play Blackjack. Once they got the hang of the game, Rodent Whisperer surprised them with a pack of Skittles, which they used to place bets as they continued playing. The atmosphere became fun, and everyone was laughing and telling jokes. It was apparent that they just wanted a short break from all of their worries and impending challenges.

Fic watched the group talking by the tables. He wandered away from the group and walked around the wayside. He saw something through some trees, and he headed over to check it out. He came to a large low structure that was the Shenandoah Visitors Center. There was a large statue of a Civilian Conservation Corps man outside the building. He looked in the glass doors and could see some exhibits and other displays inside. The doors were firmly locked, so he just looked around for a while then headed back to The Party.

They hung out for about two hours before they determined that they should get some more miles in. Since yesterday had been a long hard day, they had decided to only go a little over twelve miles today. Eventually, everyone was packed up again and they headed back up the blue blazed trail, and soon enough, they were back on the Appalachian Trail.

#

The last four miles seemed to breeze by and they found themselves rolling into camp with the day almost done, but still enough daylight left to get set up and make some dinner.

About fifty meters away from the shelter was a cabin that was maintained by the local hiking club. Kitsune had gone down to check it out and he reported back that the cabin was unlocked.

The Party all went down to check it out and were impressed by the rustic old building that had four walls and a wood stove, but not much else.

"I want to sleep here tonight," Daisy said, with Joey nodding his desire too.

"I'm sure we can bunk down here for the night. I'll sleep with you two, if that is cool," Kitsune said.

"Perfectly cool," replied Daisy.

Brown Shades and Class Room also decided to stay in the cabin, but Fic and Rodent Whisperer opted to stay up in the shelter. The night was still going to be warm, so they were hoping for a breeze to help keep them a little cooler than a four walled building. Kitsune already had his hammock set up on two posts on the cabin's front porch.

Everyone set up their bedrolls in the place they had chosen, before sitting around the table and preparing their individual dinners. They kept their meal light as they were all still full from the blackberries and food concoction that they had eaten at the wayside.

Fic had started a small fire and they all sat around, staring into the flames. Class Room walked down to her pack in the cabin and came back with a bag of marshmallows she had found at the wayside and secretly snuck into her bag. Everyone got excited at the prospect of catching a white puffy tube of sugar on fire and then eating it, trying not to burn their mouths on the liquified sweetness. She had also brought Yuk up with her and she serenaded the group as they enjoyed their treat. Joey drew in his tattered sketchbook as he nodded along to the music while Kitsune and Daisy got up and tried to create a dance that would complement the music. Kitsune twirled Daisy in a circle before she broke off and improvised a little jig of her own. She ended her dance with a pointed finger at Kitsune, indicating it was his turn to take the stage. The two went back and forth in an impromptu dance battle. Rodent Whisperer couldn't resist joining in after a few minutes while the others cheered them on.

Afterwards, each of the hikers went to their beds, happy and satisfied now that their — usually constant —hunger was sated for once.

Fic sat looking out into the forest, wondering how his wife and children were doing. Hoping they were okay and knowing that he was getting closer and closer every day. They didn't have many more miles to go, but if he rushed off now, he would feel that he would be betraying his Tramily. They had come to mean a great deal to him as he had made his way north. Without them, he wouldn't have made it this far, he was sure.

#

Fic fell asleep quickly. He was dreaming, he could tell, but was powerless to control the way it progressed.

He was in his kitchen at home, but it didn't have the usual decor. It all looked more rustic. His wife, Lori, and two grown kids were sitting at the table talking. He could see their lips moving, but not understand or even hear what they were saying. He tried to talk to them, but when he looked at his hands, he could see through them to the kitchen floor. He was transparent. Ghostlike.

The threesome talked for a bit, Fic still not understanding what they were saying, then they stood and moved towards the door. Both his kids were suddenly wearing shiny armor. They placed metal helmets on their heads and picked up two long swords, sliding them into long sheaths. As they left the kitchen, lightning flashed, followed immediately with a long crash of thunder that Fic could hear and feel.

As they walked across the farmyard, the sky grew dark and ominous. Suddenly a large grotesque man came riding up their driveway on a horse wearing a full set of black armor. He had a large spear in his right hand and his horse's breath was steaming out of its nostrils. An evil laugh came from this dark knight's helmet and he pointed at his daughter. "You will be mine," the man said, and Fic could almost smell the foul odor of his breath.

His two children drew their swords and ran towards the dark knight. The knight hefted his spear and threw it towards his two children. The spear was heading right for his son —

Fic woke up with a start. He was sure he had called out in his sleep, but when he looked over at Rodent Whisperer, he slept undisturbed.

Fic rolled over, wiping a sheen of sweat that had peppered his brow. Shaking his head at the weird dream. "Just a dream," he reassured himself softly as he faded back into an uneasy sleep.

CHAPTER 21
HOME FRONT VI - FRIDAY, AUGUST 3RD TO SATURDAY, AUGUST 4TH

Lori was sitting in the kitchen. A new day had arrived. Rain was in the forecast, as far as she could tell. Large thunder boomer clouds sat on the horizon to the west. She could see them from the kitchen window. Her children were upstairs. She could hear them moving around, so she deduced that both were awake and starting their day. She had made a large pot of coffee, using the gas stove to heat the water and a large French press to turn it into coffee.

Brittney came down first, went straight to an empty mug that was waiting for her on the counter, and poured herself a cup of steaming fresh brewed coffee. She added a splash of whole milk, traded with Mr. Cooper for some of their vegetables that had been growing nicely through this tough summer. Lori had brought the milk in from the old spring house they had just to the right of the barn. Lori was so happy to have that feature from times past. It made things last much longer without electricity. They had been working on gathering parts to set up a compact solar panel system, just to keep a few basic things running, but they were still missing a couple key items.

Brittney sat at the kitchen table and smiled at her mom. "Good morning, mother," she said happily.

"Good morning, daughter," was her reply, a small smile coming to her worried face. "What are your plans for today?"

"Shane and I will be going out for a short patrol over to the east today," she replied. "The BMP quads are all down, gas is getting low and some of it got contaminated, so we will be walking our patrol today. We plan on heading down towards the highway, follow Millwood Road towards the mountain, then circle back using Tilthammer Mill Road and Clay Hill Road, checking the five or so farms along the way."

"Better take your rain gear," Lori advised. "Those clouds look heavy off to the west. It looks like a wet day."

Shane came into the kitchen, still rubbing some sleep out of his eyes and repeated the same motions his sister had done to get that precious Go juice into their system. He appeared to be in a slightly foul mood.

"You guys be careful today," Lori said.

"We will," they both replied in unison.

After a quick breakfast of old stale cereal doused in that exquisite, fresh milk, the two siblings rose up and gathered their small patrol packs — filled with necessities to keep them going for a long day's patrol and enough gear and supplies to spend a night or two away from home if needed. Each picked up a shotgun and shouldered it.

They went to the door and turned to say goodbye to their mother, then headed down the driveway towards the road that led to Route 50. A slow roll of thunder came to their ears as they moved off. Lori was right about the coming storm, and it was going to be an intense one.

#

Lori went about her morning chores, trying to get as much done as possible before the storm hit. She checked the garden, gathering some ripe cucumbers and tomatoes; then went to check the chicken coop and gather any eggs the ladies had left them. She began to do a little bit of weeding in the garden when the rain started. Large wet drops started falling in ones and twos. Then more joined the fray, and suddenly she was getting soaked as the heavens let loose. The storm had arrived.

Lori kept herself busy inside the house as the storm raged outside. It would rain very hard for a stretch with lots of lightning and thunder, then the rain would slacken off, but never stop. Then it would pour again. This was definitely a large storm that was coming from the southwest.

When darkness came and the rain continued, Lori started to worry about the kids. Sometimes their patrols lasted all day, and on a few occasions, they had stayed out overnight when they found themselves too far away to get back before dark or they were busy with a time-consuming task.

When they still hadn't come home at midnight, she tried to go up to bed, but knew sleep wasn't going to come.

She tossed and turned for several hours before she gave up on getting any sleep and went downstairs to make coffee. The sky had started to lighten up by the mountain to the east as she finished her second cup.

The bulk of the storm had passed, but the sky was still cloudy and low hanging and a few sprinkles would fall every twenty minutes or so.

She decided she was going to walk down to the main road and see if she could find any sign of her returning children.

She made her way down the long driveway and turned left, the direction that they were supposed to finish their patrol. She walked the road for about a half of a mile, stepping around the large puddles that pooled on the shoulder. A soft wind had picked up from the south. It was warm, but wet.

She turned around and started back towards the farm. As she was approaching the driveway, she saw someone come over the rise, walking down the middle of the road. The person was staggering and having trouble walking. She watched as they fell to the ground and lay motionless.

She hurried towards the person. When she was about fifty meters away, she realized it was Shane. She started to run to her son and the first thing she saw as she came up to his prone body was a lot of blood.

He had been beaten about the face and most of the blood was coming from a wound in his side. She didn't think she could carry him up to the house, so she tried to bring him back to consciousness. She called his name a few times and his eyes fluttered. He stared at her for a few seconds, as if his eyes were taking too long to focus and finally whispered, "Mom." Tears were coming down her face as she smoothed the hair from his brow. "They took Brittney," he continued in a halting voice. "I tried to stop them, but ...," his voice trailed off.

With Shane's weak help, she was able to help him to the beginning of the driveway. They walked about fifty feet towards the house when Shane stumbled again and went back to the ground.

Lori ran back to the barn and looked around. In the corner was a large wheelbarrow. She grabbed it and started pushing it towards Shane's rag doll body.

She was able to get him into the wheelbarrow and pushed him up to the house. He was coming around again and they were able to get him inside and onto the couch in the living room.

"What happened, Shane?" she asked her son, her voice raising in panic and fear.

"A soldier — and Jim," he said softly. "They surprised us by the river ...," his voice faded off again. He was unconscious.

Lori got to work cleaning his wounds and bandaging him up. The wound on his side looked like a stab wound. She fixed it up as best as she could with some butterflies, but he was going to need a doctor. Probably stitches and antibiotics, too. *Where was Brittney?* she thought as the panic and fear came back a hundredfold.

CHAPTER 22
SHENANDOAH II - FRIDAY, AUGUST 3RD TO SUNDAY, AUGUST 5TH

Dawn came, but it was hard to tell. The sky was full of angry looking clouds and after The Party had packed up and ate a simple breakfast, the rain started. The drops were big, and thunder announced its presence all around them. Everyone donned their rain gear, and they started out.

Last night's dream was still a foggy memory in Fic's mind that put him in an uneasy state. He felt like they should keep moving as fast as they could. He had a strong feeling that something was wrong at home. "It's just a dream," he told himself. "Just a dream."

The trail was still easy to manage, and they moved along as best they could in the rain which had become heavy at times. After a few miles, they came to the scorched remains of what used to be the Skyland Resort. Destruction and devastation were becoming a common sight as the chaos raged on. They picked around the ruins for a while before moving on, finding nothing of value.

#

As The Party ascended Stony Mountain — the highest point on the trail in the park — the storm started to worry Fic some. The lightning seemed to be all around them — the thunder quickly following the flashes — the storm was on top of them.

They hurried along, getting away from the high point as fast as they could. They came to Birds Nest Hut and decided to take a long break and eat a late lunch. The group huddled in the shelter. The air was warm, but they were all soaked. They decided to cook something warm, to help their insides fight off the damp coolness of being wet.

They all sat in the cover of the shelter, looking out into the forest where the rain just kept coming down in buckets. The trail had once again transformed into a river, and no one wanted to go back out into that torrent.

An hour passed before the rain seemed to slack off, and after a short discussion, The Party decided to get a few more miles in. The road to Luray was only a few miles ahead, and once they made it to that point, there was another shelter nearby where they could stop for the night.

Compromised rain gear was thrown over wet shoulders one more time and packs were hefted and buckled into place. Onward they went.

#

When they arrived at Thornton Gap, the rain was coming and going periodically. They gathered in a picnic pavilion at the parking area near the road that went into Luray.

Fic looked over at Daisy, who had taken off her soaked hiking shoes and was gingerly picking at a couple of blisters that the wet day had aggravated. "Are you sure you don't want to go into Luray to check out your house, Daisy?" Fic asked. He was hoping she would say no, so they could keep heading towards his family. That uneasy feeling had returned.

"No," she replied. "There's nothin' there I need. It's a pretty far walk to my house anyway," she added. "Besides, these blisters are kind of slowin' me down."

"Okay, then," said Fic. "If everyone is okay with the plan, we can head to Pass Mountain Hut for the night. I think it is only about a mile more."

Everyone nodded their heads, and it was clear that they just wanted to get the day's hike done. The storm and steady rain had taken all their energy on this rainy day. They just wanted to get into their down bags and get some more warm food into their wet bodies.

The last mile seemed the hardest as they made their way to the hut. Daisy started to limp a little as the blisters she was nursing had become more painful. The trail was taking its measure of pain and blood that it always demands. No one felt good, but she was feeling the worst.

They finally arrived at the shelter and set up camp. Kitsune and Rodent Whisperer went and gathered some wood. It was very hard to find anything that wasn't damp or downright wet, but they managed to gather a stack of wood that could possibly be coaxed into some kind of fire. After working at it for over thirty minutes, they had a small flame kindled. The fire struggled to stay lit and put out a steady hiss of water turning into steam and ash. Everyone gathered around the pitiful blaze and tried to warm their wet, wrinkled hands. Stoves were fired up and dinner was made and consumed in silence. It had been a hard day.

With the sun going down and the rain reduced to sprinkles from time to time, some of The Party retired to their beds. Fic, Kitsune and Brown Shades huddled around the struggling fire, feeding small damp sticks to keep it going.

Fic decided to tell the other two about his dream. "I had another strange dream last night," he began. Brown Shades gave an understanding nod.

"Was it about a Dark Knight and two brave warriors?" he asked, already guessing at the answer. "I'm assuming those two warriors were your children."

Fic looked at him for a long while as Kitsune nodded in acknowledgement that he too knew about the dream. "Yes," Fic replied. "I'm not feeling too good about this one, as we have seen how the others have played out. I feel that I really need to get back home as quickly as possible. We are only a few more days away."

"I understand your concern, and I understand if you want to move ahead without us," Brown Shades began, "but I think we need you as much as you need us right now. Daisy is dealing with some blisters and who knows what is waiting for all of us along the trail. It's your decision again, but I hope you stay with us and we can arrive at your place. Slow going will be the remedy for Daisy's feet."

Fic thought about Brown Shades' wisdom and ultimately agreed with his logic. He tried to relax a little. For now, he would stay with The Party.

"So, where is your farm again?" Kitsune asked Fic. "I know you mentioned Millwood as your town, but do you live in the town or nearby?"

"We are a little outside of the town proper. Past a small stream called Sprout Run about a half mile or so. We have a long driveway and a large red barn next to our small farmhouse," Fic described his homestead.

Kitsune seemed satisfied with the details and grew silent again, placing another small stick into the fire.

Eventually, there were no more semi-dry sticks to put into the fire and it slowly reduced itself to ashes.

The three men retired to their sleeping places. Kitsune had set up his hammock to the side of the hut. Away from the others, but close enough if needed. Brown Shades had elected to stay in the shelter again so that he did not have to deal with a possible sopping wet hammock in the morning.

A small sprinkle fell around Kitsune as he climbed into the hanging shelter. He lay in his hammock for a short while before getting out again and walking into the nearby forest, disappearing from view.

#

The Party stirred and arose from their beds. They started slowly getting their things together. The storm was gone, and the sun was shining through the trees. They sat together for breakfast and then packed all their gear. When they were ready, they hefted their packs and started heading back to the trail. Today Fic was hoping to hike out of the park and get as close to home as they could.

Fic went over to Daisy — who was standing with her pack still on the ground beside her — to ask her about her blisters. Her reply wasn't very positive.

"I think I can hike, but they're still a little sore," she said. "I had to put a pin in another one last night, but the two on my left foot seem to be gettin' better. Hopefully I can keep my feet dry today and that'll help."

Fic patted her on the shoulder and said, "Just let me know if you are having any trouble. I'm hoping to get out of the park today, if we can."

She nodded and hefted her pack. Moving out behind the others. Fic stood watching The Party move back to the trail and start to spread out. He followed behind.

This day had a much brighter outlook than the stormy hiking of yesterday. The unsettled weather had moved away, and the sun was shining. Most of the puddles were drying up and the few that remained were easily avoided. Fic was walking drag, trying to walk slow enough to not overtake the others, but his worry had increased. He just couldn't get his family off of his mind and wanted to walk as fast as he could to get home. Keeping his pace slow was becoming more of a struggle as the hours rolled by and his anxiety only grew.

The sun had passed its zenith when he came upon Daisy sitting on a log, her right boot and sock were off. She was inspecting the side of her heel. Fic stepped up and saw the red rawness of one more blister that was starting to rise there.

"I'll be fine, Fic," Daisy said. "I just gotta put a pin in it and put some mole skin on it."

Fic helped her tend to her foot and after a few minutes, she was ready to go again.

They walked together. Fic stayed behind her to keep her company and make sure she really could make it. After another thirty minutes, he started to worry that she couldn't.

She kept trying to hide her pain from him, ensuring him that she was okay and could go on. Fic saw right through her ruse and when they came to the road where the others were waiting, he suggested they head to the nearby Elkwallow Wayside to see what they could find, take a break, and eat some lunch. Everyone agreed, and they walked a short way down the road to the wayside.

The building seemed intact but had been breached like the other waysides they had passed. They went inside and looked around. They found another coveted can of blackberries, a six pack of Coke, some candy bars, and more chips and pretzels.

The Party moved to the picnic tables and showed off their finds. Class Room and Daisy did rock, paper, scissors over an extra snickers bar. Daisy won the contest, but cut the bar in half with her knife and gave Class Room her own share of the prize anyway. Everyone enjoyed their special lunch. It wasn't the most nutritious, but the sweet variety was a welcome change from the bland trail food they had been eating lately. When the found food was gone, it was time to go.

Fic looked at Daisy and asked, "Can you make another five miles to the last shelter in the park?"

"I think so," she replied, a stubborn look on her face.

"Okay, let's get going," he said.

The Party moved along with Daisy in the middle, intentionally walking slow, so she could make it without too much pain.

#

After a few hours, they had arrived at Gravel Springs Hut, the last shelter within the park. After leaving the park boundaries, they would pass one more before hitting the road.

They set up camp and gathered wood for a fire. The day had been nice, and they were in a better mood. All except Daisy and Fic. Daisy's pain was all over her face and Fic's growing unease was starting to physically affect him. When he stood still, he would almost quiver with the need to keep going.

While Kitsune and Brown Shades made the fire, Class Room nursed Daisy's feet. She cleaned everything up, drained another blister that had popped up on her little toe, and placed mole skin and band-aids where they were needed. Class Room put a pair of her own socks on Daisy's feet that were thick and dry. A look of relief was now on Daisy's face, she thanked the young woman and gave her a hug.

Everyone ate their dinner and sat around the fire for a while before moving off to bed one at a time. Just like the night before, Fic, Kitsune and Brown Shades were the last ones left around the fire.

Fic started telling the other two that he was feeling anxious and really wanted to get home. It was so close now. He had hiked almost a thousand miles to get to this spot and he could see the end. He brought up his dream again and how it had increased his unease.

"The power of our dreams and the fact we are all sharing them is something to take notice of," Brown Shades said. "There is no denying that they have had a prescient note to them." Kitsune looked on with a slightly concerned expression on his face, but he said nothing.

"I don't want to keep pushing Daisy. She tries to hide her pain, but I know she is hurting. I'm playing with the idea of heading out alone, while you guys follow behind at an easier pace, helping Daisy along the way."

"I don't think you should go alone," Brown Shades said as Kitsune nodded his agreement. "You know there is a lot of danger out there and having backup can be the difference between success and failure."

"I'll go with you," offered Kitsune. "I can be your backup."

"I can come too," said Brown Shades, "but my knee has been hurting some and I have to say, the easier pace today felt good, so it may be hard to keep a quick pace."

"I think you would be better leading the others to my place," Fic suggested. "I'll ask Rodent Whisperer if he wants to come tomorrow."

A voice came from the edge of the shelter, "Come where?" Rodent Whisperer walked over to the others, scratching his long, shaggy beard. "I heard my name mentioned."

Fic relayed his plan to Rodent Whisperer, and he agreed to come with the other two before Fic could finish his explanation.

"Ah, you're worried about your two warriors and the Dark Knight," he said as if it was completely natural to know each other's dreams and to share them each night.

"It's settled then," said Fic. "Tomorrow us three will head out after breakfast and try to get as far as we can. I figure it is about thirty-three miles. I don't think we can do all of that, but hopefully most of it."

The others agreed with nods and assurances.

The fire was stirred into steaming coils of smoke, and everyone went to their sleeping places.

Kitsune went to his hammock and sat inside for about thirty minutes as the forest darkened. When he had deemed the wait long enough, he exited his hammock and walked into the forest. Disappearing behind a large pine tree.

#

The cardinal was flying in the dark. The clouds had broken up from the storm and a gibbous moon shone in the sky. The bird was flying north steadily on a path. A mission.

The cardinal flew down near a highway that crossed the trail. There were a dozen Jeeps and Humvees parked along the road. As the cardinal circled around the convoy, many soldiers could be seen moving around the vehicles and up and down the road. There were several tents in a field to the west of the trail. Lights shown all around. The bivouac was bustling and crowded.

The red bird climbed up into the air and headed north again. He followed the mountain as it rose up and down, and eventually he came to a mountain pass with a road running through it. Off to the left the cardinal could see a river, and he flew towards it. The bird followed along the river until he came across a tributary and veered off in that direction. The creek eventually led him to a road, which led to a driveway, and finally to a farmhouse with a red barn next to it.

The cardinal landed next to the porch of the farmhouse.

He had been there the night before but was unable to see anything as the house was dark and the curtains had been drawn.

The cardinal pecked at the ground for a bit and then looked at the house. There was now a light on at the back. The bird flew onto the back porch and fluttered up to the windowsill. It appeared to look into the window.

Inside was a woman who looked frantic. She was pouring water into a basin next to the stove. She picked up some bandages that were lying on the table and went back into another room.

The cardinal took flight and circled around the house until it came to another window. Inside, the bird saw the woman working on a young man who appeared to be unconscious. He pecked at the pane once and she turned to look towards the window, her eyes landing on the red bird on the sill. The young man mumbled something in his fevered state, and she looked back to him.

The cardinal turned and took flight, disappearing into the darkness to the south.

#

In the morning, Fic waited until everyone was up and had eaten their breakfast before telling the others of his plan to move ahead with Kitsune and Rodent Whisperer, and the rest of The Party would come as best they could with Brown Shades and Class Room leading them. Fic had given them detailed directions to his farm.

Kitsune appeared a little concerned and said to Fic, "I don't know how I know, but I have a strong feeling we might have some trouble today. I think the rogue soldiers are up ahead somewhere. We may have to sneak around them."

Fic stared at him with a strange look in his eyes. "How strong is this feeling, Kitsune?"

"I think there may be a roadblock up ahead. Or a trail block if you will."

"We'll figure that out when we have to," replied Fic.

Kitsune nodded his head, but he knew that they would be dealing with something today. The worried look remained on his face as he stared back at Fic. He seemed to want to say more, but instead, rearranged his face into a neutral expression and remained silent.

Fic, Kitsune and Rodent Whisper were all ready to go while the others were still finishing up their packing. Fic looked at the two men, raised his eyebrows and said, "You ready?"

Two nods answered him, and they all donned their packs and headed out as a trio. The rest of The Party said goodbye for now and promised to move as fast as they safely could with their injuries and unknown obstacles ahead.

The three men moved off at a fast clip. Fic was leading now, and he felt like he was being pushed from behind by an invisible hand. He kept up the pace for a few miles before calling for a short break.

When the break was done, they moved on once again at a hurried pace, but now Kitsune was leading the threesome.

Another few miles down the trail they came to a small kiosk that marked the border of the park. They were now back on regular Appalachian Trail property.

A little further along, they came to the Tom Floyd shelter. They stopped here to eat a quick lunch, and after a short break to stretch out and loosen overworked muscles, they continued on their forced march.

They passed a forest road and a small footbridge over a creek before the trail started up a smooth incline, climbing a hillside. Moving away from the babbling stream, brought their attention to a different kind of sound. The unmistakable commotion of road noise filled the air around them, but the vehicles emitting the cacophony resembled large trucks or construction equipment of some kind.

Fic looked over at Kitsune who remained quiet but raised an eyebrow, almost as if he was saying "told ya so."

The men continued, growing more cautious as they got closer to the noise.

The trail topped the rise, and they could tell the road was near, as the sounds were coming from just over the hill.

Carefully, they crept up to the top and looked down towards the scene.

Down below was a huge camp that straddled the road and spread up both sides of the hills surrounding the cut. There were bulldozers off to the left, and the entire area was swarming with men in uniform. There were several tents on both sides of the road and an impressive looking roadblock on Route 522. They even had a gate that they could raise and let a vehicle through, if they so chose. There were sandbag barriers on either side of the barricade, and both had manned machine guns by the looks of it.

After taking a good look at the strength and location of the setup, Fic motioned the other two back below the rise and off the trail to have a little parley.

"This looks pretty big," said Fic.

"I agree," said Kitsune. "I think it goes at least a half a mile each way." Revealing detailed knowledge that seemed too precise based on what they had been able to see.

"Did you see those machine guns?" Rodent Whisperer asked, a look of concern on his shaggy face.

"We will have to try and circle around," Fic said. "Which way would you recommend, All-Knowing Kitsune?" Fic asked the young man with a small grin.

"To the east," he replied confidently.

"Alright, let's go," said Fic, moving off to the right to try and pick away through the thick underbrush on the side of the trail.

They briefly bushwhacked through the wild terrain before the forest opened up some, making travel a little easier. They continued downhill and east. Staying far enough away from the road to keep out of sight.

After pressing on through the woods for a stretch, Fic headed towards the road. As they got close, the brush was thick again. They slowly made their way through the brambles and small trees.

The brush thinned near the road, and they came to a clearing. Fic cautiously continued forward, and as he went to take another step towards the highway, he was startled by a sudden shout from his left.

A soldier was standing there with his rifle pointed at them. "Don't move," he shouted in a shaky voice. "I will shoot you."

Fic looked back at the men behind him and only saw Rodent Whisperer. Kitsune was nowhere in sight. Fic had shouldered his shotgun to make his way through the brambles and knew it would be foolish to try to swing it around. The boy might be nervous, but he still had the drop on them and all he had to do was pull the trigger and then all his plans of getting back to his family would go up in smoke.

He raised his hands and said quietly to Rodent Whisperer, "It's just us two."

Rodent Whisperer understood what he meant and nodded his head as he, too, raised his hands.

The soldier approached the two men and told them to place their weapons on the ground at their feet, step back, and get on to their knees.

They complied, and the man came closer and gathered the shotgun, small axe, and two knives. He conducted a quick frisk of the men and found only a wallet on Fic and another knife on Rodent Whisperer. He pocketed the items and looked back at the men.

"What are you two doing out here?"

"Just hiking, Private," said Fic.

"With a shotgun?"

"Yes, we were looking for some squirrel or something. Food is scarce nowadays."

"I need to take you to see the Major," the soldier continued. "He can decide what you are doing out here with weapons while trying to sneak by our checkpoint."

The soldier had the two men walk in front of him back to the edge of the military operation. There was a large tent on the side of the road, and he motioned for them to enter.

He pointed to the corner of the tent where there were two folding chairs in front of a crate that was acting as a table. "Sit there."

The Private went over to a locker and pulled out a small handheld, turned it on and said, "Delta one, this is East Side Sentry. Do you copy?"

The radio answered back, "*Copy East Side. Send your traffic.*"

"I need to talk to the Major. I picked up a couple of stragglers who were trying to sneak around the checkpoint."

"*Delta six is off sight currently. Keep the captives secure and stand by for further instructions.*"

"Roger that. Standing by."

He hooked the transceiver on his vest and came over to the men.

"Y'all just sit tight there for a bit. We will sort this out ASAP. Just don't try to get tricky or anything."

"What base are you out of, Private?" Fic asked the soldier in his Sargent voice.

"We are outta We — Hey, that is not any of your business where I'm outta. Th-that's classified," he stuttered a bit. Looking suspiciously at Fic for a good five seconds.

"You look familiar, do I know you?"

"Never met you in my life," replied Fic.

The soldier waved his hand at him in a dismissive gesture and moved over to one of the three cots in the other corner of the large tent.

He sat on a cot, his weapon still slung and at the ready.

Fic looked at Rodent Whisperer and gave him a nod. "We need to get away from these people," he said very softly. "They are probably from Mount Weather, and they may know me."

"Quiet," the Private yelled from across the room.

Fic wondered who this Major was. He had no idea if the soldiers who were stationed at Mount Weather were in on the coup, if they had been caught up in it somehow, or if these were brand new rogues who had taken over the base. He needed to find out. He also realized that his military ID was in that wallet the Private had taken from him. He kicked himself for still carrying something that could identify him so easily.

An hour went by, and the three men just sat there silently. Rodent Whisperer decided to lay on the ground next to his chair, using his pack as a pillow and catching a few winks. Fic could feel the seconds ticking away and each minute made his anxiety about getting home more intense.

#

The rest of The Party had taken their time getting ready to go but got onto the trail only an hour after the other three had left.

Their aches and pains were thankful for the leisurely pace they were maintaining as they followed in the tracks of their preceding companions. Daisy even reported that her feet were feeling much better when they took their first break.

They had just arrived at the Tom Floyd Shelter to eat lunch, when Kitsune came walking quickly down the trail from the north. He had a worried, but determined look on his face as he came into the camp and took a seat. He didn't have his pack with him.

"The soldiers, they got Fic and RW," Kitsune panted. "I got away and stashed my pack a ways back. I was able to see where the soldier took them. We need to get them out."

He filled them in on what had happened at the road and what to expect over the next rise.

Brown Shades looked concerned, as he weighed options on what to do. "Well, I guess we need to go save them. This is a lot like what happened to Fic and me at Fontana Dam, when we met Class Room and Gnobbit had to come rescue us. Now it's our turn to do the rescuing."

The Party quickly finished off what was left of their lunches as they hurriedly got their gear back together and ready to go.

Kitsune led the way towards the roadblock up ahead. He veered off the trail at the same point the trio had earlier and led them to where they had been discovered.

Hanging back, he described the area in great detail. He drew a picture in the dirt of the road, the tent, and the other nearest structures. He gave an estimate of how many soldiers were in the general area and where they were positioned.

Brown Shades studied the drawing and stroked his beard as the wheels turned in his head.

"Can I borrow your shotgun, Joey?" he asked the boy.

"I want to come on the rescue mission," Joey insisted.

Brown Shades turned to the boy and bent down so he was eye to eye, "I need you to stay back in reserve while Kitsune and I go and attempt the rescue. You, Class Room and Daisy will observe our progress and come to our rescue if needed."

Joey thought for a second and handed Brown Shades the shotgun. Daisy took out her revolver and handed it to Joey. "Here, you can have mine until this is over."

Brown Shades explained his whole plan to the others. He looked at Class Room and gave her a nod. She understood that she had to keep the kids safe. She drew her pistol, Kevin, and kept it in her right hand at the ready.

Brown Shades handed the shotgun to Kitsune, who turned and entered the bush again. He headed towards the tent at an angle, so that he could approach it from behind, near where he thought Fic and Rodent Whisperer were being held inside.

Brown Shades waited until he saw Kitsune come up to the edge of the brush next to the tent. He steadied himself, stood, and started walking straight towards the tent, making no move to keep concealed.

He walked up to the tent and tapped his staff on the wooden frame. "Hello, in the tent," he said. "Can you help an old man out?"

Inside, Fic and Rodent Whisperer watched the soldier give a start when the knock came. He got up and said to his captives, "Stay put."

Brown Shades heard some movement in the tent and a muffled voice that he couldn't understand and then the door opened.

The Private looked out at the tall man with the dark glasses and scowled, "What do you want, old man?"

"I just have some questions. I was walking up the road and I think I may have missed my turn."

He continued telling the guy a long — surprisingly convincing — made-up story. He played the confused old man to perfection. The soldier listened for a while, but it was evident he was starting to think of some way to get this guy with his big walking stick to go away.

As the two detainees looked around trying to improvise a plan while Brown Shades acted as a distraction, they noticed a slim blade puncture the tent and slice down to the ground, making a large hole in the tent.

Fic and Rodent Whisper grabbed their packs and slipped through the slit as quietly as they could.

The Private saw some movement out of the corner of his eye and looked back just in time to see the dark-haired, shaggy guy slipping out of the tent.

"Hey!" he yelled, turning back inside the tent and hurrying to the corner. Seeing the hole, he started to head towards the ragged opening when a large wooden staff came swinging down, connecting with the left side of his face and dropping him immediately.

"Sorry about that," Brown Shades said. "You had my friends, and we can't let you keep them."

Just then, the flap opened and in came Fic, Kitsune and Rodent Whisperer.

As the group were smiling at each other in victory, the radio on the soldier's vest squawked. *"East Side sentry, this is Delta one. Delta six has returned and wants you to bring the captives to the command tent."*

Fic quickly went to the unconscious soldier and removed his rifle and sling. He looked in his vest and grabbed an extra magazine for the M-4 and also grabbed his 9mm he had holstered at his hip.

Rodent Whisperer grabbed Fic's shotgun and his hatchet and made for the door.

"Do you copy, East Side?"

Fic grabbed the transceiver and keyed the mic. "Roger that, Delta one. I'll be there in five mikes. East Side Sentry, out." He shoved the radio into his pocket and followed the others out the tent door.

"We have about ten minutes before they figure out I wasn't the Private. Let's get outta here."

The three reserve hikers had seen the commotion and had come down to the tent. The reunited Party crossed the road and entered the forest moving as fast as they could in the thick undergrowth. They wanted to get far away from that area before finding the trail again.

Daisy moved quickly, without a limp. It looked as though the excitement had made her completely forget her blisters.

The Party moved deeper into the woods and disappeared from sight. Fic realized that in the intense action of the rescue, he had forgotten to retrieve his wallet. *Oh, well*, he thought. *Can't go back now.*

#

Fic led The Party along the side of the hill, checking his compass every so often to ensure he was still paralleling the trail about a half of a mile to the east. They came to some residential streets and followed them past empty looking houses that had long driveways and wooded lots.

The street continued, leaving the bulk of the houses behind. When Fic noted that the road was turning south again, he led the group back into the woods and up an incline.

As they moved through woods and roads, they monitored the radio. The command had radioed the soldier a few times, asking where he was and why he was taking so long. About ten minutes later, more traffic came over that clearly indicated they had found the unconscious soldier and discovered the captives had escaped.

Fic listened as they issued orders over the net, sending patrols in all four directions — most likely right along the trail where they were making their escape. They would have to move fast for a while to put some distance between themselves and the checkpoint.

After climbing up the mountain for a few hundred meters, they came upon the trail. Fic let out a sigh of relief when he saw the white blaze on the big oak tree in front of him. He turned right and told everyone that they needed to make some good, fast time for a while to get away from the search.

Fic's radio squawked a few times and he learned they had sent vehicles out to try and head them off at the next major road crossing.

Fic was starting to recognize a lot of landmarks now. This was his usual stomping grounds. He had hiked out here many times, both alone and with family and friends. He was getting so close; he could taste it.

Time passed and when Fic started feeling a little better at their progress, he slowed the pace some. They came to the entrance trail to the Jim and Molly Denton shelter. Fic called a halt in order to rest, check their weapons and gear, and discuss the plan. They had hiked over eighteen miles already today.

"How are the feet, Daisy," Fic asked the girl.

She nodded her head and said, "They're fine. I guess adrenaline is a healin' hormone — or at least a pain killer. I think I can keep goin' for a while."

Fic took stock of their weapon situation. Things were getting intense, and he wanted to make sure they were as prepared as possible.

He retained the M-4 with two full clips of thirty rounds. By far their best weapon. Kitsune had given Joey his shotgun back and had taken the 9mm that Fic had relieved from the soldier. Rodent Whisperer had grabbed Fic's shotgun when they hightailed it out of the tent and Fic gave him the shells he had in his pocket. A hatchet will no longer be sufficient in the current peril.

Class Room still had the 9mm she had used on the guy who had attacked her so many miles back. Daisy had retrieved her revolver from her cousin. Brown Shades was the only one in the group who didn't have a modern firearm. His staff could be potent; it had been wielded by him and others to extreme effect and he was okay with keeping it as his weapon.

They quickly replenished some energy that their adrenaline had burned off. Everyone was eager to keep moving. Each hiker now looked like a warrior, keeping their weapons ready or within easy retrieval. They had turned their alertness up to an eleven. Fic could see that today was taking its toll on the group. Their weary faces saying the things that they held back to keep the group going. Their short breaks were filled with silent panting instead of the usual banter.

"Let's move a little further on and make sure we haven't been headed off at the pass," said Fic. "I haven't heard anything on the radio in a while."

They walked across a shady country road and as they moved back into the forest on the other side, they heard a vehicle driving towards the place they'd just vacated. They stilled as the vehicle passed nearby and then moved off as the sound faded away to silence. All they could hear now was the late day birds singing to each other and the whistling wind in the large pine trees that grew near the trail.

Kitsune was walking drag and he pulled back some, letting the rest of the group move ahead.

The young man stopped and moved off of the trail. Sneaking back the way they had come, moving very quickly, but quietly through the forest.

It didn't take long for him to see what he suspected. He swiftly turned and moved back to the trail, taking off at a run.

Kitsune overtook the group, telling each of them what he had seen back by the road. "They're coming from behind," he told each of them.

Unexpectedly, a shot rang out, coming from in front of them. It was way off target of any of the hikers, but it was clearly sent down range in their direction. "Quick! Off the trail and down the side of the mountain," Fic ordered the others. He was impressed how quickly they responded, moving away from the trail and hopefully out of sight of whoever was shooting towards them. *These guys are great*, Fic thought fondly as he moved quickly down the mountainside away from the trail.

Fic had a quick sense of deja vu as they moved down the hillside. Almost the exact thing had happened to his squad when this whole thing started. It had been scared locals that time, not these rogue army soldiers, but that attack had separated him from his men. He hadn't seen any of them since that fateful day when the attack started with an arrow striking his pack, followed by a forest full of gunshots.

"Stay together," he commanded, scared of the same outcome as the first time.

They moved away and a few more shots sounded in the forest from the position in front of them. Suddenly, shots answered the first, this time, from the direction they had come from.

It appeared these two groups, both hunting The Party, had opened fire on each other, thinking they were fighting the escaping hikers, but actually fighting each other. Their incompetence amazed Fic, but he was going to take advantage of their mistakes.

The hikers moved further down the hill until they came to another residential road. This way was mere gravel. They huddled on the shoulder, everyone at the ready, while Kitsune went out along the road and did a quick scout. He moved back and forth from bush, to tree, to shadowy nook, before disappearing around the bend.

The firefight had stopped, but nothing had been said on the radio. Fic tried a couple of the other channels, but nothing produced any traffic to give them any hint of what was happening on the hillside.

After a few minutes, Kitsune came back. "There's a farmhouse just up ahead. It appears to be vacant," he reported.

The Party moved along the road and cut across a field to the back of the farmhouse. Kitsune had led the way and he went to one of the back doors and pulled it open. "I took the liberty of opening this up on my scout," he said, disappearing into the dark house.

The house looked like it had been vacant for a while, but it appeared that some kind of trauma had happened just before it had been abandoned. There was a half-eaten meal sitting on the kitchen table, with pots and pans on the stove. There was something staining the floor — either dried blood or maybe spaghetti sauce.

They checked out the rest of the building and decided to bunk down in the large living room.

Class Room found some dark sheets and covered the windows to keep any light from escaping, ensuring that no evidence of their presence would be noticeable from outside.

The sun had gone down and the last of the light of day was fading to the west on the top of the mountain. They each set up their place for the night, Class Room and Brown Shades claimed the two large sofas and the rest of the group placed their sleeping pads on the floor.

"We will need to keep a watch tonight at the door, or maybe outside," Fic said.

"I'll take the first watch," Kitsune said. "I'm not the slightest bit tired for some reason."

Everyone gathered in the living room and ate a quick, cold dinner. Headlamps were used sparingly and only on the red setting. Everyone talked in hushed voices as the intensity of the day showed itself as frayed nerves and shaky hands.

Fic handed the M-4 to Kitsune. "Do you know how to use this?" he asked.

"Yes," replied Kitsune. "My father is a cop. We've shot many different weapons together." Kitsune went to sit next to the door. Weapon at the ready, but at rest.

Silence came to the house and eventually everyone fell into an uneasy sleep. There was lots of tossing and turning as the night deepened.

Kitsune sat at the back door for a couple of hours. He looked back at the sleeping hikers and quietly opened the door and slipped outside. He sat on the porch step and gazed out into the woods. Wondering what was actually happening at Fic's house and thinking again about the dream. He felt the same urgency that Fic felt and knew they would need to get him home tomorrow some time.

CHAPTER 23
HOME FRONT VII - SUNDAY, AUGUST 5TH TO MONDAY,
AUGUST 6TH

It was past midnight. Lori sat in the kitchen, a lantern on the table next to her sending a soft glow across her face. She looked worn out and tired. Streaks of dried tears were visible on her cheeks and her hair was disheveled. It had been a long day since her daughter was taken and her son wounded. Darkness looked into the windows from outside.

She rose from the chair and moved over to the gas stove that had a small pot of water warming over the flame. She turned off the flame and poured the water into a basin. She grabbed a few clean rags and took the basin into the living room.

Another lamp, burning low, revealed Shane asleep on the couch. He had a pained look on his face as if his suffering chased him in his uneasy dreams.

Lori placed the basin on the table next to the couch and dipped the rags into the water. She removed the bandages from her son's wound in his side and used the rags to clean the area. In the dim light, she could see the wound wasn't doing very well. She rebandaged the wound.

Lori was torn. Her daughter was missing, but her son was here, and he was seriously hurt. No one had come by to check on her, so she had no easy way to go find Doc Miller, who lived about three miles away. She didn't want to leave her son for that amount of time, but knew she was going to have to do something soon.

An infection in that deep wound could possibly kill her boy and she wasn't going to let that happen. But without some help and meds, her cleaning and re-bandaging was only going to do so much good. She was almost out of bandages and was planning on cutting up some sheets soon.

Lori heard a noise at the window, and her gaze first went to the shotgun in the corner, gauging its distance if she needed to get it quickly, then at the window.

A cardinal was on the windowsill looking into the room. She thought it strange that this songbird was out and about in the dark. She couldn't remember ever seeing one during the night before. Shane mumbled some incoherent words and shifted restlessly. Lori looked away from the window and to her son.

The bird flitted around at the windowsill for a few more seconds, then flew off.

Lori checked Shane's forehead and his skin felt warm. Not too bad, but she reckoned a fever was starting to try to burn the inevitable infection that she was fearing. If it got worse, she would have to take action, even if it meant leaving Shane alone in the house.

She lay down on the floor next to the couch where she had set up a sleeping pad and a light blanket for the slight chill of the early morning hours.

#

She slept uneasily, but did manage to get a few hours of restless sleep. She got up, made some more coffee on the stove, and fixed a light breakfast.

She spent the day trying to keep busy as she worked in the garden for a bit and cleaned more bandages, checking on Shane every half hour or so. He slept on. Sometimes deeply and sometimes light and restless. In the afternoon, she walked up the road again past where she had found Shane, hoping for some sign of Brittney, but the roads and fields were empty. Nothing moved but the leaves of the shoulder side trees in the soft summer breeze.

As the sun went down, she noticed that Shane's fever had gotten worse. His skin was hot and dry. There was no question, infection was here.

Lori went to the kitchen and poured some cool water onto one of the rags and returned to the living room. Placing the rag on his forehead to try to help cool him some.

When she changed his bandages again, the wound appeared red and angry. A smell that did not bode well wafted up from the wound. Infection had set in. She was going to have to go for the doctor. She would go as soon as the sun was starting to lighten the sky.

#

Lori spent another night on the floor next to the couch. As her worry for her son and daughter grew, her tossing and turning became more vigorous and in the early morning hours before dawn, she finally gave in, got up, and started packing a small pack with a few items that she may need for this trip to the doctor.

She checked on Shane one more time. He too was sleeping restlessly. Soft mumbles escaped his lips from time to time, but he appeared stable for now. She placed a note she had written on the table beside the couch, explaining to Shane where she had gone. She took one last look at her boy, grabbed the shotgun, and headed to the back door. She left the house and started walking down the driveway. When she came to the road, she turned left and started walking as fast as she could towards Doc Miller's house.

The way to the doctors was fairly straight but rolled up and down on this fertile farmland near the Shenandoah River. She pushed up the up hills and started to jog on the downhills, but the day was heating up quickly and the humidity was oppressive.

The road took a slight turn and as she moved around the corner, she could see the doctor's place. Something wasn't right. She stood staring at the front of the house. There was an army Humvee parked in the front yard. Suddenly, she realized that she was standing out in the open. Even though she had been an army wife for decades now, she could no longer trust that those wearing the uniform were safe. She moved off of the road quickly and rushed into the bushes. She skirted the low scrub and moved off into some thicker trees, then started moving towards the house, un-slinging her shotgun.

As she got close to the house, she tried to get a better look into the front yard, searching for a first-story window to get a peek into the house.

She got to the edge of the small, wooded copse and crouched, looking. Her heart was beating rapidly in her chest as she saw movement in the house. Three men came out of the front door. The one on the right was an army Private, at least he had an army uniform on.

He wore the black arm band that she had come to know meant that he was a rogue soldier, serving that fascist asshole, Richard Flaherty, who was holed up in Mount Weather. At least that is what they had deduced — that he is most likely in Weather, pulling his strings, ordering people about, killing indiscriminately, and taking whatever he wants.

The second guy was Jim Henry, the leader of the Blue Mountain Patrol. Something was definitely not right here. The BMP had been trying to stay away from the army, but Jim and this Private had a familiarity between them that suggested they knew each other and were actually working together.

Between them was Doctor Miller, a despondent look on his face. Each of the other two men had hold of one of his arms as if they were moving him along against his wishes.

"Where are we going?" asked the doctor, fear making his voice high and squeaky.

"You'll find out when we get there," replied the soldier. "We require your services on a little side job. Our fun went a little too far and we need you to fix someone up for us."

Doc Miller somehow caught sight of Lori looking at them from the bushes. He did a little shake of his head, warning her off. She stood tight.

Jim let go of the doctor and opened the back of the Humvee. "Get in, Doc," he ordered. "You got everything in your bag, right?"

With one arm free, the doctor shook free of the soldier, dropped his bag and started running toward the side of the house. He was hoping to get to the back where a trail led into the forest. If he could just get out of sight for a bit, he could try to lose them on the maze of paths that he knew intimately from years of hiking them. There were several different ways to go in the dense woods and he had actually made quite a few of the routes himself.

The soldier brought his weapon to the ready and sighted down on the running doctor. He pulled the trigger sending a three-shot burst towards the running man, just as Jim Henry screamed for him not to shoot.

The doctor fell to the ground in a pink spray of blood as all three of the bullets found a target in his back.

"What the fuck!" yelled Jim Henry. "We needed him, you stupid asshole. He is the only doctor in the area."

The man looked over at Jim, shrugged his shoulders and said, "He ran."

"Have you ever heard of chasing and catching alive?" Jim continued the anger in his voice was steely and hard. "Now we are going to have to splint her leg ourselves. Do you know how to splint a fucking leg?"

"Naw, but we can figure it out. It doesn't have to be perfect. Just good enough"

"Don't you have any medic friends up in Weather?"

"Naw, they're all assholes. Besides, this op is covert. No one in Weather knows we have her."

"Fuck!" Jim yelled one more time, his frustration a clear sign on his face.

He picked up the bag, opened it and looked at the contents. His dumb stare revealed that he didn't really know what he was looking at. He closed the bag and put it in the back of the Humvee.

Both men got into the Humvee and the soldier started the engine. Neither man went to check on the doctor. They had already written him off.

The Humvee pulled out of the driveway and moved down the road that Lori had just walked up.

She waited until it turned the corner in the road, and then took off running towards the side of the house.

She went up to the doctor. He had fallen face down with his arms and legs spread out like he was trying to do a belly flop into water.

She turned him over and the wounded man sucked in a long shaky breath. The sound was like a gurgling brook. He was alive. Lori checked the man over, pulling his bloody shirt away revealing three leaking holes. All three of the bullets had gone through and through. Who knows what kind of damage they did as they passed through the man.

He coughed and blood sprayed out of his mouth in a fine mist. He opened his eyes and focused on Lori.

"I–I, didn't want them to find you," he said hoarsely, as blood ran out of his mouth and down to his chin. "I think they have your daughter," he slowly continued on. "I should have just gone with them. I think she is hurt." He coughed again and closed his eyes, trying to breathe as blood filled his lungs. "I thought I could get to the woods."

Lori tried to make the man comfortable as the life continued to drip out of him.

"Shane is hurt too," she told the doctor. "I came to get your help. It was probably those guys that hurt him. Brittney was with Shane when he went out. He came home bleeding with a wound in his side and said that someone had taken Brittney. I need antibiotics and more bandages." She didn't know if he even heard her, his breathing had slowed a lot and his eyes were still closed.

His eyes fluttered a bit again and he said, "I have supplies hidden in the house." He coughed again. "Find the key — red tape — kitchen — walk-in closet." His voice was growing fainter and quieter. Then it stopped.

Lori checked him again, tears flowing from her eyes as she tried to stop the bleeding of the wounded man with a makeshift bandage made from his torn shirt, she saw that he had stopped breathing. His eyes had opened again, but no life remained in them. He was gone.

She checked his pulse to confirm and moved away from him.

Lori went inside the house. His last words ran through her head. She found the red taped key in the kitchen and then a bulky chest in the back of the large closet in his bedroom. She opened it and saw that everything she needed was there. This stash would be paramount during these desperate times, but she wouldn't be able to carry all the supplies back, there was more than her pack could hold.

She filled her small pack with as many of the supplies as she could, locking the chest and hiding it a little by throwing some clothes on top of it. She put the key in her pocket.

Lori went back down to the doctor and slowly pulled him into the house. They were close to the back door, so she carefully maneuvered his body into the kitchen. She found a blanket on the back of the doctor's couch in the living room and covered his body.

"Once I get Shane stable, I'll come back and bury you, Doc," she said with some more tears. "I promise."

She went to the front door and carefully looked up and down the road to ensure the Humvee wasn't coming back and then she headed south. She stayed off the road, moving parallel and staying in the woods. This slowed her down a little, but she couldn't be discovered before she got back to her son.

"Hold on Brittney, I'll find you as soon as I get Shane stable," she said to the wind as she made her way south, back towards the farm.

#

Lori walked for about a mile in the brush and trees next to the road. She turned another bend and saw several vehicles, all military, blocking the road. She looked at them for a few seconds, frantically thinking of what she should do. She hunkered down in the brush and observed the scene.

The three Humvees stood across the road and there were about six or seven soldiers milling about. Another Humvee was sitting perpendicular to the three blocking the road. It was the vehicle Jim and the Private had been in.

Jim's soldier was outside the vehicle, and he was talking to two of the other men.

Lori couldn't hear what they were saying, but the Private seemed pretty worked up and he kept gesturing back at his Humvee where Jim sat silently.

Eventually two men jumped into their vehicles and moved them backwards, letting the killer's Humvee through. Once they moved past the blockade, they pulled forward again and the men went back to milling about the road.

Lori thought for a while, visualizing a map of the area in her head, and then decided she needed to detour towards the river and then work her way around the roadblock. She couldn't figure out why they had set up a block seemingly in the middle of nowhere.

Following her plan, Lori walked until she figured she had gone far enough, then headed back towards the road, continuing to parallel it in the brush and trees.

The sun had been continuously getting higher in the sky as she moved along and the heat had increased again, if that was even possible.

Lori was almost home, her eagerness to be back with her sick son increasing her pace as she neared the last road crossing before her property. She reached the pavement, and looked both ways before venturing out into the open, turning left and jogging towards the driveway.

As she approached, a group of people came over the rise that was south of their house. They were jogging too. Lori counted seven people, a couple of them looked quite young.

She slowed to a walk, swinging her shotgun off of her shoulder and making it ready. She noted that they all carried a weapon and were wearing backpacks.

The man in front slowed as he saw her, he looked at her standing in the middle of the road, then he sped up again. He looked ragged and haggard. His beard was a good four or five inches and his clothes were worn and tattered.

There was something so familiar about his run.

CHAPTER 24
HOME - MONDAY, AUGUST 6TH TO TUESDAY, AUGUST 7TH

Fic sat on the porch of the farmhouse, weapon in hand, and watched the sky start to lighten to the east. He got up and went inside the house. He had relieved Kitsune after a few hours' sleep and had been wide awake the rest of the night. He just couldn't sleep with his family being so close, and yet so far away with all the obstacles the soldiers presented between home and him.

He went into the living room and saw the others already stirring. Everyone had felt his urgency and wanted to get him home as fast as they could. When Fic had relieved Kitsune, the young man had said that they should get an early start. He had a feeling that things weren't good at Fic's home.

Fic had stopped wondering how the boy knew so much. After his predictions and warnings had been confirmed many times over, he had just come to believe that the boy knew things. Maybe he could see the future or other places or something.

As the sun was just starting to peek into the valley, they set out — the road steering them to the north. Everyone kept their weapons at the ready and remained alert to anything out of the ordinary.

They made their way back to the road that they had almost reached the day before and quickly returned to the woods. Shortly after that, they had to cross Interstate 66, and then a creek that ran in front of them. They noticed another smaller stream was entering this one from the direction of the highway. They followed the creek upstream and saw that it passed under the highway in large five-foot-high culverts. They used that tunnel to get under the highway and lessened the chances that someone who may be monitoring the road would see them.

Fic used his compass to find the trail again, though he already had a good idea of where it would be. He knew the lay of the land here. Not just the trail itself, but the surrounding woods also. He had hunted in these woods with both of his kids and his wife.

They moved as fast as they could. Fic checked on Daisy a couple of times, but each time she said she was feeling good. "I think I finally got a handle on those blisters," she explained. "They are hardly hurtin' at all."

The morning's miles went quickly, with only one short break to rest and eat a quick snack. The day was hot, starting off that way before the sun had risen and growing more intense as it rose in the sky.

They could tell they were getting close to Highway 50, the road that led to Fic's farm, when they started hearing traffic. This was the most road noise they had heard in a long time, and they sounded like heavy vehicles and buses.

When they got close to the road, Kitsune did a quick scout and came back to report that crossing the road was going to be a challenge. The traffic was quite heavy, and they seemed to be looking for something. Maybe they were looking for The Party.

"I have an idea," Fic said. "I know these parts pretty well, follow me as we sneak around these idiots."

He moved off to the left, paralleling the road.

They crossed a few country roads and saw a house or two as they went along, but the area was well wooded and they kept out of sight of the road — which continued to announce the presence of vehicles driving up and down.

After about a mile, they could smell the river. Fic moved down a small incline and there was the great Shenandoah River.

They were following a small dirt road that went straight to the river. Fic stopped and gathered the others around in a circle as he explained the scene.

"Okay, my house is on the other side of the river. We will need to go up on the road and get across as fast as we can. We'll be out in the open for longer than I'm comfortable with, but if the traffic lets up some, we should be able to make it."

"I'm gonna have a look around," Kitsune said and disappeared into the brush before Fic could say anything.

The group crept closer to the road. There was a steep embankment going up from where they were hiding to where the bridge started across the river. They would have to perch at the top, hiding behind the guardrail until they saw an opening.

Kitsune found them at their new hiding place. He had a paddle in his hand. "Maybe we can paddle across," he said, holding up the paddle for the others to see. "I found two canoes down by the river. This road is a boat launch and people store some boats down next to the water. They have locks on them, but I figured RW's axe should be able to cut the cable easily."

Fic was happy with this new plan as he was having second thoughts as to how fast they could get across the open bridge.

The Party went to the water's edge and found the canoes. There were two of them and three more paddles under one of the watercraft. Rodent Whisperer was able to cut the cable that held both canoes secure with only a few hacks of his blade. They quickly divided themselves into two groups, deciding that Fic and Brown Shades would paddle one boat with Class Room and most of the gear. In the other canoe, Kitsune and Rodent Whisperer would paddle with the two tweens as passengers and the rest of the gear.

Both boats rode low as they started paddling. They intended to stay under the cover of the bridge the whole way across, hoping that no one up on the road would see them crossing.

This started out fine, but as they moved into the main channel of the river, the current started to pull them downstream. Both canoes turned into the upstream side and paddled hard to stay under the bridge.

The heavily loaded canoe that Fic and Brown Shades were crewing started to lose the battle with the current and was pulled downstream and out in the open.

Kitsune and Rodent Whisperer's canoe was able to make the shore while still under the bridge and the occupants watched helplessly as a few Humvees passed overhead. The other two canoeists paddled as hard as they could and finally they reached the other bank about fifty meters downstream of the other canoe. Fic wiped a sheen of nervous sweat off of his brow as the canoe's bow scraped into the sandy bank.

They all quickly disembarked and pulled the canoe into some bushes. They had made it.

Fic started off across the fields and away from the road. They moved into a large forest and Fic led the way, quickly finding one of the trails and following it for a while, before veering off back into the woods in the direction he wanted to travel.

They came to the end of the forest and saw a large swath of fields, with brush borders and stone walls dividing them and a few fences showing the property lines. Fic led The Party straight through one of the larger fields. They crossed a couple of roads, carefully checking first to make sure they were empty.

At one such crossing, they heard a vehicle coming down the road. They hid in the darkness of a small clump of trees as a Humvee came driving by. They waited for the sound to die, then continued on.

They were crossing one more field and Fic could see the highway up ahead. That was the road that went to his house. His pace quickened.

He hopped the last fence and turned onto the road. He started off at a slow jog. The rest of The Party did the same until they were a wave moving up the road. Together and at the ready.

They moved over a rise and as they went over, they saw a woman standing in the middle of the road shouldering a shotgun. The person stopped and looked at them, swinging the weapon to a ready position.

Fic saw the figure in the middle of the road and immediately recognized his wife. Lori was right there. It had been two months and a thousand miles since he had last seen her. She looked as good as ever. His pace quickened and a smile came to his face as he ran to meet her.

"Hey, darling," Fic said, his voice hitching. "I'm home."

Lori's shotgun clattered to the ground as she realized that crusty old man was her husband. She ran into his arms, shouting his name, forgetting that urgent business needed to be taken care of, at least for a few seconds.

#

Fic and Lori stood in the middle of the road. Hugging each other. Talking over each other. Looking at each other. Lori reached up and pulled on his beard. "Nice beard, soldier," she said. "Is that regulation?"

Fic reached up and touched the side of her face. "I sure did miss you, lady," he said. "It has been a long walk home."

Suddenly, Lori remembered why she was out in the middle of the road. Her son was hurt and needed her. "Quick," she said. "We need to get home. Shane is wounded and Brittney is missing." She turned and started for the house while Fic stared at her in shock at what she just reported so nonchalantly.

"What?" he asked as he hurried after her.

The others followed behind, completely forgotten for the moment.

Lori ran up the drive and into the house, Fic right behind her. She led him to the living room and towards the couch and stepped aside as Fic approached Shane.

Fic saw his son on the couch and at first, he thought he was dead. He lay still, his sunken eyes closed in a pale face, his breathing apparently non-existent. As he kneeled next to his son, he saw that his eyes had lied to him. His son did breathe, it was shallow and slow, but it was there.

Lori had dropped her pack and was rummaging through it for something. She pulled some bandages and a vial of pills. She opened the vial and shook out two pills. Lori went to her son. Softly talking to him and rousing him from his sleep. His eyes fluttered and he saw his mother in a blurry haze. "Ma," was all he said.

She gave him the pills and helped him drink them down with the glass of water she had left by the couch. After that feat was complete, he looked behind her to the man kneeling next to her. The guy looked a lot like his father, but older and with a full beard. "Dad?" he whispered before his eyes grew too heavy to keep open as he fell back into an uneasy slumber.

Lori turned to her husband and told him what had happened the day of the storm. Bringing him up to speed on how Shane had gotten wounded and Brittney abducted.

At this point she remembered that the living room was full of people. She looked past her husband and asked, "So, who are your friends?"

Fic remembered his Party and introduced each of the hikers to Lori. The hikers would give a little wave or bow as Fic told their name and how he had met them.

"I wouldn't have gotten back here without their help."

"Are you guys hungry?" Lori asked the group.

"We're hikers," said Rodent Whisperer. "We are always hungry."

Lori led the group to the kitchen and put a bunch of fresh produce and other foods on the table. She sent Fic out to the spring house to fetch the milk and butter.

She grabbed a skillet and some eggs and started cracking them into the pan as Brown Shades offered to help with the cooking.

"Ma'am," said Rodent Whisperer

"Call me Lori," she said with a smile.

"Lori, I have some healer skills. I could take a look at your lad if you like. Maybe change his bandages?"

"Thank you," replied Lori. "That would be nice. I don't know what else to do. I had gone to fetch the doctor but witnessed his execution instead."

Fic came back into the kitchen as she said this and was shocked. "What has been going on here?" he asked. "I know it is crazy out there now, but if I had known, I would have come faster."

Rodent Whisperer walked to the sleeping young man and started checking him out.

Lori continued with her story. She told about what had happened in the area after the bombs, and how they had joined the Blue Mountain Patrol, and how they were all working together.

She told about how something was happening up on Mount Weather and all the coming and going of the vehicles and buses all the time. How the soldiers had mainly left the community alone until recently.

Lastly, she told them about what she had seen at the doctor's house. How it appears that Jim Henry was working with the soldiers, or at least this soldier and from what she had heard, they may be the ones who took Brittney, and she may be hurt too.

"I never really liked Jim that much, but he was the leader of the Blue Mountain Patrol. Brittney had complained about his advances several times."

"Okay, I know where to start the search for Brittney. The Henrys live out on Clay Hill Road, right? That's where I'll start."

"I'm coming with you, Fic," Kitsune said, Brown Shades and Class Room nodding their agreement and volunteering their help as well.

Lori looked over at her husband, her eyebrow arching and a half smile coming to her face. "So, we are Fictilibus again?" she asked, looking at him closely.

Fic smiled and nodded. "Yeah," he said. "It seemed appropriate when hiking the Trail. When I met Gnobbit and she introduced herself by her trail name, it just came naturally that I replied with mine, even though I hadn't worn that name for many years."

"Who's Gnobbit?" Lori asked.

Fic briefly told her about Gnobbit and Finn and how they had left them in Pearisburg way down in the south of Virginia.

Concentrating on the emergency at hand, Fic started thinking of a plan to find his daughter.

"So, is the truck running?" he asked.

"It runs ... if it had some gas," she replied. "The soldiers were confiscating any car or truck that drove out of the neighborhood, so we used the gas for the quads that the BMP were using. I don't know where we could get some more."

"Well, I've been walking for two months," Fic said. "What's a few more miles? It isn't that far."

Fic went into the dining room where they had dropped their packs and stowed their gear, and started checking his weapon. Kitsune and Class Room came in and started checking their weapons. When Joey went to check his shotgun, Fic said, "I think you should stay here, son. I need someone to guard the house and my son while we go find his sister."

Joey looked at Fic with a sad expression. "I'm a good shot, ya know," he said.

"I know that. That's why I need you here."

Joey nodded and went to place his shotgun near his pack.

Fic looked to Brown Shades as he sat massaging his still aching knee, and asked that he stay here too, to help Joey with security. Brown Shades nodded and threw Fic a quick salute with two fingers.

Rodent Whisperer came in and Fic asked him to come along, just in case his daughter needed his healing skills. Rodent Whisperer nodded and went to get his pistol and a small pack that had medical supplies. "Your son appears stable for now," he said.

"I'll help your wife with the chores here," said Daisy.

Fic looked back at his group of friends and was proud how they all prepared for the mission just as good as a well-trained platoon.

When all were ready, he stood and said, "Let's roll."

The four team members went out the kitchen door and headed towards the drive. When they came to the road, Fic led them across and into the brush on the other side. It was time to do some more cross-country walking.

#

The four hikers cut across the land. Through fields and small forests until they came to Clay Hill Road. They walked along, keeping close to the shoulder, so they could jump into the edge bushes or trees if they heard a car coming down the narrow country road. The pavement made a small turn and started heading down a hill towards the river.

They came to a compact, paved driveway heading up an incline with a wooden fence lining the house side of the drive. The top of a house could be seen above the rise.

Fic called the group into a huddle.

"Okay, I don't know if Jim is here, but his mother, Maybell, might be, if she's still around. She may be a handful, but we should be able to reason with her. It all depends on how much she has had to drink so far this morning."

Fic gave each of his warriors instructions on how to approach the house. He sent Kitsune off to the left, to circle around in the woods and get close to the back door. Rodent Whisperer he sent to the right to cover that side, hidden from the house by the rise of the land.

"Come with me Class Room," Fic said to the woman. "We are paying old Maybell a visit today."

Fic and Class Room started walking up the driveway. Rifle hanging loosely in its sling and pistol holstered. They were trying to look peaceful and somewhat harmless.

They came to the front door and Fic knocked with a hard rap. They waited a good two minutes with no answer, so he knocked again. A little louder this time.

From inside they heard the clatter of something and a shouted word that they couldn't quite understand, and eventually, they heard footsteps coming to the door.

The door opened a few inches, stopped by a chain from the inside and a bleary, red eye looked out at them.

"Hi, Maybell," said Fic. "Is Jimmy around?"

The woman looked at him blankly before questioning, "Clayton Collier? I ain't seen you in months. Where have you been?"

"Yes ma'am. I just got back, I'm here on Blue Mountain Patrol business. Is Jimmy around?"

"That no-good son ain't here," she said with a slur. They could smell the alcohol reeking from her mouth, she was unmistakably heavily inebriated.

"He wouldn't get me my 'medicine', so I kicked him out."

Fic knew that her preferred 'medicine' was vodka, but anything containing alcohol could be part of the prescription when desperate.

"Do you know where he might be?" Fic asked the drunken woman.

"Probably at the cabin," she replied.

"Where is this cabin?"

"Down off of Ellerslie, along the river. About a mile and a half down to the left from where Clay Hill runs into it. There is a big rock next to the road that marks the trail to the cabin."

"Thanks, Maybell," Fic said. "We'll go look for him there."

"You say it was BMP business, what kind of business?" She looked side-eyed at Fic.

"Yeah, my kids were involved in an incident while on patrol. I need to talk to him about it."

"You wouldn't have any hooch on ya, would ya?" Hope crept into her bloodshot eyes.

"Sorry, Maybell," Fic answered. "We are all out at the moment. Thanks for the info on Jimmy."

Fic and Class Room moved off of the porch and started back to the driveway. As they fell out of sight of the house, they hunkered down until Kitsune and Rodent Whisperer re-joined them near the road.

"Just a little more walking, guys," Fic said. "He may be in a cabin down by the river."

They made their way to Ellerslie Road and followed it along the Shenandoah River. They walked along silently, the fear Fic had for his daughter emanating from him. The worry gripped the entire group, feeling for their friend and his family.

The quiet was broken by a vehicle heading in their direction. They quickly moved off the road on the river side, which had a sharp embankment that dropped about ten feet very rapidly into some brush and then the water.

Everyone was well hidden when the vehicle came rushing down the Ellerslie from the direction they were walking towards. Fic had an obscured view of the road, but he easily recognized the vehicle as a Humvee. He had already suspected, by the sound, but he got a quick look at the man driving. He didn't know his name but recognized him as one of the personnel stationed at Mount Weather.

When the sound of the Humvee faded, they moved back on the road and continued on. After about fifteen minutes, they came to a large rock that sat next to the road away from the river. Next to it was a path that led up the hill and into the woods.

They could tell they were close. The group steeled themselves, ready for whatever lay ahead. They moved up the path in single file. After about a hundred meters, they could see a dilapidated cabin sitting in a small clearing in the woods. It was made of logs and looked like it had been there for at least a century. The roof needed some work and there was a lot of broken equipment, buckets, and pieces of wood laying around the clearing.

The patrol got their orders and executed them with precision.

Fic told Class Room to stay hidden and cover him in case anything started happening.

She nodded and held her pistol at the ready.

Fic approached the cabin, using the cover of some bushes and a couple of trees, then ran to the corner of the building. He crept around to the front window and peered inside. At first it was hard to tell what was what in the dark building. It looked like there had been a commotion in there with stuff strewn about everywhere.

Fic looked at the door and saw that it wasn't closed completely. He ducked under the window and moved to the opening. Using the tip of his rifle, he pushed the door open and waited, listening.

He looked back at Class Room who was watching from the edge of the clearing and signaled to her that he was going in and that she should advance to his position when he moved in.

She nodded her understanding and got ready to move. He looked to both sides of the cabin and saw Kitsune and Rodent Whisperer were in position. She signaled to them her next move, and they too nodded in understanding, getting ready to join if need be.

Fic moved into the cabin, keeping low and sweeping his weapon across the room. There was a small bed in one corner, and on it, Fic saw Jim Henry. He was either asleep or unconscious.

Fic quickly moved toward the prone man keeping his rifle at the ready and said, "Jimmy, wake up." The man gave no response, and as Fic moved closer to prod Jim with the muzzle of his weapon, he saw that he had recently suffered a severe beating.

Both of his eyes were swollen shut, and he had a large cut on his left cheek. The severity of the wounds revealed there may have been some torture involved.

Seeing the man was in no state to offer resistance, he let his weapon fall into its sling and came closer. He shook the man's shoulder and said closer to his ear, "Jimmy, wake up."

Jimmy stirred and tried to open his eyes with little success. "Who's that?" he croaked, coughing a little.

"It's Clayton Collier, Jimmy. I just got back from Georgia. I came home to find my boy wounded and my daughter missing. They went missing while working for you. Do you know where Brittney is?"

Understanding came into the man's beaten face. He tried prying his eyes open once again, and this time he was successful in getting his right eye open a little. He looked at Fic and fear was clearly the main emotion he was feeling now.

"No, I don't know where she is," he replied, coughing again and trying to sit up and move further away from Fic.

"What happened here?" Fic asked. "Who beat you?"

"I — fell down," he replied. He had gotten his other eye open now and seemed to be looking around the room for something. Fic noticed his actions and did a little looking around himself. The other three members of his patrol entered the building, weapons ready. Fic gave them the all clear sign, and they relaxed, standing by.

At the foot of the bed on the floor, Fic saw a small black bag. He went over and picked it up. It was one of those medical bags the old tv shows used all the time. There was a metal plate next to the zipper; on it was the name *Dr. Michael Miller*.

Fic opened the bag and saw a plethora of medical supplies.

"Jimmy, I know what you did to Doc Miller," Fic started. "Who did you need the doctor for, before you killed him?"

"I didn't kill him," Jimmy said. "George did." He was still looking around the room. His face was becoming frantic as he understood that Fic knew what he had done, and he had just admitted that he was involved.

"Who is George?" Fic demanded.

"A soldier from up on Weather," Jimmy replied.

"What's his last name?"

"I think that is his last name. That's what is on his uniform, George."

"So, why were you looking for the doctor, before George killed him?"

Jimmy snapped his swollen lips together and looked away guiltily, as if he had just realized again who he was talking to. He offered no answer.

"I swear Jimmy. If you don't give me some answers, I'm going to make you look a little bit worse than you already do, if that is even possible."

Suddenly, Jimmy jumped up and started running for the door of the cabin. Class Room stuck her foot out as he tried to run past her and he tripped over the outstretched appendage, slamming onto the floor just before the door, which Kitsune was swinging shut. He slid forward and slammed into the now shut door, falling unconscious.

"Let's get him into the chair," said Fic. "I think we will need to tie him up, so he doesn't accidentally kill himself trying to get away."

Rodent Whisperer and Kitsune lifted the man and sat him in the chair, he slumped over, still groggy and out of it, but regaining some semblance of consciousness.

Fic found some rope in a box next to the bed. There was also a knife and a roll of duct tape. "Hmm," he said. "It looks like you have the perfect tools available for tying someone up. Who were you tying up, Jimmy?"

The restrained man looked blearily at Fic and said nothing. "Okay, I guess we have to do this the hard way," said Fic, reaching up and squeezing his cheeks together. He held the grip for about ten seconds and new blood started leaking out of the cut under his eye, where Fic's thumb was.

Jimmy let out a long groan and then said. "Okay, Okay, Okay."

Fic let loose his grip, wiping the blood off of his thumb on Jimmy's shirt.

"George had taken a prisoner and he asked me to keep her — I mean him — here until he could transport him somewhere."

"Him?" Fic asked. "It sounded like you said 'her' first. Don't lie to me Jimmy, I can tell." Fic reached up and squeezed his face again. This time it was a little bit harder, and Jimmy screamed.

"Did you take my daughter, Jimmy?" The look on Jimmy's face was all Fic needed for an answer. He took a half step back and backhanded the young man with all his strength. Jimmy and the chair fell to the floor.

"Was my daughter in that Humvee that drove past us before we got here?" Fic yelled at the dazed and confused man, laying on the floor tied to a chair.

"Yes," said Jimmy as blood flowed out of his mouth. "Some Corporal took her. He did this to me. I was trying to rescue her."

"Rescue her?" Fic looked sternly at the man. "You fucking took her, you idiot! Was she hurt?" Fic stepped on Jimmy's lower leg between the ankle and knee. He pushed just a little, but was ready to increase the pressure if Jimmy tried to be stubborn.

"She fell down a cliff near the river," Jimmy said. "We weren't sure if her ankle was broken or just badly sprained, but she couldn't walk on it."

"Was she trying to get away from you when she fell?" Fic asked, leaning forward on his foot that was on Jimmy's leg.

"Yes! Yes! Please stop hurting me. I liked her, but she wouldn't give me the time of day. George thought it would be a good idea to take her and … convince her," he started blabbering, his words no longer understandable.

Fic looked down at the man, sobbing on the ground. "Please don't kill me," Jimmy blubbered. The disgust was clear on Fic's face.

"Where did they take her?" Fic asked.

"Weather," was the whispered response.

Fic looked at the other three and said to Kitsune, "Cut him loose. I may need him later." Fic looked at Jimmy as Kitsune cut his bonds. "I'll be back for you later, Jimmy. If my daughter dies, so do you."

Fic motioned to the group towards the door, and they all headed out, walking back to the road. Just as they were about to turn on the road, a shot rang out and Fic felt a bullet whiz past him next to his ear. He turned and saw Jimmy, pointing a small pistol at him and trying to take aim with his swollen eyes.

Shots echoed up and down the river valley as Jimmy fell to the ground.

Fic walked back up and looked at Jimmy's bullet riddled body. He wouldn't be of any more help to them now.

"Should we bury him?" Class Room asked.

"Birds gotta eat, same as worms," Fic replied, finally finding a situation where he could use a clever line from a Clint Eastwood movie.

No one caught the reference, and they all turned to walk back to the road.

Fic addressed the others as they started moving back the way they had come. "We need to return to the house and make another plan. I think I have an idea, but I won't know if it will work until I try it."

Fic started to jog and the others followed suit as they moved into the late day's light with long shadows trailing behind them.

#

The patrol moved across the fields and came to the road that Fic lived on. As they were moving towards the pavement, crossing a rocky gully next to the shoulder used for draining rainwater, Class Room stepped on a large rock that shifted and rolled, taking her foot with it, and turning her ankle. They walked slowly to the driveway, helping Class Room make her way, and headed to the house. They went around the back and entered the kitchen.

Lori, Brown Shades, Joey and Daisy sat around the table. They were drinking chilled water that was from the spring house, the glasses had a good sheen of condensation covering them.

They all looked at the warriors and were disappointed that it was just the four and not five.

Seeing Class Room limping and being helped into the room, they all jumped up to see what had happened.

"We just walked about five miles and I stupidly twisted my ankle not a hundred meters from your driveway," said Class Room. "I'm such a klutz."

Rodent Whisperer took her to the side to check out her ankle, now that they were safely inside and out of sight.

Lori looked at Fic in despair,"You didn't find her?"

"No, but we know where she is," Fic responded. "Though it is going to take some effort to find out exactly where and I may need to do some sneaking."

He started to tell her about talking to Maybell and then Jimmy. How he got Jimmy to admit taking Brittney and how it all ended with Jimmy's bullet riddled body.

Just then, a moan came from the living room.

Rodent Whisperer rose to go check on Shane, Fic and Lori following close behind.

Shane lay in a sheen of sweat. He didn't look good. Rodent Whisperer checked the boy's vitals, started rummaging through the backpack, and asked Lori to rinse out a rag for Shane's forehead.

He got the boy to swallow some aspirin, and another dose of antibiotics. After fussing around with the boy for a while, Shane seemed to settle down and fell back into a troubled sleep.

#

Darkness came to the farmstead and a couple of lamps were lit around the house. Fic set up a watch schedule for the night. Although Lori had said that the soldiers had mostly left them alone, he had a feeling that they were going to start paying a lot more attention to the residents near the base than they had before. Roadblocks, and now the taking of the citizens, may just be the start of something worse.

With guard duty settled, Fic set up a watch on his son. The boy wasn't doing too well, and they wanted to have someone nearby, checking on him for changes to his condition.

The group that wasn't assigned the first watch tried to get some rest.

Fic and Lori sat at the kitchen table. Rodent Whisperer was in with Shane and Class Room had the watch on the back porch.

"What's your plan, Clay?" Lori asked her husband.

"I will go into details tomorrow when everyone is well rested, but I will tell you that I will be more recognizable to you. A little less shaggy."

Lori smiled at her husband and reached over to tug on his beard. "I'm starting to get used to this old rag. It reminds me of when we met. A little less sparse, but still nice."

"If Brittney is in Weather, I will need to get into the base and find her. I think that if I can blend in, I may be able to get further into the base. As far as I can tell, they are still following some kind of good order and discipline. All the rogue soldiers we have encountered so far seem to be following grooming standards."

The couple stood and Fic killed the lantern. He pulled up his head lamp to his forehead from where it had been hanging around his neck and turned it on.

They headed to bed and lay cuddled together in a spoon shape, seeking some relief in each other's arms after so long apart. The parents agonized over the danger both of their children found themselves in. They whispered worries and hopeful reassurances back and forth for hours, knowing they wouldn't get a good night's sleep while both of their children's lives hung in the air.

#

Fic was awoken by someone shaking his shoulder, seemingly only seconds after he'd finally fallen into a restless sleep. He looked and saw Brown Shades in the dark room. His face was illuminated by the lantern he was carrying.

"Your watch," Brown Shades said, turning to leave the room. "Both of you."

Fic unspooned himself from Lori and placed his feet on the floor. He got up and threw on some pants and a shirt. Heading down the hallway to the stairs from memory in the dark house. Lori sat herself on the edge of the bed, trying to knock the sleep out of her head. She was exhausted from her lack of quality sleep. Anytime she'd been able drift off, her anxious brain only unsettled her even more with horrible nightmares. Fic went into the kitchen where Brown Shades waited for him. Daisy was standing at the doorway to the living room, looking like she was ready for some sleep herself.

Brown Shades handed the M-4 to Fic, gave him a half-hearted salute and turned to go up to his sleeping space, which was in Shane's room on the floor.

Lori came into the kitchen next, and Daisy smiled at her. "He's been sleeping peacefully during my watch," she updated Lori. "I'm off to bed for a couple of hours of sleep." She gave Lori a quick hug and followed Brown Shades up the stairs. She was sleeping in Brittney's bed, her cousin on the floor next to her.

"I'll bring you out some coffee," Lori said to Fic. He gave her a peck and went out on the back porch.

The night was loud. Insects called to each other, and a few early riser birds were starting their morning songs. Fic sat on a rocker on the back porch. Weapon across his knees. He looked into the forest surrounding the back of his house. A slight breeze was swaying the limbs of the forest edge, but it was a warm breeze, offering no cooling effect at all.

Lori came out and handed him a mug of coffee. Their watches will take them into daylight, so they were starting their day early. She gave him a peck this time and went back inside to watch over her hurt son.

Slowly, light started to enter the backyard of the farmhouse and Fic was able to make out more and more details of the area. It was good to be back in his home, but he was uneasy. His plan, which had started to come together just before Jimmy's life ended, had matured and morphed during the night. He spent a lot of time in his head as he thought about what they could do to find and rescue his daughter. Jimmy had been a creep, but he did show some small sense of honor when he tried to keep the soldier from taking his daughter. The man he had seen in the Humvee, although familiar, did not conjure any names to Fic's mind. The fact remained that she was in Weather, and he needed to get inside and find her. If he had to kill a lot of soldiers that had at one time been part of the same command, he wouldn't hesitate for a second. The worst thing about killing is it starts to get easier after a while. It was a part of himself that he didn't like but had come to accept as part of the job when he was deployed. He found he had quickly settled into that mindset when people started shooting at him. That attitude had been set into overdrive with the wounding of his son and the taking of his daughter.

Fic waited until he saw the sun peaking over the mountain before heading into the house. Some of the others were already up and getting their own coffee and Class Room was cooking a bunch of eggs on the gas stove. "How's the ankle?" he asked Class Room.

"Better," she replied. "But still pretty sore."

Fic set the M-4 in the corner of the kitchen, and grabbed a pitcher of water that he had poured from the large jug filled from the hand pump they still had out in the barnyard.

He went up to the bathroom and found his battery powered razor. It hadn't been used in months, but still had a charge. He went to work on his hair and beard.

After ten minutes using the electric razor and then a Bic razor, he was once again Sergeant First Class Clayton Collier. Grooming standards compliant.

Fic went into his bedroom and opened his closet. In the left corner of the large walk-in, hung four full uniforms. He took one off the rack and started putting it on. After he was dressed, he went over to his dresser and picked up a key card with a metal clip on it. The ID had his picture, name, rank and a red stripe to mark his access level in the building. It also had a magnetic strip and IC chip. "I sure hope you still work," Fic said to the key card.

When Fic came into the kitchen in his uniform and with a clean face, everyone did a double take and stared in awe for a few seconds. He smiled and sat at the table.

"So, I guess this uniform is part of your brilliant plan, huh?" Rodent Whisperer said.

"Yes, it is," Fic said, placing the key card on the table. "Hopefully this will still work, and I will be able to just walk right into the base. I have extensive access to the whole site due to my duties on the security team."

Fic started to finally explain his plan.

"So, as you can tell, I'm hoping to blend in with the rogue soldiers in order to get onto the base. I'll have to do this part alone because I don't think any of you could wear one of my uniforms since the poor fit would make you stand out more than anything. Once I've made it on base, I have a few ideas where they could be holding large groups of prisoners, so I'll start there and hopefully find Brittney and Joey's mom and brother quickly. After I've seen exactly how they are all being detained, I'll have to come up with a way, on the spot, to get everyone out and back here safely. That's just my end of the objective, I will still need everyone else's help, too.

"Class Room, with your ankle issue, I need you to stay here and help Lori take care of Shane. Hopefully, he is over the hump, but we still don't know if we got the infection under control yet. Constant monitoring and treatment is still needed.

"Joey and Daisy, you will be in charge of watching the boats we will use to get across the river. I saw two or three canoes at Jimmy's cabin when we were there. You will need to guard them and have them ready when we get back with Brittney, your mother and brother.

"Brown Shades, Rodent Whisperer, and Kitsune will be my support team. You will come with me up to the border of the base on the forest side and will stand by until I get back out. You're to provide cover for our escape and if anyone needs any medical help, that's where you come in RW. Kitsune, your eyes, knowledge and knife will be needed as we move along."

The three men nodded, and Brown Shades asked, "When do we leave?"

"We will head out as soon as everyone is ready and make our way to the river. After we get the canoes and get them to the water, we will see if we can get across if it is clear. If not, we wait until it is, but there shouldn't be very many people in that area.

"After leaving Joey and Daisy with the boats, we will move cross-country up the ridge. Once we find and cross the A.T., we will find the back road that ends at the rear of the base. Not too many people use this route, but we will still stay off the road and undercover as we make our way to the back gate.

"When we are about a hundred meters from the gate, you three will take cover and set up an ambush, monitoring the gate for when I come out.

"I will walk in that gate like I'm reporting for duty. If my keycard works, we are in. If it doesn't then we will have to shift to Plan B."

"What's Plan B?" asked Kitsune.

"I haven't figured one out yet, but I'm pretty good at going with the flow. We'll cross that bridge when we come to it.

"Once I get our people, we will make our way back here, pick you guys up, head to the boats, cross the river, and back cross-country to the house. Easy Peasy," Fic finished with a smile.

The group sat in silence as they processed all the information Fic had just thrown at them. Then Kitsune said softly, "I'm ready, but I need to borrow your razor first."

Lori had gotten up when she'd heard most of the plan and went into the other room. She came back with a small bolt of black cloth, went up to her husband and wrapped it around his right arm over his uniform sleeve. "You'll need this," she said. "All the soldiers wear one now, to show they are with that asshole in Weather."

Fic looked at the black arm band and smiled at his wife. "What would I do without you?" he said as he caressed the side of her face with his hand.

CHAPTER 25
ASSAULT ON WEATHER - TUESDAY, AUGUST 7TH

Six people walked through an open forest. There were fields on each side of the small grove of trees and the sun was bright out there, but soft and shaded under the trees. Green shadows flitted about on the silvan floor as a soft and warm breeze hit the walkers in the face. The wind smelled of the river.

This new party had a different look then the one that had traveled the trail. Fic was back in uniform. A weapon at the ready in a sling around his neck and his pistol belt on his waist. Brown Shades had traded his staff for a shotgun. Rodent Whisperer also carried a shotgun and a pistol had replaced his axe at his belt. The cousins had pistols holstered at their waists. Kitsune was armed with a scoped, hunting rifle, and was sporting a fresh haircut and clean shaven face.

The group came to a road at the edge of the woods. It ran along the river which was in front of them. A steep embankment leading to the water's edge.

They turned left and moved up the shoulder. Fic brought them into a slow jog, so they could shorten the time they would be exposed.

They came to the large rock with the trail leading to Jimmy's cabin. Fic stopped and turned to the group. "Kitsune and I can get these two canoes. The rest of you head back about fifty meters to that driveway that goes towards the water. I'm pretty sure I saw another canoe down there that we will need for the mission. Go see if it is secure or if we will need to figure out how to free it for use." Fic really didn't want the kids to be traumatized by seeing Jimmy's body which had been out in the heat for a full day.

Fic and Kitsune headed up the trail while the others backtracked to the driveway. As they approached the cabin, Fic was at the ready, with Kitsune backing him up. He expected to hear flies as they got to where Jimmy had fallen, but all he heard was birds.

They came within sight of the cabin. The place where Jimmy's body had been left was just a patch of grassy dirt with some stains on the grass. Jimmy was gone.

"Let's make this quick, Kit," Fic said to the young man. "Whoever took Jimmy may still be around."

They moved to where the two canoes were stored next to the cabin and were relieved to see they weren't locked up. They looked around for some paddles, but none were in sight. Kitsune entered the cabin and scoured through the mess that all the commotion had stirred up. He swiftly found two paddles and noticed a board lying next to the bed, grabbing that as well. "That'll do in a pinch," he said to himself.

Kitsune met back up with Fic, waiting with the canoes at the front of the cabin. He threw the two paddles and one makeshift paddle into the canoe, grabbed the two front handles of the watercraft as Fic grabbed the back two and they headed down the trail.

The two men found the others at a tired-looking red canoe that was chained to the post of the porch on a small cabin near the water's edge. They were trying to figure out how to get it loose.

They dropped the free canoes at the water's edge and Kitsune searched the cabin and a shed that was back by the road. He came back with a claw hammer, a crowbar, and two more paddles.

Rodent Whisperer went to work on the lock and chain and after a few sharp blows and some prying, the canoe was loose.

Joey noticed they lacked enough paddles for three canoes and went looking around in the woods, finding a thick stick that would act as the sixth paddle.

They lined up the canoes and looked out at the river, which was empty of any traffic. No one could be seen on the other side of the river. Everywhere seemed deserted.

"I'll cross with Daisy," instructed Fic. "You can use the board as a paddle," he said to Daisy. "I'll only need a little help to get us across. RW, you go with Joey and his stick paddle. BS and Kit, you come in the third canoe with the real paddles."

The three canoes set out into the river, going barely fifteen feet before the current picked them up. At that point all three of the canoes turned upstream into the current and the paddlers dug hard.

Fatigue made their arms feel weak and heavy as the canoers finally managed to reach the other side of the river. The waterway was making an oxbow bend where they crossed and there was a nice stony beach that Fic had been aiming for. He'd managed to hit the target, only a little downstream of the middle of the spot he had chosen. The group quickly disembarked and pulled the canoes all the way up the shore and into a stand of trees near the water's edge.

They found some branches and fronds to cover the canoes to try to disguise them and then Fic gathered Joey and Daisy. "Okay, this is your part of the mission," Fic started. "Hide in that large bush over there and keep an eye on the canoes. If anyone comes, first, just try to observe. If there are only one or two people, you can engage if you feel you can get the drop on them. Don't take any chances. If you appear to be outnumbered, just retreat up the ridge to the A.T. From there you should be able to shake any kind of pursuit. We are going to wait until dark to enter the base, if we can, so we should hopefully be back before midnight. You have gear to spend the night here, so if we haven't returned by first light, take the canoes and head back to the farm."

Both tweens nodded their heads together, a determined look on their faces. "Please find my Ma and brother," said Joey. They were happy to be doing their part in this rescue effort. If they lose the boats and get chased, the river would become an obstruction instead of their means of escape. They went to the bush and hunkered down, pistols in their hands now and senses alert.

Fic motioned for the others to follow and started moving away from the river towards the tall ridge that was in front of them.

They found a country road and started following it as it passed a few houses before the woods came in close on either side as it moved up in elevation.

They reached the top of a rise and the road turned to the south following the small ridge top. Fic kept going in an easterly direction, moving into the woods and starting to bushwhack.

They could see there were several small hills that ran from south to the north. "There's the roller coaster where the trail runs." Pointing to the ridgeline. "We should be able to get to the path on that drawl to the left. Crossing on the downside. After that, the back road to the base should be on the other side and will take us up the next larger ridge."

They moved through the woods passing a small man-made pond and came to the road that led to the base. They followed along near the edge, ready to get off if they heard anything. They were moving fast now. Fully alert and ready for trouble.

Suddenly, they heard a vehicle coming from the direction of their target. Fic quickly waved everyone off the road. They jumped over the side and started moving downhill. Crouching and sitting still as the vehicle passed where they had been just moments ago. "I guess this road is getting some use now," said Fic, noting that it was another Humvee that had passed them.

Fic motioned for them to come down the hillside with him, and as they moved along the side of the ridge, they came to a path moving from left to right in front of them. As they stepped onto the trail, Fic saw the tell-tail white blaze that he had been following for the last several weeks.

Fic called a halt, and everyone gathered around him. He pulled out the handheld he still had that he had taken from his captor down near Shenandoah and turned it on. Immediately, he heard traffic on the channel he was on.

"Searcher three, this is searcher four. What's your twenty?" A voice came out of the radio.

"Search four, searcher three, I just left base and am heading down Morgan Mill Road. Going to patrol around to the west and south. So far, no sign of any insurgents," another voice replied.

"Roger that. Searcher four out."

Fic turned the radio off and stowed it in his cargo pocket. He started off again on the other side of the trail and began climbing through the woods.

They're looking for someone, he thought to himself. *Are they expecting us?*

He shook off an uneasy shudder and continued on.

#

They climbed the ridge away from the road and trails. The brush became thick, and they had a lot of blowdowns, slowing their progress, but Fic didn't mind the delay since there were still several hours of daylight left. They approached a fence crested with barbed wire that ran through the woods. They would've needed to sit on the tallest person's shoulders just to see over the top. To the left, would be the gate that opened where the road came into the base. To the right, the fence stretched out of sight in the thick forest, but Fic knew it turned to the east and headed to the road at the main entrance to the base.

Fic came to the fence and crouched down, the others following his lead. He looked up and down the border, debating whether they should head towards the gate, or try to breach the fence somewhere along this length.

Kitsune looked to the right and said, "I think we may have a way in." He walked in the direction he'd been staring before anyone had a chance to respond.

They followed him until they came to a blowdown that had fallen across the fence, destroying a section and squashing it to the ground. The tree created a convenient bridge right over the fence.

Normally, the perimeter is patrolled daily to find things like this, but Fic guessed — even though they appeared to be keeping their grooming standards — not all the duties from before the bombs were being adhered to. The next part of Fic's plan became clear.

"Okay, this is where I will head into the compound when it gets dark," Fic said, looking to the southwest to see how long they had until the sun went behind the ridge. "It looks like we have about four hours at least." Traveling overland and getting across the river had taken up a lot of the day, but they still had to wait a while.

"We will wait here until dusk, and this is where I will leave you three. Once I find Brittney and Joey's kin, I will come back here, and we will be able to head west to the river straight from here." Fic looked around the area. "Stay hidden over there," he pointed to the top of the fallen tree which was still full of dead leaves. "You can build a little nest in that and be able to keep watch on the fence line to look for my return. Until then, we stand by, to stand by."

After about an hour of sitting and staring into the forest, Kistune said to Fic, "I'm going to take a little scout." At first Fic thought he should deny that request, but decided to let him proceed; Kitsune really was a capable scout, and he seemed to have skills well beyond their knowledge.

"Okay, but be careful and stay out of sight. Don't get too close to the gate and don't make contact unless you have to. We need that element of surprise. Or, better yet, to get in and out without them ever knowing we were there. Take Rodent Whisperer's shotgun instead of that rifle."

Kitsune gave Fic one of Brown Shades' two finger salutes, traded weapons with Rodent Whisperer, and moved off into the woods as the others hunkered down in the nest they had carved out of the fallen tree.

The young man moved down the ridge and circled around towards the gate. The thick forest hid him from view after a few seconds.

#

Private George used his key card to disengage the lock and moved through the unguarded back gate. Security had become pretty lax, he thought to himself as he started down the road away from the base. That's good for me. Let's me do my business in peace.

George had been a regular army Private when the bombs fell. Just minding his own business, standing his watches in the Operations Center as a radio operator and staying out of trouble and under the radar. All the better to do the things he wanted to do, he wasn't going to let the strict rules of the army hold him back.

He pulled a large joint out of his breast pocket, put it up under his nose and took a long sniff. "Ahh," he said. "Mother Nature's finest." After the stress of the last couple of days, he needed a break from his mind.

He walked off the road into the woods to the left. Following a light trail that he had made from his many visits to his hiding place.

When the bombs fell, everything went crazy. At first, they went into alert and prepared for the government leadership to arrive as planned in order to continue operations in this unexpected state of war. But no one ever showed up.

Eventually, a large group of soldiers came to the front gate and demanded to see the commanding officer. When Colonel Gifford came out to talk to the men, he was shot in the head like a piece of meat. When the Executive Officer rushed over to see what was up, he met the same fate. All the men in the group had drawn their weapons and had launched their takeover of the base. It was the perfect surprise. The base was completely caught off guard when rogue soldiers showed up.

They had put all the crew into the mess hall and guarded the doors. One by one, they brought the captives to see a man named Richard Flaherty. He would ask a list of questions — sometimes seemingly unrelated to their situation — and then he would announce that he was the new leader of this ruined country, and they could either join the rogue army and serve him, or ... He always left the rest unsaid.

George wasn't stupid, he had seen their ruthlessness with the Commanding Officer and Executive Officer, he readily joined the rogue army, and just as he'd guessed, things had gotten a little easier for him. He could come and go as he wanted, only needing to check in with Sergeant Wheeler every couple of days, and he could sneak out for a quick smoke before going on watch in the new operations center. So much had changed since the bombs. Not all of it good, but for him, it was better. He had a little more power and freedom than a lowly Private doing his duty.

He could interact freely with some of the locals, like Jim Henry, and make his own way in this new world. The last thing he did with Jim went to shit though. The girl. The doctor. Then, Corporal Richard had found out they had the girl and took her, beating Jim in the process. He knew when to choose his battles, and that was one he had let go. More opportunities would come for him, he was one of the people in power.

He sat on a log that was familiar and comfortable and pulled out a lighter. He fired up the joint and sat puffing it every once and a while, looking out into the forest in the late afternoon light.

He took a large pull on the smoking spliff and started coughing. When the smoke cleared from in front of his face, he saw a cardinal, sitting in a tree not ten feet away from him, looking right at him. The bird sang a few bars of cardinal song and continued to watch him as he finished off the joint. Stubbing out the small roach and putting it back in his pocket. "I'm fucking starting to get paranoid, I swear that bird is watching me." he said out loud to himself.

"Hey bird," George said. "What do you want? I ain't sharing." He started to laugh at his joke that was only funny to his addled brain.

The bird took flight and flew over his head, appearing to dive toward him and making him duck down. "Holy Shit!" he exclaimed. His paranoia increased.

George sat on the log for a while and looked at the forest as his buzz intensified. He looked around for his weapon and realized that he had left it in his locker. *Oh well*, he thought. *I'm safe out here so close to the base and that bitch is heavy.*

He stood unsteadily and started to walk down the path. He took three steps and discovered that he was looking down at the barrel of a shotgun. He followed the barrel back to the owner and saw a young man on the other end of the shotgun.

Fear crossed the soldier's face as the young man gestured with his gun, "That way."

George saw no option but to follow his orders. He was so high, he surely didn't feel coordinated enough to fight him for the weapon and he wasn't positive he could even run if he needed to. He turned and started walking the way the man had pointed.

#

The three men sat, each looking in a different direction. Fic was watching the spot where Kitsune had gone when he saw some movement. Loud rustling preceded a soldier emerging from the bushes, his hands were up, and he was glancing over his shoulder. Behind him, Fic saw Kitsune with his shotgun pointed at the man's back.

Hmm, he thought to himself, *time to alter the plan a bit again*.

When the man approached, Fic noticed that his name was George. "What do we have here," he said softly to Kitsune as they walked up to the hideout. "Private George, I presume."

They sat the soldier down in the middle of the group and started asking him questions. Fic started by asking about the situation in the base. How many personnel? Were there guards? Are they keeping prisoners in the west side stockade? Then, he started asking about Jim Henry, the doctor, and finally about his daughter. He didn't let George know that Brittney was his daughter and George was so dazed, he would just answer the question without even realizing that he was giving up vital information.

"Yeah, we took a girl," he said groggily. He was confused and thought that the guy in uniform asking him all the questions was one of Flaherty's Rogues. "She was pretty hot, and Jim wouldn't stop talking about her. She's lucky we'd even give her the time of day, really, with our reputation and power. She pretended like she wasn't impressed, so we had to convince her otherwise. Too bad she messed up her ankle."

It took all of Fic's energy not to slap this wasted scum silly. He took a deep breath and moved back away from the smiling lowlife. He thought for a moment and looked at Kitsune, then at George. "Take off your uniform, George," he ordered the soldier.

George stared blankly at Fic with glassy eyes and a gaping mouth before saying, "Take off?"

"Yes, we need your uniform," Fic said firmly. "That woman you abducted is my daughter. We are going in to get her out. You will stay here, and my friends will take care of your wasted self."

He turned to Kitsune and said, "Put on his uniform. I may need some help and your freshly groomed face will fit in nicely. It's like you knew you would be coming in with me." He smiled suspiciously at the young man.

Kitsune nodded, took the guy's uniform, and changed into it. Stuffing his clothes into his small pack.

They tied up George and sat him in his skivvies in the center of the blowdown.

Fic handed his rifle to Brown Shades he would only be able to rely on his pistol inside Weather. Kitsune returned the shotgun to Rodent Whisperer and took his pistol, placing it in the small of his back under the uniform shirt. They didn't want to draw any unwanted attention, and in the close corridors of the base, a long gun may be a hindrance.

Kitsune held up the soldier's key card. "At least they are still using the key cards. If yours doesn't work, maybe this one will." This card had a blue stripe instead of Fic's red one. Not as much access as his, but it should help them get through the gate at least.

"Good observation, Kit," Fic said. "I just hope mine works, because I had some killer access in the base. This lackey only has a few levels of access."

Fic gave Rodent Whisperer and Brown Shades a final update and nodded to Kitsune to signal his readiness for the next phase of the plan.

The two uniformed men followed the light path past the soldier's smoking stump and came to the road. Turning right, they walked towards the gate as if they belonged there.

#

Fic approached the fence line and pulled out his key card. The large gate spanned the road, had a chain keeping it shut, and was locked with a large padlock. To the right of that was a person sized gate with a card reader that had a red light and a keypad below it. If all went as planned, Fic's key will be scanned, and the gate should open.

Fic held his key card for a few seconds, getting ready to try it on the scanner. After thinking about it for a bit, he put his card away and retrieved Private George's from Kitsune who had clipped it to his shirt pocket flap. He held it up to the scanner. The device beeped when it read the card and then nothing. The red light continued to shine at them as they stood there. Apprehensively, Fic started to reach for his key card, when the device beeped again, the light turned green and there was a loud click.

Fic quickly reached back to the gate and pulled it open. They had access.

There was a small courtyard and then the walls of the base rose above them. It looked like a one-story building with no windows. What wasn't common knowledge to the civilians was that this building went down, not up. Ten levels dove deep into the mountain. Carved out over the years.

The door had another card reader. Fic scanned George's card again and this time the light turned green quickly, and Fic pulled open the door. They'd made it inside.

From what Fic had gathered from George's rambling, all the prisoners were being kept on level three on the west side. The infiltrators walked along the corridor and passed the elevator, Fic motioned to the stairwell instead. He pushed open the door and the two men entered and started down the steps. "We need to avoid running into others as long as possible," he explained to Kitsune.

After going down three levels, Fic opened the door to another hallway that looked a lot like the one they had just left. He turned left and they came to several doors that had a square window in each. Fic walked to each door and looked inside. As he was glancing into the third window he came across, a soldier turned the corner. After a few seconds of panic, Fic just started walking towards them as if he had somewhere to be.

The man coming towards them was busy looking at a clipboard and didn't notice them at first. As they got closer, he looked up at the two men approaching them. Showing no recognition, he nodded, mumbled a soft "Good evening, Sarge," and looked back down at his clipboard, continuing down the hallway. The ruse was working so far.

Fic smiled to himself as they passed the soldier, glancing at Kitsune and nodding his head. The soldier turned a corner into one of the cross hallways and moved out of sight. Fic continued to check the windows.

The final door in the hallway had a card reader and a small sign above the door that read, *Stockade #1, Secure Area, Authorized Personnel Only*.

Fic held up George's card and the red light remained red after the first beep. Fic handed George's card back to Kitsune and tried his card. The light turned green almost immediately, beeped, and clicked open. Miraculously, his card still worked.

The guys entered a large space with several small rooms lined up all around the edge of the area. Tiny windows were on the doors.

There was a clipboard hanging near each of the doors. Fic went over to the first one and saw a list of about fifteen names.

He looked in the window and saw several people sitting on the floor, on a couple of beds, or on a chair or two. It looked to be a group of about fifteen adults.

He scanned the list and didn't see his daughter's, Joey's mother's, nor brother's name on the list. These were most likely the people who had been forcibly taken by the rogues to be used for whatever they were doing here. He stood and thought for a few seconds. He wanted to free them all, but doing so now would cause a commotion that may hinder him finding the three people he came to rescue. He moved to the next door and looked at the clipboard there. Still no luck. There were six more clipboards to check and after checking five more, he found Joey's mother's and brother's name. He looked up at the sign above the door, noting the designation. Turning to Kitsune, he said, "Okay, Joey's kin are in here. We can't let them out just yet, I need to find Brittney first."

Kitsune nodded his understanding, also noting the door label and moving to the last clipboard. Brittney's name was missing from that one too.

"There are two more rooms like this," Fic said. "Let's go."

They scanned into Stockade #2 and repeated the process. Fic arrived at the last clipboard in this room, and with a sinking feeling, still had not found Brittney's name.

"One more room," Fic said to Kitsune.

They entered the corridor and started walking towards the last room of the Stockade area of the base.

Before they reached the next scanner, two soldiers came around the corner just past the last room. In between them limped a tall young woman. Her ankle had a bandage wrapped around it, but there was no cast and she wasn't using crutches. Fic looked into his daughter's pained face and tried not to show any reaction. Kitsune immediately noticed the subtle shift in Fic's energy, and knowing what it must mean, waited for his next signal as they moved along.

Fic's heart started racing, but he quickly decided to try and get past these guys and then follow them to see where they were taking her. If they could get out without making a fuss, they'd have a much easier time getting back to the river.

The two soldiers barely acknowledged Fic and Kitsune, but as they started to pass each other, Brittney looked up and scanned the faces of the two other uniformed men. Her eyes grew two sizes as she recognized her father, but quickly went neutral as she saw the quick shake of his head in warning. She understood immediately that he had a plan and she needed to remain quiet and composed. She was pretty quick on the uptake when it came to nonverbal cues.

They moved past each other and down the hallway. Fic waited until they turned the corner, motioned to Kitsune, and then turned back to follow them. The shot of adrenaline he received when he recognized his daughter had made his senses razor sharp and he was hyped up. He took a deep breath as he came to the corner and peeked around. They were waiting at one of the elevators. He paused until the doors opened and the trio entered the elevator. Fic heard one of the soldiers tell the other to hit the five button. As the doors closed, Fic ran to the stairway with Kitsune at his heels. They threw open the door and started down two more floors.

The elevators were pretty slow in the building. Fic was looking out the window of the stairway door when he saw them exit the elevator, turn right, and head down the hallway away from them.

#

Fic exited the stairwell with Kitsune right behind him. Carefully coming to the corner, Fic saw the two men and Brittney stop at the third door down and knock. A muffled voice came from inside and the men entered, escorting Fic's daughter in front of them.

They waited at the corner for a full minute. The door opened and the two soldiers came out. One turned and walked away from the infiltrators and the other stood at the door, on guard. Fic looked back at Kitsune and mouthed, "follow me."

They turned the corner and started walking towards the guard. This time, the man looked up at the two approaching soldiers and was intently staring at Fic. His expression turned from suspicion to alarm as he realized something about Fic. The man started reaching for the microphone of a hand-held walkie talkie clipped to his belt. Fic sprinted the last three meters and hit the man in the face. Kitsune was right behind Fic and he grabbed the man in an advanced hold that looked like some sort of martial arts move. He tangled the man up with his arms, keeping his hands away from the microphone and causing him to struggle to get free. The hold was so intense, it was stopping the blood from flowing to his brain, and after about thirty seconds, he became limp in Kitsune's arms. Fic looked at the young man with a respectful expression. The kid was full of surprises.

Fic opened the door quietly as Kitsune held the unconscious man. There was a sign above the doorway that said *Engineering.* Fic entered the room with his hand on his pistol, getting ready to draw it. Kitsune slipped in behind him, still holding the man. Once inside, he silently let him slip to the floor off to the side and closed the door.

The room they had entered was small. There was an empty desk opposite the door and an open door leading into a much larger room on the right. Fic turned and headed for that door as he heard a man's voice talking in a smooth, silky hiss.

"I know who you are. Your father used to work here, didn't he? We have all the records that were in the base. He has been flagged as a Resistance fighter down south. A traitor to my cause. I need to know where to find him and I'm willing to hurt you to find out."

"I don't know where my father is," Brittney lied. Her voice was shaky and had a high pitch which denoted her stress level. "He was away from home on a training exercise when you did your takeover, and we haven't heard from him since. I don't know how you 'flagged' him, but we have almost given up hope on his return."

Fic felt a bit of pride in her acting, but he wasn't too surprised. His girl was a very smart cookie.

Fic pulled his pistol as he passed the threshold, sweeping the room as he entered and saw only one man standing behind a large wooden desk. "I'm right here," said Fic, drawing his bead on the man's forehead. "Who the fuck are you?"

The man was about six foot four inches. He had dark hair cut in a severe high and tight and a thick mustache of the same dark color. His eyes were hypnotic, almost crazy looking, and his smile exposed very large teeth. He was dressed in all black. Black pants with a black long-sleeved shirt that had the sleeves rolled up. When Fic walked in and addressed him, he only showed surprise for a second before his face went blank. It was almost as if he was expecting him, but still shocked to see how easily he had gotten into this room. Noticing that he was in uniform, he quickly deduced just how he had made it this far.

"Sergeant First Class Clayton Collier, I presume," the man said, a smug look on his face. He started to sit in his chair, reaching for the edge of the desk as he did so.

"Don't fucking move, asshole," Fic ordered. "I know there is a button on the back side of the desk. If you really know all about me, you would know I was Chief of Security here before the bombs. I know every level in this place and every security alarm and safeguard. If you move one more inch, I will shoot you."

The man froze and looked at Fic with hard eyes. His smug look lost a little bit of his sleaziness — and was that a touch of fear Fic just saw flicker across his face? This man's attitude revealed that he was someone who wasn't used to being told what to do.

"Move away from the desk and sit in that chair over there," Fic said motioning to a chair in the corner of the room. The man did as he was told, keeping his eyes on Fic and his pistol the whole time. Brittney came up to her dad and gave him a quick peck on the cheek, careful not to distract him from his aim.

"Hi, Daddy," she said. "I knew you would find me." She moved off behind him and looked at Kitsune, not recognizing him, but understanding he was helping her father. "I'm Brittney," she said to the young man.

"Kitsune," he replied softly.

As he sat down, the man noticed Fic's companion. "So, you are in on this too, Private George," he said, reading the name tag on Kitsune's uniform. Kitsune stared at him for a few seconds and decided to just go with it. "I sure am," he said.

"So, you know me, now why don't you tell me who you are?" Fic said.

"I'm Richard Flaherty. I run this place," he said, that smug smile was back. "Actually, I run the whole entire country now."

"Seriously," Fic said, not believing the tall man. "Who the fuck are you? And why were you interrogating my daughter?"

"I assure you, sir, I am Richard Flaherty. I picked this office because I wanted to be out of the way. A little hard to find. I don't like having guards around all the time. I don't trust them." At this point, he looked over Fic's shoulder into the outer room, he caught a glimpse of the unconscious man lying in the corner and shook his head in disgust. Pointing at the guy, he raised his eyebrows in a "see what I mean" look.

"I'm the one who took over the country overnight. A feat never before accomplished until I came along. I'm the greatest leader of my time. Of any time. You should be bowing down to me."

The man really had an ego. Fic had seen news reports of Flaherty when he was first stirring up trouble, but he hadn't paid a lot of attention after he figured out that he was a kook. He looked different then. Longer hair and no mustache. If this was really the guy that had caused all the trouble in this country, then this was really a lucky turn of events. Fic's plan shifted in his head.

The man continued. "I had received reports that some ex-army guy was causing trouble down south, and after some investigating, we figured out who you were and where you were heading, but we must have underestimated your movement. If you open that top left drawer in the desk, you will find something that I think you lost a bit south of here." Flaherty said with a wry grin. Fic opened the drawer and saw his ID card sitting there staring back at him. He grabbed it and placed it in his shirt pocket.

"Just a half hour ago, my security guys said that your old key card had been used at the stockade rooms and was in the base. I didn't really think it was you, but maybe your wife, so we decided to move your daughter from her cell and be on the lookout for a woman roaming the halls. So, you understand my surprise when you showed up. In uniform. Bravo, Sergeant."

Fic's plan shifted once again. This was turning into a shit show, but he had found his daughter and knew where Joey's family was. The bonus was that he had the monster that had caused all the trouble in this country down range of his weapon. He could take him out right now. Would that set the path of the country back on track, or just make it harder to get out of here with his daughter? He was going to find out soon enough.

"How is your ankle, Britt?" he asked his daughter.

"It hurts, but I can walk. Let's get out of here."

"Okay, world wrecker," Fic said to Flaherty. "You are coming with us. You will go in front, and me and my partner will escort you out of the base. We will head for the stairs and move up to level one, then out the back gate. Once we are free of the base, I'll let you go." Fic explained, effortlessly lying without a hint of hesitation. "You are our ticket out of here. If you cooperate, we will cut you loose once we are safely away from the base," his lie expanded.

Fic went up to Flaherty and plucked his key card off of his shirt pocket. He looked at the card. It was blank, had no picture or other information, but Fic would bet that it would open every door in the complex. He took his own card and flung it into the corner. They knew he was here and were probably tracking his movements. They knew he had been in the Stockade rooms. He hoped that they didn't deduce where else he had gone.

The four people moved out of the Engineering Office, through the reception room, and out into the hallway. They moved along with Flaherty in the lead, followed by Fic, with his pistol covertly at the ready. They made it to the stairwell and headed up the steps. When they reached level three, Fic told Flaherty to stop.

"We need to do something first. You have some people here being held against their wishes. We are going to let them out now."

They moved on to level three and made their way to the Stockade rooms. Using Flaherty's key card, they entered the third room and went to the cell where Joey's mother and brother were being kept. Leaving Kitsune to cover the prisoner, Fic used Flaherty's card to unlock the cell and pulled the door open. Standing at the door, he said, "Are Melissa and Davey Dunning here?" At first no one answered. Fic started looking around the small cell that was jammed with people, he noticed a boy that looked a lot like Joey, but a few years older. He was standing next to a woman with blonde hair and a slight resemblance to Daisy. Looking at them, he asked again, "Are you Joey's Ma?" I came here with him and his cousin Daisy. We came to rescue you."

At the mention of her son's name, her eyes grew wide, and she nodded her head. "You came with Joey?"

Fic nodded and waved them over. "I'm Clayton. Joey and Daisy are waiting for us. Come with us and we will take you to them."

The two captives moved behind Fic and gathered with Kitsune, Brittney and Flaherty. Melissa looked at Flaherty, confusion on her face at first, and then some anger, and finally understanding. He was their ticket out of here.

Fic tossed Flaherty's key card to one of the captives that was standing next to him. "I need you to do me a favor," Fic started. "I need you to open all of the cells in this room and in the two others that are out the door and to the right. Once everyone is free, tell them to go up two more levels and find a door to the outside. We need to spread out as much as possible to cause confusion and increase the odds of everyone getting out." Fic left out the fact that he needed the distraction to help cover their escape. He hoped for the best for them, but right now his priority was his daughter and Joey's family. He couldn't rescue everyone himself. He needed everyone's cooperation.

The man nodded his head and went to open the other cells in the room.

Fic turned to his small group and ushered them out as the people he had freed went to find their own families that they had been separated from in this complex.

The five escapees and one captive moved back down the hallway and into the stairwell. Moving up once again, they came to the first level where the door to the outside was located.

As they were making their way towards the back door, a soldier rounded the corner, her pistol drawn. Just then an alarm started sounding in the complex. Fic grabbed Flaherty and placed his pistol to the side of his head.

"Hey, Sarah," Fic said, recognizing the woman. "What the hell is going on here? I go away for a couple months and the whole place goes to shit."

Staff Sergeant Sarah Murry was a friend of Fic's. They had had each other's families over for bar-b-ques and birthday parties. They had known each other for several years. They had been in the sand pit together.

"Clay?" the woman said, a confused look on her face. She raised her pistol and pointed it at the group, trying to figure out what was going on. Kitsune trained his weapon on the Staff Sergeant.

Sarah recognized Flaherty right after she recognized Clay. "What are you doing, Clay?" Indecision racked her face.

"This asshole had Brittney," Fic replied. "You know this is the guy who caused this whole mess. We're here to fix it."

Sarah stood staring for several seconds, then lowered her weapon and said, " I'm only here because he threatened my family, I felt like I had no choice. I suggest you leave his body in the ditch outside." She looked disgustedly at Flaherty; hate filled her eyes. "I'll try to cover for you here. There is a group of us who are fed up with these traitors. We will re-establish control of the base. Just get rid of him. I assure you, he is way too dangerous alive."

"I just need him as insurance to get out of here with everyone safe. I most likely won't have to hurt him," he said looking at his captive, trying to give him a little bit of hope so he didn't do anything rash. It was always easier to control people when they thought they had a chance of surviving.

Sarah approached Fic and pulled out a pair of handcuffs she had on her belt. "These might come in handy." She handed the cuffs to Fic and started heading back the way she had come. "Hurry," she shouted back at them as the alarm continued to sound. Other sounds were reaching them now. Shouts and the banging of doors. A shot rang out deep within the structure.

They exited the building and moved to the gate. It was dark now. They went through the gate using George's card and moved down the road to the little path. Fic grabbed Flaherty's arms and cuffed his hands behind his back. The group made their way back to their meeting point, casually strolling along with one of the most evil men in the country, currently. As the fallen tree came into view, Fic realized that he could not see Rodent Whisperer, Brown Shades or George anywhere.

The sound of the alarm was banging down the mountain, echoing through the forest. That was the only sound he could hear. Every bird or insect that had been making noise before was silent. The alarm rolled on.

The group circled around the blowdown and Fic saw Brown Shades motioning to them from another covered area down the dark hillside. He quickly moved over to Brown Shades, keeping a grip of Flaherty's shirt as he went.

"We heard the alarm and decided to move a little downhill, but still within sight of the blowdown," Brown Shades explained.

George sat in the corner of the covered area, in his underwear, hands tied behind his back. He'd gained a blindfold and a gag since they'd seen him last. Fic looked at Rodent Whisperer with a questioning expression and he shrugged, "He just wouldn't shut up."

"Do you have another bandana? I want to put one on 'President' Flaherty here," Fic said, sarcasm dripping from his voice at the fake title.

"Flaherty?" Rodent Whisperer and Brown Shades said in unison, looking at the man dressed all in black. "*This* is the man who caused so much chaos and death?" Rodent Whisperer asked incredulously.

"Yep, this is him, but I think we need to put things right," Fic said. "Maybe it's time we took our country back."

Rodent Whisperer brought a bandana over and Fic covered the man's eyes. This might slow them down, but he didn't plan on having either of the soldiers with them for much longer.

Brittney recognized George sitting in the corner and she quickly went over and kicked him in his chest with her good leg. He toppled over and moaned through the gag.

"You monster!" Brittney hissed, continuing to kick his prone body before stumbling back on her hurt leg. "You and Jimmy will pay for abducting me and treating me the way you did."

"Jimmy already paid, " Fic said to his daughter. "I'll fill you in on all the details, when we are safe at home."

"We better get away from this place now." He grabbed Flaherty by the shirt and guided him along. Rodent Whisperer pulled George to his feet and started guiding him by the shoulder. They bushwhacked straight down the mountain until they crossed the Trail.

The sound of the alarm faded, but now they heard constant gunshots from up around the base. A large firefight was taking place at Weather. They moved off the trail and entered the gully they had come up just a few hours ago. Going back down in the dark was an extra challenge.

Fic called for a quick stop to assess everyone's ability to keep going in the dark. Brittney was still limping pretty badly, but her anger at George was still steaming which numbed her to the pain a bit. The two captives had fallen a few times and were a little banged up. Fic decided they were slowing them down too much. He expected they'd arrive at the country road that led to the river where the kids and canoes were waiting soon. It was time to do what he had been delaying until he felt safe enough in their escape.

They came to the road and stopped. Fic told the others to start following the way to the left and he would catch up with them soon. "Leave George there," he said, pointing to a spot on the shoulder.

Rodent Whisperer sat the man down and moved away, trying to gauge Fic's intentions. He seemed to wrestle with his thoughts for a moment before he finally turned and started helping Brittney along, asking her about her injury so he could assess how bad it was. Melissa and Davey quickly followed, eager to be reunited with Joey and Daisy.

Brown Shades and Kitsune regarded Fic. "What are you planning, son?" Brown Shades asked, a worried look on his face.

"I just need to do my part to get us back to normal," Fic explained. "This is on me. You guys go with the others. I will catch up in a few minutes."

Brown Shades nodded his head and started after the others. Kitsune hesitated for a few more seconds, before following behind Brown Shades.

Fic was alone with Flaherty and George. He stood there for a full minute, letting the others get far enough ahead before he did what he knew he had to do. He looked at the pistol in his hand. *This would do the job fast and clean, but the sound will travel and if there are rogues out looking for us ...* He didn't take the time to finish the thought.

"You're not going to kill us," Flaherty insisted. "You don't have the guts. I'm too important. This country can't run without me." Fic was astounded at this man's audacity, his ego really made him believe he was invincible.

Fic stood looking at the man with disgust on his face. This guy was a total piece of work. He was the reason he was separated from his family for so long. The reason his son was lying wounded in his home and his daughter has been taken. With him gone, maybe the country can find its way again.

Fic holstered his pistol. "You're right," he said to the blindfolded man. "I'm not going to kill both of you." He pulled his long knife, grabbed Flaherty's hair, pulled back his head, placed the knife on the left side of his neck and drew around until he was on the other side. "I'm just going to kill *you*." Blood spurted on George, and he started to scream under his gag. "This country was just fine before you came along. It will be fine after."

Flaherty fell to his side, trying to say something, but his efforts only made him bleed out faster. After another minute, he stopped moving.

"George," Fic addressed the sobbing, half naked man. "I'm letting you live. Eventually you will get out of your bonds, and I suggest you get as far away from here as you can. If I see you again, I will let my daughter do to you what I did to Flaherty. Nod if you understand."

The man nodded briskly and repeatedly, saying something from behind the gag that Fic couldn't understand.

Fic wiped his knife on Flaherty's pants leg, sheathed it and started down the road at a slow jog, catching up to his friends.

#

Fic caught up to the others after a few minutes of jogging. Everyone noticed that he was alone. No one said anything about it.

They followed the road back to the river. The four with head lamps lit the way for the three without. Rodent Whisperer moving along slowly at the back, still helping Brittney with her walking.

As they moved along, they heard more far off gunfire. A few explosions had added to the fray. It appeared that the situation up in Weather had grown even hotter. The thundering sound of battle was their backdrop as they ventured on.

"I guess Sarah must have got her soldiers together to fight off the rogues," Fic said. "That's good for us. If they are being kept busy, they can't come looking for us."

As they neared the area where they had left the canoes, Joey and Daisy came out of the shadows. Joey ran to his mother and threw himself into her arms, hugging her fiercely as Daisy exclaimed, "Aunt Missy! Davey!" She gave Davey a hug. "We came for you," she said, giving her Aunt Melissa a hug once Joey let go.

They dragged the canoes out of their hiding place and back into the river's edge. They divided themselves into three groups of three. Davey asked if he could paddle for Daisy and she agreed, moving to Kitsune and Brown Shades canoe. Brittney joined Fic and Davey while Melissa went with Rodent Whisperer and Joey.

They got situated and shoved off, starting to paddle across the river. Suddenly, a huge explosion lit up the night. They could see a white light growing bright up on the mountain, right where Weather was. The brightness made spots form in front of their eyes and they all looked away from the glow. A large cloud of smoke and flame flashed out of the light rising into the air and turned a dark red. The group froze for a second and looked at each other, worried expressions on everyone's faces. A few seconds later, two more explosions went off, from each side of the main building of the complex. Their rumble sent a shiver through the group. Three more explosions erupted on the mountain. These were much closer than the original blasts. Panic had officially overtaken the group, their rowing motions became erratic and a scream escaped Melissa's mouth. Two more detonations shook the earth — one far off on the other side of the mountain, the other entirely too close to the party.

Fic yelled for everyone to keep paddling like their lives depended on it, which seemed to actually be the case. When they were about thirty-five feet from the river's edge, a final violent bang erupted right next to the river bank. The blast enveloped the fleeing canoes, sending them all tipping over and pitching the passengers into the river.

Fic groggily came to and realized he was underwater. He burst through the surface, coughing and sucked in a large gulp of air, waiting for it to burn his lungs, but it didn't. The blasts had subsided and even though the whole hillside appeared to be aflame, there were no more explosions.

He looked around and saw heads bobbing in the water. The current had grabbed each of the swimmers and the canoes were being drawn down river. Fic had lost his paddle and he couldn't see any in the dark water. All he could do was start heading for the far side of the shore, looking for others as he went.

The first person he came to was Brittney. She was swimming towards the shore just like him. He swam up to her and asked if she was okay. She signaled she was unhurt and kept moving towards shore. She was a strong swimmer, and he was confident that she would make it with no problem.

Fic caught up to Davey and noticed he was having trouble swimming. He grabbed the boy, hefted him onto his back, and kept heading to the western side of the river, away from Weather. Away from the explosions.

Fic got himself and Davey to the river bank, arriving at the same spot as Brittney. He assessed their situation and Davey was holding his arm. His shoulder had been twisted as he fell out of his canoe. Brittney had a cut on her leg, but it wasn't too severe. Luckily it was a warm summer night and there was no danger from the slightly cool water of the river.

"Stay here but keep looking for others. If you see anyone, give them a shout and help them get to shore," said Fic. "I'm going to move downstream to see if I can find anyone that way. The current was strong out in the middle."

Fic took stock. He still had his pistol but had lost his head lamp and rifle. His small pack with a few odds and ends in it had stayed on his back. Surprisingly, he appeared uninjured, except for a few bruises.

Fic walked along the shoreline heading downstream. He came to two people huddled on the shore. Rodent Whisperer was bending over a figure lying flat on the sandy shore. As Fic drew closer in the darkness, he realized his companion was performing rescue breathing on Melissa, who wasn't moving at all.

"I think she hit her head when we flipped over," Rodent Whisperer said in between giving her a breath. "I pulled her to shore and when we got here, I noticed she wasn't breathing." Just as he was about to lean over and give her another breath, she started coughing and a spurt of water came out of her mouth. Melissa moaned and tried to sit up.

Rodent Whisperer gently stopped her from moving too quickly before he knew the extent of her injuries. Reassuring her, he helped her slowly rise to a sitting position and clear the water she had taken in. Rodent Whisperer started working on stopping the bleeding on her head wound. Her coughing enabled Joey to find them in the dark. He came running up and kneeled in front of his mother, holding her hand and patting her on the back as she continued to cough and sputter. Melissa looked at Joey and then around the area as she continued to cough. "Davey?" she gasped out between coughs.

"He's fine, ma'am," Fic said. "He's up stream a ways with my daughter."

Fic quickly tended to a nasty burn that Joey had on his arm and, noticing that his head lamp was still around his neck, asked to borrow it. He put the lamp on his forehead, looking out over the river and down the shore for the other missing members of the group. The whole side of the mountain appeared to be ablaze, lighting this side of the river and helping him search some.

After moving about a hundred meters, he came upon Daisy, sitting on the shore hugging her knees and sobbing. Beside her lay Brown Shades. His glasses were gone, and his eyes were open, but he wasn't breathing. Fic quickly moved to his side and started checking his vitals, finding no pulse or breathing. He started CPR on his hiking companion who had become a loyal friend, but Fic was worried that his condition was too dire. He maintained his rhythm, pressing down on his chest and trying to keep the blood circulating in his body, hoping that his heart would start up again and he would suck in a breath, just like Melissa did.

Fic told Daisy to move up the shore to the others and to get everyone back here, tossing her the head lamp.

She grabbed it and started north, looking for the others.

In five minutes, everyone was gathered around Fic and Brown Shades, as he continued trying to revive him. When he grew tired, Rodent Whisperer took over. Everyone watched and prayed that Brown Shades would start breathing again, but that didn't happen. They rotated turns, desperately trying to bring Brown Shades back for over an hour. Davey and Joey were taking their turn together, when Fic finally accepted that their efforts were futile. Not wanting the burden to fall on the boys, he cut in, gave a few final pumps, and then stopped, resting his hand on the man's shoulder. The wise and courageous wizard was gone.

Everyone stood by their fallen comrade as the river came rushing past in front of them and a fire raged on the mountainside across the river. The burning base lit up the night. The smoke from the burning forest choked their lungs.

Daisy frantically looked around at the group, "Where's Kitsune?"

The group was horrified to realize that they were still missing a member. Kitsune hadn't shown up.

After searching the shore up and down stream for several hundred meters until well past midnight, they were all exhausted. Fic decided to wait until daybreak to resume the search for Kitsune. Fic directed the group to move up to the house where they had found the third canoe. "We are going to have to wait until first light to continue the search," Fic said. "Let's get Brown Shades up to the house and we can place him there until we can come back and transport him to my place."

They carried Brown Shades up to the small cabin, broke into the building and placed him on a small bed in the back room. Melissa and Daisy wrapped him with a sheet, creating a shroud.

Everyone gathered in the large main room of the cabin and took stock of their situation. They had lost most of their weapons. They still had three pistols, but all of the long guns were gone. They only had one headlamp now. Everyone huddled together and let their body heat dry the river water that had soaked their clothes. Melissa comforted Daisy and Joey as they quietly sobbed, mourning the gentle, grandfatherly mage.

No one slept.

CHAPTER 26
MANY PARTINGS - WEDNESDAY, AUGUST 8TH TO SEPTEMBER
AND BEYOND

The sky was starting to lighten in the east. The light from Weather had died down, but some of the forest around the base was still on fire. Smoke rose and blew towards the sunrise and away from Fic.

Fic was sitting on the porch of the cabin, his thoughts in turmoil. A lot had happened in the last several hours. His body was just now realizing the shock of everything, and for a few minutes, he couldn't move at all. He felt frozen in place. The events that had happened kept running through his brain. Rewinding and replaying again.

The job wasn't over yet. They still had to get everyone back to the farm, and he needed to find Kitsune. Brown Shades' passing had hit him hard. The mission had been a complete success up to that point. Then, with the explosion of Mount Weather, everything had gone sideways. The distraction they wanted to help them escape had triggered something much worse than they expected. They didn't know what was going on up there, but the explosions had destroyed everything.

During the night, they had heard rampant gunfire on both sides of the river. Some of it was not too far away.

Fic got up and went inside to find everyone ready to resume the search for Kitsune. He grabbed his small pack and threw it on his back. Just as they were all spread out along the driveway, they heard a vehicle moving at a high rate of speed coming down the road.

Fic could see bright lights shining through the trees that lined the way.

Everyone scattered to the side of the driveway, looking for cover.

A Humvee came screeching down the road and skidded to a stop in front of the cabin. The engine turned off, but the lights stayed on, and a soldier exited the driver's side of the vehicle with an M-4 in his hands.

Fic pulled his pistol and took aim at the edge of the vehicle. Waiting for the soldier to enter the headlight beam. As they did, Fic aligned the sights of the pistol on their chest and saw that it was Kitsune. "Hold fire," Fic yelled to the others. "That's Kit!"

He stood and waved to Kitsune, who spotted Fic and raised his hand. He came walking over to the others with a smile on his face. "I found us some wheels," he said.

Everyone expressed their delight at seeing Kitsune alive and well. With a heavy heart, Fic told him what had happened to Brown Shades. Kitsune stood in shock for a few seconds, then took a swallow of air and nodded his head. "He was a good man," was all he could think of saying.

"So, how did you find this Humvee?" Fic asked.

Kitsune told them how the force of the blast had knocked him unconscious. "I guess I floated face up for a while, because after several minutes, I came to, looking up at the stars, wondering how I had become weightless. As the fuzziness left me, I realized what had happened and made my way to shore.

"I got to the shore and tried to figure out where I was. Looking around, I saw the bridge we had floated under just yesterday, and quickly got my bearings.

"I had lost everything. The shotgun. My pack. I gathered my wits and started walking north.

"The brush was really thick next to the river here, so I had to make my way inland trying to find a way through. I came to a small road and just blindly stepped into it. I was still pretty out of it.

"All of a sudden, a spotlight shone on me. It was this Humvee," Kitsune said, gesturing to the vehicle. "Two soldiers called to me, thinking I was one of them. Instead of trying to bluff my way through it, I ran back into the woods.

"They started chasing me. Of course, they could never catch me. Not in the woods. It did take several hours to completely lose them, but I had led them far enough away from their vehicle that I was able to fl– uh … get back to the Humvee before they did and drive away. Not only had they left the key, but this M-4 was also in the back.

"I drove back towards the area where we got separated. I was going to start looking for you guys around these cabins, but knew you would be here when I pulled up. It was just a feeling."

Finishing his story, Kitsune stepped back and said, "Let's get everyone home."

Kitsune and Rodent Whisperer went back into the cabin and brought Brown Shades' body back out. They placed his body up on the roof of the vehicle. Then everyone else piled into the Humvee. It was surprisingly roomy inside, but still a tight squeeze with eight passengers. Fic elected to ride up on the roof with Brown Shades to make sure he stayed secure and to act as lookout for the one vehicle convoy.

They started off towards the farm. When they passed the Henry's place, they saw that it had burned to the ground. Another Humvee sat in the barnyard, a dead soldier on the ground next to the open door. Looking next to where the porch used to be on the house, they saw Maybell, lying dead in her front yard. A shotgun in her hands.

Kitsune pulled into the barnyard, and they inspected the situation. They moved Maybell and the soldier into the barn. Placing their bodies in the corner until they could come back and bury them.

Davey and Joey gathered the shotgun, M-4, and 9mm pistol that had been laying by the bodies, and placed them in the second Humvee, which conveniently still had the keys in the ignition.

Everyone repositioned. They moved Brown Shades' body into the new Humvee and Fic drove that with Davey and Joey.

The day started to brighten as Fic led the two vehicle convoy down the country roads towards his house. They still heard continuous shooting coming from all directions.

As they came to the end of Clay Hill Road, Fic saw a parked Humvee blocking his turn. A single soldier stood at the front of the vehicle, weapon in hand, but not at the ready, watching their approach.

Fic stayed at a steady, slow speed as he closed in on the blockade, trying to look as though he was planning to stop. When he was close enough, he floored the gas and headed straight for the lone soldier. The man panicked and jumped behind the Humvee.

Fic turned his Humvee into the parked vehicle and clipped its front bumper as he sped past, pushing it out of the way. This also had the effect of knocking the soldier into the ditch on the other side of the road.

Fic saw the man crumple into the ditch as he moved down Bishop Meade Road, watching in his side-view mirror for any movement and to ensure the other Humvee made it through the open blockade. They sped away from the scene.

Fic pushed harder on the gas now, worried about all the soldier presence in the area and eager to reach home. In a few minutes, they were pulling into his driveway.

Lori and Class Room stood on the porch with weapons in their hands. Seeing her husband getting out of one vehicle and her daughter jumping out of the back of the other, she broke down with relief.

Running to her daughter, she pulled her into a tight embrace. She never wanted to let her go. Fic came walking over and joined the group hug.

Everyone disembarked from the vehicles and Melissa and Davey were introduced to the home front women.

Fic told Lori and Class Room about Brown Shades. Class Room ran to the back of the Humvee and crawled in with the body. Her sobs reverberated through the open air while everyone gave her a moment to grieve her friend.

"Let's get these vehicles into the barn and out of sight," Fic said to Kitsune.

Kitsune nodded his head and moved towards the Humvees. They moved the vehicles into the barn and placed Brown Shades in a long wagon. Tomorrow, they would lay him to rest. They joined the others inside and Fic asserted, "We need to lay low for a couple of days and be vigilant. It seems we may have helped initiate a countercoup. I'm hoping this means the beginning of the end of this fascist regime, but I can't be certain yet."

As Lori got everyone some breakfast, Fic went into the living room to check on his son. Rodent Whisperer was in there with him, checking him over. With a sigh of relief, Fic saw that Shane was awake and alert.

"Hey Dad," Shane said with a raspy voice. "When did you get back?"

Fic kneeled down and took his son's hand. It felt warm, but not hot. He pressed his hand on his son's brow, feeling a cool surface. His fever had broken.

"I have been working on getting back here since the day the bombs fell," Fic told his son. "I just had to walk all the way back. I used the A.T. to get home."

"Cool," Shane said softly. "I always wanted to hike up from Georgia. Maybe we can do it again, together."

Fic ruffled his son's hair and said, "Sure." Smiling at him with a tear in his eye.

#

Fic found himself in a large banquet room. Large mounts of elk, moose and other game festooned the stone walls of the building. A thatched roof was above and bright lanterns hung from the rafters. A roaring fire danced in the hearth and the long table was covered in a feast of food.

At the head of the table sat a wise wizard. His long staff with the glowing gem leaning on the table beside him. To his right sat a pointy eared rogue. Gnobbit in her finest, but still black, jerkin and pants. Across from her, sat a tall elf, Finn also wearing the

*same bright clothes he wore at their going away banquet. Along
the table were all his friends. The halflings, now numbering four
with a slightly larger Melissa, tending to their hungry needs. The
Dwarf in his regal dress, cracking jokes that had everyone in
stitches. Kitsune wore a hat made of reeds that resembled a fox's
face and clothing of crimson felt. At his feet lay a fox, curled in
a ball and sleeping in the warmth of the hot fire. A bright red
cardinal perched on Kitsune's shoulder. The beautiful Class
Room stood in the corner, playing her lute. The music filled the
room and the warmth of her song brought everyone joy.*

*Fic sat at the other end of the table and beside him sat Lori,
his wife. She was dressed in a beautiful dress with flowers
interwoven into the fabric. On the other side sat the two armored
knights. One female, one male. His children. All healthy and
alive. The dark night was nowhere to be seen or felt.*

*The feast seemed to last a long time. Food was eaten, stories
were told, and Brown Shades was alive and happy and full of
laughter. At one point he called across the room to Fic. Telling
him not to fret and that he had done good. "Don't worry about
me, my friend," he said to Fic. "I'm okay. All is well."*

The dream faded and Fic came awake in a dark room. He
was disoriented at first, but then everything came back to him in
a crash. He thought back to the dream. Smiled as he recalled the
mage's hearty laugh and drifted back to sleep, a slight grin on
his lips.

#

The next morning, after that wonderful dream, they took Brown
Shades up behind the barn on a small hill where a large oak
grew. They buried him close by, where the shade from the large
tree would cool his resting place on the hot summer days.

Tears flowed freely. Class Room played a sad melody on
Yuk, soothing everyone, but also producing even more tears.
Daisy and Joey had made a small cross from some wood they
had found in the barn. Decorating it with flowers they had picked
in the meadow behind the house. They laid Brown Shades' staff
next to him, nestled in his arm, and sprinkled some dried flowers

on his shroud. The flowers had been nestled in a side pocket of Brown Shades' pack, most likely being saved to produce some special color for a future campfire.

After everyone had told their favorite story about the old mage, Fic, Rodent Whisperer and Kistune stood and gave one final two fingered salute to their fallen comrade.

Lori looked up in the tree and spotted a wise, snowy owl with mysterious markings around its eyes that looked like brown glasses. It stood and watched the procession for several minutes, then flew off into a thicker part of the woods surrounding the open hill.

#

They spent the next several days laying low. Staying inside the house or close to it. Eating what they had on hand and quietly observing what was happening around them in the countryside.

They had taken a quick trip the next day to visit the nearby places that had seen death and laid to rest the Doc, Maybell Henry and even the few soldiers they found rotting in the sun. They never did find Jimmy's body.

The sneakiest members of the bunch would take turns going out on scouting trips. They would silently reconnoiter the area, never engaging and deliberately remaining unseen.

Kitsune reported that he saw several buses coming down the mountain, crossing the river and heading for the highway to the west.

No soldiers came around. They didn't see any Humvees or other military trucks at all on any of the roads. It was as if they had departed the area completely.

After a week, Fic and Kitsune donned their uniforms again and pulled one of the Humvees out of the barn.

They navigated up to Mount Weather. The trees were burned over the whole mountainside, but it had burned itself out a few days after the blast.

The road was still passable, and they were able to drive up to the main gate. Fic still wasn't sure what had caused the blasts but they had been extensive. All they found was wreckage. It was hard to tell that buildings once stood where now there were just ruins. Small whiffs of smoke still rose from the charred hole that used to be the main complex.

They saw no sign of people. There weren't even any dead bodies lying around. Nothing.

They returned to the farm and reported their findings.

After the second week, the group started moving about the area. Looking for other families that were still around and seeing what they needed or if they could help.

Slowly things started to get back to normal again. They pulled out a small radio and started scanning the airwaves until they started finding local stations that reported what was going on.

One report said that Richard Flaherty had left the country, abandoning his coup and giving up all he had taken. A few other reports would say he was dead; killed in the blast on Mount Weather. As more news started to flow, things started to get back together again.

A majority of Flaherty's followers started to jump ship as the word went out that he had abandoned them. The die-hard cultists had to deal with The Resistance, which had grown far beyond the confines of Appalachia. Their numerous spies infiltrated The Regime and conducted counterintelligence operations, hastening the Regime's complete collapse.

The Vice President had been found. She had been hiding in New Mexico, trying to plan a way to get rid of Richard Flaherty. She re-assumed office when it was confirmed that the President had been killed in the initial attack on Washington, D.C. and was sworn in as the new President in Albuquerque, New Mexico the new National Capitol.

Trucks started running and stores were opened again. The electricity came back on and they were able to move around more. One day, a US Mail truck came down the road and actually delivered some mail to their box. Fic walked down with Lori and inside they found a letter from Gnobbit and Finn. They took the letter to the kitchen and gathered all of The Party to excitedly listen to Fic read it. The letter told about how things had gotten worse for a while in Pearisburg. The two hikers had stayed out of sight for a while at the house, but the Flarmy caught wind of them, and they had to retreat up into the nearby mountains to escape capture or worse. After a couple of weeks, they had snuck down to check on Gnobbit's mother and found that the Flarmy had pulled out. Leaving the forced workers behind. By the end of August, everything had finally started getting back to normal. In the euphoric aftermath of the war, the two hikers had become engaged.

Everyone laughed with delight at the news and all who knew them had to tell a story or two of their exploits together. It was a bright spot in a still dim world.

Later, they were all sitting around on the back porch, enjoying a sunset that had given a spectacular show. The sunsets had been amazing since the bombs had caused so much dust and smoke to get up into the atmosphere, but the cause of those spectacular colors was also a poison that could hurt them all.

The battle wounds that were acquired mended as time went on. Class Room's ankle was fine within a couple of days, followed by Brittney's severe sprain. Shane was walking around the house some now but was still weak and on the mend. Davey's shoulder had healed and all the cuts, burns and bruises had mended or faded.

"I think I'm going to be heading home to New Jersey soon," said Class Room. "Traveling should be easier now."

"I need to go check on my folks, too," added Kitsune. "I know my mother is worried sick. Once I make sure everything is alright, I think I'll come visit, if that's okay?" Kitsune looked towards Fic.

"Of course, son," Fic said. "You are always welcome here."

Shane 'whooped' as Kitsune smiled at his new friend. They had formed a close bond, one strengthened by surviving something horrific together at a deeply impressionable age. As his wound began to heal, Shane had started standing watch with Kitsune. They would trade stories about their separate adventures, competing for the most outrageous experience, and tell each other jokes that only young men in their late teens would understand.

"I think I may go see if I can get a flight back to Scotland," Rodent Whisperer said. "I do miss my homeland."

Melissa and the kids were sitting in the yard on some chairs. "We should be heading down south soon, too. I know our house is gone in Waynesboro, but that is still our home. We need to go see what we can recover."

Fic stood looking at his Party as they all made plans to move on with their lives and try to get back to some new normal. Everyone here was family. His real family and his Tramily. Those he had picked up along the way and helped to break free of the crazy that Flaherty had brought to this land.

Thinking back at all that had happened to get him back here with his family, Fic was filled with emotion. The Trail had provided. The Trail had brought him home.

The End

ACKNOWLEDGEMENTS

This story started kicking around in my head not too long after I first set foot on the Appalachian Trail. The beauty of the wilderness, the challenge of a long distance hike, the power of nature, all inspired me as I pried the story out of my head and onto the page.

The hikers I met along the way gave me the fodder I needed to create the characters for this story. Their wealth of personality was hopefully translated into interesting hikers who were a lot like the kind of people I met on the trail. Gnome, Grade School, Mouse King, Firefly, Huck, Baltimore Jack, and others each contributed a little bit of themselves to my creation of characters.

To my brother, Tom, who's critical feedback pissed me off enough to get me moving on the story.

To the National November Writing Month (Nanowrimo) challenge, which let me actually sit down and spend a month concentrating on nothing more than getting the words down on paper.

To Lulu.com for providing a vehicle to get a first draft out into the world. Still raw and unfinished, but *Out There*. Where I wanted it to be.

To Aunt Barb, my biggest (only) fan, who voraciously read my chapters as I slowly released them on my blog. Giving me the feeling I needed that maybe someone else besides me would enjoy this story.

And lastly, to my daughter, Shauni, my editor. She meticulously went through each chapter, keeping my boomer ass on the straight and narrow. Giving me better ways to say the things I wanted to say. Without her, the raw version probably would have been the last version.

There is one more acknowledgement. To you, the reader. If you have gotten this far, then I guess I have actually done something.

Peace, out.

ABOUT THE AUTHOR

Joseph "EarthTone" Harold was born and raised in western Pennsylvania. Joining the Coast Guard at age 20, he soon found himself in Cape May, New Jersey where he met his lovely wife, Lisa (LoGear). They set out on an adventure called life. Moving around the country, raising two wonderful daughters and eventually finishing a 30 year career in the military. From there the Appalachian Trail called and they both shouldered their packs and walked most of its miles. Now they continue their adventure together, still traveling the country, but going where whim desires and not where orders dictate.

Made in United States
Orlando, FL
10 May 2024

46728507R00232